INFORMER
The Wars of Men

INFORMER
The Wars of Men

To: Aville

Fr: R....

Rhoan Flowers

THANKS & Enjoy.

authorHOUSE®

AuthorHouse™
1663 Liberty Drive
Bloomington, IN 47403
www.authorhouse.com
Phone: 1-800-839-8640

First published by AuthorHouse   6/7/2010

ISBN: 978-1-4490-4170-0 (e)
ISBN: 978-1-4490-4168-7 (sc)
ISBN: 978-1-4490-4169-4 (hc)

Library of Congress Control Number: 2010907315

Printed in the United States of America
Bloomington, Indiana

This book is printed on acid-free paper.

Introduction

Informer is a fictional tale based upon the lives of two men who took separate routes to achieve riches and power. No civilization was ever constructed without the treachery of powerful men, intended on profiting and ruling the governments of the land. This epic adventure describes such puppet masters and the enforcers of the laws they appoint, overwhich these two seekers of riches must conquer.

Kevin, the eldest of the two, became involved with a drug kingpin from Columbia, who found use for his diverse skills within his organization towards exterminating one of his greatest foes. Through said kingpin, Kevin acquired the means and measures to implement his drug empire, which he established in a separate country. The friendship between Kevin and his mentor became a lifelong journey, where through business aspects derived serious drama that could have left either deceased, but their friendship and admiration for each other prevailed. The young apprentice finds himself in a country where the products with which he deals are primarily controlled by a ruthless gang of bikers who refuse to have any form of opposition join their market. Through roughhouse tactics, the gang attempts to force Kevin to purchase their products as every other ethnic group that operated in the city had done. With a fearless stance against Canada's biggest biker gang, Kevin becomes the idol for all who have suffered beneath the corrupt system, which is primarily enforced by Montreal's police. The reality with which he was dealing brought Kevin to a separate world within the confines of the one he lived, and, through said friends, he was capable of strengthening his empire.

Kevin's primary nemesis was Martain Lafleur, a lavishly wealthy son of a business tycoon who inherited his position as the head honcho for the most ruthless gang in Canada from his deceased uncle. The massive membership list of the biker gang had many secret, influential members whose contributions to the club aided the daily running of the underground. There are certain secrets that, if whispered, are rewarded with instant death, and there are the lives of the darkest living forces in every city for which someone has to account. And then there are those who attempt to rule it all by draining every pit of resources known to man. Information is priceless, and thus any informant with the proper item himself either becomes a commodity or a threat. The extent of corruption and stench that evolved in the underworld extended to the rulers and elected officials, who pay a higher price for concealing their garbage.

Kadeem comes along during an era when he could provide, with his form of badmanisme, exactly the assistance Kevin needed to accomplish a certain feat. Kadeem camefrom a dog-eat-dog world where only the toughest and most skillful survive. Never one to fear blasting his weapon, Kadeem, after a mean beginning to life, attempted to change his gunman ways after relocating to another country. Surprisingly, there is never an exit from badness for certain individuals whose talents with a weapon are like Michael Jordan with a basketball. Perfect! Kevin and Kadeem are notoriously known and are referred to by different names as are most thugs who often operate under their street names.

Beyond the corruption, murders, and every illegal money Ponzi schemes there was, the two warring factions bump heads in one spectacular event, where your chosen animals of demolition are thrown into a fighting pit, and only the winner is slated to exit the battlefield. Inherently, even when matters appear clarified, there is always that one hidden secret which you will protect with your last breath.

Part 1

MAXWELL BISHOP COULD hardly conceal his anxiety as he stormed up the staircase toward the third floor of Building G at the El Greco Tropical Resort. The sun had been blasphemous throughout the day, yet with the shades of evening came a mild tropical breeze. Jamaica's land temperatures during the latter part of the year were divinely soothing, and so was the funding with which Maxwell perceived. He shouted adieu to a hotel groundskeeper on the second floor before weaseling his way up the final flight of stairs. There was a scruffy-looking hotel employee standing at the top of the stairs. Maxwell immediately asked him for directions while harboring the thought that said person appeared slightly out of character.

Suite D-316 was almost to the end of the corridor, and Maxwell spent his few seconds to the door properly grooming himself. Before knocking, however, Maxwell noticed that his shoelace was untied and bent over to correct the problem, which landed him a chrome, 9 mm nozzle to the rear of the head. With the gun to Maxwell's scull, a separate hand came through the mist of air that surrounded Maxwell and knocked on the door.

A bass-toned voice whispered from the rear, "If you breathe anything but you name, me a-splatter you morrow all over the front door. You feel me my youth?"

By then, a Latin-toned voice sounded behind the door, demanding the visitor's name. Maxwell barely conjured up the strength to announce himself after first swallowing a huge lump of saliva that had sneaked up the back of his throat. The sudden jolt of terror that shook Maxwell's very foundation had him clenching his ass in an attempt to avoid defecating himself.

The visitor exclaimed, "Bishop! It'sIs me, Maxwell!"

With the clack of the door lock came a huge, size fifteen boot that smashed the door into the small man on the opposite end. Before anyone could protectively manoeuvre themselves, Maxwell was tossed into the condominium head over heels, andas he went crashing against the centre table.

The taller of the two intruders threatened, "Nobody move, nobody get hurt, seen?"

The sole person inside the room, whose mannerisms were those of someone important, exclaimed, "What's the fucking meaning of this? This is disrespectful! How dare you barge into my suite?"

"Th-th-th-this ie-ie-is a fu-fu-fu-fucking st-st-st-stick-up," said the shorter man in his stammering lingo.

The boss, who'd settled back into his seat, asked, "What the fuck did he just say?"

"Him just say we accept all credit cards, jewellery, and money. Or, in layman's terms, fill up me blood-clatt bag," translated the taller man of the two robbers.

The sixth man inside the room asked, "You fools have any idea who y'all trying to rip?"

"An-an-an-any bo-bo-body a-a-a-ask yu-yu-you an-any ti-ti-thing?"

The five-foot-six Spanish bodyguard shot back, "What?"

"Just keep you blood-clatt shut before somebody put a shell inna it," warned the young robber. "Stammer, me a-go check out the rest aof the place. Just keep everybody covered 'til me come back."

With the taller of the two robbers away checking each individual room for additional victims, Stammer remained in place while surveying the entire room. *The centurion left in place is that scruffy-looking worker,* thought Maxwell to himself as he slowly regained consciousness. He immediately turned to the man he'd come to meet with and began apologizing profusely.

"Mr. Lopez, sir, I have absolutely nothing to do with this robbery. I'm sorry I didn't notice them coming up the stairs, and I'm sorry I brought them into you place, but them did go kill me boss!"

"You would be a fool to bring anyone here to rob me. Obviously these men have no idea who I am, or they would tuck their tails between their legs and run out of here like the chumps they are," stated Mr. Lopez.

The initial guard who attended the door was bloodied and wobbly. The man rolled over onto his back and attempted to sit up before he was forced back to the ground by a sturdy boot to the left temple. Instead of further aggravating his intruders, the guard simply wiped the blood from his eyes and remained tranquil. After reasserting their control, Stammer hollered at his partner to ensure his safety.

"Everything is everything, Stammer," advised his partner. "Now, weahhere the money, big man? A the money we come for, so give it up before things start get ugly in here."

"Ki-Killa, se-se-see t-t-them ha-ha-have a bre-bre-bre-briefcase o-o-over de-de-there so," pointed out Stammer.

"All right, before all that, tie up them blood-clatt before someone start feel like a hero," said Killa.

At that point, Stammer removed his backpack from his back, unzipped it, and removed a few pieces of rope and a roll of duct tape. The bleeding guard, who was the closest, was the first in restraints. At session's end, the man resembled a calf that had been hog-tied by a cowboy in a rodeo. The second of the two guards leaped to his feet following his thoughts of receiving a bullet in the back of the head, execution-style.

"You fucking Puta-Marricons ain't gonna execute me like some fucking butcher slaying cattle. Fuck them guns, I take you fuckers with or without them guns," threatened the guard.

"A wha yu feel like?" *Boom!* Killa's 9 mm cannon exploded, hitting the guard directly in the kneecap, which forced him back to the seat of his pants. The impact of the bullet blasted out the guard's knee as Stamma ran over to him and immediately gagged him before hog-tying him, despite the injured knee. The big boss, who wished for no added injury to befall his mates, immediately tossed the briefcase Stamma spoke of at his antagonists.

Killa said, "If anybody else in here feels like Superman, let me know. If not, shut the fuck up and we'll be gone as soon as we get paid for our deeds. We feel each other?"

The young thugs bound each one of their captors securely before turning their attention to the briefcase "Ching-ching!" exclaimed both robbers as their faces lit up like Christmas trees. The briefcase contained more U.S. presidents on paper than they'd ever witnessed. As Killa went about maintaining order, his partner began transferring their newly acquired wealth to the backpack he'd brought.

The sound of the condominium's telephone startled Stammer, who immediately grabbed for his pistol. Killa signalled him to continue his task as he peeked through the window for uninvited guests. Once he was satisfied that there were not any law enforcement officials around, Killa walked over to the phone and paused before answering.

"Do-do-don't a-a-a-answer th-th-the f-f-f-phone, Ki-Ki-Killa!" Stamma instructed.

Again, Killa signalled him as he lifted the receiver from the base. Mimicking their captives' Spanish accents, he said, "Si, can I help you?"

"Hello, sir. Excuse me, but we received a complaint from several guests who reported hearing some sort of banging from your unit. We're just checking to make sure that everything is fine with you guys, and if you guys could please offer our other guests the same courtesy they do you, it would be greatly appreciated," stated an employee.

"Si, señorita, excuse us. There will be no more noise. Thank you!"

With that, both thugs finalized their dealings and casually exited the condo. The thugs walked to the elevator and rode the car down to the street before hopping a taxi down to the Gully Market. With the sidewalks crammed with Iglers seeking sales, Stamma stopped to purchase some vegetables and fruits for his grandmother, who had raised him throughout his life. Both Gully thugs chewed on sugar cane as they made their way home through the rough Gully neighbourhood.

On the edge of Canterbury and Gully was a wooden shack convenience store that belonged to Hatchet. Hatchet was considered the Gully don because of his interaction in the daily affairs of the poor and the needy. Hatchet would prepare large meals for himself and everyone in need as his daily contribution to ensure the hungry had food. The many personalities of Hatchet were known throughout;so too was it evident he was not one to be fucked with. Hatched controlled the only ghetto business that remained open after 7:00 pm, as vendors were aware of the turbulence brought on by nightfall. The Gully don was the face of hope, as well as the face of despair, considering he operated the underground sales of armaments and drugs which he chose to sell outside his poor neighbourhood.

Stamma and Killa arrived moments after the evening meal was served to find a slew of thugs and others eating their proper fill. Hatchet was, as usual, behind the counter of his store as he paused his food-scarffing to serve a client. As soon as the returning thugs walked into the store, Hatchet directed them to come around to the rear door of the store.

"Onnou want two flour?" Hatchet demanded.

Killer greedily answered, "But of course Iah!"

"See two plate yah, the food over there in the pot," Hatchet directed.

Killa and Stamma were intelligent enough to maintain their poise and composure around the kennel of wolves, as there were those within the group who were vindictive and conniving motherfuckers. The thought of there being one hundred thousand U.S. dollars in the knapsack on Stamma's back would be motivation enough for someone to attempt something sooner or later. Both Stamma and Killa collected their food and joined Hatchet behind the counter.during which They all demolished their food while discussing the ordeal.

The Gully don had a hand in every major business affair to translate from Bottom Gully to the edge of Canterbury. Hence, a portion of every gross intake by Gully soldiers had to be paid to the "Feed the Community Fund." That was how Hatchet provided such nutritious meals for starving Gully folks. Stamma donated five thousand to the "Feed the Community Fund" before paying Hatchet another five hundred for the 9 mm he negotiated on consignment.

"So, Killa, you a go pan the move with Justin and Stamma them later?" Hatchet asked.

"Naw, man, me nice for today!" Killa exclaimed.

"Congratulations, mi buoy. You just purchase you first toy," Hatchet declared.

Stamma tapped the weapon attached to his waist and let off a huge grin before an embarrassing burp shot from his mouth. Killa broke out in laughter as his accomplice covered his mouth and mumbled, "Excuse me." After dinner, the thugs individually rolled their separate marijuana joints as music bounced from the jukebox in Hatchet's grocery. Killa and Stamma soon continued their journey toward home a few yards up some hell-forsaking climb. The terrain up the hill was rocky and dangerous, yet the thugs trotted up as if it wasn't of consequence.

On their way up the pathway lined by sheets of rusted zinc and torn down fences, Stamma's cellular sounded with his uncle on the other line. Stamma's Uncle Rev was the orchestrator of the theft, although he hadn't the testicular fortitude to physically rob someone at gunpoint. Rev was a closeted homosexual who occasionally slept with Maxwell Bishop. The idea for the heist was originally devised by Maxwell, who was of the upper-class region with zero ties to the thugs of the ghetto. Hence, Maxwell decided against proceeding with the plot that he'd braggingly brought to Rev's attention.

"Didn't I tell you fucking dummies not to hurt anybody? What kind of shit is shooting out a man's knee? What if security or the police did come to check on what was going on? You idiots probably would be giving me up now! You know something? Make sure my cut reaches me within the hour!" Rev argued.

Killa knew Stamma was a little scaredy-cat when it came to his elder uncle, who at one time was the only person financially assisting Stamma's grandmother. Rev was twenty-four years Stamma's elder, who was raised on the Gully side before relocating in fear of what would happen to him should anyone around the neighbourhood discover his sexual preferences. What may had been considered rumours prior to Rev moving away soon became facts as the ex-Canterburian moved in with a man in West Green.

"If you want that, you have to come for it, a can't bad man you a call and a demand things! We naw pay you a cent batty buoy, go suck you man an go way!" Killa garnished.

"That's why I don't deal with hood rats! You want fuck with me? Let's see how you like me sending some of my bad batty buoy police friends after your ass. I go make sure say you get yours, because me go get mine one way or the other!" Rev commented.

"You a go get yours, one fat shot inna you blood-clatt!" Killa threatened before disconnecting the call.

After their antagonists had departed, the two guards shuffled themselves across the floor to each other where they untied each other's ropes before setting everyone else free. The injured guard moaned and groaned as his fellow companion rushed him a towel filled with ice cubes. While the guard attended to his mate, Maxwell continuously apologized for the mishap that transpired.

Ernesto said, "Listen to me, my friend. If you have anything to do with this robbery, I will find out, and then you will be no more. Until then, I need you to find me a doctor to come treat my assistant, and as for our original deal, I'll have someone here by tomorrow with the agreed payment. Until then find me a personal physician to summon for my friend, I suggest you go, and hurry! I don't want him to lose his leg."

Ernesto was a drug smuggler whose operations extended from South America to the Great White North. Following the seizure a few metric tonnes of cocaine by the DEA, Ernesto decided to open a new pipeline that would flow through the Caribbean and back into the United States. The trip to Jamaica was the first leg of Ernesto's travels, and he planned to implant similar routes through Haiti and Cuba. The sensitivity of the journey was one that demanded secrecy, which was Ernesto's reasoning for demanding a private physician. With the different bureaus such as the DEA breathing down his neck, Ernesto knew the grave implication of a member of his realm being reported injured, especially with a gunshot wound.

Within two hours, Maxwell had returned with a qualified physician, an off-duty doctor who was fifty years old and who practiced medicine around the Rose Hall District. The doctor was a roots man who asked little and behaved as if the gunshot wound was a regular fracture. Ernesto walked over to the physician as he performed his duties and spoke candidly with him, considering his immediate financial status.

"This man works for me, and I'm afraid to say that I won't have your exact fees until the bank opens in the morning. If you could please take my Rolex watch as a temporary payment, I will pay you in full once the bank opens in the morning, and you can then still keep the watch," negotiated Ernesto.

The doctor, who was by then simply bandaging the guard's leg after repairing the torn cartilage, looked up at the watch and was stunned at the offering. It was an eighty-five thousand dollar watch with lavish diamond studs throughout the centre point. The doctor nonchalantly accepted it without hesitation. Ernesto charged a bottle of Petron Tequila to his suite before making an overseas call to his assistant in Florida in order to arrange the replacement of the funds. After the drug kingpin got through with his phone dealings, the men inside the suite drank the night away as if nothing faulty had occurred. The next day, Ernesto made good on his promises as he paid the doctor in full and awarded Maxwell a second briefcase filled with loot.

Part 2

KEVIN WALSH LEFT Jamaica at the tender age of thirteen to reside with his single mother in West Palm Beach, Florida.Tragedy soon struck his family with the untimely death of his mother after Kevin's third year in the United States. The death of his mother at the hand of some would-be bank robber attempting to empty her cash register sparked a flame under Kevin that blazed throughout the remainder of his natural life. After discovering that, due to technicalities in the case, the murderer received only thirty-six months of imprisonment, Kevin decided to judge for himself the man who killed his beloved mother.

Kevin lined up calendars for the next three years and kept a constant check on the prisoner through the prison's online services. Once Kevin found out that his mother's murderer was awarded early release some nine months before his scheduled date, he knew the time had come to settle the score.

After more than two years in Broward County State Prison, Hector Dominguez walked out a free man. With a slew of his essays at hand to greet him at the entrance, Kevin watched his first opportunity slip agonizingly away, as he had planned on slaughtering Hector once he stepped foot from protective custody. Kevin trailed his intended target and his thuggishfriends, who joked and played around inside their vehicles for the duration of the journey.

With his heart pounding similar to the bass omitting from his speakers in his vehicle, Kevin felt motivated to avenge mother. With blood in his eyes and revenge in his toughts, Kevin trailed the entourage back to their hood in South Miami Beach. By the time they arrived in Little Haiti, Miami, Kevin had thoroughly blessed his marijuana joint, which caused his eyes to glow a fiery red like those of a dragon. The vengeance-thirsty Jamaican followed the eccentric partiers into the heart of their gang turf, where he fearlessly drove through sections of the city, which most residents avoided.

The young hard head scoped out the scene, parked his vehicle across the street from the ongoing party, and left the engine running with the doors locked and the remote attached to his belt buckle. The roads throughout the neighbourhood were filled with obvious gangbangers, residents enjoying the evening calm, and children playing throughout. Kevin watched as his intended target walked over to a house, where they had an ongoing barbeque, before deciding to unleash his punishment. Casually dressed in jeans, a marina white T-shirt, track shoes, and a backpack on his back, Kevin walked directly across to the festivities and unveiled a pair of nickel-plated 9 mm pistols.

With both eyes plastered on the man who murdered his mother, Kevin began shooting each individual that stood between himself and Hector. However, Kevin's earlier, inaccurate assessment of how many people were actually inside the three-bedroom house soon hindered the promise he had made to his deceased mother, because the welcoming crowd went from celebrative to survival mode. The gang of Cuban thugs were, as Kevin had expected, fully armed to the teeth, and after his initial scare wore thin, a shoot-out between he and his antagonist arose. Before a single shot was returned at Kevin, three thugs laid dead, with a fourth screaming at the top of his lungs that he'd been hit. Hector quickly ducked from Kevin's vision, narrowly escaping the shells logged at him. However, once the Cuban mob began laying down cover fire, Kevin was forced to rethink his attack. As the revenge-seeking Jamaican scurried back to his vehicle, four thugs from half a block down the road began racing toward him with shells from their 9 mm pistols striking everything except their target. By then, the entire street had nearly emptied as residents who'd grown accustomed to the violence fled for their dear lives. Kevin kept his head low and popped up as he reached his car door to force the four charging bulls to revise their intents, as he hammered a few shots at them. One of the five shots Kevin blasted at the thugs struck one man in the chest and forced the others to rethink their actions. Kevin then hammered a couple at the front door from which he'd launched his attack as the regrouped thugs sought the head of the lone intruder who had bravely attacked the core of their Cuban movement.

Unknown to Kevin was the fact that there had been two individuals stationed a few paces up the street constructing a small surveillance on the mob. The two men who sat and watched Kevin in action were impressed at the method with which he over-powered the ruthless bunch of thugs. . They were even more surprised at the amount of respect awarded Kevin, who, even as he departed, had each member of Hector's entourage tucked tightly behind some protective device. As Kevin departed the scene, the men inside their Trailblazer truck kept their distance as they followed in pursuit.

Kevin cruised along Interstate 95 and drove into Broward County. As he exited the highway, he took notice of the Chevy truck in his rearview mirror and continued on in an attempt to positively confirm his suspicions. The heated maniac drove down Commercial Boulevard and continued on to his friend's house in Tamarack. Kevin parked his vehicle in his friend's driveway and walked up to the single-story house, located at 439 Eastern Drive. With a soft rap on the door, an incredibly huge man soon appeared inside the doorway as he opened the door and allowed Kevin entry.

The Trailblazer truck drove up to the house and settled across the street. Inside the house, Kevin explained his actions to his friend in a calm and relaxed tone. Following a slight peek through a bedroom window, Kevin crawled beneath the bed inside the room and pulled out a huge duffle bag. Once he got through explaining about the Chevy truck that trailed him, his friend, Swarty, became enraged to find out that he'd brought unwanted company to his house. The huge, six foot four, four hundred and seventy pound man stood in the door frame and blocked all through traffic.

Swarty said, "?" Brethren, don't tell me say you make police follow you back to my house?"

"Police or not, they're fucked cause they chose the wrong day to follow me"! ," Kevin answered.

"So what you plan on doing to make sure your guests don't come back here?"

"Watch and see!"

The young maniac, after being granted passage through the doorway, tossed the duffle bag and its contents over his shoulder and headed through the main entrance. At the last minute, Swarty caught a whiff of the dish Kevin was about to serve and dashed into the kitchen. Kevin walked through the front door and began heading in the Chevy's direction. Midway across the street, Kevin unveiled the duffle bag's contents, which immediately caused the Trailblazer's occupants to exit their vehicle with their hands held high.

Swarty dashed into the kitchen and grabbed his sawed-off pump rifle from inside the oven. The huge man, who was remarkably light afoot, ran through the rear door and unnoticeably crept his way around to the other side of the Trailblazer. As Kevin got prepared to empty a few banana clips from his AK-47 into the shell of the vehicle, the driver of the truck leapt from his seat with both hands high in the air, exclaiming, "Please, please, don't kill me! We only wish to talk to you, my friend!"

Before Kevin could inquire about their actions, Swarty's voice could be heard lashing instructions in the distant. With his pump action selecting its shell for discharge against the passenger's head, Swarty could be heard ordering the man f to get his face in the dirt.

"You have five seconds to awaken my interest," declared Kevin.

"Our boss says he thinks we have the same problem, and he wants to negotiate with you," advised the driver.

With both men facedown into the asphalt, Kevin pondered over whether or not to eliminate them. As he weighed his options, a Mercedes Benz 600 luxury car turned the corner down the road and began moving toward the scuffle. "Who the hell could be so stupid", thought Kevin to himself as the vehicle continued advancing. With his foot centred in the middle of the driver's back and his weapon now aimed at the Mercedes, the vehicle came to a halt. Kevin's finger tickled the trigger of his weapon as he adjusted himself for combat. As the rear passenger window rolled down, Kevin looked to dive for the turf while unloading his first clip, considering the protection awarded the occupants.

"Hello. My name is Ernesto, and I believe we can greatly benefit each other if we have a talk. My men obviously didn't lie about your survival skills, so please, please join me," suggested the lone passenger who stuck his head out the window to speak.

The man beneath Kevin's foot exclaimed, "My boss!"

After he allowed the men to their feet, Kevin collected the duffle bag and placed the weapon back inside. Without delay, the young thug returned the weapon to its proper domain and rearmed himself with the dynamic duo which lit up Miami some time before.

Kevin asked Swarty, "You coming along for the ride?"

"Personally I'm mad that you didn't holler at me before you brought that vigilante stuff to Miami. But we discuss all that later, for now just tell the big man you riding with that when we get where we going, if you don't exit that vehicle, his boys ain't exiting this Trail Blazer"! " warned Swarty as he hopped into the Trailblazer with his favourite chess piece.

Swarty eased back and looked grudgingly around inside the Trailblazer with his weapon lying across his lap. It didn't take the airy fat man long to sequester his demands;as he immediately demanded they select Hot 96 radio station for jams to roll to. Following his demands, however, Swarty took time out to apologize for the rough treatment he and Kevin had inflicted on their host. The Spanish-American men began emphasizing their fascination with Kevin, whom they'd had the fortune of watching perform.

Kevin was in the midst of being introduced to the finer aspects of life. After meeting his true host, Kevin became aware of the real reason he was sought out. His host Mr. Ernesto Lopez wanted very much the same tyrant on whom Kevin preyed exterminated, for personal business reasons. Ernesto, unlike Kevin, had done business with the Cuban gang and witnessed first-hand their treachery. For Ernesto, it was pure business, thus his conversation was a means of convincing Kevin to join his team.

Ernesto instructed the chauffeur to drive them home, a ride that took some twenty minutes, but upon arrival, any doubts about his financial claims were immediately shunned after viewing his two million dollar home. With the rewards being as promised, Kevin passed a few hours in the graces of his host as they discussed futuristic ideas. Over the course of their discussion, Ernesto revealed his original plot being to simply hire and assist Kevin in his quest for Hector Dominguez's head from behind the scenes. Incidentally, once Ernesto shook Kevin's hand, his entire perception of him changed, and he hoped to maintain a young man with such vigour and intellect around him.

Once a few shots of Hennessy crept into the bloodstreams of the newly federated members, Kevin began discovering the real history behind Hector and Ernesto as Ernesto shared his story.

"Life has blessed me because I came from the gutter. I was born in a poor village in Columbia to hardworking farmers. When I was three years old, men from the drug cartel came to my village in search of workers to cultivate their cocaine. They shot and killed my father and took my sister, mother, and me into their work camps to work as slaves cultivating their drugs. I'll never forget the sight of my mother and sister, who were beaten and forced to work in the nude as they packaged the cocaine outside in the labs. The worst was having to watch the guards rape and molest my mother and sister as they pleased. They would simply enter our lockups and molest the ladies they desired right in front of their friends and families. Many people lost hope as well as their lives, but there were those, like my mother, who, despite our situation, decided to educate the children around the camp. Even an education, like many other things, had to be taught in secrecy, because had the guards, who were themselves dumb bush people, found out about it, it would be the end of that.

"I grew up a farmer who tended to the Pappy Plants of drug cartels because even as a child I was forced to do physical labour, or else there was no food for me. They worked me when I was a child like they did the grown men seven times my age. Every day, my hands and legs bled from picking the Pappy and walking barefoot through the fields. My temper boiled to the point where I knew if I ever got into a physical confrontation with anybody, I was going to kill them and suffer the consequences. Still, through all that, I studied the daily chemistry of the guards and their superiors, along with the smugglers and business preps who were buying, paying, or collecting. In a world far beyond the comprehension of most civilized humans, Hector's father was one of the kids who became my friend when honestly I didn't need anyone. A month after my thirteenth birthday on a foggy Saturday morning, I woke up to the sounds of machine gun fire, which was mainly being casted down from overhead by patrolling helicopters. The guards did their best to hold their own, but in the end, nearly everyone was killed except for a few workers who fell to the ground and prayed to be rescued. I ran to find my mother and sister, but found my sister holding the body of Mama, who had been shot by one of the guards. As for me, I had learned the great distance to which men would go to harvest this flower that financed the camp I'd lived in, the army protecting it, and the elaborate, lavish lifestyle lived by the cartels who rarely visit the plantation. While those slaves who had been broken over the years awaited their saviour, I moved to the only logical place I believed worth investigating, which was General Gustav's quarters. Hector's father, Raphael, was smart enough to follow me, because we found more money and cocaine than we could carry. I ran away from that horrible place as a man, which I became in my young years, and I never looked back! We found our way into the city, where I bought documents and travelled here to this great country where I've built my empire from the same product I'd sworn to hate. As for Raphael, he remained in Columbia, and we reunited six years later when I returned to Columbia to negotiate my first trade line. Raphael drove me to the Estrada Cartel estate and introduced me to Señor Estrada, who has since graciously accepted me into his family. I chose to bring Raphael back to the United States in order for him to be by my side so I can have someone who I could completely trust. Things were good for the first few years, until Raphael met Hector's mother, Loretta."

Ernesto paused as he personally reflected over the events that transpired before indulging in his alcoholic beverage. The story had intrigued Kevin to where his marijuana joint had lost its flame because of his lack of interest therein. However, given a moment of acknowledgment, Kevin soon reignited his joint and puffed away.

"Loretta was the queen of manipulation, and it didn't take her long to convince Raphael that he was worth a whole lot more than I was paying him. In fact, she had him convinced that we should have been partners because he introduced me to the connection. The next thing I knew, my right-hand man was skimming off the top and planning on ways to overthrow me. Until this day I regret that order, but it had gotten to the point where Raphael had conspired with my own enemies to have me assassinated! Loretta gave birth to young Hector seven months later, and had since raised her child to believe that I killed his father to take over the business. The woman has completely poisoned her son's mind, but after killing his father, I refuse to give the son the same treatment," revealed Ernesto.

"So what exactly do you want from us?" Kevin asked.

"I'd like to offer you and your friend a position working for me," offered Ernesto.

"What kind of a position?" Kevin questioned.

"My money collectors have been getting robbed and targeted by those low-lifes you attacked. With Hector away, they've been less successful, but I'm sure they're looking to advance their attacks. I need some no-nonsense gunners like you who will be willing to protect what is mine at all cost. I'll provide you the necessary supplies to get the job done, and if you bring any recruits, they can join the payroll and get properly rewarded!" Ernesto then motioned his personal assistant over and collected an envelope from her. The envelope contained ten thousand dollars in U.S. currency, which was a simple appetizer to tempt Kevin.

"You make the best hire of all!" Kevin shoved the envelope into his huge jeans pocket.

"So I take it we have an arrangement?" Ernesto asked.

"Without a doubt. Mr. E!" Kevin assured him.

"I'll have Alex show you the important material. You go enjoy yourself, and what's mine is all yours. Allow me to take care of some minor business and we'll talk later," Ernesto advised.

Ernesto's chief security officer brought Swarty and Kevin into the basement, where they were brought into the weaponry chambers in order to properly acquaint themselves with the various armouries. The newcomers to the Ernesto family were amazed at the selection of various weapons displayed all throughout the room. There were a number of weapons in Ernesto's armoury that Kevin hadn't previously the opportunity to fire, and being the lover of weapons which he was, the chance to do so greatly excited him.

Swarty argued that he didn't personally own a handgun before shoving a huge .357 Magnum into his waistband and a box of the accompanying shells into his pocket. Both men were elated to join Ernesto's team, which, for more beneficial reasons than harmful ones, appeased both unemployed thugs. The men returned home to find Swarty's girlfriend, Deloris, who was a professional clothes thief by trade, bargaining the sale of items she'd stolen with prospective buyers she'd invited over to shop. There were three ladies groping through the clothing that was spread across the living room furniture like a showroom exhibit.

"Dwayne, how comes youknow say, 'me gone out on the hustle' and you don't even cook the chicken me leave in the sink? We have bills 'round here and I don't see you big ass getting up and paying any of them! I saw Keith down by the Swap Shop and him say the thing ready, so tell you to check him later," said Deloris

"You get me the shirt?" Swarty demanded.

"It's in the bedroom!" Deloris responded.

Swarty dipped into his pocket and tossed Deloris a thousand dollars as he walked by with the huge, pump action weapon at hand, as hereturned the weapon to its original domain. The sight of the life taker in Swarty's hand may have aroused other females' interest, but Deloris and company behaved as if that was a regular occurrence. In fact, the ladies were more amazed by Swarty's money gesture than they actually were over the shotgun. As Kevin passed through on his way to the kitchen, Deloris intercepted him and said, "See the shirt me tell you me think would fit you nicely here," before tossing it at their roommate.

"Yeah, man, a dat me a talk bout," said Kevin as he acknowledged Deloris' exquisite sense of style.

Kevin walked directly into the kitchen and collected two Heinekens from the refrigerator, passed one to his friend, and sat around the five-piece dining set. The two friends began assessing their strategies toward ridding their new employer of the pest he so gravely wished exterminated. Given the personalities of both men, the decision was quickly made to secretly assassinate every careless member found until the poisons within were nullified. Both friends also found the time to reminisce over the past, as their friendship, which expanded since the death of Kevin's mother, moulded them into brothers.

"Tell me how you feel when you see the buoy who killed you mother head at the tip a you gun?" Swarty emotionally asked after a night of solid drinking.

"Believe me, breatherin', it was like all them years of grief and pain was about to subside! Like me mother spirit could finally rest in peace knowing that me her pay back the pussyhole who murder her! Me a tell you say me line up the buoy under a kill or be killed vibe, and it's only by the skin of him teeth that him get way! But you see the next time!" Kevin barked angrily as he removed his side arm and stared at it.

"I can't forget them cold sweat you used to wake up in when you just moved here. I told you one day you will get you chance to settle the score and you see, I was right!" Swarty exclaimed.

"Me dream about this moment for years. One time, them cold sweat dreams used to scare the shit out of me, because all me used to see was that bitch Hector pumping gunshot inna me. But over time, you convince me that him a go be the one getting bore up and that kill all them weird dreams," Kevin remarked.

The next morning, Kevin had information sent to Deloris' e-mail address concerning the prudent members of Hector's gang who posed a threat to the daily operations of Ernesto's empire. There were three members who orchestrated attacks against Ernesto's affairs during Hector's absence, with the majority of service men being foot soldiers. Hector's mates were the nucleus of a vicious neighbourhood gang called The South Hourds, who ruled and dominated the entire southern portion of Carol City. The South Hourds were renowned for expelling radical gangs like The Bloods and Crips from their turf in order to fully control the illegal activities around their hood. Kevin highlighted his means of disposing of the troublemakers to Ernesto in a phone conversation, as he believed secrecy to their involvement was important to his overall accomplishment of the mission. Once photos of the wanted men were obtained, Kevin cast an APB on the whereabouts of all the men he sought by every available personnel related to Ernesto's team.

Day One Assault - 11:20 am

Swarty and Kevin cruised by seven members of the South Hourd gang outside a local fajita restaurant that belonged to the parents of one of the gang members. The gangbangers all sported their green handkerchiefs, which was the gang's insignia colour. With Swarty behind the steering wheel of a Honda Accord EX, loaned to the pair by their employer, Kevin instructed his accomplice to circle the block. As they circled, Kevin prepared his assault weapon for work while advising Swarty on how to properly handle the vehicle during the impending assault. The Honda Accord turned back onto the road with a moderate approach, which appeased the thugs who screened every unfavourable vehicle that passed by. As the Honda drew closer to the preoccupied gangbangers, Kevin popped the nose of his M-16 through the window and began emptying the clip at the unsuspecting thugs. At the sound of the weapon, every one of the seven intended victims lay lifeless as the seventeen-inch tires of the Honda Accord screeched as it sped away from the scene of the crime.

Day One Assault - 12:19 am

The vigilante pair received a phone call from Carlos, who indicated that one of Hector's valued generals had been spotted in downtown Miami transporting his female as she revelled in one of her pampering expeditions. The assailant had brought his female friend to a manicure/pedicure appointment she had on Hollywood Boulevard for 10:40 that morning and had at that point brought her to her second scheduled stop, which was at Leann's Beauty Salon on Ives Dairy Road. The sought-after culprit had received the notification concerning the slayings of his peers, though no one had any information about who the drive-by shooters were. Hence, the gangbanger had protectively armed himself as he patiently awaited the woman he'd been chauffeuring around. His Acura Legend was parked with the building to his rear in order to clearly view everything ahead of him. Once Swarty and company spotted the Legend, Kevin instructed Swarty to drive and park behind the building, as the vehicle's positioning made a frontal attack extremely difficult. There was a street bum going through the Starbucks Cafe's garbage in search of food, and Kevin summoned him by offering spare change. Kevin offered the bum twenty dollars for every piece of his clothing, except the soiled underwear, which the man graciously accepted. With a cardboard sign that read, "Please, any little thing helps," Kevin walked staggeringly up to the Acura Legend and tapped on the driver's window. The driver initially waved Kevin off before deciding to donate a little spare change to the persistent beggar. The gangbanger tapped on the automatic roll-down button and turned his head to the armrest console to give him some change. As soon as the man turned his head, Kevin repeatedly stuck a six-inch knife into the side of his neck before leaving the gangbanger gasping for oxygen.

Day One Assault - 9:47 pm

There were more questions than answers in the South Hourds camp after losing an incredible eleven thugs in less than thirty-six hours. The sole survivor of the horrific tragedies was a twenty-two-year-old male who remained in critical condition at the General Hospital in Hollywood. The neighbourhood of South Carol City resembled a district being governed by Martial Law, where the residents were being controlled by an early curfew. Police squad cars patrolled the outer perimeters of Carol City while the after hour thugs governed their territories. Members of the South Hourds held a meeting aimed at deciphering who the lone shooter was from the day before, and what his motivation was for attacking an element in its own backyard. The meeting led those who sought answers further from the truth as a disagreement in philosophy brought everyone to finger-pointing. The gathering adjourned with confusion as members sought to defend themselves should an incident arise rather than combining to fend off whatever dangers arose. Two gangbangers went to the neighbourhood convenience store, where they sought sodas and snacks as they chatted over the way they'd mutilate any man crazy enough to attack. A scruffy-looking Jamaican with dreadlocks, a mangled beard, and a moustache walked into the store and asked the proprietor for a flame lighter and two packs of Zig Zag rolling papers in order to construct his joint Just then, the two debating thugs walked up to the cash register and waited patiently behind the man with the dreadlocks. The Rasta Man intently watched the thugs behind him through the glass casing behind the store clerk, and neither man behaved as if they believed him a threat. The dreadlocks man paid for his items and collected his change before moving to the exit as if he was about to leave. Just before exiting, he turned back to the clerk as if he'd forgotten something and began blasting humongous holes through the unsuspecting thugs. The Rastafarian, with the world of police around the territories, shoved both pistols into his pockets and walked off into the dark.

The report was unofficial, yet investigators began increasing their interest in locating the person or persons responsible for killing an undercover federal agent. U.S. Marshall Jeffrey Gains was brutally murdered while seeking to purchase some ordinary items from a convenience store. The deceptive-looking U.S. Marshall had gained the confidence of the local territory thugs, who had embraced and initiated him into their flock after he'd lived among them for nearly a year. The undercover agent's objective was to infiltrate the gang, whom law officials believed capable of controlling the valuable South Beach drug trade some time in the future. The crime scene was thoroughly combed for clues as investigators sought to collect anything which might prove valuable to solving the case. The obituary for Agent Gains read, "Killed in the line of duty." Hence, his fellow Marshalls were determined to bring to justice those responsible for killing the undercover agent.

Day Three Assault - 6:36 pm

With an APB out on the Rastafarian captured from the surveillance camera inside the convenience store, as well as a sketched portrait of the vigilante two days prior scattered throughout the counties of Dade and Broward, Kevin briefed his Spanish mates on an attack strategy he wanted them to implement. The reports from the streets indicated that terror was widely felt by residents, who, in most cases, were keeping their children from attending schools out of fear of harm coming to them. South Hourds members would join together at the basketball court inside the Ronald Regan Public Park off 47th Street for their daily basketball contest, where they'd assemble a number of teams and play for bragging rights.

The only unarmed thugs in the park that day were those immediately involved in the game at hand. Besides the ten basketball players involved in the full court game, there was one waiting team, along with a few spectators, some cheering girlfriends, and lookouts. With the spectators demonstrating their intrigue in the physical nature of play a blue 1984 Ford Bronco smashed through the fencing surrounding the court, injuring and surprising gangsters who believed they had every angle of attack well protected.

The loud screams of terrified females were only muted by the barks of automatic gunfire as the Bronco charged through the crowd with gun shells spitting through every window of the vehicle. A large number of those in the park were smart enough to hit the dirt, while others were laid to the ground. The intelligent gangsters used the protective layers of the trees to dodge bullets before in some way or form returning gunfire at their attackers. The Ford Bronco sped through and unloaded its cargo before hitting the roadway and screeching its tires as the attackers made their getaway.

Day Four Assault - 4:08 am

Hector had been getting increasingly nervous due to threatening phone calls indicating that he was the main target of all who had died thus far. At 2:00 am of the fourth day of assault, two motorbikes sped by Hector's house and sprayed it with bullets. The revenge-seeking gangster was given a business card by a federal agent who assured Hector he would one day desire their services as so may had before him. Hector didn't hesitate to utilize the number as he sought protection no one else could offer. In exchange for his testimony against Ernesto's cartel, the Feds offered to protect and guard Hector, which was an offer he could not refuse.

Three black Chevy Suburban trucks pulled in front Hector Dominguez's home moments before someone was spotted being protectively ushered from inside beneath a wool blanket. The person, who was said to be Hector, was placed in the middle SUV before being taken to the Hoover Federal Building in downtown Miami. Carlos received information from their contact inside the Feds indicating that Hector had been shaken by the recent killings and had sought protection after receiving a few death threats. For his testimony against Ernesto's organization, federal agents proposed relocation and sanctuary, which Hector wasn't that enthusiasticabout. From the Hoover Federal Building, Hector was transferred to a safe house in Key Biscayne where he was to remain under guard until official documents in the case had been processed.

Part 3

STAMMA AND TWO Gully thugs went to the Rose Hall district in order to rob the home of a prominent businessman who was abroad on business. The thugs gained access through the skylight on the roof of the house after breaking the glass and climbing down a rope. Once inside the home, the thugs collected jewellery, appliances, and anything valuable enough to bring in a buck. There was a personal safe underneath the businessman's office desk that the thugs decided to carry along considering they'd need professional help to open it. The usage of flashlights by the thieves alerted the neighbour across the street, who had promised to watch over the house in the owner's absence. The neighbour immediately telephoned the police and advised them of a crime in progress that was developing in one of the most upscale neighbourhoods in Montego Bay.

The robbers had tallied the articles desired and were seeking their exit through the rear when the loud sounds of police sirens echoed down the street. All three robbers sneaked to a front window and peeked out to find a gang of officers taking up the perimeter around the house. The robbers were all stunned to find their perfect heist detected, and the three thugs began nervously considering their options.

The nerviest of the three exclaimed, "What the fuck we go do now? The cops got the whole house surrounded!"

Justin said, "A which one of you set off some alarm or something?"

"Before you start critising check you self, maybe it was you who set off the alarm"!"

"Le-le-let's g-g-g-get o-o-outta h-h-here!" Stamma advised.

The thug who was almost in tears reasoned, "And where the fuck do you suggest we go, Stamma?"

"H-h-here, y-y-you dr-dr-drive," Stamma remarked as he tossed a pair of BMW keys at his accomplice.

"Where you find this? Lord please let there be a car in the garage. ? Fuck them shit deah, right now me just want out," exclaimed the thief, who was beginning to feel claustrophobic with cops all around.

The thug ran to the door that led to the garage and quickly jumped behind the wheel of the car. Stamma and Justin were sure to carry their work's compensation in case they were fortunate enough to escape the grasp of the Jamaican law enforcement. The three thugs sat quietly in the darkness of the vehicle before exiting as they advised each other of important messages they'd like the others to pass on to family members should they not make it through their ordeal.

Gunshots began ringing out before the officer caught a clear sight of exactly what to shoot at as the garage door to the two-story house began elevating. The garage door opened and a BMW 335I blasted out. One of the four police cruisers was parked at the foot of the garage, and the driver of the BMW narrowly missed the cruiser and the officers seeking protection behind it. There was an intense shoot-out between the thugs who were attempting to gain access to the roadway and the police officers intent on finalizing the break-and-entry case right there and then. The BMW narrowly missed the police cruiser, but the bullets being exchanged by police and thief made their way into something or someone.

As the BMW swerved from hitting the cruiser and straightened out to tackle the tough Jamaican roads, Justin, who had been barking his automatic Glock the moment they exited the garage, was shot in the right side of his chest and immediately taken out of contention before the battle had begun sizzling. The gangster grabbed for his chest and began grabbing at Stamma while imploring him not to let him die. The petty pistol-firing of the thieves was outmatched by the officers and the huge automatic rifles they carried, which were desired for patrolling the vicous streets of Jamaica. The golf balls fired by the officers on the scene pierced the skin of the BMW and made huge holes as they also blasted out the rear window and the front passenger-side window. The officers all quickly boarded their vehicles and pursued the suspects who were intent on gaining their freedom at all cost.

The chase ruffled along the Howard Cook Highway, where the fleeing BMW reached over 120 MPH, narrowly missing similar lunatic drivers who only shifted to the soft shoulder because of the sirens. The driver behind the wheel of the BMW made a judgment call to avoid going through the busier downtown district and cut across Top Road over to Albion. From there, they could run down the hill into their safe haven of Canterbury, where they knew the officers would think twice before pursuing. With his escape route plotted, the terrified driver kept his head as low as possible, while the bullets from the police popped holes into the vehicle's frame., With the threat of dying from his wound, the mercy-seeking Justin pleaded to be dropped off at the hospital.

Stamma utilized his opportunities when granted to partially keep the officers at bay by hammering bullets from both his and Justin's confiscated weapons at their followers, considering the injured thug was more concerned with attaining medical assistance. The valiant effort by Stamma through areas where the narrowness of the road was favourable to say the least kept the advancing officers from rear-ending the criminals' stolen BMW off the steep and curvy roadways. Despite the challenging roadways that keep a driver focused are humongous ditches that are detrimental to the health of any vehicle. Hence, precaution along the route was an important task being performed by both cops and robbers.

Officers from one of the Toyota trucks in pursuit opened their automatic rifles at the fleeing BMW, which forced Stamma and his operator to duck their heads or have them blown away like the wind. As the lead BMW started down the steep Cornwall Heights hill, another of the Toyota cruisers' operators became a bit overzealous and attempted to ram the BMW awkwardly down the mammoth hill. Stamma caught the rake and hammered two shells from his 9 mm, which luckily caught the cruiser's left front tire and blew it completely off the rim. The driver of the Toyota truck momentarily lost control of the vehicle as the right tire slammed into a huge pothole, which caused the vehicle to pirouette down the steep hill. As the vehicle rolled down the steep hillside, one of the officers was tossed from the vehicle, and the impact rendered him motionless. The other officers aboard all died from various injuries, while their peers involved in the chase that were bound to apprehending the suspects simply alerted emergency personnel as they scurried along.

The officers' intensity increased following the crash, and all the preventive measures previously acknowledged were thrown out the window. As the chase went along Albion Road behind the Cornwall College soccer field, which was a long stretch of road with no sidewalk, two friends walking home from a soiree were shot and killed by stray bullets being hammered at the evasive BMW. The field report later submitted by the witnessing officer indicated that the bystanders were shot by the cowardly thieves who showed no concern for the public's safety.

The thieves turned off Albion Road onto Seaview Avenue, which led to the back hillside of Canterbury. As Stamma responded to the bullets fired at his entourage, his wounded mate grabbed his thigh one last time in order to beg his allies to not allow him to die. The stuttering thief turned to his accomplice and honestly advised him that each man was on his own. Directly after Stamma warned his accomplice of his possible fate, the driver announced he was about to pull over and bail from the vehicle.

The majority of roughneck within Canterbury who stayed up throughout the nights,night bleachers, not only terrified neighbours into retreating home early but also secured their borders from exterior threats.The entire band of thugs had all but returned to the sanctity of their safe havens when the first loud crash was heard. Without any further warnings, the driver pulled the vehicle to the soft shoulder and slowed down enough to feel the dirt beneath his feet before fleeing the stolen vehicle with his acquired merchandise. Stamma was not to be outdone by the terrified driver, hopped from the vehicle and pivoted to a stop, before he regained control and fled the scene with his stolen merchandise. The BMW rolled its way into Mr. Gale's cemented wall before smashing its way to a halt. Officers were around the BMW faster than a race car on the Indy circuit were quick to corral the vehicle as they moved in on the injured thief. Stamma and the getaway driver were blazing down the hillside when three shots rang out from the point where they'd crashed the BMW. Stamma gazed at the other survivor running alongside him and shook his head in disbelief as both men contemplated what may have become of their friend.

The intensity of the vehicle chase caused four officers to become over-zelous, who gave no second thought as to where they were pursuing their suspects. With weapons at the ready, the officers bolted from their chariots and followed the fleeing thieves into one of Montego Bay's most infamous killing zones. The belief and hopes of the robbers were that the pursuing officers would realize the complexity of the situation and either retreat or call in the more dominant JDF soldiers to detain their criminals. However, with the death of their peers and an "apprehend at all cost" mentality, the four gun-slinging constables engaged their escaping thieves.

The terrain was steep, rocky, and dangerous, and presented a much greater chance of injuring one's self from a fall or from other sharp materials such as razor-edged rocks. At certain points along the trail were deep ravines where a tumble over the ledge would prove catastrophic to the victim. Stamma and his partner were well aware of such treacherous conditions as they scurried along while being extremely cautious. Hatchet and his most trusted confidante were reasoning on matters vital to the security of Canterbury when the first eruption of bullets exploded. The two thugs, like the majority of Gully youths, had been drinking and smoking throughout the night as they cohesively protected their territories. The shots heard by Stamma and his chauffeur alerted the Gully don to the existing problem as Hatchet summoned two others to join their investigative quest.

"Yow Troy and Danny, bring the heavier machines and lets go check out what's happening"!" Hatchet exclaimed as he removed the safety latch from his 9 mm handgun.

With the gleams of light from the new day dawning, the officers became equipped to properly visualize their evasive criminals. Stamma and his accomplice were a few paces ahead of the gaining officer, who began gearing up to shoot the escaping thugs in the back. There was a stretch along the rusted zinc and rotten wooden fence pathways where the path ran straight for nearly fifty feet. As the clearing materialized, three of the four constables opened fire and luckily struck the chauffeur in the left thigh. The realness of the situation forced Stamma to abandon his second accomplice as he tucked his head and fired two bullets at his antagonists. The chauffeur tumbled forward and quickly rolled onto his back to offer himself a proper firing position. With luck, the young thug was able to squeeze off a round from his Smith and Weston thirty-two-calibre, which struck the closest constable directly in the groin. The entire incident occurred so fast that the robber became overwhelmed by police before he could pull the trigger again. The constable who was shot in the groin released his SLR automatic rifle that was strapped to his body and grabbed his private area before falling to both knees and grunting like a pig. Two of the three constables ceased pursuit as they stopped to ensure that the breath of life was properly expunged from the chauffeur's body. Stamma began sucking for oxygen as he fought to maintain his running pace as the same eruption of bullets that befell Justin sounded for the chauffeur.

With fatigue setting in, Stamma thought it best to evade his pursuer by cutting through Mr. Turner's yard, scaling the twenty-foot Gully water drainage wall, and escaping through the trenches where officers seldomly followed. The problems with his closest and most diverse escape route would be Hercules and Sampson, who were Mr. Turner's pair of Doberman pinscher guard dogs. Both dogs were well over three feet tall, with solid muscles, body mass, and a viciousness that kept a bouncing ball from entering the yard and surviving. As Stamma contemplated his options, bullets from the advancing officer whizzed by, boring golf ball-sized holes through the existing zinc fences, and in some cases, sent stray bullets through the wooden wall houses of Canterbury's poor residents. Residents of the neighbourhood, who have survived countless Jamaican elections where the entire country would be at war during such proceedings, knew to simply crawl beneath their beds or find shelter and pray to Jehovah that the bullet exchange would cease as soon as possible.

Maw McPurse, who was an elderly grandmother of six, was preparing her morning coffee before she commenced her daily chores. The seventy-four-year-old grandma had just removed the tea kettle with hot water from her General Electric gas stove and was in the process of adding the water to her Blue Mountain coffee crystal when a stray bullet from the outdoor altercation struck her in the chest. The bullet killed Maw McPurse instantly, and her tumble sent the teakettle and everything else sailing in whichever direction. The sound of the huge crash inside his grandmother's kitchen, along with the loud clatters on the exterior, brought a concerned Dexter to the kitchen. At the sight of his grandmother, Dexter began yelling hysterically, "Somebody killed mi grandmother," before rushing to the cellar, where he immediately dug up a Chinse AK he had buried there. The scorching sun had not properly descended upon the island, yet all throughout the neighbourhood, even residents with cement walls found themselves crawling beneath beds and other protective materials. The sight of parents grabbing their infants and toddlers and shielding them went on from house to house as the squeezers of the triggers carelessly let gunshots pop.

The phrase, "Babylon, Babylon," began echoing down the pathway as fear invoked the normally stuttering Stamma to speak with clarity. With the constable gaining ground by the second, Stamma saw no other alternative but to ignore the beware of dangerous dogs sign and go for broke. The evasive thug leapt over the huge fence into Mr. Turner's gladiator dome and sprinted for the Gully ravine. With no dogs initially in sight, Stamma trotted along, confident that he would safely escape. However, confidence quickly shifted to uncertainty as Sampson bolted from the back of the house and began giving chase. The extra long strides of the animal made the fatigued Stamma seem as if he was running in slow motion as the Doberman caught him some ten feet before the ravine and grabbed onto his thigh.

"Arrrrrrr!" The humongous dog growled as he attempted to yank a chunk of meat from Stamma's leg.

"Ahhhhhhhh!" Stamma yelled as he quickly glanced to see if the constable had aligned him into his sight of shot.

At a point in his travels where he had absolutely no time to spare, Sampson the guard dog forced Stamma to surrender valuable time attempting to free himself. With the dog attached to his leg, Stamma thought it best to shed the dog by shooting him, and thus began shifting his weapon in said direction. Before Stamma could properly align the animal, the constable in pursuit had entered the yard and began unloading his automatic clip at his suspect. The constable shot Stamma five times with bullets that pitched the crook over the ledge of the Gully ravine. Sampson, who had his teeth sunken into Stamma's thigh, was yanked over the ledge with his captive and was lucky enough to land on top of the suspected thief.

The constable had begun moving toward the ravine to ensure his kill when the second of the two animals began charging at him from behind the house. Fright influenced the constable to aim his weapon at the charging dog, which obeyed or listened to no one except its owner. The constable shot and killed the dog before the animal placed him in the same predicament as it did his fellow companion. After killing the Doberman pinscher, the constable veered into the ravine with a sarcastic smirk, knowing he'd avenged his fallen comrades by abiding by the code of conduct and getting his man. The constable satisifinglyturned from the Gully and immediately froze, while his mouth fell wide open. The Jamaican constable had come face-to-face with Hatchet and his band of marauders, who all dispised the police force. The thugs made no suggestions nor demanded anything of the constable as they blasted the proud hero into the same ravine he'd sent their ally. As Hatchet and friends moved to the Gully to investigate who else had been touched by the Grim Reaper, an eruption of bullets began exchanging slightly up the hill toward Seaview Avenue.

"Blood-clatt Hatchet a Stamma the Babylon Buoy dem murder!" Hatchet's closest confidante exclaimed.

"What happen to Justin and Craig?" Hatchet questioned, seconds before the eruption.

Hatchet immediately got on his cellular and began calling his soldiers, who were primarily responsible for the border security. Such soldiers of the ghetto lived closest to the edges of Canterbury and were ordained the Gully's first line of defence. The Gully don had provided his perimeter defence with weaponry. The government would later admit that it had no idea such weapons existed on the island. The constables who remained at the top of the hill all protectively aligned themselves once the shooting began inside the Gully territories. Two armour-piercing automatic submachine guns, which had been camouflaged and positioned to cleanse the top road of any interference, began chopping up vehicles and everything else within their path as the order was given to secure the Gully's borders. Within minutes, another eruption of bullets began forcing the constables, who had taken up a perimeter around the Seaview area, to retreat, reconsider their stance, and return to the base of the hill. Once it became evident that the vehicles, trees, or cement walls would not protect them from the response of the ghetto, constables could be seen abandoning everything, including their weapons, as they raced to safety wherever possible. Reports were filed into police headquarters by constables who described the loss of four officers amidst a violent uprising by natives who sought to protect their own.

The first explosion to sound was from a police cruiser blowing up and bursting into flames as fifty-calibre bullets from the submachine weapons struck the fuel line. The entire ghetto fell under Bad Man's Law, and whichever resident contemplated work, school, or play knew to cancel such plans. Honest, law-abiding citizens became prisoners inside their homes as the thug militia who represented Canterbury took control of the area. Additional bombings were heard to the south along the King Street route as thugs blocked the roadway with an old car frame, stoves, a refrigerator, broken-down sofas, and other articles. The thugs set ablaze the pile of rubbish by lighting a couple of bottles filled with gasoline corked with pieces of fabric and tossing them at a distance. With every entrance to the ghetto securely blocked, thugs manned their patrol stations as they held up and robbed every motorist unaware of the turmoil, even murdering a few who were too stubborn to simply hand over the money.

The road blockages at both Seaview Avenue and King Street inconvenienced residents of the Salt Spring area, the Glendavon area, the Albion area, and everyone east of the problem area. Everyone was forced to use alternate routes, which caused massive delays. Word of the dangers surrounding the Canterbury area quickly spread throughout the territories, and civilians knew from experience to totally avoid said portion of the city. The altercation, in retrospect, caused a grave number of citizens who lived beneath the poverty line to miss out on the fundamentals of their daily activities due to the increased distance it would take to reach their destinations.

A battalion of soldiers under the command of one Major West arrived at the Seaview Avenue location at 8:23 am. The soldiers were called in as an alternative strike force to the constables, who carried sufficient fire power to tackle vigilantes on the street, yet lacked the physical training to combat ghetto thugs in their jungle environment. The soldiers immediately sealed off the area by implementing their crowd control measures, which saw them back spectators far away from the danger zone. Major West, however, was subdued by orders not to penetrate the borders until all diplomatic measures had been exhausted.

At 9:37 am, a survey helicopter was sent in by the army to report on the ground activities in order to provide the soldiers more information should an invasion and extraction mission become necessary. The two-passenger helicopter came over from the south with a single pilot and an observer aboard. From the initial entry, the observer reported and recorded the position of six border guards who were all scattered across the entryway in their camouflaged and articulate hiding spots. As the helicopter swooped down into the midst of the Gully, the observer saw and reported on a few thugs with weaponry so huge they had to transport them about on hand carts referred to as Ballawoo carts and wheel-borrows. At the sight of the humongous machines on the Ballawoo carts, the observer caught his fright and instructed the pilot to take the helicopter to a higher altitude. As luck would have it, Killa, who was an apprentice with the bazooka rocket launcher, was taking aim at destroying the intruders' spyware when Craig, who had taken up a position in the huge ackee tree along the pathway, opened fire at the chopper with his AK-47.

As bullets struck the tail end of the helicopter, the observer yelled, "We're being fired on! Retreat! Retreat! Let's get the fuck out of here!"

Killa had the launcher aimed at the chopper, yet was unaware of the fact that he needed to adjust the sensor tracking. As the helicopter crew resorted to exiting the area, Killa released the rocket, which narrowly missed its mark before crashing and exploding in country man's vegetation gardens. Had anyone translated such occurrence by word of mouth to someone else on the island, the receiver of the tale would certainly shun the teller as an exaggerator of the truth, yet fortunately for such doubters, there was a JBC News helicopter covering the story with explicit orders to remain more than three hundred feet away from the altercation. At the sight of a rocket exploding after missing its target, government officials thought it best to utilize their diplomatic policies in order to quickly bring such a massive standoff to an end.

The MP for the area, Mr. Trevor Balan, contacted Hatchet, who was an important political figure in his gaining an electoral position, and spoke with the Gully don regarding a termination to the conflict. The People's National Party had long since controlled the Canterbury region with legions of thugs stupidly willing to die for the party's cause. The majority of the barrage of weapons, controlled by Hatchet and his legion of thugs, were donated by their favourite MP as a strategy to maintain control over the people through fear. Hence, like many other MP and Gully dons before them, Hatchet and Trevor made a much more cohesive unit than people were led to believe.

"Hello, Hatchet. What is all this standoff business me hearing about happening over there?" Trevor asked.

"Bigger Boss, you want see is like some idiot police run dung inna the ghetto and murder off three a mi soldier them! Obviously them naw go escape, so right now is like we have three a batty buoy tie up pan di base," Hatchet replied.

"Listen to me before this thing go escalate pass the point of no return. Mi want you see to it that nothing harmful don't happen to them constables, 'cause right now them boys a look for a reason to infiltrate Canterbury!" Trevor advised.

"Everything depends on how them boys go about dealing with the business," Hatchet responded.

"Another thing. Who is Kadeem Kite and Ron Powers? Me get word from some top police executives that them rip off some tourists outta El Greco and them want fi them share of the profits!"

Part 4

"**L**ISTEN, I KNOW everything about this guy's operation, from where he smuggles his drugs to where he distributes the shit. All the undercover investigations you guys do—the stakeouts, the spy intel—will never in a million years produce the info that I got on this guy!" Boasted the FBI's newest informant.

"Well, you called us, so let's hear what you got on Mr. Lopez," the agent inside the interrogations room exclaimed.

"Wait a minute, not so fast. I want to hear what you guys are willing to do for me before I start talking. I used to think my gangbanging partners would extend my life span, but right now they got no idea where the hits are coming from. You fellas gotta assure me that this dying craze that's hitting the south isn't getting anywhere close to me!" Hector argued.

"It all boils down to what your testimony does. Mind you, as a criminal yourself, your word against a prominent businessman like Ernesto Lopez isn't worth squat, but if you got enough goods on him to help us nab him with his hand in the cookie jar, then we'll fix you up nicely with a house and a fresh start somewhere, like Nevada," said the agent.

Hector gazed into the eyes of the two federal agents inside the room as he inhaled a lump of cigarette smoke into his lungs. The informant thought there might be an added reward for a smuggler of Ernesto's calibre as he proceeded to negotiate his information for more riches.

"So, you guys are trying to tell me that Crime Stoppers or one of those organizations ain't got some sort of a reward out on this guy?" Hector asked.

"Okay, listen up. This is the way most of these affairs usually unfold. The informant in high profile cases like this one gets our full protection during the proceeding and an honest reward should a stiff conviction result. We're aware of the fact that Mr. Lopez and your father were partners until his untimely death, so you should know a little about their business affairs," answered the senior agent.

"You mean *killed* my dad over jealousy! I was young, but my mother told me the stories about my father being the one with the true drug connection back home in Columbia before Ernesto killed him to gain everything. My mom said she vowed after my father's death to never take a dime from that man no matter how hard times were, and she never did! She advised me to never work for that man and help his empire get bigger. I would have destroyed it myself, but his money and influences make him hard to get a target on," Hector began.

Hector sat and told the federal agents both true and fictitious stories about one of the agency's most sought-after smugglers in the United States. With their recording device capturing every detail of their informant's accounts, the agents questioned and heckled Hector for chinks in his story. Once the agents were satisfied that they'd acquired the knowledge they sought, they immediately arranged for their newfound friend to be transferred to their version of Club Med.

Ernesto was irate to hear that Hector had decided to turn state's evidence by offering the Feds valuable information about his empire. A complete overhaul in business affairs was immediately implemented as Ernesto, who always thought safety first, chose prevention rather than having to search for a cure later. The Columbian drug lord sat uncomfortably inside his office among his associates contemplating the major effect certain information would bear on his business. Said occasion was the only time Kevin ever witnessed Ernesto unravelled as he smacked items from his desk and tossed articles about the room.

"I want this punk dead at any cost! Why is it we don't have someone working inside that federal building to give us information on what is going on in there?" Ernesto demanded.

"Don't worry, Boss E. I have an idea how to find out where they plan on hiding him," Kevin suggested.

The newest addition to Ernesto's lynch mob used his cellular phone to telephone the operator for the main number to the Hoover Federal Building. Kevin then blocked his number to remain anonymous as he imitated an informant calling to report valuable information about Ernesto.

"Hello, you've reached Hoover Federal Administration. How may I direct your call?"

"Good afternoon, madam. I would like to speak with the agent in charge of the Ernesto Lopez case," Kevin responded.

The receptionist asked, "Do you have an extension number, or are you aware of whom you wish to speak to?"

"I'm sorry, Miss. I have no idea who he is, but some agent gave me this number to get in touch with him when I recalled something," replied Kevin.

"Please hold while I scan through my directory to find the agent you're interested in talking to," the receptionist said.

"No problem, ma'am," said Kevin.

The lady was off the line for a few minutes before returning with the desired information.

"Can you recall whether you spoke with Agents Carbonelli or Agent Dunn, sir?"

"I believe it was Agent Dunn," Kevin answered.

"Agent Dunn's extension is 2258. Would you like me to transfer your call?"

"Yes, thank you," Kevin accepted.

The phone rang several times in Kevin's ear before a mild-toned voice male responded to the call.

"This is Agent Donald Dunn. How may I assist you?"

Kevin chose to remain silent as he disconnected the phone link, while the agent on the other end repeated his hail before hanging up his phone, annoyed. Kevin used his newfound information to stroll through the pages of the local telephone directory in search of an address to accompany the name. There was no information about the agent's residence in the telephone directory. However, the agent's name was all Ernesto's hired hands needed to complete the findings. Through an informant at the telephone company, the information regarding the living coordinates of one Agent Dunn was easily acquired, and Ernesto's gun hands were immediately sent to stake out the agent's residence.

Agent Dunn was a seven-year veteran of the agency, which he joined shortly after returning from serving his country as a soldier in the United States army. It had always been the agent's dream to become a federal agent, and once the army granted him the opportunity, Dunn quickly jumped aboard. His salary from the government granted him a comfortable living, which he enjoyed in his three-bedroom condo located in Lauderdale Lakes, Florida. Further information about the agent revealed that he lived with his pregnant fiancée, and she was due to give birth any day.

Hugo Ramerez, who was undoubtedly Ernesto's fiercest warrior, disguised himself as an employee of the Florida Hydro Company and went to Agent Dunn's front door. After the third ring, a fatigued woman, whose belly was so huge she had to turn sideways to reach the narrow door handle, answered the door. Hugo convinced the woman he was doing some sort of water testing to determine whether or not the water from the tap was sanitary enough for the forthcoming baby. Once inside the condominium, Hugo withdrew his weapon and pressed it against the woman's temple before disrespectfully shoving her into the sofa. The mild-mannered and polite impersonator changed into a vicious beast who behaved as if the woman wasn't already in a frail position. The nervous female gazed up at her captor in the event that she was placed in the position of having to describe him later. However, the silencer attached to the end of his weapon caught her attention because she knew he could kill her in an instant without anybody hearing a sound.

"I want you to telephone your husband and calmly tell him to come home right now!" Hugo ordered.

The frightened female, who had to grab hold of her squeamish mouth, nodded her head in agreement as she pointed to the phone across the room. The thought of running to another room and sealing the door behind her crossed her mind, but reality quickly sat in as she acknowledged the forty-pound weight gain, as well as the little person inside her. Hugo brought back the phone and proved he was in no mood for gimmicks as he handed her the phone and pressed his weapon directly on top of the woman's stomach.

She begged, "Please, anywhere but there! It might accidently go off!"

"Any funny talks when you talk to your husband and it is going to go off!"

"Please! Please!" The woman cried as the phone rang in her ears.

After a couple of rings, the woman's fiancee answered the call and could immediately discern that there was a problem. Agent Dunn was in the process of transferring Hector to a safe house further south in the Florida Keys where they suspected he'd be well guarded and safe from assassinations or threats. The pregnant woman, for the sake of her unborn child, controlled her emotions to the best of her ability, although it was evident she had been crying.

The agent asked, "Hey, honey, how are you and my little guy doing?"

"Not so good, baby. Could you just please come home?"

"I'm just dropping off an informant with the boys. I'll have this thing wrapped up in about half an hour and then I'll head straight home," said the agent.

"Okay, just come home as soon as you can," pleaded the wife before disconnecting the call.

The phone receiver was barely on the base before a mild knock sounded at the front door. Hugo maintained a close visual as well as his weapon on the female against the sofa as he walked over and responded to the alert as if he was the head of the household. Kevin and Gustav walked in wearing uniforms similar to Hugo's to disguise themselves from inquisitive neighbours curious about their friend's well-being.

Forty-nine minutes later, the agent pulled into his parking spot and collected his personals from the car before climbing the short steps to his condominium. With a, "Honey, I'm home," the agent unsuspectingly walked into his condo, where a gun was placed to the back of his head the instant he closed the door.

Kevin said, "You see, right now, everything depends on how well you respond to commands! If you fuck with me, I'll kill both you and your little fiancée. You understand me?"

There was a table lamp in the corner of Agent Dunn's living room, which came on and lit up the room, revealing the many characters inside the room. The first person Agent Dunn took notice of was Hugo, who was standing over his fiancée with a chocked weapon pointed at her pregnant stomach. There was a person who would be considered the enforcer, who stood across the room from his fiancée, surveying the happenings with a Mack 10 automatic weapon. The male who held the weapon to the agent's head shoved him forward into the abyss, where he tripped and landed facedown into the carpet. Before Agent Dunn could attempt to reason with his intruders, a huge boot pinned him to the ground, and the boot owner began disarming him. Once the agent had been disarmed, the male dragged him to his feet and shoved him toward his pregnant woman.

"Are you guys okay? These bastards, , didn't hurt you, did they?" Agent Dunn asked.

"No, they haven't, honey. I don't even know what they want!"

Kevin brought a dining chair from the dining room and forced Agent Dunn into the seat. The agent was handcuffed to the chair with both feet tied to completely restrict his ability to move while his fiancée cried for every dreadful minute. Once the agent was properly bound, the reason for his intruders was then known to his fiancée, although the agent himself had worked the Ernesto Lopez's case long enough to by then identify a couple of the armed men inside his home. Agent Dunn also had a distinct idea of what his intruders were after as he contemplated methods of withholding private government information which shouldn't under any circumstances be leaked to the public.

"This afternoon, you and the boys transferred one Hector Dominguez to a safe house in the Keys. Where exactly is it located?" Kevin demanded as he commenced his interrogation. "Now, before you answer me, take a look at my friend over there with his gun pointed at your unborn child Fuck that bullshit they taught you in the academy. Your first wrong answer, the baby is dead, the second, the mother, and so forth so forth!"

Hector Dominguez is at 157 Old County Road, a half mile off the final Interstate 95 exit. Turn right and drive down on the beach until you come to a blue condo. There are five guards protecting him, but the beauty about where they are is that we can't get reinforcements down to them fast enough if any problems occur. I've spent a few nights down there to know it gets pitch dark at night. You boys cut off the power, throw on some night goggles and storm the place, and you're guaranteed to get him," instructed the agent as if he were a member of the strike force battlefield strategy committee.

"Thanks for the input. What is it you have against Ramerez?" Kevin asked.

"I hate murderers. Especially the ones the system allow to slip through the cracks so they can return and cause more families grief," Agent Dunn responded.

At the agent's response, Kevin thought of his mother, and he rose to his feet and advised his comrades to follow suit. Hugo argued that the information collected may be coerced and thus false because it was much too easily given. Kevin refused to debate the fine arguments pointed out by his mate as he stuck to his decision and ordered his accomplices out. Before exiting, however, Kevin telephoned their lookout positioned outside to ensure everything was proper on the front. The sound of bullets being disbursed through a silencer sounded, as Kevin, astonished, turned around to find that Hugo had shot their captives directly in their foreheads.

"Why the fuck did you kill them?" Kevin asked.

"They saw my face, and that's unacceptable!" Hugo exclaimed as he nonchalantly passed Kevin and exited the condo.

Later that same evening, two SUVs filled with Ernesto's assassins journeyed to the southern-most region of Florida where a target sat in the waiting. Hector had settled in bed after a strenuous evening of swimming, dart-throwing, table tennis, a couple hands of poker, and Chinese takeout for supper shared with his assigned protectors. It was 2:20 in the morning and Hector had been unable to comfortably fall asleep. Hence, one of the agents on duty loaned him his cell phone in order for the nervous informant to telephone his girlfriend. During his conversation with the female, the television inside the room went dark, which immediately concerned the informant. Hector sat up in bed and listened through the silence for any indication that he needed to hide himself underneath the bed or inside the closet. The silence of his bodyguards, who were all passed out in different areas around the house, soon calmed the informant, and he slowly reclined onto the mattress.

Kevin, Swarty, and eleven of Ernesto gunners coordinated their attack as they quietly gained entry into the house and veered off toward different regions of the three-story safe house. There was a LCD surveillance camera mounted in the corner that captured everyone entering through the front door, and Kevin, Swarty, Hugo, and two others fell prey to the technology. As instructed by Agent Dunn, Kevin and company wore night goggles that brightened up the darkened haven as they sought out everybody's location around the house. The agent who loaned Hector the telephone was jerking off his dick to a porno flick inside his chosen room when his television suddenly went blank. Aggravated that he was unable to complete his mission, the agent abandoned his third-floor room and blindly felt his way around the dark as he headed for the basement in order to check the circuit breaker.

Four of Ernesto's gunners were heading for the third floor when they came across an agent feeling his way through the dark. The agent was passing the master bedroom suite when he hollered a word of comfort at the informant, who had made it clear he was terrified of the situation because he believed he was being targeted.

"Don't worry, Hector. I'm going to check the circuit breaker. It might just be a little trip," the agent said.

The agent felt the rails that led to the bottom of the steps and took one step down before the blast from a pump rifle flung him backward. With that single blast, all hell broke loose as gunshots erupted all over the house. Hector frightfully jumped from his bed and felt his way around while moving toward the closet, which he'd pinpointed way before the disruption. The informant slid across the sliding door and scurried inside as the pit-pats of footsteps sounded on the stairs. With the sounds of men dying from bullets, Hector lunged into the closet and closed the door as panic began setting in.

His girlfriend asked, "What's all that banging I hear?"

"Call the cops, baby! Call the cops! It sounds like we under attack!" Hector whispered.

"Where do I send them to?"

"Oh, shit! I have no idea where this is!" Hector exclaimed.

"Then you hang up and call the cops so they can trace you, and then call me back," the girlfriend instructed, which was the last time she'd ever talk to Hector.

The nervousness of not having anything with which to protect himself, the constant gun barking echoing below, and the stress of being directly in the middle of the fire confused Hector, who forgot that the glow from an activated phone can be seen by others. As the intruders burst into the master suite, Hector, who was in the midst of dialling 911, froze as the men looked around the room. There was slight green light emanating from the closet, and as the intruders caught a hold of it and advanced toward it, Hector quickly realised what he'd done and slammed the phone shut. The men inside the room simply paused and opened fire at whoever occupied the closet, killing Hector instantly. The intruders identified the kill before moving on to securing the other rooms on the floor.

Ernesto's employed first grade people for everything he wanted handled, and this was especially true about his security personnel. The guards who protected the perimeter of his house were ex-service men who had all been highly trained in various killing techniques. Although the grounds around his house were primarily looked after by his personal strike force that also lived on the property, Ernesto believed that a certain flare was necessary for the beautification of his guard station, hence the camouflage uniforms for all his ex-military exterior guards.

At 6:25 that same morning, an array of police vehicles drove up to Ernesto's front gate, threatening to break it down in order to exercise the powers of a few warrants. Ernesto's security guards stood between an army of law enforcement personnel and their bread and butter until proper warrants were provided that stated the officers had permission to enter the private premises. The guards immediately telephoned Mr. Lopez at the main house to inform him they'd done everything in their power to deter the officers, but their warrants were legal and binding. Ernesto jumped from his bed and informed the lovely señorita beside him to alert his ace gunman as he scurried to prevent an altercation that would definitely end in turmoil.

Ernesto met Agent Carbonelli and his band of law enforcement professionals at the step outside his mansion, where he was handed the warrants for three of his employees. The government agent was sure to advise Ernesto that he'd be back to arrest him once proper evidence was obtained to identify him solely as the man who ordered the hits against both the safe house in the Keys and the Dunn family. Ernesto convinced the agents, who were to charge the residence in order to apprehend the wanted thugs, to allow him to summon the workers whom he declared wouldn't resist arrest. The U.S. Marshalls, although anguished, agreed to have Ernesto summon his employees rather than scurry around for criminals who had a genuine dislike for law enforcement personnel. As promised to Ernesto, who had children and a female on the grounds and fought to avoid a gun battle which might result in some stray bullet escalating the situation, the three men sought walked out willingly and surrendered to the Marshalls.

Swarty was home in bed with his lady when the U.S. Marshalls made a special house call in order to exercise their warrant. There were Marshalls breaking in through the windows and doors, which incredibly only disturbed Swarty's lady, who initially thought they were experiencing a tornado. Both Swarty and his lady slept naked, and she had to scramble for the sheet once it became evident what was occurring. The Marshalls announced themselves as they surrounded the huge, king-sized Posturepedic bed and couldn't believe that their loud racket plus the added screams of Swarty's frightened lady didn't even tickle the wanted man who continued to sleep soundly. A U.S. Marshall butted Swarty on the chest with the butt of his weapon as Swarty spread out across five-eighths of the bed. Swarty groggily opened his eyes and found he was staring down the barrels of huge muskets. As he wiped the cold from his eyes, he realised they'd been infiltrated by the infidels.

Perspiration ran from Kevin's pores as his grabbed onto the hips of the mid-sized woman he'd been sexing for nearly an hour and a half and jammed her as if he was trying to expel the demons from within himself. Following their successful night's escapade that transpired without a single causality, Kevin returned to the home of a female he'd had a number of telephone interactions with. The couple began having sex at 4:30 that morning and were still as heated as the moment they began at 6:03 am. By 6:35 am, Kevin's cellular began sounding constantly as the calls rolled in one behind the other from the same number. Kevin glanced over at the phone once to check the number before continuing with the sex expansion lesson he'd been teaching. The gangster tossed the female onto her bed and turned her onto her side before throwing her right leg over his left shoulder, with her left leg between his thighs. The female, who lived alone, had been moaning and groaning throughout the experience as she fought to remember the specific number of orgasms she'd endured. As Kevin re-entered her, her seductive groan sent chills up his spine. He ground his penis into her moist and juicy vagina. The woman, who had been equal to the challenge, grinned at her partner's nine-inch iron as he again hit her G-spot, which was always the prelude to her climaxing.

"Ah, yeah, right there, baby," moaned the female as Kevin pondered over the importance of the call while caressing and admiring the luscious curves of his partner.

"How does it feel, baby? You like that?" Kevin teased as he changed gears and increased his intensity, which startled the woman, who didn't believe another gear was possible.

The woman found it fascinating to conceive that someone could perform for such a long duration of time without the aid of drugs or some sort of ancient remedy. As she sucked on Kevin's penis, the female pampered the gangster's sensation tool and thought about the constant joy such a strudel would bring to her permanent life. The constant interruption of his cell phone soon got to Kevin, who finally decided to respond to the caller.

"Hello?" Kevin answered.

"Good morning, Señor Kevin. I'm sorry for waking you up, but Ernesto asked me to call you to inform you that the Marshalls are here with a number of warrants. I guess he wants you to keep yourself in a safe place and he'll be in touch with you as soon as possible," explained the woman on the line.

"Thank you," answered Kevin, and he immediately hung up and telephoned Swarty.

Swarty's phone rang with no answer due to the fact that the Marshalls had taken both he and his lady into custody for various violations such as marijuana and weapons possession. Kevin called back several times before the realisation of what might have happened to his number one ace sunk in. The wanted gangster laid back on the female's bed and pondered over his situation as his lover continued stroking his penis while tickling his fancy with her aggressive tongue action.

It inevitably became obvious that something was bothering Kevin, because his erection slowly relaxed even though his lover was performing tricks which would cause other men to curl their toes and cling tightly like a baby to its mother as they ejaculated uncontrollably. The female paused her erotic manoeuvres and rolled up underneath Kevin's arm as he threw his hand around her thick, healthy body.

"That was one of those worrisome phone calls, wasn't it?" She asked as she compassionately sought to help the man who'd been fucking the daylights out of her.

"Yeah, you can say that," Kevin answered.

"Anything you need, just let me know. Illegal or straight," declared the female.

"Listen to you!" Kevin joked as he ran his fingers through her lengthy weave. "I just got word that I might be on the Fed's wanted list."

"Then run away to Canada, like my brother did, but don't just sit back and let them catch you and bury your ass in one of those underground federal institutes where the only thing you get to do is probably read fucking books and jack your dick," exclaimed the woman.

"Isn't your brother American? Then how the hell did he sneak into Canada?" Kevin asked.

"He just walked across the border somewhere out there between California and British Columbia where it's like wide-open plains and where it's as easy as walking across a street," the female replied.

Kevin thought about the woman's suggestion as he once again began kissing her neck while caressing her luscious body which he'd enjoyed and adored. The gangster decided to abandon his worrisome thoughts and leave matters to Jehovah as he'd always done in times of great tribulations. Should Kevin get caught and receive a zillion years in prison, the knowledge of avenging his mother's death would offer him solitude, and he hoped the memories of his final moments with a female would be sufficient enough to stimulate him through his incarceration.

The first round of intercourse left Kevin feeling a bit sticky and uncomfortable after buckets of perspiration dripped from his anatomy. As the sensation of Round Two overwhelmed Kevin, the gangster rose to his feet and brought the female into her shower, where he opened the sprinkler with warm water onto them and backed her against the wall before lifting her left leg over his arm and reinserting his hard penis. Their heated passion, along with the steam from the pipes, soon fogged up the entire bathroom, through which the only object of reference pointing to people being inside the bath was the renewed seductive cries of the woman's moan and groans.

Part 5

THE CANTERBURY GHETTO standoff between the Jamaica Defence Force, or JDF, and the true sufferers of Jamaica had entered its third day with no signs of surrender from either side. The ghetto youths of Canterbury implemented a strict no-fly zone around their territory against the "Babylon System," which was how they described governing officials who represented their own special interests while the poor suffered and starved. Soldiers of the JDF took up positions to the southern portion of Canterbury, the northern portion which runs along King Street, and the eastern sections along the Gully Market. For the three days since the standoff begun, there had been repeated exchanges of gunfire from both lines against the borders, with some of the island's hugest weaponry being exercised to the fullest. With every introduction of a powerful weapon by members of the Jamaica Defence Force into the conflict, the ghetto youths of Canterbury would respond with something humiliatingly heavier. The defenders of the ghetto were hidden and defended from trenches behind houses and whatever bullet-resistant object they could find, while the Jamaican army personnel hid behind their armoured vehicles, citizens' vehicles, and trees. The Jamaican army, which would have ended the conflict overnight by simply carrying out an all-out raid with their huge battalion, was forced to work through diplomacy due to the fact that the ghetto thugs still held two police officers hostage.

God-fearing and law-abiding citizens who were forced to find protection within their own homes were forced to pray to every god known to man for the shooting to cease as the death toll slowly rose. The decibel level emanating from every home throughout the community detailed the extent of sorrow radiating through said residents as citizens remained trapped with murdered corpses inside their homes. One such voice was Kim McPurse, who woke up to find her elderly grandmother killed by a stray bullet that bored through their half-inch wooden walls and struck her grandma in the chest. Kim bawled like a cow braying for water for nearly two days as she remained fixated on the final, pleasant stare on her grandma's face.

Over by the Baker family, nine children under the age of thirteen cried for their bellies as the poor fisherman's family awaited the return of their father, who had sailed off to acquire fish to sell and to feed his family. Mr. Baker sat out the initial night of the conflict and had been unable to return home to feed his children due to the escalating violence that struck the area. Regardless of the volatile tension, Mr. Baker, after giving considerable thought to his disadvantaged children, attempted to cross the eastern JDF barricade before being physically restrained by police officers placed in charge of crowd and traffic control. For many other families throughout the ordeal, the experience was similar to that of enduring a hurricane as food rations ran dangerously thin while the devastation outdoors rambunctiously claimed lives throughout. There were homes with infuriated mothers who had newborn babies requiring formula or milk. The majority of these mothers chastised their partners for not doing enough to provide for their hungry children.

The Gibson family suffered one of the toughest losses after Pamela grabbed her three-month-old baby from the rocker to find that the child had been horribly murdered. Pamela bawled louder than an entirely packed stadium as she cuddled her baby and refused to separate herself from the corpse. Another ten households wept and grieved their losses, though they had individually assured themselves the same fate would not befall them, while everyone remained close to the ground and barricaded themselves behind some protective object.

The officers in captivity were handcuffed to a huge ackee tree in the centre of the community along the pathway up the hill toward Seaview Avenue. The officers were stripped of all their clothing, shoes, and weapons, and they could barely be identified due to the large amounts of dried blood covering their bodies. Both officers had been beaten with fists, batons, gun handles, pipe irons, and every filthy bit of material the neighbourhood gangsters could get their hands on. One officer could barely remain conscious as an ex-convict who believed he'd been mistreated by the officer was sure to clobber him over the head the moment he regained consciousness. However severe the beatings were, however, every ghetto thug was cautious to heed the warnings of Hatchet, who ordered that neither man be killed.

Dexter McPurse had a younger brother named Jimmy whom most people believed was a bit senile due to the fact that he occasionally spoke to himself. Jimmy, despite the whispers of others, had always been obedient to his grandmother, whom he praised for sheltering them while his mother acquired proper status abroad before filing documents to have them relocated. While Dexter was off with his band of marauders bleaching and fighting, Jimmy listened to Pamela scream her head off as he sat quietly on his bed, rocking to-and-fro while staring at his grandmother's corpse. The voices that warped young Jimmy's mind instructed him to fetch his grandma's machete from the kitchen and go forth in search of evil souls.

Jimmy, despite all the mayhem outdoors where even the frontline thugs had to occasionally rotate their positions, found himself carelessly wandering down the path as bullets whistled all around him. An exchange of bullets was occurring only a few feet away between the JDF soldiers and the ghetto warriors as Jimmy came across the bloodied captives that were properly shackled and handcuffed. The instructions given to Jimmy by the voices in his head were very precise, and they specifically told him to make mincemeat of the Babylon worshippers. Jimmy began mutilating the captives as if the very Bible he'd rendered devotion to didn't warn against such volatile acts. The ghetto soldiers who came across the mutilation were surprised to find the ordinarily tranquil Bible student carving the thinnest of steak slices from the officers' bodies. Dexter had to be summoned to hinder the lunatic who appeared to have lost all touch with reality as he nonchalantly hacked away at the deceased officers. Die-hard thugs who had splattered men's brain matters either threw up at the sight of Jimmy's justice or admitted to the fact that they'd never seen anything as gruesome. Dexter had to plead with his younger brother for him to release the machete before consoling his beloved sibling, and then walking him back up the path toward their home. Hatchet, who'd attempted to avoid a full-scale invasion by the Jamaican Defence Forces, simply warned his followers to prepare for Judgment Day as all gloves were removed once the officers ceased breathing.

Almost immediately, Hatchet's cell phone began erupting as if someone had a hot story to tell. The expression revealed by the area don's face gave all indications that said person was not one he wished to converse with at that moment. Hence, for the first time since the altercation began, the JDF soldiers completely silenced their weapons and ceased firing.

"Hello?" Hatchet said as he stepped away from the bunch of thugs who'd gathered.

The MP questioned, "Didn't I tell you diplomacy was in the works? Is what kind a rass-clatt thing that mi just see on the television?"

"Is what you a talk 'bout?" Hatchet asked naively.

"The-the-the rass chop thing me just witness some butcher a chop the police them like them is some cattle or something!"

"Boss man, me can't discuss them things right now, mi link you later," retorted Hatchet as he disconnected the call.

Sergeant West received confirmation from headquarters to proceed with tactical operation called "Gully Sweet." It was a military exercise developed by Jamaica's finest. With the majority of Gully thugs confused after five minutes of silence while the JDF soldiers repositioned themselves in preparation for an attack, Killa and friends reloaded their weapons in anticipation of something different. Two gunship army helicopters swooped over the horizon from Seaview Avenue and immediately began clearing the entire terrain. The huge, fifty-calibre Remington M-250 automatic weapons on board the choppers wiped out the guard posts that hindered the sergeant and his troops from entering. The chopper's engineers were sure to abstain from shooting directly at homes, as their purpose was mainly the guard posts and dropping troops deeper into Canterbury.

The invading soldiers tossed their ropes from the helicopters and began sliding their way to the ground while attempting to lay cover fire as the scattering thugs sniped off a few of them in retaliation. The threat of the gunships above persuaded most ghettorude boys to rethink their strategy and retreat, as it was obvious that the Babylon System's patience had run out. Sergeant West and his troops had fully invaded the territories and were killing more thugs than they arrested as they slowly swept the hillside of its weakened defence. The Gully thugs who were arrested were placed in the custody of the Jamaican constables on site who had alternative motives in mind for those they captured. Once the hustling constables got the opportunity to interrogate any prisoner, they'd immediately seek to find the two thieves accused of theft at the El Greco Resort. An injured prisoner who'd been shot in the elbow after attempting to flee capture was pressured into disclosing Stamma's address as the interrogating officer jammed a piece of stick into the man's wound.

Killa, Hatchet, and a number of their colleagues surveyed from which direction the true threat emerged with all intentions of gang rushing the section with the weakest link. The borderline between the Gully Public Market and Canterbury had held firm against all oppositions, and thus the decision to make it their escape route was unanimous. The Rude Buoys of Canterbury were increasingly becoming desperate as the armed forces for the country rained down on them. As the twenty-eight thugs trampled toward the borderline, those at the rear became obliged to secure the flank as a number of overzealous soldiers had to be reminded with whom they warred. The fleeing warriors struck the eastern border like a high-powered train chucking at its highest speed with grenades—weapons that sounded a *boom* instead of *pow-pow* and with a much greater force than that to which they were subjected.

Sergeant West had originally entrusted a dozen soldiers to the post with the arrangements that the constable police would back and assist the soldiers should they desire the aid. Once Hatchet and his band of marauders added their massive weaponry to the defenders along the eastern post, the clearing out of those along the Babylon border went as follows::

The police constables became scared and abandoned the JDF soldiers who were determined to hold their position, The already scanty civilians all disappeared at the sound of the protruding Gully thugs, while the

JDF soldiers who were incapable of maintaining the border without assistance, surrendered their lives. The twenty-eight fleeing disciples of Canterbury, overpowered their memesis across the market border, before scattering to safty across the island.

Stamma's grandmother believed the constables who came to call were there to ensure she'd made it through the ordeal. The constables aided the old lady to her feet and escorted the granny outside, after which they advised her they were returning to search the house for fugitives and weapons. The old lady, who'd been trapped for days, walked to her front gate and looked out at the community she'd lived in for nearly eighty years. There were two bodies lying in the bushes about ten feet away.while Granny P. threw her hands over her mouth and began asking for her boys. The tension mounted quickly as initially nobody had any inkling where the thugs were or whether they were alive or not. A few relatives of certain deceased thugs began arguing with police officials as the next of kin sought to transfer the bodies back home. Constables argued that everything needed to be photographed and documented before it was possible for any article or bodies to be moved, hence the continuous bickering.

Gloria, who was one of the hillside's most notorious gossip queens, came walking up the hill with her eyes filled with tears. The gossip queen had set out to document those who had been killed, injured, or imprisoned for adequate knowledge during her daily discussions with girlfriends. Gloria was almost to Granny P. before she noticed the two dead bodies across the way in the bushes and went over to investigate.

"Them should put about fifty more shot inna them two over there!" Gloria scandalized as she walked over to Granny P. Gloria resembled someone who had just risen from the comforts of her bed, with her hair wrapped in curlers, a plain white Mickey Mouse T-shirt that highlighted her sizable brawless brests, a skimpy little shorts that awarded her a free passport to check out whatever, with no police interruptions and her basic yard slippers.

"Them kill him, Granny P.! Them kill him!" Gloria exclaimed.

"Who, child? Who them kill?" Granny P. asked.

"Is Stamma, Granny!" Gloria declared.

"Lord, God no"!, *no!*" TDramatically exclaimed the old ladywho tumbled into Gloria's arms. "Not mi grandson, Lord! *Noo!*"

Gloria carried Granny P. back into her house and entered to find the police ransacking the domain. The ruthless gossiper began chastising the constables, who soon ran from inside the home as if a skunk had run inside.

"Is what onnou doing in the woman house after onnou kill off the woman grandson? Onnou come out onnou dirty stinking rotten shit house. If onnou plant anything inna the woman house, onnou go live to regret it. Fuck around and see if I don't put a spell pan onnou," threatened Gloria.

Killa, Hatchet, and a few others rode a minibus destined for Savlamar where they could lay low and hide out until the heat settled before returning to their domain. Hatchet had a backpack filled with money and guns, which he handed to his gun bag man to carry should they run into a police barricade. The Canterbury don was originally from the Savlamar district where his mother and grandmother still resided. The thugs who were just moments before involved in one of Montego Bay's most devastating gun shoot-outs behaved politely and tranquilly as if the incident didn't faze them in the least.

As the minibus neared West Green, which is a small community south of downtown Montego Bay, Killa yelled out, "One stop, Conductor," in an attempt to dismount the vehicle. The minibus, which was packed with adults and children returning home after a long day at work or school, stopped across the street from the West Gate Mall, and Killa paid the conductor and exited the taxi. The gangster was sure to hail and recognize his friends, to whom he offered no explanation as to his intentions. Killa looked up and down the street before yanking his Pittsburgh Steelers peak hat down over his forehead and proceeding in the same direction as the minibus.

The West Green housing development was unlike the Canterbury ghetto, where children rode about on their bicycles, lived in decent homes, and ate from golden spoons according to people of the poorer class. The more durable, concrete houses stretched out for acres and were painted with luscious colours that enhanced the beauty of the landscape. Police patrolled such neighbourhoods more often than they would such places like Glendavon, Salt Spring, Flankers, or Canterbury, even though the majority of middle-class citizens are more likely to own a weapon. Throughout the poorer ghetto sections of the city, it was almost impossible to acquire the assistance of local law enforcement, who abstained from certain volatile areas due to the crime rates.

Killa walked into the West Green community under scanty streetlights since one in every three or four light bulbs had been smashed out. The Canterbury thug had thought of his deceased friend since the news reached him, and as he wiped a single tear from his left eye, images of Stamma marching alongside him played visibly again inside the movie theatre in his head. The thoughts of him chucking Stamma or Stamma chucking him as they walked brought a temporary smile to the thug's face, although it quickly vanished once he thought about the man he blamed for his friend's death. Killa totally disregarded the fact that Stamma was attempting to escape capture after shooting his way from a foiled robbery. Hatchet had disclosed the police's interest in acquiring both he and Stamma, which for Killa proved his very suspicions.

The revenge-seeking thug stopped at the neighbourhood convenience store on Orchard Road and bought a dozen Red Stripe beers with the instructions to have them delivered to 20 Violet Lane. Killa then scurried along in advance before the delivery boy arrived in order to position himself for his grand entrance. The baptised gunman ensured the streets were relatively calm before jumping the fence to 20 Violet Lane and hid in the shade brought on by the huge trees in the front yard.

Within minutes, a slender kid came riding his bicycle up the road with the box of beer seated in a trolley attached to the front of the bike. The kid came to the gate and entered the yard before briskly walking to the house ahead with both hands on the box. Killa ducked down behind a huge column built at the front porch as the unsuspecting delivery boy went up and knocked the door.

The voice behind the door inquired, "Is who dat?"

The delivery boy answered, "Kenny, from the convenience store!"

"What the fuck you doing at my door, Kenny?"

"Mi bring the Red Stripe Beer them for you!"

"But mi never order no Red Stripe Beer. Hold on a minute. Let me see if my friend know anything about this delivery," replied the voice behind the door.

The delivery boy argued, "Listen, boss, because them beer ya pay for already, me just go leave them right here until you decide fi come pick them up. Mi buoy, Usain Bolt, about to run a race on the TV and mi naw miss it over some beer!"

"What you say? Pay for already?"

The person inside the house caught the tail end of the delivery boy, who quickly mounted his bicycle and rode off. There was, as promised, a six-pack of perspiring Red Stripe beer on the porch in front the house when the occupant opened the door to retrieve the alcohol. The insurmountable level of shock that struck the home dweller once Killa jumped from the shade caused the man to instantly drop the free beer. once Killa pointed his weapon directly at the man's head and backed him inside the house.

"Who else inside the house?" Killa demanded.

The terrified male answered, "Just Reverend in the shower!"

The brightness inside the room clarified the identity of the male frozen at the mouth of his weapon as Kadeem used his thumb to yank back the hammer. Everything became clear as a terrified Maxwell again lay directly in the sights of his aim. Killa instructed Maxwell to rise and lead the path to the bathroom, as he needed to ensure that no surprises popped out from the woodwork. By the appearance of things, it seemed as if Maxwell and his partner were preparing to celebrate an achievement with the crystal glasses and a bottle of Moet chilling on ice.

From behind the shower curtains, Rev exclaimed, "Maxwell, I told you to get me a glass of that champagne and come join me in this shower!"

Kadeem used his right leg and stumped Maxwell directly into the shower curtain, sending him and everything else collapsing against the wall. Rev immediately became irate as he began cursing Maxwell, blaming him for being such a klutz and causing him to hurt himself. A huge gash opened up above Rev's right eye, and he grabbed for his wash rag to cover the wound.

"There is no need for all that bickering, so zip it before me have to zip it for you!" Killa threatened.

"Oh, my God! Kadeem, I hope you don't think I meant anything I said to you the other day. Mi did just a run off mi mouth. You know, say sometimes mi talk too much!" Rev pleaded as he removed the curtain that obstructed his view of Kadeem.

"You send police to kill off your own nephew? How you explain something like that?" Killa said.

Maxwell started to shout, "We had a deal and you crooks want—"

Bam-bam-bam-bam! Killa fired his pistol that pistol silenced Maxwell permanently. Reverend, who already had blood gushing from his forehead, caught the explosion of blood that burst from his partner, and the gravity of the situation became clear. Killa then grabbed the person he came to assassinate and booted Rev like a dog all the way back into the living room. The naked informant begged for his life throughout the journey as he received a number of scrapes, cuts, and internal injuries during the trip.

"Kadeem, Kadeem, please don't kill me. I know say the police them a look for you, 'cause them say a you kill off them partner them during the shoot-out. But just wait, listen me out! Me have an open ticket to Nassau that me can use any time and you done know say we resemble bad, just spare mi life and me give you the documents and ticket. Leave mi tie up and by time you reach and safe, them can't do you nothing after that!" Reverend begged.

"Where you have the documents them a hide?" Kadeem demanded.

"Inna one of my bottom dresser drawers," Rev responded.

Without so much as another word, Killa opened fire at Reverend, hitting him four times in the chest and once in the mouth, which would indicate to whomever found him that he had been an informant. The satisfied gangster retrieved the materials that were being used to bribe him from Rev's bedroom before quietly slipping out through the rear entrance and disappearing.

The morning Star newspaper's first text read, "Nineteen thugs, six constables, and two JDF soldiers killed in brutal shoot-out." There were also eight arrests and five patients taken to the hospital with injuries that were not life-threatening following Montego Bay's longest standoff. Killa had some unfinished business to which he had to attend in the ghetto, and after lounging about his girlfriend's for a day and a half, he decided to briefly return to Canterbury. The entire hillside progressed in Nine Nights celebrations as parents and guardians all coordinated their efforts in remembering their fallen children. Granny P., like many other relatives about the district, had a yard full of mourners who'd gathered to celebrate the life of Stamma, who was, in all actuality, a very fun-loving individual. Killa returned to the coordinates at which he'd buried his dividends, dug up his hidden stash, and moved to join the mourning festivities.

Stamma's family members became Kadeem's over the years because Granny P. had always included him in family affairs. Once the wanted gangster materialized, every arm around the proceeding came open with sentiments of sorrow, and Killa soon found himself swinging from embrace to embrace. Drunken Uncle Eddie, who had sworn he found God in the bottom of a Wrey and Nephew overproof bottle of white rum, was preaching at the top of his lungs against the use of weapons, and he paused his ceremony to embrace and assure his nephew that he would always be there for him. Killa made his way inside to Granny P's room, where the elderly mourner was surrounded by female members from her church congregation.

The sight of Kadeem eased the nervous woman's tension, and she outstretched her weakened arm at him. Everyone inside the room sensed their desire for privacy and walked from the room, allowing Granny P. to advise her adopted grandson who was said to be on the police's wanted list for murders committed and assumed.

"You okay, my boy? Them no hurt you or anything?" Granny P. asked.

"No, Mama. Me fine," Kadeem answered.

"Listen to me. I want you to find a way to go live with your father in Canada. All these years he has not been the best father, but him at least occasionally sent me a dollar to help you. Make something of your life for me, my son, because me can't afford to bury both you and Ron, so promise me you go do whatever it takes to leave this island," Granny P. reasoned.

"I promise, Granny P," Kadeem answered as they both embraced and tightly held each other.

Part 6

KEVIN STOOD ON his tailor's mantle while the young man measured him for a few garments he was having made. The midweek morning was filled with rain, and it was forecasted to continue throughout the entire week. There had been a slight fog overshadowing the city of Montreal, which brought darkness close to that of night. A loud ticking clock against the wall detailed the hour at 10:53 am, and Kevin checked with his tailor about the authenticity of the time on the clock.

The young designer was an immigrant from Jamaica who modified his apprenticeship into a rare form that was admired and adored by many throughout. The young designer, Carlton, had migrated to Canada some seven years prior in search of what many attempted to achieve. Carlton himself worked with an apprentice from Trinidad, whom he'd taught and groomed since the tender age of sixteen. The two had a modest workshop where they designed and sold the multitude of their designs. The front area of the store displayed the many garments available to the public, while the rear boasted the area from which the creations were derived.

Kevin's cellular rang frequently as that of a major enterprise, though he survived without the use of a proper secretary. His many illegal dealings saw temporary pauses by the tailor, who demanded perfection of himself and waited for the proper moments to proceed. Kevin would respond to requests demanded of him over the phone by assigning one of his three employees scattered throughout the city. Whatever the demand, Kevin maintained a constant calculation over the figures as his supply on demand business thrived.

Following the altercation that had landed the majority of Ernesto's cabinet behind federal bars, Kevin was smuggled from Florida to elude capture by government officials who sought to bury him as the main enforcer in the assassinations of federal agents, a federal informant, the fiancée to an agent, and her deceased fetus. Ernesto orchestrated a limousine for his *numero uno* problem-solver to be transported to California, where Kevin followed the instructions given to him by his final American fling and simply walked across an unmanned portion of the Canadian/United States border into a new country. Kevin was given a Manila envelope containing an English passport and a document stapled inside identifying him as a foreign student from the United Kingdom who had transferred to Canada to complete his studies. There was a Canadian driver's license, a cellular phone and an American Express card to accompany the travel documents, along with a separate Manila envelope that was filled with cash. The fugitive from American justice was picked up directly after he crossed the border by an Indian whom Ernesto befriended in an immigration jail the first time he attempted to enter the United States.

The Canadian native, whom Ernesto asked to guide Kevin through his transition in a country where two languages are recognized, was parked along the roadway with his hood raised as if he were experiencing car trouble. The Indian who arranged to meet at a specific junction along the highway, drove an old Ford F-150 truck and quickly rushed Kevin into the vehicle before advising him to buckle down for the long ride to Quebec.

"I'm Eagle Esquada. How was your trip?"

Kevin was about to roll his given name off the tip of his tongue, when he thought about the documents which referred to his new identity.

"I'm Nicholas Henry. Nice to meet you. The trip wasn't bad, but I think I'll fly the next time around," Kevin answered, and both men chuckled.

"How is my old friend doing back home?" Eagle inquired.

Both men struck up an arousing conversation, during which Eagle, who lived on the Indian reservation in Chateauguay, south of the island of Montreal, gave his perspective on living with the Frenchmen. Eagle offered Nicholas a place to stay, which he didn't brag was the Trump Plaza but hinged it was the safest territories throughout all of Quebec. The Indian disclosed to Nicholas that he lived with both his sons, who were both of manly status, and that it would be their honour to welcome him despite their cramped quarters. Nicholas refused the offer because he didn't wish to intrude upon anyone's life on account of his business involvements. The young fugitive had Eagle drop him off around the Notre Dame de Grace area, where he recognized a vacancy sign in the window of a duplex home, went in and paid the proprietor a year's rent in advance, collected his keys, and moved right in. Five months later, Kevin stood on his tailor's mantle as one of the primary cocaine distributors around the metropolitan area of Montreal.

The chimes above the front door sounded, and three huge men wearing raincoats walked into the store. Though the rain from their coats drenched the entire entryway, it was their massive structures and tattooed anatomies which grasped the Trinidadian helper's attention. The three men appeared to be weightlifters with incredibly muscular physiques, and they boasted tattoos of demonic significance on their bodies. One of the men wore his German riding helmet that had the Rough Riders insignia against the front. Carlton's helper recognized the biker insignia against the man's helmet and wondered what business they had inside the store.

"Welcome to Carlton's Creations, gentlemen. How may I be of service?"

"We are looking for Nicholas Henry," answered one of the Frenchman, who sounded like he'd been practicing the question prior to asking it.

"Is he expecting you gentlemen?"

The same biker exclaimed, "He talk to us!"

The Trinidadian continued, "But he's a bit tied up, sir. Is he expecting you?"

"Listen, *mon ami*, we hear Nicholas here from good source. Now get him, or we find him ourselves," demanded the biker wearing the helmet.

"I'm sorry, I'm sorry, but who do I say wishes to speak with him?"

The conversation transmitting from the front of the store was almost to a scuffle, and Kevin and Carlton caught notice of the loud voices. Kevin's newest identification came with a new name, which was the very person being hailed by the Frenchmen in the lounge. The curious fugitive crept toward Carlton's office door and peeked out at the men asking for him. The only dilemma for Kevin was the identity of these men who knew personal aspects of his character that he had never made public. The majority of those who knew him in this new world referred to him as Nick, or Nicholas, which were the names surrendered by him at introduction. A handful of friends from the motherland were the only true bearers of Kevin's proper identification, though they eventually joined in by addressing him as everyone else did.

If these guys were police of some sort, they wouldn't be asking to talk to me. They would kick down the door and send in all types of SWAT teams to get me out, thought Kevin to himself as he pondered whether or not to confront the intruders. *I wonder if they some bounty hunters like them fools on* Cops. *Couldn't be, or they would be looking for Kevin Walsh instead of Nicholas Henry.*

The Trinidadian helper, who'd become nervous by the manner of physicality, forced Kevin's hand as he returned to the rear of the store in search of him. Kevin began regretting not having a weapon with him;though he'd never before had the need for one on this new soil. Thoughts of an escape through the rear exit crossed the fugitive's mind before the Trinidadian professed they were possible gangsters from the Rough Riders clan. At that point, Kevin intriguingly reported to the front of the store, with curiosity being his primary motive.

The spokesperson of the bunch demanded, "You Nicholas?"

"Yeah, what's up, man?" Kevin answered.

"Your business dealings conflicting against my boss, *mon ami.* You do business with no more my boss' clients. No more business for you 'round neighbourhood," began the spokesman before Kevin rudely interrupted.

"Wow, wow, wow! What the fuck you just said? What shit 'bout boss clients you talking about, man?" Kevin argued, demanding clarification of what the Frenchman meant.

"You do business no more in NDG, LaSalle, or downtown,

comprendez? We control the major street hustlers *dans—"* continued the spokesman.

Kevin's thoughts drifted from the words being uttered at him as he confusedly misjudged the entire situation. Not believing any one entity had enough testicular fortitude to dominate the entire drug trade forced Kevin to alter his reflections on the immediate altercation. Simply stating, Kevin believed Ernesto to be the jackal responsible for the game he perceived was being played with him.

"So where's this pussy? Bring him out. Bring him out so I can tell him to his face what he can do with my dick in his mouth!" Kevin laughed.

From nowhere came a right cross that crashed against Kevin's left earlobe, ringing his ear like a church bell. Before Kevin could collect the driver responsible for the infraction's personal information for his insurance claim, a jaw-breaking uppercut landed him flat on his back, from where he could properly admire the tiles on Carlton's ceiling. Showers of licks began raining from the heavens, and Kevin was forced to protect his vital points by curling up tightly. The three men yanked Kevin from the floor and worked him over properly, with both his hands held securely by his antagonists. Kevin was only left to wonder why was he receiving such a beating.

Carlton rushed to his office and quickly dialled 911 before his entire clothing line was destroyed. His assistant, in the meantime, came up under the nozzle of a P-53 Magnum handgun after attempting to rush to assist a fellow Caribbean native. Carlton soon suffered the same fate as did his assistant, though he never swayed from voicing his opinion at the transgressions. The tailor professed the devaluing of his creations should there arise allegations of death inside his store. Carlton even pleaded with the bikers not to damage his products, citing his children's need for food as the reason.

The man who waved the pistol in the faces of Carlton and his assistant telephoned his boss with an update on what was transpiring. A faint sound from a police cruiser could be heard in the distance, and the molested began wondering if any of them were to be left alive. Through this entire ordeal, one thing remained constant, and that was the beating being laid on Kevin. The men pounded him with their fists and steel-toed boots, opening huge lacerations on his face and fracturing several bones. Kevin was knocked unconscious by one of the many blows to the head, which may had been the reason the beatings ceased. By then, the faint police cruiser sound was roaring in front the garments store, bringing hopes that everyone may survive.

A pool of blood surrounded Kevin, who lay motionless on the floor. Carlton had expected their unwelcomed visitors to vacate the premises before the cops arrived, yet the men showed no fear, nor did they panic as the sirens whistled out front. Fear and fright began setting into the captors, who prayed they would not end up in the middle of a gun battle between their antagonists and the police. The manor of Carlton's appeal could only be confronted by gun-wielding, tactically manoeuvring officers such as the SWAT team, which was whom they expected as rescuers instead of some regular street cops.

Two uniformed officers soon waltzed in and engaged in a comical conversation with a third individual. The third individual wore a simple jeans outfit, Avalanche leather boots with Zidic buckles on the side, a platinum skull ring on the right hand with a quarter cut diamond in each eye, and a platinum cross beside dog tags stringing from a beaded chain with his hell-raising tattoos to complement the style. The two officers stood to the side like spectators while the man walked over to Kevin and knelt down beside him.

"Okay, wake the fuck up! I know you can hear me in there; now act accordingly," the man instructed before slapping Kevin across the face with a backhand. "I can see your eyes. I can see your eyes! What is it? I speak better English than my boys do, or you smart enough to look at the man who will bury you in an instant? Now, I'm Martain Lafleur, and if I get word that you set up shop anywhere close to my zones, ain't no more warnings."

Carlton and his assistant looked on in total disbelief at what they were witnessing. The two metropolitan officers stood to the side with their arms properly folded while the bikers continued their rude mischief. As they looked on, the Rough Rider captain became infuriated by the insult suggesting he perform fellatio on Kevin, and he motioned his troops for something. It wasn't until one of the officers tossed his flashlight to Martain that Carlton understood the gesture that brought a closing to the entire situation. The red lights from an ambulance flashed through portions of the window as Martain caught the flashlight in midair and whacked Kevin across the temple with one sleek move.

Martain left Kevin as he found him, unconscious and unresponsive with blood gushing from every portion of his anatomy. As he rose to his feet, one of his enforcers tossed a blouse from a hanger at him in order to cleanse himself of the blood which tarnished his manicure. The weapon that paralyzed Carlton and crew had been removed from their vision, yet both men remained motionless as they stared down at Kevin with their mouths wide open. The shorter of the two arrogant police officers finally awarded recognition to the ambulance technicians who'd been demanding proper clearance before entering into the unknown. Both officers and gangsters saluted each other as Martain and company made their exit.

The taller of the two officers shouted, "You Carlton, aren't you? Hey, I'm talking to you. You Carlton?"

Carlton looked over at the officers with disgust and nodded his head. The words suggesting he would report the officers bobbled in his mouth, as terror caused his legs to shake uncontrollably.

"I'll tell you straight: if you wish to continue doing business in Montreal, you'll forget everything you just witnessed and leave it as if you never saw a thing, because if you report us or them, it's your funeral, so remember that," threatened the same officer.

Kevin was taken to the Jewish General Hospital in a coma, and he remained comatose for the next eight months. The doctors at the hospital treated Kevin for massive brain swelling, and he had to be rushed into surgery the moment he arrived in order to relieve the built-up pressure around his brain. The prognosis of him surviving was initially faint, and doctors warned he may not survive the first forty-eight hours. Kevin underwent four separate surgeries later on to repair everything in his body from soft tissue to broken bones. The nursing staff, however, became increasingly worried about Kevin after the first month and a half passed with zero visitors. The hospital contacted the police precinct with their grievance before the case was reassigned to the original officers, who were instructed to find a next of kin should the unexpected occur.

Officers Roger Pilon, a six foot three, two hundred and sixty pound ex-linebacker from Quebec City, and his partner, Guy Trudeau, a five foot nine and one hundred and seventy pound ex-cadet, went to Kevin's bachelor pad at 1315 West Broadway St. While en route, the officers disclosed their orders to Martain Lafleur, who advised them to check for any form of narcotics, which he'd happily dispose of. The officers ignored procedure, which called for them advising the proprietors before engaging in any form of search, and they went directly to acquiring the information ordered.

Kevin occupied the basement apartment of a duplex, with the proprietors residing above him and an unwed couple on the top floor. The inquiring officers tapped on Kevin's front door before forcing entry into his bachelor's suite, which was unoccupied. Officers Trudeau and Pilon made no subtle gestures to signify the apartment hadn't been searched as they ravaged everything during their search While Trudeau tore apart Kevin's mattress, along with everything else in his bedroom, Pilon tossed produce from the refrigerator to the floor and messed up the room. Kevin had a quarter-pound of marijuana in the cooling storage area of his refrigerator, which, after discovery, convinced the officers there was far more to be had.

The loud ruckus coming from the basement was overheard by Mrs. Brittle, who was the senior proprietor. The vibrant, sixty-nine-year-old woman had not seen for some time the kind young man she rented her basement apartment to, and she curiously went to investigate. With her seventy-two-year-old husband terminally ill, Kevin would assist the tender old woman with her groceries and certain chores whenever possible. Mrs. Brittle admired her young tenant for understanding her husband's need for peace and tranquillity, and for his providing such without prior demand.

Mrs. Helen Brittle was surprised to come across two officers sworn to protect and serve destroying the belongings of a Canadian student. The old woman had never encountered an event as such during her fifty-odd years of being a landlord. Mrs. Brittle was cognizant to the regulations regarding interfaces with public servants, yet did not comprehend why she hadn't been informed prior to the officer's raid.

Mrs. Brittle demanded, "What are you gentlemen looking for, and where is Mr. Henry?"

Office Pilon asked, "Is there something we can help you with, madam?"

"Yes, there is. I'm the proprietor of this establishment, and I would like to know why it is I wasn't informed before you boys kicked in my door," replied Mrs. Brittle.

"We, ah, did attempt to contact you, ma'am, but we received no response," Officer Pilon responded.

"Bullshit. I've been home all day with my sick husband and no one rang the door or telephoned. By the way, where is Mr. Henry?" Mrs. Brittle repeated.

"Well, that's why we're here, ma'am. See, Mr. Henry was in an accident, and we're here in search of any documents of health insurance for the doctors," said Officer Pilon.

"If paperwork is what you're looking for and you did this to the man's apartment, I wouldn't like to see what the place would look like if you were searching for drugs!"

The second officer, who'd ignored the conversation between his partner and the proprietor, materialized from the bedroom with a Smith and Weston hand gun, which he'd found taped to the bottom of Kevin's nightstand drawer. Officer Trudeau's elation at finding the weapon was quickly dispelled by the proprietor, who knew the officers' corruptive intentions from them not advising her prior to their search. The vibrancy within Mrs. Brittle orchestrated her fury as she slandered the officers and threatened her intentions to testify against them should any legal actions be taken against Mr. Henry. With her constant yelling of "police corruption," it wasn't long before other neighbours began peeping through their windows at what was transpiring.

The officers soon became frustrated after confronting the notion that they'd be unable to accomplish their mission. Without the proprietor's intrusion on their dealings , the officers had Kevin's coffin sealed. They could use the evidence collected to rid Canada and Martain Lafleur of Mr. Henry permanently by having him deported back to the place from where he came. The officers figured on collecting a handsome payment from Martain Lafleur for somewhat of an exportation job, which would land a silent victory for their alternate boss.

Officer Trudeau threatened, "Madam, do you realize we could arrest you for obstruction of justice? Now, I suggest you return to your confines before I'm forced to do something I'd really like to do!"

"Arrest me for standing up for my door being knocked down? You boys are not working with a full deck, and I'd appreciate your names and badge numbers before you boys leave," stated Mrs. Brittle.

The word "arrest" brought a number of complications into the altercation between Mrs. Brittle and the police as neighbours of the proprietor, who were also her bridge game competitors, joined the fight against the corrupt officers. Madame Francoise and Mrs. McGraves respectively left their humble abodes in support of their neighbour and friend, who sounded as if she had her hands full in dealing with the agitated offices. All three Caucasian elderly ladies blasted the officers into submission to the point where they mounted an immediate retreat and vacated the premises.

Nicholas Henry awoke from his coma to find himself handcuffed to the bed rails. There were three other individuals soundly asleep with IVs fastened to their veins. The fugitive attempted to recollect what got him into his present predicament. Nicholas began moderately tampering with the handcuffs before he started dragging against them once his freedom couldn't be attained. All three men inside the room appeared handcuffed, although the loud racket he created didn't manage to startle any of them. Nicholas could remember nothing due to the humongous headache scrambling his brain as his trials at dragging the depths of his memory failed to produce the reason for the handcuffs.

A French nurse soon entered to perform her scheduled examination of the comatose patients, and Nicholas began pretending his status hadn't been modified. The lesbian nurse had recently lost her female partner of six years to a firefighter assigned to Fire Station 22 outside of Laval, and she was somewhat bitter at the entire male population. Nicholas was accustomed to people whistling or singing while they worked, but he found the nurse's conversation with herself slightly abnormal. The idea of the nurse asking herself questions wasn't what puzzled Nicholas, but rather the answers she gave in response to the questions.

Nicholas peeked through the slits of his eyelids as the nurse began examining the second male over toward his left. The nurse's grief magnified immensely once the door closed behind her with no witnesses to testify as to what transpired. She did her duties, which consisted of temperature checks, heart function assessment, and limb assessments, before finishing with a personal examination of her own. The nurse removed a pair of pliers from her white gown, clinched onto the man's genitals, and dragged the patient's privates from his boxers. Then, as if possessed by some sort of demon, she placed the patient's penis between the grip and squeezed with all her life force. The manoeuvre startled Nicholas, who grabbed for his penis in order to check for minimal sensation.

The nurse moved on to her second victim, and Nicholas began wondering how many penis vice-grip treatments he'd endured since his coma. With no one at liberty to yell or scream for mercy, Nicholas wondered which torture treatment facility he was being housed in. With this maniac nurse victimizing the helpless, Nicholas planned to rid himself of the shackles and chains before attempting his escape from wherever he was being held.

The second patient, as the first, didn't even grimace from the shocking pain that sent lightening bolts screeching down Nicholas' groin. *I ain't gonna just lay back and let this bitch crunch my shit. I got somme for your ass, bitch!*

Nicholas allowed the nurse to exam his vitals while patiently awaiting her grand finale. The touch of a woman's hand on his penis almost spoiled the surprise as his soldier stood at attention. With his penis fully erected, the lesbian nurse sought to castrate its empowerment as she reached into her pocket for her pair of pliers.

"What the fuck!" Nicholassaid as sat straight up like a frozen corpse resurrected to life.

"Ahhhhhhh! Ahhhhhh! Ahhhhhhh!" The nurse's eyes nearly popped from their sockets as she grabbed her chest and stormed from the room.

The troubled nurse soon returned with two other specialists who all went to work on different sections of Nicholas' body. The attending doctor allowed his team of physicians to attend to Nicholas' paralyzed limbs while he examined whether the patient suffered any form of memory loss during his coma. The doctor began asking Nicholas a series of questions as his memory of the incident slowly returned. With his revival to the world came the return of the immense hurt he'd forgone during his coma status, and he quickly demanded pain relief. However, Nicholas couldn't understand the reasons behind the huge glow glistening on the faces of the physicians, though he was indeed happy about being cared for by professionals without whom he wouldn't have survived his ordeal.

The doctor said, "Hello, I'm Doctor Sung. Could you please give me your entire name?"

"My name?" It Kevin said, while stalling to remember the information he'd used. "Ah, the pain!"

"I think I should inform you that you were in a terrible fight a while ago, and as a result, you were in a coma for eight months. Nurse, the injection please? Now, before we continue, I'd like to know if you remember your name," explained the doctor.

"Yeah, yeah," whispered Nicholas softly, as he pondered over the news given to him. "I'm Kevin. No, sorry, Doc—Nicholas Henry!"

"Where are you from, Mr. Henry?"

"I'm from England, in the United Kingdom."

"How old are you, and what's your date of birth?"

"I'm twenty-eight, and my birthday is on the twelfth of June."

"Interesting accent you have. It sounds almost Caribbean."

"My mother was a Jamaican national before moving to the United Kingdom."

"Do you remember your parents' names?"

"Miss Monica Henry and Mr. Pussyhole."

The doctor burst out with laughter. "Interesting description of your father. I take it you guys never got along."

Nicholas stared at the doctor with a blank stare before rattling the handcuff attaching his right hand to the bed frame.

"Those we'll get to once I've finished asking you a few more questions."

"Naw, fuck that, my memory is fine. Now why am I attached to the rails?"

A well-decorated government official walked into the observation room and stood near the foot of the bed. Nicholas could only catch glimpses of the man through the attendants who encircled him, though the high-ranked officer remained out of harm's way. The light green uniform the officer wore was that of the Immigration Bureau, and Nicholas began wondering about what information they possessed. It wasn't long before the INS officer debriefed Nicholas on his latest predicament, which was that the government had begun processing documents for the immediate deportation of one Nicholas Henry.

The immigration officer waited for the doctors to award him clearance before commencing with the task he was sent to accomplish. The gentleman officer was courteous and polite, avoiding being the bearer of unpleasant news as he informed Nicholas of his impending dilemma. At the termination of his presentation, which he began by first placing the patient under arrest, the immigration officer handed Nicholas documents explaining the reasons for his detainment, along with solid advice on how to proceed in his defence. Nicholas, who had limited use of his limbs, demanded assistance to sit up in bed as he examined fully the short list of charges against him.

Once everyone had left and everything was settled, Nicholas telephoned Ernesto, who became elated once the operator announced the collect caller. Ernesto had solicited Eagle and his native friends to find his prized partner after his disappearance. However, once Nicholas' dilemma was revealed to him, the results cast him into a severe state of depression. The voice of one of his top dogs snapped Ernesto into what seemed like a terrible nightmare, and those around him watched him transform into the tyrant they were accustomed to him being. Both men chatted for an hour, with Nicholas disclosing the entire story of how he wound up in an immigration medical ward, while Ernesto brought him up to date on the trials of all his former gun hands charged with the murders of multiple U.S. Marshalls, witnesses, and informants.

Later that night, Nicholas fell asleep, fatigued after willing himself to manoeuvre his aching limbs despite his handcuffs. The detained fugitive, of whose identity immigration officials were unaware, awoke in the middle of the night from a horrid nightmare. The sudden jolt from his relaxed position cast a shocking pain down the sacral plexus, forcing him to buzz the attending nurse for pain medication. After swallowing the Motrin pills handed to him, Nicholas laid back in bed and thought of the man responsible for nearly paralyzing him and terrorizing his dreams every time he'd close his eyes.

Physiotherapy was the first order of business on Nicholas' agenda, and he willed himself to reclaim the proper use of his body. With minimal use of his body came the news of a preliminary hearing to justify the government's rationale for warranting a deportation against the accused. The law offices of Bradley and Carter provided Canada's most revered and expensive attorneys, which were provided for Nicholas by Ernesto, who had also began making arrangements should deportation be ordered against Nicholas. Private Counsel Ian Carter visited with his client that evening and briefed him on how he expected to proceed throughout the hearings, motions he planned on filing, and his honest opinion on Nicholas' chances of seeing the streets of Montreal again. Nicholas became confident his attorney could deliver on his promises, and therefore he chose to withhold the information of him being an American fugitive.

The preliminary hearing was brought before Senior Judge Courtney Sylvester, who was a mild-mannered immigrant from Germany. The seventy-six-year-old senior judge was a product of Adolf Hitler's Nazi regime, which imprisoned and tortured Jews during his childhood years. Courtney was rescued by a German woman who pretended he was her child before fleeing the dreadful tyranny for Canada. The young Jewish boy grew up in a foreign country, which laternaturalized him, though his mother withheld his personal history until his fifteenth birthday.

The courtroom was the second domain of justice Nicholas had visited, with the first being the criminal trial of the man who killed his mother. Special assistance was provided for Nicholas, who scurried along in a wheelchair due to the slow recovery of his limbs. Once Nicholas was wheeled in, the judge became increasingly interested in finding out why a molested individual who was beaten within inches of this life was removed from the streets and brought into his courtroom for deportation proceedings. The documents presented before the judge appeared legitimate, although communications with the United Kingdom had thus far neglected to substantiate Nicholas' claims.

The prosecution argued that Mr. Henry had voluntarily agreed to reconvene his studies in Canada, and should thus be removed for not complying with the arrangements previously agreed into. Chief Prosecutor Edward D'avinche also speculated that the Municipal Police of Montreal believed Mr. Henry a danger to the public, although he provided no substantial evidence to back his allegations apart from an unfired handgun that was speculated to come from the defendant's apartment. Following the government's presentation, Judge Sylvester listened to the defence's arguments before citing negligence against the prosecution for bad judgment. The judge recounted his personal tales from law school, where he talked about himself refusing to attend school until he'd gained the affections of the woman who would later became his wife.

The judge asked, "What percentage of mobility do you have right now, young man?"

"Sir, I'm in more pain than I've ever known. I'm slowly regaining strength in my legs, but it's going to take some time before I'm a hundred percent," Nicholas answered.

"Do you remember what happened to you?"

"It's kind of a blur right now, but I think in time it will come back to me," Nicholas answered.

"Mind you, should you appear before me after today, and I find out that whatever happened to you had to do with drugs or anything illegal, I will see to it you end up somewhere you don't want to be," the judge assured.

"Yes, sir," Nicholas answered.

"Understand also that a firearm is a viable reason for me to have you removed from this country, but considering the circumstances under which the weapon was found, and the fact it had never been used, I'll disallow the matter into evidence because I'd like to see a young man like yourself make something of your life," said the judge.

"I understand, Your Honour," Nicholas answered as if responding to his parent.

"I also recommend that since you're in this country to advance your schooling, you immediately enrol into a facility. Education is the key to a solid future, so don't squander you opportunity. Am I understood Mr. Henry?" The judge emphasised.

"Definatly sir." Nicholas sighted.

Without the dramatic events of a trial, Nicholas was set free without having to post bond, although he received instructions to enrol at an academic facility within a month and then present valid evidence of schooling to the courts thereafter.

Part 7

THE CHIEF PROSECUTOR telephoned Martain Lafleur with an immediate update on a case that intrigued the biker leader. Monsieur Martain Lafleur was accustomed to acquiring whatever it was he desired and believed failure to be an utter disgrace. With the power to enter any commercial facility and take whatever he wished, Martain would often engage in large shopping sprees where everything he acquired was stolen, given with contempt, or taken under serious duress. The underground boss of one of Canada's most notorious gangs owned and operated two Harley Davidson super bike stores, the shipping dock by the Old Montreal Pier, three Ultramar Gas Stations, and a Metro Supermarket. Despite all of that, he still found time to extort protection benefits from small business owners, manage the largest drug distribution north-east of the U.S. border, export stolen, high-end model vehicles to customers abroad, smuggle guns from Russia that were later sold on the U.S. black market, run an exclusive escort service, and pimp a number of females around Montreal. In business as well as his personal affairs, Martain was a relentless beast once it came to the acquisition of money. Once any agreement was entered into with the biker boss, any payment made late or short the exact amount came with consequences usually harmful tothe client.

Martain shouted, "What the fuck do you mean he's to be released with conditions? I didn't grease your whole division's pockets to have this man left in my country!"

"I'm sorry, Mr. Lafleur, but that's the way things go at times. I presented my case on the grounds that Mr. Henry was a threat to Canadians, and thus should be deported, but we weren't prepared for the judge to seek vital evidence at a preliminary hearing," explained Edward D'Avinche.

"I thought you said the mere fact that he was arrested and was being held automatically warranted an investigation which comes after the preliminary hearing! So why was this fucker released on my streets before you got to convince the judge otherwise?"

"Sir, the judge Mr. Henry passed before is the toughest immigration judge on the eastern seaboard. I've worked with him for years and have never once seen him come to such an irrational decision so fast. Personally, I believe it's due to Mr. Henry's physical condition at the moment," stated Edward.

"Do I sound like I'm in the mood for your assumptions? What I want is a fucking refund on my investment!" Martain rudely disconnected the phone line.

The biker boss was furious after hanging up the phone and went directly toward his liquor cabinet. Martain toppled two bricks of ice into a glass, and then added a dose of his favourite Jack Daniels whiskey. Without so much as a flinch, Martain downed the glass of liquor before addressing some of the members of his cabinet around the room.

"I paved the way for this incompetent lawyer who does nothing but fuck shit up! Well, I want *him* fucked up; if he believes he's just going to enjoy my money without me enjoying satisfaction, he's got something else to look forward to. Jean, I want you to pay Mr. D'Avinche a visit for me and see to it he spends a little time in the ICU," ordered Martain.

"What's up, *mon chum*?" Martain's second-hand man, Yves Buchard, asked. Yves and Martain became lifetime friends during Yves' preliminary years at James Lynn High School, where he single-handedly muscled the two goals desired for a victory during a hockey match against their school's local rival. In the dying seconds of that match, an opponent of the visiting team orchestrated a foul play against Martain where he illegally ran the defenseman into the boards, fracturing his left shoulder and forcing him to leave the ice. Yves ran to his defenseman's aid, dropping his gloves before knocking down the opponent who'd prematurely began celebrating. After the match, an appreciative gesture landed Martain an anchor support throughout the remainder of his life, and the two became inseparable, though Martain would later become Yves' boss.

Martain answered, "They failed to deport the Englishman."

"So, what's the big issue?" Yves asked.

"I don't know why, but I got a funny feeling about this guy. Something tells me he's not going to just sail away into the wind like everyone else we've influenced," stated Martain.

Yves joked, "I don't see a problem!"

"See, you don't know the numbers, so you definitely won't see a problem. This guy single-handedly, through the quantity of his products, increased sales around NDG by at least 1.5%. Since we've recaptured the people he supplied, business is back up with a modest increase in sales. We got lackadaisical in monitoring our affairs, and that opened the door for this Englishman to move right in, but the door is now closed and we are going to keep it that way," exclaimed Martain.

"I sure don't see any man coming back for seconds after we've shared him a plate," professed the muscle head that landed the first punch at Nicholas.

"You're starting to sound like you would have preferred partnering up with this guy instead of escorting him out of town," exclaimed Yves.

"That's not it, *mon ami*, I would love to have taken his suppliers, you know, to maintain a balance in the business. Instead, I know far less about who this stranger truly is, no relatives of importance, nothing. I promise you, though, he better leave this city, or I want him buried beneath it," insisted Martain.

Nicholas traded the finest rehabilitation equipment available in Montreal for an ancient Indian treatment system boasted about by the friends who had taken him in. Though only physically capable of manoeuvring 78% of his body, Nicholas opted to reject the advice and abandon the facilities of the physicians who had played a dramatic role in his recovery thus far. The belief that someone aimed to cause him bodily harm saw Nicholas gain distance between the public servants of the government and himself once the doors of bondage were ajar.

The Indians, who rescued Nicholas from the jaws of the Babylon, brought him back to their reservation land where the rules and regulations ran contrary to those of the mother city. The prior arrangement between Ernesto and certain patrons of the Kagnawagi Indian tribe, which landed Kevin inside the Canadian borders, had extended far beyond the knowledge of regular Joes. Through the smuggling systems of the Kagnawagi people sailed the impurities of pleasant immoralities intended on strengthening the financial attributes of Ernesto's enterprise. Hence, the Esquada family, with whom Nicholas stayed during his recovery, had become close acquaintances of his and his associates.

The Esquada family consisted of Eagle Esquada, the fifty-six-year-old aboriginal father to Danny Esquada, thirty years of age, and his younger brother, Kane Esquada, who was twenty-five. The Esquada family lived primarily off the vegetations of the earth with luscious crops produced on their five-acre property. The mother to both of Eagle's sons had died after being struck by a drunk driver some fourteen years prior, leaving him the lone parent to raise his boys. Through farming and an occasional stint at trafficking, Eagle earned enough to offer his children the finest education, though they inevitably followed the path of their father.

Danny Esquada was a mere portrait of his father, with similar features and attributes. The two men walked similarly to each other, had similar posture and physical structure, and would have been considered twins had it not been for Eagle's added decades. Danny was a serious individual who graduated from being a bully to become the enforcer of Danny's Laws. During high school, "The Pitbull," as students would refer to him, fell in love with boxing and quickly became a promising talent among young Canadian athletes. With a record of nine wins, no losses, and a draw, Danny was selected to the 1986 Canadian Olympic Boxing Team to display his talent and skills. During his semi-final match against a boxer from Russia, Danny knocked out his opponent with a fierce blow that broke his right wrist. The adrenalin flow after the match saw Danny shrug off what he believed to be a slight twitch, due to his eagerness in competing in his gold medal match that was scheduled for the following day against the Americans. A slight inflammation occurred around the fractured area which Danny kept iced over-night, while giving the assumption he was in perfect health. A Canadian native had never before advanced to the gold medal rounds, and Danny sought to make his people proud by winning the gold.

At the gold medal match the following evening, Danny fought mainly one-handed and made an adequate showing of himself despite being injured. The American fighter dominated most of the fight, with Danny gaining grounds in the final rounds. With the American back-pedalling in an attempt to survive the final round, Danny faked the right hook and brought a left cross that landed the very moment the final bell rang. The American boxer fell like a log as his trainers and staff rushed to his side. With Danny jumping in the air believing he'd been victorious, the referee began waving both hands in the air while rushing toward the judge's table. An array of boos were cast by patrons inside the arena once it was announced the fight had been awarded to the fighter who was then struggling to regain his coordination.

Kane Esquada was the fragile temperament inside the Esquada house after the lovely Keisha Esquada passed away. The resemblance between Eagle and Danny had always earned numerous comments, but Kane who was the splitting image of his mother, resembled a total stranger considering Keisha was of the Navaho tribe. "Mama's Protégé," as he was often called, had carried the memories and sorrows of his deceased mother in the deepest trenches of his heart, and the graphic pictures of Keisha's body forever tormented his dreams. Kane believed there were demons sent out to collect his mother's soul, and that said demons had in turn cast their interest at him. Kane, who was proud of his heritage as the ancient of Canada, abstained from alcohol and drugs with the intent of being alert and prepared for the demons he presumed were coming to attack. Two prior incidents, one where he was stabbed in a racial dispute by ignorant French skinheads, and a second, where he survived being in a crashed car that was totalled, had Kane convinced he had been marked by demons. A supernatural consultation with the local healing doctor confirmed Kane's suspicions of demonic integration, yet the doctor also advised him that Keisha would never allow the demons to tamper with his life.

After two weeks of physical endurance with the native people who work hard from sunup until sundown, Nicholas regained one hundred percent of his mobility and was capable of accomplishing normal tasks. With Danny's workout regiment from boxing, assisting with the heavy-duty labour around the yard, and his personal aspirations of fully regaining his mobility, Nicholas' body remarkably responded and healed itself. However, his terrible nightmares involving his newest nemesis continued to plague his every unconscious moment, awakening him from dreams and causing him to yell out in tormentduring.

The Esquada boys and Nicholas would often hike into the hills of Du Prairie, where Nicholas and Danny would comfortably indulge in a marijuana joint before target practicing with Eagle's home protection pistols. As their friendship grew, the men became tight in all aspects to the point where criticisms were not demoralizing comments but rather signs of thoughtful admiration. It was during one their getaway hikes that Kane chose to address Nicholas' horrid dream state, a problem with which he was all too familiar. Though Kane selfishly chose to forgo the ritual that Indians had successfully used for centuries to rid themselves of evil torments, he still caringly suggested that Nicholas undergo the spiritual treatment so as to fully rid himself of that which tormented his dreams.

On the first full moon of the new month, Eagle Esquada's entire household attended the Aboriginal Ceremony of the Ancients, which was a gathering of the community to celebrate life and the richness thereof. The festivities were in full gear, featuring natives wearing their porcupine headdresses and costumes while dancing around a huge bonfire chanting and beating drums. Nicholas had never before witnessed a gathering of such force and spirituality, nor had he heard the Ojibwa language, which is the aboriginal tongue, as he and company joined the circle of Indians surrounding the festivities. There was almost one hundred people in attendance forming a huge enough circle for the medicine man and performers to dance about inside. The primary performer inside the circle was the tribe's Medicine man of Realms, who stood alone inside the circle at the commencement of the event with his staff featuring the skull of a monkey as the crown headpiece. As the ceremony progressed, various patrons seated among themasses would become engulfed by spirits, fall into trance-like states, and dance about as if freeing themselves from the bondages of the soul. There was an ancient chalice with carvings of the bear, the fish, and the eagle being passed about, though only certain individuals partook of the ceremonial pipe. The eerie vibes soothed Nicholas' nerves as he began clapping along with the masses as, the effects of the marijuana joint they enjoyed in the car had long since set the pace and enabled him to conform to the ambiance.

Nicholas received the ceremonial pipe from Kane, who, like always, refrained from confronting his personal demons. Before inhaling the fumes, Nicholas took a moment to admire the pipe, which appeared to be of ancient origins. The Esquada family was seated on either side of Nicholas to add testament to him as their honoured guest, and Nicholas looked to Eagle for consent to blaze up the pipe. A slight nod from Eagle saw Nicholas inhale the toxins, which immediately altered his emotions, giving him the ability to actually see medians gliding about the atmosphere. From the huge bonfire shot up the faces of Martain and his goons, and Nicholas envisioned himself fully dressed in native attire while savagely stalking and hunting the men who injured him in the wilds of the outback. After staring a few ghosts of his past in the face, Nicholas drew courage from his support system around him and tightly closed his eyes. With hisfists clenched tightly, Nicholas sailed back to that horrid day in the tailor's shop where he received the beating of his life. With intense anger, Nicholas stood over himself as Martain and company beat him up before leaving him to the mercies of God. Nicholas soon awoke with tears in his eyes, and a huge smile glistened on his face because he knew his fears were of no further consequence.

The joys of an entire night without his recurring nightmares had Nicholas rejuvenated and charged to tackle anything the following day. The recovered ex-deportee was up early for strength training with Danny, who was all too accustomed to his daily regiment. As Eagle began his day aimed at feeding his precious livestock, the thought of his boys warming up to anyone but him drew a pleasant smirk to his lips as he went about his affairs. Later that day, the Esquada boys and Nicholas went to the grocer's to purchase a few items for the house, as well as their personal hygiene articles. The muffler on Danny's 1982 Nissan Stanza could be heard bawling from a mile away as they sailed along the bumpy local strips. Nicholas demanded a stop as they passed the Abenaki motorbike store off St. Joseph Boulevard, where they soon traded in Danny's four-wheel rust bucket for helmets and two-wheel hammers.

Nicholas was elated that the Esquada men, who have proven to be wholesome friends, had taken the time to heal all aspects of his injuries. At supper, where typically each man retrieved his spoils from the kitchen before planting himself before the television or whatever activity he had engaged in, Nicholas offered to take the entire family out for a night in the city. Eagle had made prior plans to visit an old friend who had fallen ill, and he insisted the younger men have a ball without him.

The Esquada brothers and Nicholas fired up their Kawasaki motorbikes and swerved through traffic on Boulevard St. Francis and along the Pont Mercier Bridge on Interstate 20 before exiting the highway at Rue Guy, and then cruising the St. Catherine strip. The Gentlemen's Desire Nightclub housed some of the finest beauties in the city of Montreal, and also catered to a man's every need. As the fun-seekers parked their bikes against the sidewalk, the urge to secure their property was enhanced by the trail of bikes already parked, as well as the goon left to watch over them.

The classic ambiance inside the Gentlemen's Desire Nightclub catered to the heterosexual male's desires, which are women and lots of them. Women were all over Nicholas and his partners the moment they walked in through the front door. Kane quickly scooped up the sole coloured female to attack the bunch, leaving Nicholas thought-provoked as he lingered along behind the two brothers. Danny found himself a dynamite redhead with astonishing rear beauty, and an ass that said, "Hold on for a bumpy ride!" The trio package that attacked the young lads forced Nicholas to self-consciously draw for the weakest link, who was a young French girl from Thunder Bay named Stacey. Each man had their lovelies lead the way as they remained in the rear, casually adoring each sexy figure before them. The choice of seating was a booth table toward the rear of the club where there was proper surveillance of the entire flooring. .

Despite the club's logo, which symbolized the sort of customers they'd prefer entertaining, there were very few suits in the house, and a large number of drunken, loud-mouthed bikers gawked at the exotic performers while enjoying themselves. Their rude antics, however, didn't mitigate the fact they were spending a large array of money in commemorating the birthday of one of the members. The birthday boy was on stage being whipped by a mob of females who'd successfully ripped off his clothing before tying him to the pole and bringing out the straps. The beating that left the biker's buttocksredder than the planet Mars was at its grand finale as Nicholas and friends made their way to their seats.

"If that's the initiation process to get with you ladies, I'm definitely in!" Kane commented.

The coloured female answered, "That little act on stage? You ain't seen nothing yet!"

"Listen!I told you the kid has no idea how to talk to the Berries," joked Danny as he nudged a grin from Nicholas.

"Berries!" Nicholas mocked.

An account of everyone's beverage was taken by a waitress who wore a bunny suit and did it justice. The cigarette smokers at the table all lit up their drugs and began puffing away while engaging in introductory small talk. The drinks came with an audacious idea from Kane, who insisted the females engage in a sexual orgy, which was an experience he'd never before witnessed. To his surprise, such was a secret fantasy of each of the ladies, who were all too happy to sexually molest each other and get paid in return. The onstage entertainment featuring the young and delectable Electra was fast replaced by the beautiful nymphs nibbling at each other. Braziers and thongs were tossed at the primary audience, who watched in amazement as the young ladies mounted a first victim atop the table and tickled her fancy until she squirted like a fire hydrant. The force with which the young redhead squirted cum against the booth's backrest stunned her audience, who had never before witnessed such a spectacle. Kane had to quickly remove himself from the path of the young redhead's ejaculation since he'd seated himself directly in the path of her orgasm. The young Mohawk from Kagnawagi was laughed at by his peers, who found it hilarious to watch him brush specks of orgasm from his shoulder.

The ladies' appetites were gruesome as they fondled each other for what seemed like an eternity. Their moans and groans soon captured the attentions of other patrons, who wished they'd concocted such a marvellous scheme. As Nicholas and friends looked on, each man thought tohimself "what had the vicinity been different" as they drooled over the luscious bodies before them.

Nicholas brought his double shot of cognac and cranberry juice drink to his lips as the manager of the establishment vacated his office to oversee the proceedings. The well-built Caucasian male walked by Nicholas' dark table and smiled at the guests who'd put on such an amazing event. Over the rim of the glass, Nicholas watched as a true ghost of his past waltzed right by the table he'd acquired. The shocking memories from his whoop-ass session flashed through his mind, and he began reminiscing on the amount of licks he received from the male who passed before him.

"Who that?" Nicholas demanded of one of the ladies.

"Oh, that's Pierre the manager, otherwise knownas 'Moose.'" Stated the red head who finally came up for air after licking the coloured female's clit for nearly fifteen minutes.

"Who is the owner?"

"He's never here. I think he runs too many businesses, but that's his clan over there. The all-mighty Rough Riders gang," stated the redhead.

Nicholas wondered if everyone else could hear or feel the pounding of his heart, which intensified the moment he laid eyes on the manager. Without hesitation, Nicholas turned to Danny and said, "I need to borrow your pistol?"!"

"No problem brother." Danny answered.

claimed Danny.

As Nicholas collected Danny's self-protection, he took time out to explain the situation to his amigos, who hated to see proficient pussy go to waste. The twitch beneath Nicholas' armour desperately needed scratching, and he handsomely awarded the ladies, who insisted they be allowed to properly finish. Following the brief, mediocre farewell between Nicholas' entourage and the luscious strippers, the men waited for the overzealous females to retire to their changing room before commencing with their antics.

Nicholas insisted both brothers exit the club and await him by their bikes, as he refused to have any harm befall them. While ushering his wishes, Nicholas casually inspected the weapon he'd acquired beneath the table by removing the safety lock and placing a shell into the firing chamber.

"Come on, man, there are at least two dozen guys over there. I'm staying to help you just in case, bro," Kane declared.

"No way. If anything goes wrong, it's my ass again, though I do appreciate the offer," Nicholas answered.

"You got this?" Danny asked, who had grown ever closer to Nicholas while training over the past few weeks.

"Yah, man!" Nicholas answered as they shook hands.

The three men rose from their table and began walking towards the exit, before Nicholas parted ways and moved towards the bikers' celebration. Though the honoured guest chose a private booth to celebrate, bikers were scattered throughout every facet of the night club, gaping at the many exotic dancers who pranced around wearing their skimpy outfits. With his liquor in his left hand and a tight grip on the Glock's handle in his pocket with his right, Nicholas made his way across the floor toward the VIP Champagne Room, which housed the honoured guests.

At the front door, Danny handed Kane the keys to his and Nicholas' Kawasakis before instructing his younger brother to "keep the motors running." The ex-professional boxer remained inside the club and out of sight while preparing himself to help in whatever fashion possible. Danny watched Nicholas through his peripheral vision while simultaneously maintaining coverage over the remaining bikers inside the club. The man on a mission walked directly into the Champagne Room and stood behind the waitress, who was in the process of tending to a customer's request.

The birthday boy shouted, "Whoo-hoo! This is the best birthday ever! Yow, Moose man, thanks for everything, mon ami ! I think I finally lived out my dreams today. Whoo-hoo!"

The waitress asked, "So, you guys want another bottle of Baileys for the ladies and?"

The birthday boy shouted, "Yahoo!"

"One more bottle of Jack Daniels with another two litre of Coke?"

The birthday boy again shouted, "Yahoo!"

"Forty-eight chicken wings with mega fries, jumbo salad, and bread. Was that all?" The waitress demanded.

The birthday boy again shouted, "Yahoo!"

The waitress collected the orders and turned to a complete stop as she bumped into Nicholas. "Oh, I'm sorry, sir!"

Nicholas remained silent to the girl's apology as he maintained a visual on his target. The darkness throughout the club made it increasingly difficult for Moose or any of his four honoured guests inside the Champagne Room to clearly recognize Nicholas, who was simply on a mission. The drunken birthday boy mistook Nicholas for an ally and told him to "acquire his own bitches," as he was not about to share any of his prizes. A rotating disco light attached to the ceiling some twenty yards away cast a reflection that made it possible to visualize Nicholas' features. Moose's mouth fell wide open as he quickly grabbed for his protective weapon, which was shoved into his waistband behind his belt buckle.

The first two shells released by Nicholas were launched unexpectedly at the biker to Moose's left, who had managed to arm himself faster than anyone else inside the Champagne Room. The blaster was pointed toward Moose's chest within the twinkle of an eye as the club's manager struggled to remove his weapon from his waistband. In his drunken state, the birthday boy could only manage to toss the females in his lap to the floor before flinging his hands in the air, signalling that he'd surrendered. With his eyes detecting every motion of the bikers inside the Champagne Room, Nicholas took one step forward, placed his weapon directly on Moose's forehead, and pulled the trigger. In expectance of a total assassination attempt, the biker to the left of the birthday boy tossed the sole female in his lap at Nicholas, who stumped her to the ground with his foot before she could reach him. The man then attempted to run from the room while screaming the word "assassination" in order to alert his friends of their predicament. Once again, Nicholas sounded the Big Thing, which tore away the man's chest cavity as it sent the biker airborne, landing him across the bar in the head-over-heels position.

A number of bouncers began cautiously approaching the demolition scene, and Danny caught the bar attendant reach beneath the counter for a high-powered, pump action rifle. In the commotion that saw innocent customers breaking for the exits, exotic females screaming as if they were in danger, fellow bikers arming themselves with broken bottles and so on, Danny sneaked behind the waiter who appeared to be Nicholas' greatest threat and incapacitated the man with a bone-crushing punch to the centre of his spine. The waiter tossed his weapon high in the air as he groaned while crumbling to the turf. Danny snatched the pump rifle from the air and jumped on top the bar with one sole command.

"Get on the fucking floor!"

It was through his altered view of the crowd that Danny was able to realise that far more patrons were armed than he had previously calculated. The loud music blanketed the sounds of a weapon being dispursed at Nicholas from the south-west section of the club, which Danny highlighted by the sparks gashing from the mouth of the weapon. The Indian spun the high powered riffle towards the sparks and blasted at the biker, who was taking cracks at his friend. The deed took two attempts, but with the second blast from Danny's riffle, the biker was sent smashing against the slot machines inside the club. Danny was forced to blast another hole through the biker in charge of security, as the man who was conversating with his club members ran to his friends' aid.

The two warriors reunited after Nicholas snatched the birthday boy as hostage before using him as a protective shield to cross the battlefield. Nicholas apologized to the terrified strippers who had been screaming their heads off after witnessing Moose get his dome blown off. The vengeance-seeking roughneck had to encourage the birthday boy to convince his peers to lower their weapons, before his greatest day ever changed to his worst.

"Talk to your boys, talk to your boys! We all go home to our families. This got nothing to do with anybody else!" Danny repeated to his hostage as the birthday boy pleaded with his peers not to retaliate.

The streets were serene as Nicholas, Danny, and their hostages emerged from the club to find a vacant St. Catherine Street. Kane had punctured the tires of the long line of Harley Davidson motorcycles outside the club, and he had also knocked unconscious the guard left to watch over them.

"Get low on you knees and tell you boss say him should have killed the Englishman when him had the chance!" Nicholas commanded as he and his allies mounted their bikes and rode away.

The Aftermath

Eagle was forced to remind his overzealous bunch of misfits that they weren't the sole living organisms inside his home at 2:40 am after they had returned from their rowdy escapade fully excited from what had taken place. Once Eagle returned to bed,the three marauders continued their celebrations with his bottle of Canadian Whiskey,ofwhich Danny and Nicholas partook while indulging in marijuana joints constructed by Kane. Nicholas knew and expected their actions would escalate the tension between himself and Martain, although he chose to ignore the seriousness of the situation.

Eagle arose from his chamber the next morning to find all three men strung out in various sections of his living room. The early bird went on to commence his day by preparing himself a freshly brewed pot of coffee and reading the local newspaper, which was delivered to his porch every morning, before beginning his labour. The subtitle to the newspaper's primary story, which read Gangbang in Gangster's Town, was Eagle's first inclination of what his pupils did the night prior before reading the first two sentences.

"Get your asses up now! Get up, get up!" Eagle screamed. He turned on the bright overhead light before continuing to slap anyone in arm's reach, from his sons to their honoured guest.

The young men all attempted to shield their eyes from the blinding light before discovering the need for evasive actions against Eagle's unexpected onslaught. Nicholas found himself crouching behind Danny like a child avoiding a parent as Eagle interrupted their peaceful calm.

"Y'all think this is funny? Think this fucking shit is funny? I know you all had something to do with this shoot-out!" Eagle exclaimed while waving about the morning's newspaper. "Any of you have any idea who these people y'all decide to fuck with are?"

"What are you talking about, Pop?" asked Danny, who didn't believe their actions would have landed them in an article on the front page of the city's main newspaper.

"Damn it, damn it, damn it! Why, boys? Y'all could have left it alone. Now that y'all spilled blood, ain't no turning back," stated Eagle as he sat on the edge of the sofa with his face buried into his hands.

Kane grabbed the newspaper and began reading aloud the article about what transpired at the Gentlemen's Desire Nightclub. The reporter who wrote the story appeared bias towards the bikers in his coverage, as he'd lessened the blame to the two attackers, who he would later describe as "hired assassins for an alternate cause." The reporter went on to convey that the identity of the assassins was gathered from secret video footage that the bikers refused to hand over to police, citing internal problem-solving methods of their own. The story also disclosed that the bikers would seek out and administer their brand of justice, described by one member as, "with utter hate and malice."

The tears gushing from Eagle's eyes caused him to choke up as he lectured his squad on whom they were confronting. From experience, rather than gossip, was the knowledge Eagle had about the gruesome force his boys had engaged. However, with each fallen tear, Danny and Kane, who were only witnessing their teary-eyed father for the second time since birth, understood the magnitude of the shit they'd stepped in.

"You boys are seeking a war you can't win against an enemy you can't defeat. These are the people who moved into Canada, saw a nation of proud people living here, and took this bitch over like it was theirs to begin with. They stretch from the government to the lowest form of ghetto species known to Canada. I've seen the bravest of Indians go against these people, only to have the lives of their entire families, as well as their own lives, taken without any form of sympathy. You boys are my life, the only reason I've existed since your mother passed away. See, in my younger days, I was a hell of a rebel, and no one could say a word to me, especially one of those French boys. I used to beat their asses and take their money like they owed me allowance. But one day I met your mother, and she changed my life. She corrupted it so bad I turned pussy over time. Then you boys came along with my old fiery temper, and you take no shit. I never changed that in you boys because I wanted you to change that in yourselves. I see the same fury burning beneath your skin, Nicholas! You and my boys gotta care for each other to do this right, because the time y'all falter is when it's all over. I'm not about to stand by and have these French fuckers take another thing from me, so this no one alert no one on guard bullshit ends now. To your feet, boys. Indian combat training is in process. Get up, get dressed, and outside right now!"

Part 8

"**S**COUR THIS ENTIRE island and make sure these fuckers are on the evening news, or someone is going to take their place in the obituaries tomorrow!" Martain warned after watching the surveillance video from the attack the night prior. "I should have killed that fucking tar baby the first time I saw him. Now I gotta explain to Moose's little kids why my boy isn't coming home."

"I'll personally find them. A black man and two Indians won't be hard to spot in Montreal," Yves Buchard assured him.

The word went throughout the city like the expectations of a first place finish in the National Hockey League's championship finals to determine the bearers of the Holy Grail. The Rough Riders considered the attack against members of their coalition forces on home soil a family matter and disclosed no identity of the intruders to the police. The flamboyant crew of Harley Davidson riders instead plastered the photos of the three wanted men across their website, knowing that a sighting or information on one of the men was imminent. Within an half hour, a member of the biker crew's southern division, who surveyed the photos over the bikers' Internet page, recognised Danny Esquada's photo after combating him some time prior in the boxing ring. The crewmember who phoned in the information remembered being knocked out by Danny in the fifth round of their exhibition match, and insisted he be inserted among the assassins chosen for the mission. Martain had the biker escorted to his haven, as the biker boss sought to acquire every bit of information possible about his newest nemesis.

Eagle Esquada was a man who lived for his sons after the tragic death of the only woman he'd ever truly loved. The elderly father of two had fought against the government of Canada and over the rights of aboriginals throughout his tenure as the oppression of his people persisted. Eagle had been taught by his forefathers to abstain from the calamities of the world, although his personal losses through life caused him to stray from such righteous teaching. Eagle hated the man he'd become after vowing at an early age to abstain from such a path. The oppression fighter rarely drank in public, though the same could not be said for him in the privacy of his own home. The spiritual Indian warrior joined in countless rebellions against the tyranny of the government by blocking railway lines, bridges, and highways that passed through Indian reservations, and yet his prized knowledge of the Rough Riders sacrament scared him most.

Eagle had insisted that Nicholas deal his poison across the river since the day he smuggled into the country. The proud Indian Eagle had always been caused him to compassionately consider the economic bearings such cosmetic drugs would have on his poor people who already had nothing to survive on. Nicholas had heeded the requests of Eagle throughout, although his sons weren't as optimistic about the people as their dad. Kane had entered the underground market of substance trafficking with the backings of Nicholas weeks prior, and he fought hard to maintain secrecy from his father. Kane Esquada dealt drugs through his entrusted friends, who did all the physical labour without complaints after receiving the products on consignments with minor penalties. The financial ruin cocaine would bring to the Indian people, according to Eagle, was eventually introduced to the same people he attempted to protect by his own flesh and blood.

The three friends had spent most of the morning in the hills, where they practiced with 9 mm handguns, practiced evasive fighting manoeuvres, exercised, jogged, and played around with each other. On their way down the mountain, Samuel, whose mother was Eagle's younger sister, rang Kane's cell phone and insisted they meet at once. Kane advised his cousin to meet with him at their regular spot, which was along the trail heading home. The urgency of Samuel's tone bothered all three friends, who decided to attend the meeting.

"There are some biker guys approaching the local crackheads and offering them free rocks for information on where to find you guys. They're saying they know that you guys supply the reservation. I assume they're friends of yours," informed Samuel.

"I assure you, cousin, they're no friends of ours," said Kane.

"Well, it's only a matter of time before they get an address. With the free shit they're giving away, someone will give up their mother real soon," said Samuel.

"All right, cousin, I want you to bring me the bag I hid by your mother last week," Kane said.

"By the looks of them guys, I'm already ahead of you, because they don't seem like they looking for conversation," Samuel exclaimed.

The news of strangers on the reservation swept through the communities like the atomic bomb on Hiroshima. By the time the men returned to Eagle's house, the warrior had already received word of the exact infraction he'd expected. Adam Cardozer ran a local corner store where a large percentage of the community frequently transacted business. Martain Lafleur, Yves Buchard, and three other goons sought information regarding the exact whereabouts of the three men who'd disrupted his adult lounge. With a population of three thousand, Martain expected the grocer to have adequate knowledge of the community and the people residing in it.

"Good day to you, sir. I'm looking for the Esquada ranch or home, and I know you can definitely help me," said Martain.

"Who did you say you're looking for?" Mr. Cardozer asked.

"Esquada family. Two sons with a black friend of theirs," Martain answered.

The store operator looked the tattooed individual up and down over the rim of his glasses before denying ever hearing the name *Esquada*. Martain signalled his goons to man the front door while he extracted valuable information the only way he knew how. Yves and another biker member walked behind the counter and dragged the fierce shopkeeper from his comfort zone. Both men brought him front and centre to Martain, who was no mood for gimmicks. Mr. Cardozer kicked and fought, knocking over articles as the two gangsters brought him to their boss.

"Settle him down, enough of thechildish bullshit!" Martain ordered.

Yves grabbed the shopkeeper's fax machine/telephone from the counter with both hands and smashed it over the man's head. "You didn't hear the boss say to shut the fuck up!" Yves yelled as the revolting proprietor ceased his uprising.

Martain stepped over the shopkeeper and pressed his right foot against the Indian's neck. The leader of the Rough Riders waited for the proprietor to begin gasping for air before instructing the man on exactly how to proceed. Martain advised the proprietor that any response apart from the absolute truth would result in the loss of his store, his family, and his personal life. With the alternatives offered Mr. Cardozer, the proprietor answered truthfully all questions posed to him in fear of any retribution should they not succeed. Adam waited for the roars of Harleys to dissipate before calling and advising Eagle of what transpired between he and the Rough Riders' captain.

Danny, Kane, and Nicholas returned home to find Eagle making preparations for an attack. The Indian was busy reinforcing and barring windows, creating open areas to shoot through, and setting outdoor traps around the yard before inspecting and preparing his weapons for battle. Eagle summoned his boys and advised them to prepare for the war he'd advised them of, though he knew they were terribly outnumbered and outgunned.

"I have fought a demon in my dreams since the death of your mother. For years, I've been seeing this huge battle that I once believed came from the demons in the bottle of alcohol I slept in every night, but now I know that vision was a true prophecy, for the day of that great battle has come. My sons, I have taught you to embrace death when it comes, and I know is a trait of your young heart, Nicholas. We are outnumbered against this enemy who have showed up at our door, but we will not be defeated by this enemy. Such is the prophecy this land and my heart have revealed to me. I know of this enemy, for my ancestors ran them from our lands with their liquor and drugs. There is no sense running from these people, for it will only be a matter of time before they find you. Whatever happens on this day, know we battled like warriors, and never surrender, or you surrender your life!" Eagle said.

"All that is understood, but what is that you mixing up?" Nicholas asked.

"Before an Indian enters a battle, it is said that the war paint transforms the normal man into the braveheart desired to accomplish his task. With the war paint, a cheetah becomes a cheetah and a bear a bear. I am known as the Dark Eagle, and tonight I shall soar one final time before I join my beautiful wife and the rest of my ancestors," Eagle exclaimed as he designed his war paint to make him look like an eagle.

Unlike Eagle, there was no motivational speech before the Rough Riders' march against Nicholas and his band of Indian warriors. However, the haze of darkness had stilled the furious natures of the awaiting warriors, who camped by windows around the house with a constant view of the perimeter. The younger men inside the house conversed among themselves to combat drowsiness as the hour grew later. At 11:49 pm, Kane found himself succumbing to the pressures of fatigue and decided to fetch himself and others a drink from the fridge. As he passed by the corridor that led to the bedrooms, Kane checked the status of his father, who had been camped near the window at the end of the hall. Eagle had vacated his post, taking with him his bow and arrows and an Apache knife while abandoning his Winchester rifle by the foot of the window. Kane ran to his father's post and looked frantically through the window. There was no sign of his father anywhere in the vicinity, and Kane immediately alerted his companions of the situation.

"Eagle left his post!" Kane whispered.

"What do mean? He's gone?" Nicholas asked.

"He means Dad saw them coming and decided to take the fight to them, so keep your eyes open. They aren't too far away!" Danny exclaimed.

Eagle counted fifty invaders seventy-five feet away from his surveillance tower high among the branches of a maple tree. The Indian warrior withdrew his first arrow from the sachet around his shoulder and took aim at the last man toiling in the background. The silence of the wind guided the arrow directly into the man's chest and brought him down without a sound, and Eagle reloaded his weapon of choice and continued his assault. Eagle knocked off nine consecutive rear targets as the invaders sneaked their way closer to the house. Forty feet away from the house, one of Martain's troopers stepped into a bear trap, which snapped its jaws like teeth into the man's leg.

"Ahhh! My fucking leg!"

"Shut him the fuck up before he tells all the animals where we are!" Yves instructed.

A man stopped to assist his comrade by first placing his hand over the injured man's mouth to prevent any further outbursts. The assisting medic watched his friends continue on their mission before attempting to free his comrade's leg from the trap's jaws. The gangster succeeded at removing the contraption from his comrade's leg and turned to ask about the man's well-being when he observed an arrow lodged into the back of the man's neck. The gangster quickly turned to warn his friends, and he, too, received an arrow directly through the neck. The biker began checking the grounds around for his weapon as his friends had completely disappeared from sight. The arrow had lodged itself into the man's throat without disrupting any critical organs, although he was forced to gasp harder in order to fill his lungs with oxygen. There was in the distance the shadow of a man hidden among the leaves of a tree, and the injured gangster raised his Walter PPK automatic weapon into firing position and took aim at the Monkey Man. The Monkey Man seated in the tree had not lost focus of the gangster, whose eyes widened once he realised he'd already been targeted. The gangster quickly yanked on the trigger repeatedly before he realised that but he'd neglected to remove the safety switch. An arrow lodged directly into the man's right eye, killing him instantly with only the sounds of broken twigs to be heard as his body collided with the turf.

Eagle boldly slammed an arrow that nearly ripped the chest cavity from his target, who was at that moment walking within inches of his allies. The closest man to Eagle's latest victim observed him fall to the ground and realized a sniper was about the area. The gangster quickly calculated the trajectory from which the arrow came, although the darkness of night made it increasingly difficult to pinpoint the sniper.

"There's someone firing arrows from the tree over there!" The biker began pointing directly in the vicinity where Eagle was hidden.

The Mohawk Indian who was born on the Kagnawagi reservation fired a final arrow from his stakeout position, which landed in the belly of a biker who was in the midst of locating the sniper's position. Eagle wrapped his hands around a rope he'd used to hoist himself into the tree and attempted a quick retreat. An avalanche of bullets ripped off the tree limb that offered him protection, and he narrowly escaped the total onslaught. A bullet from an intruder's AK-47 ripped through the warrior Indian's shoulder, which was wrapped around the rope for support. Instead of a casual swing from one maple tree to the next, Eagle plummeted awkwardly towards the ground, before breaking his fall and changing his trajectory so he couldn't be located.

"Whoever he is, I want a few of you to find him and kill him!" Martain ordered, who'd went along to ensure the job was done properly.

The remaining bikers continued pressing on toward their target since Martain would not have them discouraged under any circumstance. A second biker soon screamed out in pain as he, too, experienced the clinching pains brought on by the bear trap. The closer Martain's gang of misfits got to the house, the deadlier the traps set by Eagle to offset oncoming foes. The hand-to-hand tactician shoved his hand beneath his clothing and checked the bullet wound he'd recently received. Eagle placed his ear against the ground to determine the number of assassins trailing him as he thought of ways to rid himself of the mini-Delta Force at his heels. He ran down the trail that led to the main roadway, knowing his only chance of ridding himself of his pursuers would be with the assistance of a grenade trap he'd planted along that trail. The darkness made it difficult to pinpoint the exact burial point at which he assembled the mechanism for the sabotage. The invader who led the charge against Eagle was getting increasingly closer as the Indian's wound slowed him down drastically. The bikers tracking Eagle opened fire at the fleeing warrior, who was forced to duck low behind the first available tree.

Eagle pretended he'd been struck by one of the barrage of bullets being spat at him from the thug's AK-47 and tumbled behind a huge tree. From his knees, Eagle peeked around the side of the tree to catch a glimpse of the gangsters shooting at him. Once a man became visible, Eagle tattooed him with an arrow that propelled the attacking invader back a few paces. The allies of the fallen gangster scattered and dove for the turf as if their lives depended on it before erratically scattering bullets at everything in front of them. Eagle had reconvened his track session down the hill and could not get out the way of the unseen bullets which tore chunks of flesh from his right rib cage. Eagle toppled to the ground in a similar fashion as the first time he got shot while the gangsters advanced all the while maintaining their barrage of fire in case the Indian was up to his old tricks. As they carefully advanced, one of the five trailing Rough Riders unknowingly stepped onto the grenade trap that Eagle had planted. The blast that erupted sent all five men flying in every direction as an utter calm fell over that section of the woods.

The initial eruption of gunfire advised the awaiting team of the position of three of their enemies, and it awarded them ample time to formulate an evasive plan. Danny had been taught by the best and used his warrior intellect to decipher what occurred at the first sounds of weapons. The young Indian could sense that their foes had been reduced in numbers, hence the bullet uproar that sounded was an attempt to eliminate the threat the invaders seemingly faced. Danny decided to bring the battle to his enemies, as did his father, and yet work cohesively with his brother and friend by flanking the enemy after they'd dug their trenches. The traps laid out by Eagle announced the enemies' approach since every few feet gained by the enemy produced an injured combatant. Apart from Eagle's infamous bow and arrows were his bear traps—spiked limbs that were triggered after an invader unknowingly molested it, as well as a few grenades, which also erupted once triggered..

The woods surrounding Eagle's home was already filthy with dead bodies all throughout, as another grenade erupted thirty feet from the house. Nicholas watched as the huge ball of fire that plumed into the sky blasting four motionless bodies onto Eagle's front lawn. Kane, around that point, opened fire at elements through his viewpoint as Martain and company began dumping bullets at the house.

"What the fuck? They think we don't have any guns?" Nicholas yelled as he aligned his night vision scope onto a biker's forehead.

Hollow point bullets spat from Nicholas' assault riffle as he sniped off a biker member nearly forty feet away from the house. Kane could be heard running from his assigned position, as he was forced to secure the exit which Eagle had originally occupied. Before the youngest of the Esquadas could reach the window, an intruder entered and began inspecting the room for dwellers. Fright brought Kane to create his first ghost as his nervous, twitchy trigger finger yanked on the trigger after the invader surprised him by walking out of the bathroom and directly into his aim. Kane froze for a millisecond after drilling the intruder full of holes before rushing to the window where he executed two different passersby who believed the area had been secured.

Dressed in a full camouflage outfit, with his face war-painted in black, Danny laid motionless in front of a log as a biker rushed in to use the fallen wood stump as a shield against bullets. Eagle had blocked a number of the windows around the house with plywood, although he was certain to allow shooting pockets for those inside. Rider members were not sure of the exact amount of hands they were up against, and thus avoided rushing the house in case an army awaited. The young Indian was so well camouflaged that the biker's closest ally ran by the stump of wood and even stepped on Danny's left hand, forcing him to bite his tongue without offering up so much as a whiff against the stump. The biker's ally went and took up aim a few feet from the rear window and began unloading his magazine as Danny quietly sneaked his knife up underneath the biker's friend's chin only yards away without alerting the trigger-happy shooter. The warrior Indian, although not as skilful as his father, had the training and ability to disfigure foes, and he crept up on the biker to the right, grabbed him around the mouth, and slit his throat before flinging his knife in the neck of the biker who'd stepped on his arm. Another of Eagle's deadly traps erupted as four bikers who took up positions around the outdoor shed tripped a wire that caused the shed to explode. Eagle had packed canisters with nails, sharp objects, and marbles inside the shed, which, once exploded, sent dangerous debris flying, killing instantly three others who were within close proximity. Martain immediately ordered his declining biker force to shoot up the house and everything inside as the developments thus far infuriated the gangster who hadn't ceased firing since assuming the single knee plant position a few yards away from the house.

After calling to his friend, who, by all accounts, appeared to be holding his own against Nicholas and whoever was trapped inside the house, the biker who initially led Martain across the Champlain River found that the abrupt stoppage in his friend's firing was due to a bullet which was lodged in his cranium. There were booby traps being set off around the house, all of which resulted in the death or injury of Rough Riders attempting to achieve their goals. With the decrease in bikers, Danny began playing opossum by lying on the ground and screaming for help as if he were an injured biker who'd been wounded by the enemy. As soon as anyone became naive enough to fall for the trap, the Indian would roll them up while either cutting their throats or stabbing them to death. The biker, who sought to even matters up with Danny, was manoeuvring to find a less dangerous entrance to the house when he came across a wounded biker who was beseeching anyone for help. The biker seeking assistance was the opossum-playing Danny, who had exchanged his attire with a deceased biker and cleaned up enough to lure his victims. The darkness assisted Danny, whose red skin and long porcupine hair would have easily given him away to his foes, and they would have skinned him alive had they caught him. By the time the biker realized his executioner was that close, his neck had been slit wide open, and Danny left him hunched over as if he'd fallen asleep in the middle of the battle.

Danny was determined to find his father, who failed to answer to the family's ancient summoning method which mimicked the calls of the great owl. Before he could set out in search of his father, Danny knew he had to eliminate a few more thugs from the equation before he ended up with neither family nor friend. The junior athlete of the year in 1984 at St. Augustine High School on the reservation loved the javelin event, and he still possessed a rocket of an arm. Danny wasn't seen as he crept around the grounds with precision stealth while armed with his native knife, an Uzi automatic, and a few wooden spears. As planned, Danny waited until his enemies had sunken into their trenches with their attention on those inside the house before utilizing the opportunity to slit the throats of anyone within arm's reach., The precision atwhich Danny tossed his spears, slaughtered those at a distance after connecting through some vital points about his enemies' bodies.

"Where the fuck are those idiots I sent around back to blaze them out front so we can end this cowboys and Indians bullshit? Where's

Mystro? Someone tell Mystro to grab few a men and take the house from the side!" Martain instructed.

"Mystro can't be found anywhere, boss. As a matter a fact, a lot of people can't be found anywhere," Yves answered, who kept his body shielded while bullets tore at the tree that protected him.

Martain began assessing the strength of his troops, which had dwindled dramatically without anyone noticing. Every top-ranked biker Martain summoned had either suffered a tragic accident or was being aided back to safety from the war zone. The massive pressure Martain envisioned unleashing on his antagonists seemed only a fairy tale dream as he watched his braves cower behind the protection of trees. A fierce expression fell over the biker boss' face as he counted over the remaining eight gladiators of a force once fifty strong. Martain looked around and began wondering if his legion of thugs had cowardly deserted the fight as he considered their ratio for success. While pondering over the idea, Martian witnessed a spear as it pierced through thin air before pasting one of his bikers to the tree he used as protection against the golf balls being fired from the house.

"Fuck! They've had us surrounded all this time and we didn't even know it! Retreat! Let's get the fuck out of here before we all get left here!" Martain yelled as he headed the pack back toward their vehicles once he observed the trajectory the spear had taken.

Danny knew they could outsmart the bikers into believing they were a much larger and rugged bunch before he started through the woods in search of Eagle. The number of deceased bikers scattered throughout the woods told the tale about who truly cast the decisive blow that defeated the biker army. Nicholas and Kane scurried out of the house once they noticed their antagonists had retreated. The two friends cautiously swept the dark woods with their automatic weapons to ensure the bikers had left. Danny soon walked from the dark trees with his father's body, and everyone assembled around the great warrior, praising his spirit for living before ushering him off to the Spirit Realm.

Part 9

THE HEROIC ACTIONS of Nicholas' Rude Buoys bunch spread through the streets of Montreal like tales printed in the papers from which we receive our daily updates. The most notorious gang in Canada had long ruled the world of underground crime on the island of Montreal with their well-known, fierce vigilance and unyielding tactics in battle. Hence, intrigue and suspense surrounded the man credited for temporarily simmering a gang of misfits who weren't accustomed to failure. The long-time tailor to Nicholas Henry overheard the account that transpired while altering an evening jacket for one of his customers. With the feeling of desertion still haunting his every dream, Carlton sought to lessen the burden with which he'd clothed himself by merging two entities of similar mindset and futuristic vision.

The tailor was not a close acquaintance of Brogan Alfonso, who was the voice behind the Defenders of the West Island territories, yet Carlton knew the majority of his cabinet and professed confidence in the fact that he'd stitched his way into their inner midst. Carlton perceived the merger between Nicholas and the Defenders to be a marriage for the ages, yet postponed his initial phone call to set the wheels in motion because he feared something tragic developing in their affairs where he'd end up bleeding from one group's knife as they tortured him for information about the other. The topic went unmentioned for another week and a half until, one day, Lester, one of the Defenders' most vicious gunmen, walked into the tailor shop with Scotty, who always found a mirror to check and make sure that his face was decent.

The gangster left his chauffeur in the front of the store to go to a standing mirror hoisted against a changing room door, and he proceeded on to the business at hand. Lester never wore off-the-rack clothing from department stores because he hated the idea of seeing someone else in a piece of clothing identical to what he was wearing. In addition, he demanded loose-fitting clothing to conceal his weapons. The main intimidator factor for the Defenders crew hailed the tailor and his assistant before beginning to remove the hardware he carried. Lester took off his jacket and threw it against the back support of a chair. He then proceeded to unbuckle the straps to his Uzi attaché case attached to his back, laid it on the seat of the chair, withdrew two 9 mm from his rear belt, and shoved one in his right side pocket before laying the other against the Uzi on the chair. Lester began walking toward the measuring platform before realizing he'd forgotten something in the pockets of the Uzi case. The gangster collected two magazine clips for his weapon and shoved them in the opposite pocket before indicating he was ready to proceed with the measurements. The most feared arbitrator in the Defenders crew was never a man of too many words, yet Lester spoke admirably about Nicholas, whom he'd heard of and knew was a friend to Carlton.

"You know, only recently I found out about that jumping that happened in here over a year ago!" Lester began.

Not knowing what to expect from the conversation, Carlton nodded in response and simply pointed at the area in which the beating occurred.

"Tough thing to happen to a man, especially with others around, but I respect you boys for not getting involved and for leaving people's business alone. Hah, I don't think you'd still be here had you interfered," said Lester.

Carlton sensed a bit of empathy from Lester toward Nicholas, although he maintained discretion should there be an enticing piece of bait being dangled from a string. The tailor found himself arguing within himself after only surviving the urge to facilitate an introduction a few days prior.

"Believe me when I tell you, my breathrin', Nick is the real McCoy when it comes to getting your types of products. The man is mild and has a decent temper, and he's a cool youth who deals with the real business and not the fuckery, if you know what I mean," Carlton described.

"So, you and him really tight like that?" Lester asked.

"A few times them white boys run up in here, trash the place, and claim they heard he was in here. A few of them slap me around a couple times and claim I know where he's hiding, but even if I did they'd never get it out of me," Carlton declared. "Good youth who believe inna him gun and him God."

"Apart from our business, I'd like for you to make some money hooking up some other business for us, I believe my boss could really profit from dealing with this English-man" Lester offered.

"Anything you want, boss, me a listen!"

The Unifying

The idea of Canada's native people killing their white counterparts was never an issue that sat well with the lawmakers of the land. Thus, those who are knowledgeable of their history know for certain there would be serious retribution following any situation of a white man dying at the hands of an Indian. Following the slaughtering of forty-two of Martain's Rough Riders, the three remaining combatants gathered up the corpses and loaded them into Eagle's old Chevy truck. It took four trips of twelve corpses to scurry away the lifeless bodies that Eagle and company left scattered all across the woods around their house. The three survivors transported the bodies deep into the woods, dug a massive hole, and dumped the bodies of the fallen Rough Riders within. A ten-gallon jug of gasoline was poured across the bodies before setting them ablaze like a huge barn fire. The three friends watched the bodies burn as they individually thought about Eagle's brave sacrifice during the previous night, as well as their tasks ahead should they wish to survive.

Without Eagle, the word *moral* took on less meaning in the life of his youngest son, Kane Esquada, who increased his drug trafficking around the Indian reservation. Kane developed a flock of young soldiers eager to earn their piece of the Canadian pie that is not commonly served to Indians or immigrants from other countries. The modest drug market around the reserves soon blossomed, and quality products swept through gutters and ghettos like poisonous snakes in search of a mate. Nicholas' interests in the wealth on the island of Montreal soon grew as his profit margin soared while controlling every aspect of the distribution on the reservation. It wasn't long before the wealth and power brought forth by the money began purchasing law officials from both the Federal Police Bureau or the Royal Canadian Mounted Police as well as the Native Police Bureau, which were the governing law forces policing the reservation.

The Indian reservations has always provided stiff competition against the Canadian government, with respects to the sales of cheaper generic cigarettes, which was impossible for the government to tax. These cigarettes are often smuggled across the American/Canadian borders, and sold in souvenir gift shops located off the soft shoulders of every Provincial Interstate highway surrounding the reservations. Smokers from across the river in Montreal often voyage across the bridge for cheaper native cigarettes sold in smoke huts throughout the reservation. The illegal smuggling of cigarettes was one of Eagle's secretive hustles, but his sons opted for the more financial gains that came through tougher drugs. Apart from the cheaper non-taxed cigarettes, there are also those conservative motorists who commuted to petrol stations on the reservations in order to save the extra two or three cents on the gasoline sold there.

Nicholas' empire, which grew from the gutters and pits of the native Indians of the Twelve Nations of the Native Council of Canada, was agreed upon as the place for the introductions between two entities with one common enemy. The location was kept secret between the two bosses, who knew the high compensation for treacherous espionage, especially one with such high profile personnel. Both bosses navigated their individual drivers from home to the meeting point, which was underneath the Mercier Bridge that crosses onto the Indian reservation.

Nicholas' entourage was modest yet complex.featuring Danny his right-hand shooter, Damian his cousin from Florida , Tank, a new driver, who was settling in after his first month on chauffeur duties, and two dozen Indian braves, who were invisibly scattered among a patch of tall grass a few paces off the shores of the river. The venue was perfect for a sit-down conversation, while offering patrons a clear view of oncoming traffic with areas to manoeuvre should the situation get hot and sticky. Nicholas rolled with a light infantry because he knew he had a number of trump cards at his disposal should he find himself in desire of a rescue. In place was the locking-the-bridge tactic, where, should an ambush plot be successful, the ambushers would find themselves stuck in traffic at a perilous point on the bridge before either being struck by missiles from a bazooka, or they would find themselves overwhelmed with bullets the size of which, once impacted, shredded vehicles like diced cabbage. There was the law enforcement factor, where Nicholas would call in the cavalry and have the local law enforcement administer their brand of aggressive punishment. Then there was the smash-mouth method, where modern day Indian warrior braves would get summoned, charge in to battle with their arrow-sailing, rifle-blazing, axe-throwing, and scalping tactics designed to hinder and maim one's opponent.

Brogan's entourage was fairly large, with a Denali and a Tahoe SUV, and two female riders saddled on a pair of Suzuki high-powered motorbikes, bringing their total count to the grand number of ten. Brogan's feet had hardly touched the soil before he signalled the female riders to patrol the perimeter while the gentlemen conducted business. Nicholas and Brogan approached each other without any personal guards and with affections toward each other as if they'd known each other for decades. Both businessmen walked freely along the shores of the Champlain River, discussing business proposals, ways to assist each other, and strategies to defend against their nemesis the Rough Riders.

"I sometimes think I roll like the president, but damn, you put us all to shame!" Nicholas acknowledged.

"If you've had as many attempts on your life as I have, you'd never chance it with a small motorcade like yours knowing the vultures are always seeking to attack," Brogan laughed as the two men respectfully walked alongside each other.

"I heard your family originally emigrated from Italy," Nicholas said.

"Yeah, over forty-five years now, and they even changed our

nationalities and got sworn in as Canadians. Someone told me you were British, but you sound more like some Jamaican home boys related to my family."

"I'm one hundred percent Jamaican, but for immigration purposes, it is what it is."

A stiff breeze lifted the Rastafarian's gold and green hat from his head, although he quickly caught it before it got soiled after fluttering to the ground. The ten-inch locks atop Nicholas' head appeared to come alive under the luscious breeze that blew tranquilly from the river, and he shook them free before replacing his hat.

"These bastards wish to tell us how to live, how to make money, how to do everything. They think because we weren't born here we don't have rights like them. Fuck them. I will live to see the last of them or die trying to make it happen. You fellas brought back the dream that everybody lives for but can't get to because of these fucking riders! For us, due to the fact they control the docks and shit, we can't seem to get a shipment in for the past few months because they keep intercepting our cargo and seizing the fucking thing," Brogan declared.

"So with thousands of cargo ships coming in every day, how do they specifically find your shipment?" Nicholas asked.

"Changed up everything from the sender, place it's coming from, and no matter what we try they keep finding the shit. I hear you can provide whatever weight your customer's desire. If so, I think we can do a lot of business," Brogan said.

While the bosses discussed business and properly acquainted themselves with each other, Damian and Danny kept a close visual on Nicholas while ensuring their new allies behaved honourably. The two centurions stood well armed with fully loaded extension magazines sticking out their AK-47 assault rifles, while their counterparts stood across from them, fully armed and undaunted. The unnecessary tension between the two outfits was soon disrupted by Tank, who emerged from behind his getaway driver position with five marijuana joints, gave two to his partners and handed the rest to their counterparts. The men lit up their joints and passed them around where necessary, and the barrier walls slowly began disintegrating. Within minutes, the guards' entire postures changed, and they became more relaxed and open toward each other while debating which NFL teams were going to be victorious that

Sunday. A few serious wagers inherited their picks from the discussion, which was both heated and passionate by true lovers of the sport.

The argument soon shifted from sports to aspects of business, beginning with the sole dark-coloured male amongst the Defenders establishing a marijuana connection with Tank, whom he claimed "ripped off his dome" with the hydroponic high grade he presented. Tank was more than willing to engage in dealings, especially after discovering the quantity being sought after. The Indians had the freedom and capability to produce their own cannabis, and countless Indians grew their own crops, yet instead of flourishing the drug trade to the north, they chose to smuggle their high grade across the border into upstate New York for a larger cash pot. With the U.S. dollar valued more than the Canadian and a higher price being paid for exotic hydroponic marijuana in the States versus Quebec, more Indians most likely tackled the well-policed waters of the Outaouais River.

Unlike the Indians, who smuggled everything from alcohol to tobacco, Tank, like most of his counterparts, was banned from legally entering the United States due to the fact that he had criminal records within the country in which he resided. Therefore, given the fact that the product was widely available on the reservation and hustlers simply must get paid, an arrangement was quickly reached on the price of each shipment as well as the delivery proceedings.

The two motorbike surveyors, who were instructed to patrol the perimeter of the meeting grounds, came terribly close to the camouflaged Indians whom Nicholas posted in the brushes, yet rode by the warriors several times without the slightest inclination that they were present. The female riders atop the Kawasaki iron horses handled the powerful motorcycles quite handily as they rode about in their tight leather outfits with their automatic weapons across their laps. After riding by her counterpart midway semi-circling the negotiating entourages, one of the female riders came across a herd of men who'd ridden onto the grounds and positioned themselves at the main entrance. The female surveyor came within thirty feet of the Harley Davidson riders, who'd muffled their tailpipes with silencers, quieting their hogs enough for them to sneak in close to their targets. The female rider dug her heel into the ground as she flung the tail end of the motorbike around, kicking up dark sand as the bike railed its front end high into the air and screeched off the rear wheel. As the motorbike began accelerating, a couple of clappers sounded in the rear that tossed the female rider from her saddle as she took an awful spill at the turf.

"Oh, shit! They got Shanann!" The female atop the second Kawasaki immediately sped toward the nucleus of her team.

The report echoed through a Bluetooth device that Brogan had implanted into his left ear, and he immediately demanded whether she was killed or injured. The female in search of added security couldn't quite elaborate on her partner's status, and everyone began scattering to find the safest vantage point from where to counter. While the combining forces scattered to find structures that would provide a defence against oncoming bullets, their unwelcomed antagonists unstopped their dreadful-sounding machines, which they perceived jolted the hearts of their foes. Brogan was still interested in knowing the fate of his surveyor as further reports on the estimated amount of combatants came in to the Defenders' boss.

There were an estimated forty bikers, and both bosses drew their arms and retreated to the bridge's huge support pillars, which were the closest protective structures available to them. Nicholas listened to Brogan's concerns over his fallen guard as he pondered over who exactly among their entourage was the informant who not only led their enemies there, but also had been sabotaging the gang's shipments. While racing to the support pillars beneath the bridge, Brogan, who ran with both his German Luger pistols at hand, moved his hand to his earlobe to adjust his earpiece when he looked up at the bridge above and realised there was an audience of two watching the events. Brogan immediately knew that one of the leather jacket-wearing spectators had to be Martain Lafleur, whom he'd disrespected and called a coward on two separate occasions. Brogan was especially shocked by Nicholas, who reached behind his back and ripped an Uzi automatic weapon attached by straps from his back and quickly put the first round into the firing chamber.

Martain Lafleur had his bodyguard place orange cones indicating roadwork or failed motor vehicle ahead, which disrupted traffic heading into the city. The biker boss sat atop his Harley with a Labatt Blue beer in hand while his companion joined in after readying the video camcorder for image capturing. The two men soon resembled spectators at the movies with terrific seats and adequate beverage—well, minus the popcorn.

The bikers revved up their motor engines and stirred up more noise than scare as the Defenders and Nicholas' entourage prepared for target practice with the expectation of the targets responding. With Martain and friend expecting a total slaughter and the expectance of a few causalities, the bikers charged both the bosses as well as their trusted companions with their total available force, which they perceived would overwhelm their targets. The female rider, who was the first to hit the soil, hadn't moved since she struck dirt, and the attacking bikers rode directly by her, as if they presumed she was dead.

The Rough Riders had celebrated the attack as "the day they rid the earth of their foes," during preliminary toasts where they got insanely intoxicated and heightened each other's morale before the actual battle. Martain who believed his troops were about to surprise their opponents, prematurely celebrated his precieved ambush, , which actually was the other way around, as they were the ones heading into the trap. The attacking bikers who noticed that the commanders they sought were separated from their troops, devided into two parties as they charged at their opponents. As the bikers of the Rough Riders charged into battle, Nicholas' hidden Indians waited until they'd blasted by them before rising from their camouflaged positions with arrows sprucing from bows, dismounting bikers who'd received arrows lodged from their heads to their buttocks. The displacement surprised Martain, who fell over from his motorbike and was nearly struck by a passing motorist after coming extremely close to the operational lane.

The first wave of arrows dismounted fifteen bikers from their chariots before a second wave came in and swept off another eleven. The bikers who led the charge had absolutely no idea about the fate of the comrades to the rear, and they soon clashed with the lead-spitting forces they sought. Rough Riders assassins rode through the convoy created by the Defenders and Nicholas' gun hands, exchanging bullets with their nemesis as they executed to the fullest their plan of attack. Similar to western movies involving Indians and Cowboys, where the wagons of pioneers bundled together to defend against intrusive Indians was the method of attack plotted by the bikers. Once the few to survive the ride-by shoot-out got to the point where they where supposed to turn back into the battle, the men realised their numbers had substantially decreased. The initial ten that set out to eliminate Nicholas and Brogan had dwindled to two after their preliminary drive-by, with all remaining survivors looking to each other with confusion about how to proceed.

One of the riders from the pack of two didn't flinch for long, and he turned his motorbike to the river and rode directly for it. The other five, who realised that the only exit led through a firing squad and an archery squad, immediately followed suit and sped for the river after considering swimming to the island as their only means of survival. With bullets clapping at their heels by Defenders who'd rather not have to combat the same bikers in the future, the fleeing bikers struck the river and swam like fish as they attempted to evade the reprisal. Another three swimmers were chopped off by Defenders who sought to avenge their fallen ally after racing to the shore to dump bullets at the assassins sent to terminate them.

Shanann, who was believed dead because she pretended as such, soon rolled over onto her back and slowly sat up, while her riding partner and others ran to her assistance. The furious and angry Martain, who had recorded the entire ordeal, soon mounted his Harley and quickly returned to the sanctity of the city, with disbelief over what he'd witnessed. It wasn't until Martain had left the scene that Brogan informed Nicholas about him being an overseer during the battle. Nicholas who had implemented means to capture or kill anyone around the surrounding area, was disappointed such information wasn't transferred prior as, he would have awarded Martain a taste of his own medicine.

Part 10

KADEEM WAITED PATIENTLY in line as the immigration officer chastised a young female who was attempting to gain entry into Canada. The thought that he may have selected the wrong checkpoint went through his mind as he watched the woman be escorted off to a secret chamber for further harassment. It became evident that the woman was suspected of smuggling contraband into the country after a questionable package was discovered inside her carry-on luggage. The young female initially behaved as if there were no cause for alarm before realising her situation had become dire. Suddenly, prior to entering the interrogation chamber, the woman took off racing for the exit with a slew of agents giving chase. A few minutes later, Kadeem nervously presented himself before the agitated officer while the female smuggler was returned to the chamber kicking and screaming while pleading for sympathy.

"Are you a native of Nassau, Mr. Campbell?" The immigration officer thumbed through the pages of Kadeem's passport.

"Yes, ma'am," Kadeem answered in his finest mimicking of the Nassau dialect.

"Is this your first trip to Canada, sir?"

"Yes, ma'am."

"What's the reason for your visiting Canada, sir?"

"I've recently rediscovered my long-lost dad, and he lives here, so I'm here to visit him."

"Have you anything to declare, such as alcohol or gifts received from other family members?"

"I bought my dad two bottles of rum at the duty-free shop inside the airport, but no gifts from the rest of the family."

"The rum is fine," began the officer before rudely being interrupted by the screams of the smuggler.

"I'm sorry, but I had to do it for the kids! Them hungry! Please, please, Lord Jesus, helpme! Let me go, let me go! Help me, Lord, help me!" The female smuggler argued as the INS officers dragged her into the room.

"I tell you, the nerve of some people," Kadeem commented.

"Always think they can sneak one by me and my crew, but don't worry, nothing passes through me. You have a wonderful time in Canada, Mr. Campbell, and I hope to see you again," the INS officer said before stamping the seal of approval on the fourth page of Kadeem's passport.

Kadeem scurried through the automatic sliding doors that lead to the baggage claims area, with his heart racing from the fear of being discovered. There was a meagre walk to an escalator, which brought everyone to freedom one level down, and Kadeem breathed a huge sigh of relief following his immigration experience. A man resembling the person in a photo he'd carried around for years began waving to him outside the glass casing which surrounded the escalator. Kadeem had given the INS worker his correct reason for entering the country, though the documents and evidence of whom he truly was remained confidential.

The two men gingerly hugged each other and began toward the luggage port, which according to the information screens indicated that Kadeem's luggage was set to be discharge from conveyer beltnumber three. The father and son, who hadn't seen each other for nearly eighteen years, were reunited through the kind efforts of Granny P., who continued paving the way for a youngster she help raised. Kadeem spent the last two and a half years in Nassau, where he worked honestly and sought means for a more progressive life. During his time in Nassau, Kadeem remained inconspicuous, partying little, working more, and spending an occasional weekend with a girlfriend who visited seldom. However, their long-distant relationship ended after a man from her district impregnated her and moved her into his house.

Along the journey to Jeremiah's house in Notre Dame D'Grace, Kadeem's father plastered him with rules of conduct expected of him while partaking of his generosity and home. Jeremiah professed to being a man of God who attended church regularly and expected such of anyone within his immediate circle. The use of indecent language or any profane speech would not be tolerated, and one was expected to work and to contribute to the continuing developments of the household. Schooling was cited as a waste of time by Jeremiah, who believed any goals short of a physical labour trade were unreachable at Kadeem's age. Jeremiah was himself an auto mechanic specialist who owned and operated a small garage in the Ville Saint Pierre area.

Jeremiah told Kadeem about his wife of nine years, who was a caretaker for the elderly at a privately-owned facility in Montreal. He advised his son, though, that he and his wife were incapable of producing a child; she had a son from a previous relationship who attended McGill College. *The audacity of this man,* thought Kadeem to himself before dismissing Jeremiah's prejudiced comment. The scenery through Jeremiah's Toyota Camry window kept Kadeem's mind isolated on one goal, which was to succeed at whatever task lay ahead.

Jeremiah brought home his long-lost son who would have remained as such had it not been for the thoughtfulness ofGranny P.., The old woman who was both an inspiration in the lives of Kadeem and his father, had helped in the upbringing of both men, as well as countless youths around the neighbour-hood. After dropping his son off at home, Jeremiah who had a business to attend to left for work. Jeremiah advised Kadeem, "The world don't stop rotating because you come a foreign," before scurrying off to his daily hustle.

Kadeem placed his luggage inside a small room in the basement before taking a tour of Jeremiah's first-floor duplex apartment. There were three bedrooms on the main floor, and there was an attached living room, bathroom, and kitchen that led out to a small backyard. The basement had a single room with one bathroom and appeared to be used primarily for mechanical purposes.

The fascination of the outdoors soon cluttered Kadeem's mind against anything else inside the house, and he stood by the window and watched the local traffic pass by. After a few hours of watching television, making a few telephone calls to his cousin, Auntie P., and a few others, Kadeem decided to stretch his legs for a moment and tour the surrounding neighbourhood. The dilemma over the front door came into consideration once Kadeem was prepared to exit. However, his belief that a break-in would be improbable by him spending a half hour outdoors prompted him to follow his instincts.

Kadeem took precise notes on the directions travelled and the names of streets he passed along the way. The cleanliness and order of the streets, the precision with which the houses were aligned, and the remarkable structures fascinated the Jamaican fugitive, and he took time to holler at each luscious female he passed. A student at Concordia University gave him a bit more than conversation, and she found him mysterious enough to surrender her phone number. Kadeem spent a short while with the female as she waited for her bus before finally deciding to return home before anyone got there first.

The front door was closed when Kadeem arrived home, which seemed odd considering he left it unlatched. From inside the house came the agitated voice of a female yelling at someone over the phone as Kadeem reached out for the doorbell. A few seconds of waiting eventually produced a four foot eight woman, whose thickness attributed to the fact that she wasn't shy when it came to demolishing a plate of food. The woman looked Kadeem from his Bally shoes up to his face with a despicable stare before finally stepping to the side to offer him entry.

"Okay, honey, I talk to you later!" The woman disconnected her phone call. "So, you is Jeremiah boy? You look like him. I have a twenty-one-year-old son named Junior who is about your height. Come, come give me a hug! Me is you stepmother, Doherty! You father and I married for years and I just finally getting to meet you. You hungry? You must hungry by now. Come. Me fix you a plate of rice and peas and oxtail in the kitchen, you can tell me 'bout Nassau and the rest of the islands!"

Doherty appeared caring and thoughtful despite Kadeem's expectations after overhearing her earlier phone conversation. The meal she prepared Kadeem was arguably the best plate of Jamaican food he'd eaten since fleeing his homeland some three years prior. Kadeem licked the plate and utensils clean as he answered his stepmother's questions about the beauty surrounding the places he'd been. A half hour into their conversation, Doherty's son arrived home from school and headed into the kitchen, which was his normal routine. Junior walked by Kadeem and directed his attention to the refrigerator before his mother stated the fact that there was another person in the room. The response given by Junior to his mother's suggestion that he introduce himself to his stepbrother had Kadeem wishing the young man continued on his way without any formal or semi-formal greeting. Junior's response, which was, "Mother, you always forcing me to do everything," had Kadeem confused about his reason for not wanting an introduction.

But, wait, is a batty-man them want give me for a step-brother? Kadeem thought to himself as his homosexual sibling femininly extended his hand for a handshake.

"How you doing?" Junior responded as they gingerly shook hands.

Kadeem and Doherty spoke for a few more minutes before Jeremiah's Volvo engine sounded in the driveway. Once the vehicle's engine shut off, Doherty blasted from the kitchen and went to her room without so much as a "You're welcome for the food," to Kadeem. The newcomer to Canada finished eating and was in the process of washing the utensils when his enraged father entered the house.

"Are you trying to make thief break into my house? You leave me door wide open and gone God knows where from God knows how long, for thieves to come clean out my little bit. I go check 'round to make sure nothing was stolen, and if me find anything missing you go have to pay for its replacement," Jeremiah declared before storming from the kitchen.

The rapid change in attitude by Jeremiah bewildered Kadeem, who experienced for the first time his father's furious temperament. Though the culprit who committed the infraction deterred from arguing the facts, the attitude brought forth by his father angered Kadeem, who stepped out on the back porch for some fresh air to distil his rage. The night blew a calm breeze, which suited Kadeem as he mumbled to himself while searching for the ideal spot to linger. "I refuse to have anybody deal with me like some crotches!" Kadeem repeated to himself as he walked by a familiar odour which caught his attention. *A the buoy Junior room that sweet scent a Ganja a come from,* thought Kadeem to himself as he pulled even closer to the window. *The buoy Junior burn marijuana. Sweet! Him better have at least a joint for me, to help relieve this fucking stress!*

With his temperament blazing like a furnace from his father's accusations, Kadeem knew the perfect remedy to his ailments would be a little paraphernalia, which he thought about acquiring during his walk, but had absolutely no idea where to search for it. Kadeem tapped lightly on the glass, though Junior reacted as if a shotgun had been sounded to begin a race.

"Yeah, what's up, man?" Junior asked, who didn't appear intimidated by the fact he was caught smoking weed.

"Give me a spliff, son!" Kadeem demanded.

"You smoke weed?"

"I'm from the Caribbean. Not to say that everybody from the Caribbean smokes, but I'm in the percentage that does!"

Kadeem pretended he didn't noticed the magazine clippings of a number of R&B and rap stars, such as a topless Fifty Cent, Usher, and Genuine, posted against his stepbrother's wall. The enraged Kadeem simply collected the .6 grams of marijuana, two sheets of Zig Zag, and a half-book of matches from Junior before retreating to a selected spot behind a broken-down wooden shack in the backyard. With the tactics of creativity bestowed unto him from a younger age, Kadeem constructed an immaculate cone before setting it ablaze while meditating over his present predicament. The promise made by him to Auntie P. soon subdued his rage as he looked to the skies at faces he longed to see and shouted, "Jah Rastafarri!"

Though Kadeem was not yet legally capable of working in the country due to his visitation status, Jeremiah thought it ridiculous that an able-bodied man spend his days lounging about and insisted he assist him at the mechanic shop. Hence, Kadeem began working in this new land before the twenty-fourth hour struck on his arrival clock.

Jeremiah's Auto Repair was a two-division repair shop where they repaired engines, transmissions, wheel alignments, brakes, shocks, and so on in one section, while performing frame restoration in the other. There were two permanent employees entrusted with Jeremiah's care, including Daren, a fifty-three-year-old car body man from Antigua, and the twenty-seven-year-old apprentice from Trinidad named Alwin.

Kadeem's duties at the shop were simply to assist his father while Jeremiah disassembled, repaired, and reassembled his customers' vehicles. The men worked long shifts that were anywhere from twelve to fifteen hours long, beginning at eight in the morning until the day's work was done or slightly before dysfunctional bodies hit the turf. On Fridays and Saturdays, the men would often quit early before engaging in a few games of dominos over a bottle of rum or selected beer. A small number of acquaintances would gradually fall through, simulating a fun atmosphere where friends enjoyed each others' company while either gambling for money or boastful pride.

The task awarded Kadeem offered him the ability to learn a trade, which he grasped faster than most men before him. However, it was only a matter of time before the escalating tension between he and his father rose to its boiling point. After receiving a meagre fifty dollars for the first week of which he worked three days, Kadeem withheld his objections with the expectation of a larger payment after completing a full week. Hence, the same vigour and intrigue toward his greasy duties were employed, and Kadeem returned for his second week of mechanic work.

Wages were paid out at the end of each week, and after spending his entire earnings along with a meagre personal sum on the only product which strengthened him to undergo the calamity which transpired inside the Kites residence on a daily basis, Kadeem expected his pockets fully greased after a long and hard week's work. After only a few days in Jeremiah's household, which saw Kadeem chastised constantly, the Jamaican fugitive sought independence and began thinking toward his objectives. Come payday, Jeremiah's favoured employees were attended to first as he complimented his crew of yesteryears on another fine week of service. While his peers' faces glistened, Kadeem opened the white envelope handed him to find a single hundred dollar bill and no kiss on the cheek.

"What is this suppose to be?" Kadeem demanded of his father.

"Uh, you pay!" Jeremiah exclaimed.

"Man, you can't look pan big man and give him a hundred dollar!" Kadeem argued disagreeably as he tossed the bill to the floor.

"Hold on! How much you believe you should get pay? You a forget say is my roof you staying under, is my food you a eat every day from breakfast to you late night snack them. Them calls you make to Jamaica and elsewhere that the bill don't arrive for yet, me make sure me collect for them before anything. If you did have to take the bus to work, you don't think you would have to pay for the ride? You make people even take things out of me house me have to replace, all those things add up. A what you take this thing for? Foreign a no bed a roses, we all had to pay some dues along the way," fired back Jeremiah.

"You know something? You see if I never learn to hold a higher inner meditation, me tear off you face in here for the disrespect. But I give thanks still, 'cause after all these years of saying you a crotches, me finally get the opportunity to see that you a truly one."

Before Kadeem could properly finish expressing himself, a dismantled Acura TL crept up before the huge hangar doors. The vehicle resembled something ordained to the junkyard after a lengthy tour inside a demolition pit where patrons smack into other vehicles and render them immobilized. Everyone's attention was diverted from the controversy, which was sparked a few minutes earlier, as the squeaky vehicle sporting huge bullet holes came to a halt. The three men who occupied the vehicle exited their chariot like Brinks security guards employed to secure the banking institutions' deposits made by various businesses. With hands lodged into pockets, gripping artefacts beneath their shirts with screw faces as if served shit for lunch, the men surveyed the area before entering the garage.

"What's happening, Rass Ijah?" Alwin commented after recognizing one of the men.

"You always telling me 'bout you body shop, well, me finally have some body work for you," responded the Rastafarian.

"Damn, boy, what happen to you sweet ride? Daren, come take a look at this so we can give him a quote," alerted Alwin as they began moving toward the vehicle.

"But a pure bullet holes full up this ya car ya!" Daren commented as he approached the vehicle.

"Some fools just try spray we with two Uzi up on St. Jacques road a few minutes ago," calmly exclaimed Rass Ijah.

"And with all these holes in the car nobody no get shot?" Alwin asked.

"Jah guidance alone, my buoy!" Rass Ijah boasted.

"Look like you go need some engine work too, 'cause something buss up something under the hood," declared Jeremiah, who nosily intruded to witness the damage.

"You boys lucky you have a tough car around you," said Daren.

Kadeem had privately made the decision to branch off on his own, despite what may and vowed to have nothing to do with his father after developing a feeling of being used over the past few weeks. The exiled Jamaican paid respects to his fellow co-workers before departing, emphasizing the fact he would not be returning. While Kadeem was calculating his next endeavour at the bus stop, Junior, who was on an errand for his mom, pulled over and offered Kadeem a lift, though he first had to stop by the garage for additional funds. Kadeem's frustration was evident, and not fully lashing out against Jeremiah left a discontentment in his heart, though explaining his predicament to Junior managed to slightly ease his anger. Junior offered to chauffeur Kadeem wherever, considering his luggage was fairly plentiful, as well as a loan and his documents should Kadeem decide to rent an apartment.

Refusing to exit the vehicle once they'd entered the vicinity of the garage, Kadeem sat back and awaited his stepbrother, who indicated he'd be prompt. Kadeem used Junior's cell to telephone one of his two bright spots thus far in Canada as he inhaled the toxins from his first love, Mr. Hydroponic. The young female Kadeem met on his first day out walking had been his ear of hope and voice of salvation while providing nothing less than good loving and satisfaction. The young college student shared a four-bedroom apartment with her close friend, and she eagerly offered Kadeem shelter for as long as he so desired.

With zero other offers on the table, Kadeem accepted without any further thought and assured his young lover his stay would be brief. The telephone conversation soon changed as the thoughts of being constantly in each other's presence jolted their sexual appetites. Kadeem was soon tossing about his pet name, Killa, which was anointed to him while living in Jamaica as a youngster and so desired his female companion to refer to him as such during intercourse. The young lady, on the other hand, wanted to know if there was a bit of freakiness hidden somewhere inside Kadeem where he'd be open to an occasional ménage-a-trois with her roommate and herself. Kadeem attested to the fact that he'd not be performing any oral stimulations, although he fell silent over the idea of it being performed on him.

From his peripheral vision, Kadeem caught sight of someone prancing in the air to land a dropkick at Junior, who was simply retreating with his hands up to protect his face as two other men shimmed around the corner on the attack. Another man soon landed a straight right punch at Junior, who smashed against the hood of his car before realizing he'd been circled and cornered with nowhere to run. Reactively, Kadeem jumped from the passenger side door and flung the first article in his reach at the man closest to him. Sadly, though, there went his phone conversation and Junior's link to the world, as the cell phone went crashing against the side of the young man's head.

"You bitches have to do me something, too, if onnou plan fi touch my brother!" Kadeem said in his native dialect as he pranced into action to even up the score.

The young man quickly armed himself and aimed the gun at an approaching Kadeem's head while swiping at the blood trickling down the side of his head.

"A you Chichi Man boyfriend this to you rescue? Pussy, say goodbye to you lover!" The armed thug's eyes lit up in preparation to blast.

One of the bystanders cheered, "Yes, Damian, shoot the blood clatt buoy in him face!"

"No, my breathrin', stop, stop, stop!" Alwin shouted, who overheard the disruption while departing for home and nosily intruded. "A the boss man son who just come from Mobay name Killa, me beg all you please release him.?"

"All them batty boy ya fi get gunshot!" Stated the man whose index finger massaged the trigger, eager to blast one away.

"Yeah, but him a no batty man," conveyed Alwin.

"My youth, you see how close you come to getting you life took? Watch you self next time you see bad man a handle him business, you stay out a it seen. Me should all murder you blood clatt fi buss up mi head, still a levity. You dig?" The thug saidwhile slowly lowering his weapon.

"Mi don't forget a man who point him gun in my face still. 'member that!" Kadeem stated as he helped an injured Junior into the car.

The young thug joked, "Man, you hear this guy?" He shoved his weapon into his waistband. "Say thank God I allowed you to continue breathing, bout."

A Toyota Land Cruiser pulled up as Kadeem placed Junior, who was grimacing for his ribs, in the passenger seat of his Chrysler Neon. The crew of thugs who visited the garage to have their vehicle repaired hopped aboard their limousine, leaving the butt of their jokes in anguish. Alwin, who was genuinely concerned, saw to it that everyone left peacefully before he departed the compound.

Part 11

THE LUSCIOUS PLANTS and assorted colourful flowers around Stephan D'agaruso's garden were complementary assets to the Chairman of the Rough Riders' eight million dollar mansion in St. Lazard, east of Montreal. Martain Lafleur had been an honoured representative of the east coast division of mobsters for the past six plus years, yet it was through the pioneers of the French province that the biker gang was established. Stephan D'agaruso was considered the Chairman and spokesperson for a secret, illicit group of billionaires who controlled the underground illegal markets of drugs, racketeering, and gambling while playing the legislators of Quebec's legal government like puppets. It was through these eleven giant tycoons that some of the most perilous decisions concerning the Province of Quebec were made, despite the public's belief that their anointed mayors and public servants were the governing faction.

Martain Lafleur was the only leader in the history of the Rough Riders organization to rise to prominence through blood relations. The Dominator, as he was called, was the organization's first-ever leader for nearly twenty years before his tragic death after a mercenary used a semi-trailer to run him over on one of his infamous Harley Davidson cruises. Born Yves Lafleur to prominent French parents who bore three other boys and one lone female, it was discovered that his final command was that his reign be handed down to his favourite nephew, who had always professed his desire to be exactly like his uncle. Martain had his experts scour the wreckage for clues and later found out his uncle met his demise at the hands of their fiercest enemy, who had always been Brogan Alfonso, leader of the Defenders crew.

Both Stephan D'Agaruso and Martain walked freely about the grounds while guards patrolled the surroundings. In Martain's six-years at the helm of the Rough Riders gang, he'd only been summoned to the nest on one other occasion, which had been a very nerve-wrecking visit. With slightly more fierceness in his arsenal on said visit, Martain expected intense scrutiny after the Gazette reported that s Nicholas' gun hands had struck another severe blow to the Rough Riders.

"Here's another list of people in need of persuasion," Stephan began as he handed Martain a piece of paper containing seventy-eight names. "This war that's been ongoing for more than three years needs to come to some finalization. We advised you to come to the table with this ruffian you've been trying to eliminate for over a year now. Because you insisted on burying this adversary of yours, we awarded you additional time to handle your business. However, following these recent losses of yours, we're now compelled more than ever to sit down and come to some business terms with this Nicholas. There are greater matters of importance on the table presently, and in order for us all to continue our tradition of excellence, we simply must fortify peace for the greater good," Stephan advised.

"How does the topic of discussion even come up while strategizing? After all, we've toiled for all these years, and you gentlemen simply want to give a portion of that away. Not while I'm still breathing! It's either that bitch or me, but we'll never be on the same team!" Martain argued.

"Nobody expected you to grasp the situation, which is simply the fact that we've watched an annual gross of more than three million dollars dissipate to half that amount over a three-year term. We have investors to satisfy and partners to persuade that this bickering will not spill over into affairs that are more urgent. I don't need remind you of our obligations this time around. The bottom line is this: it's either we read about Mr. Henry in the obituaries, or some sort of arrangements will be made," Stephan instructed.

The eighty-four-year-old Stephan D'agaruso held Martain's arm and used his support to bend forward in order to pick a white rose from its stem. The old tycoon that rose to power through real estate as well as an assortment of many fraudulent businesses collected an assortment of coloured roses until he'd gained enough to assemble a bouquet. Both men walked to an exquisite gazebo that was encased inside an assortment of flowers and pine trees before sitting and chatting for an additional few minutes.

"You remind me so much of myself as a young man growing up. Take no shit, deal with matters as they come. Though I can't say I was quite as fierce, I can say I did have a lot of fun with the ladies." The men looked at each other and chuckled for a bit. Martain's cellular began vibrating continuously, although he chose to ignore the caller. "The Martain I know hasn't been around for a while now. When was the last time you rode one of your Harleys? Your uncle lived to feel the wind blow through him while riding, but this war of yours prevents you from having any fun." Stephan paused and looked at Martain, whom he'd known since the day of his birth The blank stare by Martain supported Stephan's assumptions, though the gangster neglected to comment.

"You see this bouquet of roses? Before I met and married my wife, I wasn't able to see the beauty in one rose, not to mention a colourful bouquet. Life is always going to be about choices and changes, no matter which corner of the world you live in. There is beauty in everybody thus people strive to have it, which is why the most evil and vicious people I know are the ones running the world. People do what they do because of personal gratification or loved ones—nothing else. When was the last time you spoke to your father? I think it's time you start mending some issues in your life. Hah! It's funny—my wife used to always tell me to bring her roses and leave them here after she was gone. I used to tell her, 'Don't hold your breath,' but look at me! Ha, ha!"

Martain thought about everything the Chairman had urged as he looked through the thick, bulletproof glass of his Hummer H2. The leaves on the trees along the interstate outside were transforming to a beautiful golden colour, as the change to autumn caused them to flutter to the ground. His personal bodyguards knew of their boss' furious nature and remained silent during their forty-five minute trip to the cottage. The cottage was a two-story bungalow located in Laval, where biker members would often take prisoners slated for torture. The biker boss received a phone call from Andre, who called to relay information about an incident that occurred during the late hours. With his cellular phone pressed against his ear, Martain grew very aggravated at the word of an attack against his drug shipment yard on the South Shore that resulted in the complete destruction of his hangar, as well as the products it housed. The biker boss began stumping the rear of the front passenger seat as he yelled out Nicholas' and Brogan's names while swearing he'd personally dirt them both.

"It's like they came to steal the stuff, but once they saw that they couldn't come close because of our fire power they altered their plans. Then they came at us with gasoline and torches and lit up the warehouse. While we were busy waiting for the counterattack, they first lit up the blind side of the building before moving to the back and right around. We had to shoot our way out of the building to safety because they intended for us to burn inside with the rest of the shit." The person on the line paused before releasing a huge sigh. "With everything going up in smoke, we had to get our asses out of that burning building, so we started shooting our way out, but by time we got to safety behind the huge garbage container to the right of the building, there was like three of us left. Those fuckers were out to destroy everything, though, boss, because even after all that, they still threw two or three bottle bombs into the blaze. I don't know through what exit Gilles snuck out of that abyss, but I'm glad he did because they weren't planning on leaving any witnesses, either. If Young Buck hadn't snuck around on them and picked a few of them off, we wouldn't be here to say shit. I guess when they started to run away, the fuckers got in a lucky shot on Young Buck and hit him in right arm, and with the sirens getting closer, we just hightailed it out of there before the cops showed up. But the kid had shot one of them who couldn't get away in the knee and—"

"How the fuck did they even get that close to the hangar? You idiots must have been partying when you should've been paying attention!" Martain commented.

"No, no, boss, that ain't how it was. We—"

The phone line went dead as Martain slammed his Motorola flip phone shut. The biker boss planned to rid the planet of Nicholas and his allies, who had begun integrating and supplying the Haitians around

L'acadie and the eastern regions of Montreal. This was no great issue as the bikers had always provided the Haitians their controlled substances, although it was never expected that a man of dark complexion would ever join the exclusive, all-white club. With his biker soldiers perishing at a disproportionally high rate compared to those of their nemesis, the biker boss coupled with the Haitians purely as a temporary strategy, which he perceived was a valiant chess move. Biker or Caucasian assassins hired by Martain to assassinate his nemesis had all failed, and his enemies were always pleased to return a dismembered portion of the anatomies to ensure that Martain understood the fate that befell anyone he sent.

A Haitian native pretending to be of African descent befriended a young shotta who hustled around the downtown area as one of Nicholas' representatives. The young shotta was within his element, and his existence was purely on a "who-knows-who" basis. The Haitian convinced the young shotta that he was directed to deal with him specifically by Spuggy, who had recently begun serving a bid in the Boudreaux Penitentiary. He ordered five kilos of cocaine, and he handed the young shotta ten thousand dollars in cash, entrusting him a sneak peek into a leather laptop case that contained the remaining funds. The young shotta collected the money and placed the order in to the head office, after which he gave the Haitian specific instructions on where to meet in order to complete the transaction.

The Haitian was early to the meeting spot. The young shotta, Bruce, who transported the product from across the native reserves and a female the young shotta was eager to conclude the day with arrived in Nicholas' delivery boy's two-door Toyota Celica. The limousine-style tinted windows around the vehicle made it practically impossible to see the female in the rear of the car as they rode up into a vacant parking lot of Ontario Street east of downtown. The young shotta and Bruce hopped out the vehicle with the products being sought in a regular plastic bag and their weapons concealed, and the buyer stood beside his Acura TL with a thick and attractive red-boned female to his left. Bruce was almost fixated on the beautiful and sturdy stallion who was brought along to serve as the decoy.

"It is good to see you are a man of honesty," the Haitian declared.

The young shotta answered, "I'm a businessman, baby. I see you brought your bodyguard with you! Hi, how you doing?"

"Hello, hello," acknowledged the female.

The young shotta cheered, "Oh, I can smell that money!"

The female, who was in possession of the laptop case with the funds, began handing the young shotta the case before all hell broke loose. Tires from two SUVs screeched as they raced around the corner that led into the parking lot. The young shotta and Bruce took their eyes off their business associates and began reaching for their weapons before they were halted by the Haitian and his bitch, both of whom quickly jammed their weapons against their heads.

"Toss them guns over there nice and easy!" The Haitian commanded, and the young shotta and Bruce obeyed orders.

The SUV trucks were filled with bikers who all hopped out with baseball bats, pipe irons, and batons in expectation of beating those subdued. The driver of one of the SUVs walked over to the Haitians and collected the plastic bag of cocaine before calling his boss to inform him that they were successful. The female inside Bruce's car ducked down as a biker veered toward the vehicle, yet was unable to see her. The female had to cover her mouth to avoid screaming as the bikers all began beating the daylights out of the young shotta and Bruce. Both men were beaten to death by the bikers, who sought to send a permanent message to Nicholas and his band of thugs. Once they'd completed disfiguring their enemies, the Haitian tossed a biker insignia atop the young shotta before yelling, "Rough Riders forever, bitch!"

The leader of the eastern division of the Rough Riders gang walked in through the cottage door with two massive humans behind him. It was apparent that Martain had his mind focused elsewhere as he marched by bikers snorting cocaine, loosly engaged in sexual oragies, drinking liquor and playing video games, without acknowledgment and went directly to the basement. There was a room set up for torture with blades ranging from scalpels to swords, piercing objects from shanks to spears, chopping weapons from machetes to axes, chains, hooks, and electrical connections for shock treatments all built in a room where you could scream for God without even the Almighty hearing you. The stench of decomposed anatomies caused the faint at heart to vomit up their prior meals and bloodstains spackled across the walls.

"Ivan!" Martain exclaimed, raising both his index and middle fingers in the air while sitting only a few paces in front the prisoner. Ivan was Martain's personal do-boy, and he was the one who constructed Martain's marijuana joints laced with cocaine, his cranberry mixed with Hennessy drink, tended to his banking and accounting, and so on. Ivan brought over a joint and placed it between his boss' lips before sparking the lighter to set it ablaze. Martain sat quietly intoxicating himself with a poison he'd grown to love while staring at the young prisoner who'd been knocked unconscious after his debut servings of licks, kicks, and more licks.

Martain began thinking about the delicate position in which this unexpectedly lengthy war has placed his affairs while contemplating degrees to retain his governing body's confidence. Over their three years of warfare, both sides had surrendered grave amounts of warriors in shoot-outs, fights, stabbings, and so on, yet Martain remained the sole gangster lobbying for job approval. The thought of what may become of him should the council vote to terminate the bloodshed through negotiations and diplomacy left a foul taste in the back of his throat. Martain began considering mutiny about his ship should he fail to bring the disputes between himself and Nicholas to a close. Apart from the messenger and the Chairman, Sir Honourable Stephan D'agaruso's, Martain knew little of the secret society he represented or of its members. Furthermore, without knowing the members of the group, it would be impossible to confirm from whom such an order would come, considering the high-ranked billionaires they secretly represented.

"Yow, wake up, bro! Wake up! Get his fucking ass up, Ivan!"

Ivan walked over to the unconscious lad and slapped him across his bloodied face before scornfully fetching his hand towel to cleanse his hand. "Can't you hear someone talking to you, boy?"

The young lad, who bled from areas throughout, peeked through the tiny window of visibility left him through his left eye since the right eye had been totally swollen shut. Immediate flashbacks on his ordeal appeared to frighten the prisoner, who flinched terribly after Ivan simulated the intent to slap him across the face.

Martain said, "Do you have any idea what we do to people here? People have given up their grandmothers in hopes that the pain will stop once we've begun dislodging body parts. Notice you're not gagged or anything? Believe me, screaming is encouraged down here. In fact, the louder you scream the hornier we get, if you want to get technical. Let's see, just the other night we had your partner Gringo down here. I know you recognize the ring." Martain tossed a ring at the lad. The young man's eye opened wide as he looked down at the ring that landed in his lap.

"Yeah, I know; the big question is, 'What happened to the rest of good old Gringo?' You damn sure look a lot more worried about what's going to happen to you right now. Tell you what—I'm feeling a little generous today, believe it or not, and I'm going to give you a little scoop about what happened to your friend Gringo and your possible fate."

Martain used a knife to cut the ropes that bound the lad to the chair before dragging the prisoner halfway across the room. There was a refrigerator in the far left corner of the room with liquid residue resembling blood on the floor in front of it. Martain walked over to the refrigerator and pulled a man's entire leg, from the hip to the sole of the foot, from within before returning to his guest. The prisoner, who was left on his buttocks, utilized the sole moment of freedom awarded him since his capture to formulate an attack at the leader of the Rough Riders.

"Sit the fuck down. Did I tell you that you could stand?" Martain exclaimed as he whacked his prisoner across the temple with the body part.

Martain went over to the lad with the semi-frozen leg and pinned the prisoner to the floor with it against his neck. The lad looked up at the biker boss, whose rage mounted following his idiotic attempt and immediately began pleading with apology.

"I'm sorry, man. Please, I just lost my head for a second. It's back on straight now! I promise I'll never try some bullshit like that again!"

Martain stepped to the lone door a few paces from the refrigerator and turned the key already in place before drawing the thick mahogany door open. There was a steel gate with half-inch-thick bars spaced a few inches apart and a small latched port built in the middle of the gate. The stench that breathed from the room immediately engulfed the entire basement, forcing the lad to cover his nostrils with his hands. Martain opened the latched port built into the gate and tossed the human leg into the chamber.

"You wanna find out what happened to your partner Gringo? That was his right leg, and the majority of him, I guess, has already been crunched up and shit out." Two scavenging hyenas rushed the meat and fought over it before they devoured it.

The young prisoner crawled into a corner after witnessing a sight he'd only observed on television programs like Animal Planet. "Wha-wha-what the fuck is that?"

"Come say hello to Laverne and Shirley, my babies from Africa," Martain declared.

Ivan laughed aloud after watching the lad scurry for safety once he saw the hyenas attack the body part, although he refused to advance any further himself in fear of the gate accidentally falling open. "Bitches! I tell you, boss, look at how scared that fool is. They only tough in numbers, trust me!"

"Right about now, we would normally be carving off parts of your anatomy and have you watch while we feed them to my pets. But today I'm on a different program, because I believe that you not only want to continue living, but you are also a smart man who understands the concept of life," Martain said.

The young lad envisioned screaming men surrendering limbs before they died, possibly by heart attacks, while their oppressors toyed and gamed.

"What you want me to do, man?"

"Don't get me wrong, and believe that this isn't a positive gain for you, because at the end of all this, there is going to be nothing but wealth for everyone involved with the right crew." Martain paused and closed the mahogany door. "Ivan, get me ten G's from the safe upstairs! Now, I'm going to give you a down payment on some information work I want you to do for me. I understand you're just one of the gun hands so I won't demand too much, but cross me and I guarantee I will feed you to my hyenas," Martain said as his assistant returned with the funds and dropped it on the bloodied thug.

Part 12

FOH NUEY, THE biggest Cambodian cocaine dealer in Verdun, Montreal's southwest, thanked Nicholas for the deal as he exited with his companion. Nicholas reclined on his leather sofa inside his home office while his two-and-a-half-year-old son crashed his Tonka toy trucks into each other on the Persian carpet next to him. Although the majority of his interest was in his son, Nicholas occasionally peeked at the television's newscast for reports on the attack his troops launched against Martain's drug warehouse. Instead of any groundbreaking news, the CTV News was recognizing the ever-charismatic Monsieur Michel Lafleur for donating an entire eastern wing to the Jewish General Hospital for cancer research. The old business tycoonalso donated medical equipment and aided in fundraising that brought in another $1.7 million dollars in contributions.

Michel Lafleur was born in Alberta, Canada, in the early 1930s to a crude oil developer and a romance novelist who taught their children proper respect and family values. Michel, Yves, Christopher, and Lorry Ann lived royally as their upper-class parents spoiled them with everything they desired. The senior Monsieur Lafleur suffered a tragic accident before his children's teenage years when an explosion at one of the refineries he supervised left eight families without fathers. Mrs. Loraine Lafleur moved her family to Quebec six months later, where she bought a house and changed her occupation to that of a successful realtor. Her children grew with the tenet that guides each of us along the way into becoming the rebel/goody-two-shoes types of people we each amount to. Michel grew with the gentle grace taught to him by his father, whom he'd so admired, to become the country's most successful realtor and businessman after his mother entrusted him to head her million dollar empire upon retirement.

Yves was always a ruthless individual who squandered money and lived lavishly while occasionally engaging in slap boxing incidences with officers of the law. At the tender age of nineteen, Bad Boy Yves was inaugurated the president of the Rough Riders, and soon dominated the underworld as they grew in strength and popularity.

Christopher maintained a childhood fascination for the law, which saw him complete the bar exam to become a very powerful lawyer. Loraine got her son employed by Brooks and Clarion, which was the city's premier law firm, before the young stud even received his law degree.

The woman the Canadian Globe and Mail once referred to as "The Iron Curtain of Quebec" received her heart's desire the fourth time around with the birth of her only daughter, Lorry Ann. The youngest of her four children was equally spectacular in beauty and brawn, being the only female tossed in the den of lions. Lorry Ann would enter fashion as an aspiring designer, and moved to Paris before capturing the essence of the fashion world.

The wealth and power attained by Michel over the years had placed him amongst the all-time five wealthiest tycoons in Canada. Business associates and investors convinced the business mogul to enter the 1982 Provincial Election to become the mayor of Quebec. With soaring popularity ratings and a commanding lead in the polls, news of a scandal was released that brought Michel's political aspirations to a screeching halt. Thetelevision program W5 did an exclusive on the violent undertakings of the Rough Riders gang where theymentioned a ruthless Martain Lafleur, who was said to be the first offspring of the soon-to-be mayor. Despite his claims of having no affiliation with his son, whom he claimed disgraced his family, Michel forcibly withdrew from the election and politics altogether.

"That old boy better be happy him have no dealings with him son, or else me would surely kidnap him bombo clatt and use him as bait!" Nicholas exclaimed to his son, who simply looked up at his dad with baby drool running down the side of his mouth. "What up? My little shotta want some milk?"

There was a slight knock at the door, and Nicholas looked over his shoulder and waved the young thug inside.

"Yow, Boss Man, we went to collect the parcel from the Elder Dread up on Decarie Boulevard like you asked. We parked behind the building and enter through the back door, run upstairs and go deal with the business. But when we a leave them Haitian boys from the east end, show up out a nowhere and start blaze shot after we. By the grace a God none a we didn't get shot, cause even when we a try escape along St. Jacques a pure bullet exchange, until we shoot out the fool them front tire and drive off leave them. Normally them fools deah exit once we arms up, but today them come well prepared, cause a pure AK and sub-machine riffle them have a fire after we." While speaking with his hired gun-hand, Nicholas' cousin hurried by the door and went into the bathroom.

"What happened to Damian?" Nicholas demanded after the young thug scampered directly into the bathroom with blood splattered across the left side of his face.

"Oh, the mechanic son fly to him batty buoy brother's side and try tear off Damian face. You know D always a fuck with people, but the little man took exception and give him a telephone to the dome," commented the thug with a slight chuckle over the details.

"Don't tell me say him put the man in the hospital or kill him," Nicholas argued.

"No, boss, everything crisp after what happen to twitchy fingers Spuggy, man start make sure dem a fire dem gun for a reason!"

Damian was Nicholas' sole relative in Canada after Damian's mother moved back to Jamaica to assist her ailing mother after the death of her husband. Nicholas upheld the wishes of his great-aunt and taught Damian the different aspects of the game, street survival, and the guerrilla tactics necessary to survive the harsh streets of Montreal, as well as that polite gibberish his mother demanded. The Kid, as he was referred to by his peers, had a degree in chemistry obtained from the University of Florida where he completed his studies before entering the wonderful world of crooks.

"A who mash you up, Pops?" Nicholas joked, although he was relieved his overly-sensitive cousin hadn't added another charge of battery or assault to his credit.

"After me a get ready to put some kicks under this batty boy, him pussy-hole brother Killa attack me from back and buss up my head. My boy Alwin save them momentarily, but me personally go make him trip to Canada the shortest ever," exclaimed Damian, while wiping the dried up blood from his hair.

"His brother who?" Nicholas demanded.

"Some cat they said was Killa."

Nicholas summoned the maid to attend to the baby before suggesting they go in search of this vigilante who was disrespectful enough to harm his sole blood relative in Canada. Although Nicholas neglected to mention it, the refugee/vigilante withheld personal thoughts where he'd hoped the man they sought was someone from his years passed. Damian, on the other hand, began celebrating by boasting to his fellow shottas that his status exempted everyone from laying a finger on him. "Yeah, a boy a go get fuck up now," was the sole sentence reverberated by Damian all the way to the vehicles.

Kane pulled closer to Nicholas as they walked through the long hallway to the front door and began informing him of other business matters which weren't discussed. Kane briefed Nicholas on the loss of their two combatants who never returned from the detail awarded them, though reports from the sole survivor painted a picture that was not reassuring. Another member of the invading force had to be taken to Nicholas' personal physician, who occasionally administered doctoring far beyond his normal practice for wounded soldiers of his premier client. The material articles, such as vehicles, guns, and so on, that were lost during the battle were inconsequential to Nicholas, who'd created an empire large enough to sustain losses or combat any rivals.

Two Chevy Suburban XLTs were brought up from the garage and parked in front the main entrance. The five men who emerged from within the lofty four million dollar mansion separated as they approached the vehicle. Nicholas, Kane, and Rass Ijah opted for the rear transport, while Damian and Tank hopped into the first SUV. Damian could still be heard bumping his gums over what he believed was about to transpire once they found the patriots for whom they searched.

"Yow, Bobby, link up you boy and find out where Jeremiah the mechanic live and get us there ASAP, 'cause a boy about to get fucked up!" Damian said to the driver who was already inside the truck.

Doherty arrived home to find Kadeem assembling his personals and sniffed her nose at him en route to her bedroom. The lady of the house was quick to dial her husband's cellular phone in order to inform him of what was transpiring. Jeremiah was elated to find out his son had decided to no longer remain a burden on him.

"Make sure the boy no take nothing of mine!" Was the sole comment Jeremiah added to the news of his son's departure.

Although she remained silent while occasionally snooping to make sure their precious artefacts around the house weren't stolen, Doherty was especially happy to finally be rid of Kadeem after a few weeks. Doherty was in the midst of ensuring her husband's wishes were fulfilled when she bumped into Junior exiting the bathroom. The darkness around her son's left eye first caught her attention, and she immediately proceeded to demand who had injured him. The idea of Kadeem overhearing him cry to his mommy caused Junior to shrug his mother off by suggesting it occurred accidentally from a basketball to the face. Doherty marched back to her room, convinced Kadeem had something to do with her son's misfortune, as Junior had always been the sort of person to abstain from violent confrontations.

With a slight nudge on her bedroom curtain, Doherty secretly watched as Kadeem loaded his luggage into Junior's car. The thought that she would finally regain full control of her household brought a smile to her face, while she slightly closed the curtains to remain unnoticed. Once Kadeem re-entered the house, Doherty scampered from beside the window as if her interests were elsewhere. With respect, Kadeem knocked on his stepmother's door and asked to have a word with her. The Jamaican fugitive proceeded to thank the conniving manipulator he knew Doherty to be for allowing him the opportunity to reside among them. Doherty listened to Kadeem while remaining seated at the foot of her bed before waving goodbye to her houseguest, instructing him that, should he have any problems, it would best if he avoided involving his father.

Junior's American racing muffler tip roared as he fired up the engine and rammed the gear stick into the first gear of his economy-sized vehicle. The four-cylinder engine was about to take off when the Chevy Suburban with Damian onboard blocked its path. Damian pranced from within the Suburban with his 9 mm in his hand and went directly to the driver's side. The agitated thug, who still had sprinkles of dried blood around his earlobes from the cellular to the head, jammed his weapon at Junior's temple and asked if he remembered disrespecting him.

Time stood still as the eavesdropping Doherty watched the young thug threaten her only begotten son, who had volunteered to transport Kadeem to his destination. The frantic mother raced to the front door and out into harm's way without a second thought. Nobody could at that moment deter Doherty from believing that Kadeem was responsible for the black eye she noticed around Junior's left eye earlier, and she began screaming for the release of her son.

"Junior! Junior! Not my son! What did he do to you? Leave him be! He's not a violent person!" Doherty screamed as the sight of added armed gangsters froze her in her tracks.

"My lady, I suggest you go back inside, because if I start shooting out here everybody dead!" declared Tank.

"You pussy-hole, come out the car right now and make sure you hold you hands them high where me can see them!" Damian ordered as the second Suburban pulled up.

Kadeem removed himself from the car while ensuring his hands remained visible. The thought that matters would be reversed if he had a weapon scampered across his mind, and he dreaded the idea of being harmed by such toy soldier type thugs. Damian forgot that he'd put a bullet in the chamber of his 9mm automatic earlier, and expelled that bullet by attempting to select another. The slight chuckle toward Damian's mishap by Junior bought him the butt of the gun handle, which intensified the screams of his mother, who was quite aware the slayings which occurred around the neighbourhood.

Damian began making his way toward Kadeem, who expected his earlier actions to be repaid in full. The idea that her son was out of the immediate threat of danger saw Doherty move slightly toward Junior before getting refrozen by the huge 9mm automatic that adjusted her course. With his gun handy and filled with anger, there was absolutely no telling what Damian was about to do to Kadeem, who stood tall and stared down the infringing thug.

"You didn't think I was coming back this soon did you? You go get fucked up right now!" Damian stated, two steps from knocking Kadeem's lights out.

"Damian, don't touch that youth!" Nicholas shouted with conviction.

As Nicholas emerged from the Chevy SUV, there was absolutely no doubt in the minds of those under persecution that he was the head honcho. The untrimmed facial hair rounded off by his luscious dread locks that pranced off his shoulders cast a gloomy shadow over Nicholas' identity as he removed the dark glasses from his face. Doherty began feeling a bit faintish under the stress of the moment and fell to her knees with her head held high, praying to the Lord for His help in the matter. The vengeful look that covered Damian's face was replaced with confusion as he halted his actions and took one step back for precaution.

"What you mean, 'don't touch him?' 'Cuz this the motherfucker that I told you about before," exclaimed Damian.

"Mi say back up off him," Nicholas repeated.

Even with the slight temporary vote of confidence that nothing harmful was about to happen to them, Kadeem prepared for the worst knowing the volatile nature of gangsters once they've received motivation and sought to impress others. The mystery man who emerged from the SUV walked halfway toward Kadeem before halting his advance for whatever reason. Not wanting to totally lose his view of Damian, whom Kadeem perceived the point of the threat, foiled his ability to cross-reference Nicholas' features with those stored in his memory banks. However, to distil the fears developed by those involved after what Nicholas considered a drastic error in judgment, the American fugitive came forward and ended all tensions.

"Killa, you don't recognize me?" Nicholas asked.

"You know this fucker?" Damian asked.

"The man is family, of course mi know him!" Nicholas responded, with his face glowing from ear to ear.

The acknowledgment that anyone referring to him as such must be an ally caused Kadeem to fully bring his attention to this mystery leader, who brought the entire grudge affair to a close with one phrase. The idea that his boss/cousin had prior dealings with this intruder who embarrassed him earlier grieved Damian, who turned and began toward the vehicle from which he came. Nicholas was mystified by the sight of Killa, whom he'd heard countless war tales about and understood the forces against such individuals departing Jamaica with detrimental criminal records.

"Bombo-clatt a lie. Mr. Walsh is it really you!" Kadeem smiled as he hugged Nicholas following a fist bump and a firm handshake.

"You still a beat up people years later, me see. My boy, mi did sorry to hear 'bout Stamma, but it's good seeing you!" Nicholas exclaimed, initially neglecting to mention his identity change in this new world.

Damian had his hand on the door handle and was about to take a seat when Nicholas summoned him and had him introduce himself to Kadeem with an apology. The tension had subsided by the time Damian and Kadeem shook hands, yet the nerves of everyone involved had not fully transformed back to their original forms. Doherty took her freedom of speech rights to another level as she began cursing the gangsters who'd begun concealing their weapons while familiarizing themselves with one another. Junior, who'd become aggravated by the amount of cheap shots taken against his sexuality preference, stormed from his Stanza and ran into the house crying. As Junior trotted by Doherty, sobbing with his hand covering the damaged area of his face, the mental anguish of her son saw the temperamental Doherty add his qualms to her message of discontent aimed at people who paid her no interest.

Jeremiah arrived home minutes later to find his wife wailing at youngsters who weren't heeding a word of her message. Doherty's Christian beliefs conflicted with her Caribbean nature and the ideals of her message, from God's penalties that await those who harm others, to threats of summoning the police should they not vacate the premises. Kadeem, Nicholas, and company behaved like long-lost partners who hadn't seen each other in quite some time as they partook of marijuana joints pre-rolled for convenience.

Jeremiah wasn't pleased to find the gang of thugs courting in front of his domain. The final report he received from Doherty saw him shorten his regular Friday night of drinking and gambling with the boys, and he raced home to ensure the nucleus of his household was safe. The gang of "young hippie hoppies," as Jeremiah referred to Kadeem's associates in an earlier conversation, were the very same wasted sperm the mechanic warned against inviting to his house. As such, Jeremiah was quick to confront his son about the choice of people he perceived Kadeem invited to the house.

"What is all this in front my house, some kind a convention? I want all of you gone from my place right now. I don't want you back at my place, you hear me? Is long time I see that you worthless and you rather rob people money than work for it. The Bible say whatever you sow, you surely will reap, so you can go on out into the world with them evil thoughts and actions. Don't make anybody call my phone. From police to morgue attendant, you make sure you tell them stay far from 6648 Terre Bonne Boulevard. If I did know you would be so disappointing so soon, me would never agree to Auntie P.'s suggestion that you come up here. Look on the set of nobodies you want hang around with, for each one of them there is a hundred more capable souls on the island who would represent where them come from much better than them gun-shooting thugs. The Bible say that, 'he who live by the sword shall die by the sword.' Take that message with you and get the hell off my property before me go call the police them to come move you up!"

Kadeem remarkably remained tranquil despite the lengthy dose of tongue-lashing he received from Jeremiah, who refrained from heeding the advice of his wife, who fought not to have someone who was agitated shoot her husband. There had been numerous reports of people getting killed for reasons far less ridiculous, and with her knowledge of the amounts of weapons surrounding, fear sparked Doherty to calm her raging husband. Thoughts of lashing back at his father provoked Kadeem, who saw in a vision an image of Granny P., who yelled at him 'to never disrespect the hand which feeds you.' The young Jamaican exile simply walked over to Junior's Nissan Stanza, removed his luggage and handed them to Nicholas' driver for him to load them aboard the SUV. The poise and composure shown by Kadeem exemplified the type of warrior Nicholas aspired to have within his cabinet, and he welcomed Kadeem with open arms.

Part 13

DANNY TRANSLATED AN account to Nicholas told to him by Crazy Horse, who used to smuggle cocaine to the Inuit people dwelling in northern Canada before the Royal Canadian Mounted Police snuffed out the operations and closed down shop. The account was about his sole nemesis' rise to fame, which wasn't a tale loosely discussed. Nicholas would have had to surrender or abandon his quest for revenge against Martain years before due to the overwhelming number of members that represented the Rough Riders gang versus he and the Esquadas. The suggestion to form an alliance with the Rough Riders' smost prudent nemesis was made by Danny and Carlton, who both cited the similar aspirations between Nicholas and a local crew of thugs called the Defenders. Brogan and the Defenders, who were the muscle behind the slaying of the Rough Riders' first crew leader, Yves Lafleur, reached a mutual agreement that saw Nicholas expand his business and work force by supplying allies who served their exact cause. The Defenders were homeboys from the West Island who chose to dominate the drug trade around their neighbourhoods despite the city-wide unwritten law that prohibited anyone but Rough Riders from distributing. The Rough Riders crew took notice of the merger between its enemies, who were still then too feeble to mount a convincing resistance. The years since have, however, strengthened all facets of the merger between Nicholas and the Defenders, though the members' game still slightly favoured the Rough Riders.

Martain possessed the power and respect desired by many throughout the city of Montreal, with a status almost celebrity-like. The bad boy of Quebec appeared in a number of local magazines, which found the flare and danger surrounding the gang boss intriguing. With a popularity rating only overshadowed by that of the Prime Minister's, it was said the underground boss controlled more than simple thugs since they attributed numerous public assistance employees to the payroll.

The loss at the warehouse was Martain's most significant of the campaign thus far, yet Martain was not about to have a story of his demise told to anyone. Both sides had surrendered a grave amount of soldiers over the years of fighting, and neither general contemplated throwing in the towel. Young entrepreneurs who would prefer hustling for themselves sided with Nicholas and acquired the products desired for the works, from any of his many distribution factors throughout Montreal. The Defenders emerged from independent workers, who sought to break the chains of entrapment cast by the bikers, who would sell to dealers then tax them for hustling where-ever they sold. The Biker's zone tax was viable in the sence that hustlers never had to worry about interference from police, however the quality of their products was always poor and the purchasing rate damn expensive, which made it difficult for hustlers to get ahead. Rough Riders were also renowned for robbing their clients, once any hustler they serviced began making advancements or increased the quantity of their orders.

With the distruction of his warehouse Martain lost over ten million dollars in illegal narcotics. The biker boss therefore insighted the public servants of the police bureau who moonlighted as bikers, to raid a couple of Nicholas' drug bases and sieze for the biker club whatever narcotics available. . The twenty-fifth police precinct, which was considered Martain's house, was the forerunner in administering sanctions in order to retrieve valuables. A large number of the workforces at the station were Quebecois who were born and bred in Montreal. The men were childhood friends, schoolmates, church mates, and acquaintances of these bad boys who later formed the Rough Riders crew. There were a few police officers that were actually undercover members of this

Harley Davidson riders' group, and they would often form convoys of hog-roaring cyclists menacing the streets of Montreal.

Station 25 was located in Centre Ville, where the junkies, drunks, and prostitutes flocked; peep shows exhibitionists and strippers paraded, while the thieves and hustlers schemed for the almighty dollar. Therefore, information on anything or anyone was always either a bribe or a toke away. Two police cruisers and a patty wagon pulled in front the La Matador building on the corner of Peel Street and Du Maisonneuve Boulevard slightly after dusk. The officers all stormed the building based upon information implying that Nicholas housed a drug base on the fifteenth floor of the twenty-story building. The small-scale independent hustlers that sold their products along street corners and alleyways would often resupply their stock from this private drug base.

The security system to the building provided residents the opportunity to scan visitors from the lobby area before granting anyone access into the building. Apart from the building's security system, Nicholas provided his employees with a steel door that matched the mandatory design of the others on the floor, which was almost impenetrable once residents anchor the steel beam behind it into the floor. The three youngsters on duty that evening fucked up in all regards, and instead of watching the building monitors on the TV, were busy battling each other on their X-Box Def Jam video game. The worker that completed the last transaction neglected to reconnect the crossbar that gave the door its immovable backing.

The door to apartment #1525 got blown off its hinges by a group of police conducting a search and seizure without a valid warrant. Seven armed representatives of the law stormed into the apartment waving their high-powered weapons and barking orders for those inside to "get the fuck on the floor," while stumping residents to the concrete. The pressure applied by police since the destruction of Martain's warehouse had been unyielding, with instructions to intensify their vigilance.

Apartment #1525 was a single-bedroom bachelor suite with a bathroom, kitchen, and everything included. The apartment provided a spectacular view of the surrounding downtown area, which wowed viewers watching from the balcony at night. Nicholas had supplementary spots around town from where he dealt his poison in the French-speaking province, yet none as progressive as that of the La Matador base. One of the three workers inside the apartment that evening had only recently been released from lockup after being detained for possession of an illegal substance three days prior. The young worker was a twenty-one-year-old felon named Ninja who had only recently received his second consecutive strike according to the courts of Canada. The knowledge of his lengthy criminal record, along with his recent stroke of misfortune, gave the young thug a claustrophobic sensation as the officers stormed the apartment. The urge to escape saw the young thug race to the balcony, where he sought refuge from his tormentors by fleeing the scene. Ninja scaled the protective barrier around the balcony, and with the confidence and fierce belief in the agility given him by naming him Ninja, attempted to leap to a neighbouring balcony in order to escape.

The two employees who worked with Ninja later told separate stories about what actually happened out on the balcony, although neither of the men were able to properly view the incident. According to one of the workers, Ninja ran out on the balcony and attempted to evade capture by leaping onto a neighbouring balcony, which was eight feet apart. The worker sighted that Ninja's feet slipped from atop the concrete barrier, while he attempted to balance himself before jumping. The drug dealer told his peers, that the ledge of the barrier was damped from the heavy rains which fell the day prior and claimed the incident an accident.

The drug dealer's partner described a separate account, where he claimed that Ninja was pushed off the ledge by one of the intruding officers. The young man told Nicholas their boss that Ninja gave him the accounts on his arrest, which occurred some days before and that the same officer who arrested him was in fact the man who shoved him over. "I saw it with my own two eyes, Officer Betrice ran out on the balcony and caught Ninja in the act of escaping. The officer said, 'I told you the next time I caught you that I was going to fuck you up', before shoving Ninja over the ledge". Stated the worker. The conflicting arguments by both workers puzzled Nicholas, who was furious at his workers for surrendering his money and drugs to police, who were out on a robbery spree.

The blasphemous heat applied by the treacherous officers forced one over the balcony, while leaving the others terrified, not knowing whether that would be their demise, as well. With little time to waste, the invading officers began interrogating the workers on the whereabouts of the products they were convinced had been safely stored away. Ninja's body fell to the rear of the building and landed inside a construction waste container under the shadows of the gloomy Montreal night sky. The workers attempted to play hardball not wanting to surrender the drug paraphernalia or the cash retrieved from sales, which would defiantly stiffen their punishment once they stood infront the judge. Before long, the police were threatening to throw the workers into the dump along with their friend should they not decide to corporate. Excessive force, which is the policeman's forte for retrieving information, wasn't interjected following Ninja's tragic accident, not to mention the officers had no viable permission for invading the premises. A balanced offer that suggested both workers remain at large with no pending charges sweetened the bitter taste inside their mouths, and the employees surrendered the products and funds to their tormentors. The officers collected the products they came in search of and quickly exited the apartment in hopes that their traces to the building plus the foul play that occurred would never be linked to them.

The mediocre celebration of their success was delayed until the officers returned to their vehicles, where they properly inspected the volume seized before high-fiving each other on a job well done. Halfway to their next scheduled appointment, the emergency dispatcher began alerting emergency personnel of the possible suicide which had been reported by a resident of the building who was out on her balcony smoking a cigarette when she observed the young thug falling. While listening to the alarm being raised by the dispatcher, the comrades in arms laughed feverishly as they mimicked the fashion in which Ninja toppled to his death.

Words of precaution were given to fellow dealers around the area by the two hustlers from the La Matador building that were spared, thanking and praising God for not having them meet their untimely demise. Mad Max was among the first to receive word of the officers' treachery, yet stubbornly remained the only Alliance dealer to conduct usual business. Without the first-class novelties provided by landlords who managed quality housings such as La Matador, Mad Max began consealing the dope and money where it was impossible to detect, knowing the total lack of security around the dump in which he resided. The front door to the building was a standard-sized metal frame that had had the glass centred in the middle broken out by vandals. The walls along the corridors had strips of wallpaper hanging to the floor, the elevator had become the primary domain of roaches and rats, and drug addicts were often found strung out in various sections of the six-story building while the superintendent withered away in liquor and desolation.

Mad Max had been harassed by the boys in blue numerous times over the years and had grown familiar with police policies and procedures. However, news of Ninja's death agonised the usually mild-tempered Rastafarian, who had formulated oneness through the love of Jah with his deceased brethren. After securing away the materials that were being sought by the most crooked the MPD had to offer, Mad Max uncharacteristically armed himself after he began experiencing visions in which he actually envisioned Ninja pleading with him to avenge his death. The local protectors of the Montreal streets arrived as advertised with zero tolerance notification claims. The officers knocked on the door and demanded entry, surrendering a sheet of paper they claimed had been written up as a warrant to search the premises. With tears in his eyes after considering what an eyewitness told him about his friend's death, Mad Max demanded the officers slide the warrant beneath the door so that he could fully inspect it before allowing them entry. There were seven officers aligning the hallway in their tactical riot gear, with guns drawn for precautionary measures, yet only three were positioned within the perimeters of the peephole. Mad Max maintained a close watch over his antagonists through the only means awarded him while manoeuvring his weapon to where he believed a prized shot existed.

"Before I open this door, you boys slide that paper under the door so I can make sure that warrant is legal."

"Open the fucking door or I'm gonna staple this fucking warrant to your forehead when we get in there!" The officer holding the fake warrant threatened.

"Man, y'all don't have any warrant to search my shit! Whenever you bitches come here with one, ain't never no knocking on my shit. The door would a been on the floor by now, motherfucker!" Mad Max declared.

"Well, I'm giving you 'til the count of three before I do kick this shit in," the officer advised.

Mad Max peeked through the peephole at the officers who were becoming agitated by the dealer's disrespect. Thoughts of the tumble suffered by his friend Ninja had the hustler procrastinating whether or not to empty the magazine of his Desert Eagle pistol through the wooden door. The tension between Nicholas, Rough Riders, Defenders, and law officials had escalated over the years to a point where the trust between ordinary civilians and police had grown frail. Infractions that were once dangerous yet negotiable had advanced to events that worried the minority group leaders who sought measures to reunify all parties. Mad Max had himself endured the discriminative pressures of the local police, who brought him along their scenic route one night before bringing him in for processing. Officers of the twenty-fifth precinct were highly praised for suspected offenders confessing in detail their crimes way before the investigating detective got the opportunity to interrogate. Local criminals, from whom officers sought information, were brought along to the abandoned warehouses and desolate sections of the Old Port, where officers would duct tape thick phone books to the men's subdued bodies before beating the daylights out of them with their police battons. Hence, false stories were told and confessions were signed by a number of innocent youths to whom the justice system showed absolutely no remorse.

"You know something? I wish one of you fuckers accidentally do kick in my front door!"

An officer along the hallway thought of using the art of persuasion to convince Mad Max to open the door by surprising him with a huge bang that would normally frighten the typical resident into opening. With the back of his boot, the young genius kicked the door and disobeyed the dealer's order. Bullets began raining! The first huge bang saw a veteran in the force drop his firearm and grabbed for his shoulder as the bullet tore through the strap of his vest and hit his collarbone. The officer fell into shock once he realised he'd been shot and began hysterically racing for the exit like a stomach grumbling human running for the toilet. His remaining choir began their roars of discontentment as they carelessly opened fire through and around the door frame of Mad Max's apartment. The thug on the other end of the barrier was forced to retreat behind his kitchen counter as bullets slammed into and through the articles inside his apartment.

The officers became tactical in their approach as they quickly kicked in the door in order to properly identify their target. The dread locks man flew into action once the front door got kicked in by first hammering two shells through the doorframe at thin air. One of the bullets fired by Mad Max as he attempted to change his position blindly struck the left arm of an officer who was peeking into the room. The loud groan by the officer was the thug's first indication that his bullets had made contact with skin, and he raced into his bedroom while reloading his pistol. The thunders like those of the heavens roared once more as the invading forces turned into marshmallow everything inside the apartment. Had Mad Max not abandoned his place of refuge behind the counter, the onslaught delivered by the forthcoming officers would have surely sealed his fate.

"Mad Max is a psychopath," is what anyone who'd ever met the man would tell you. Most people related his stay at the Douglas Mental Institute, where he underwent treatment after professing to interactions with spirit mediums, as the evidence necessary to cast judgment of his insanity, while others believed he he should be incarcerated and removed from civilised society. Whatever possessed Mad Max blessed him with balls the size of Hayden mangos, and he shoved the Desert Eagle pistol into his waistband and muscled the mattress from atop the box spring. Laying on the box spring was an AK-47 automatic assault rifle, and he grabbed it up and aimed directly at the bedroom door.

The Rastafarian cranked back the selector of his AK-47 and let bullets fly as officers were forced to hit the turf or find protective measures. Valiant men who perish defending stupid causes aren't looked upon as heroes, especially after being persecuted by the defenders of the law. Regardless the consequence, Mad Max valiantly charged the police, who were busy scattering for cover, and peppered them with what seemed like a never-ending arsenal assault stemming through the extra-long banana clip attached to his weapon.

The summons for the entire cavalry could be heard transmitting through officers' radios as the emergency dispatcher yelledcontinually, "Shots fired—all available officers approach with caution!" The dispatcher also summoned ambulances to the scene after receiving reports of injured officers awaiting medical attention. Within minutes of the call, an astounding twelve cruisers had surrounded the entire building, and with reckless abandonment, officers raced into the war zone.

At the centre of the controversy was Mad Max standing firm, with his disorderly dog barking while cowering from the brave attempts of the Montreal Police Department. The officers along the hallway knew their allies were under serious duress as the only weapon sounding for what seemed like an eternity was that of the assailant. Thus, in order to award their comrades freedom to respond, a few of Montreal's finest began returning fire in the direction from which the AK-47 sounded as they were unable to verify the shooter's exact position. There were three officers inside the apartment clinging to whatever article it was that awarded them protection as their mentally ill host spat countless gunshots at them. The AK-47 soon made a loud click, which indicated the need for a magazine exchange. The officers who were placed in precarious positions hesitated after the momentary shock, yet seized their opportunity to regain full advantage of the situation. Mad Max was caught attempting to reload his weapon, and two of the three officers inside the room shot him at pivotal points of the body, killing him instantly.

At 3:30 that morning, three members of the Defender crew exited the Pussy Katz Strippers nightclub on Gouin Boulevard in Côte-Vertu after the birthday celebrations of one of the posse's members. The men laughed and joked with each other as they gossiped about the lovely females who took their money while offering them whatever it was they spoke of. Although they behaved like children at an amusement park, the men were cautious in their actions, knowing the terrible inner-city gang warfare their squad was involved with.

The three friends were twenty-six-year-old Jacques Carter of Montreal, twenty-seven-year-old Trevor Balan of Montreal, who was the person celebrating his birthday, and twenty-six-year-old Al Miner of Rigeau, Quebec. The Pussy Katz nightclub was a favourite hangout spot for members of the street gang, who customarily spent a large amount of money on liquor, not to mention the exquisitely-shaped women who paraded their sexiness around the club. The birthday boy was properly serenaded by a number of big booty women who dragged him on stage and stripped his down to his undies before proceeding with the festivities planned. Trevor was teased and molested by five women of Caucasian, Asian, and African descent who pushed the club's policies with their antics of seduction. Mr. Balan exited the nightclub a few hours later with the same erection he'd obtained while his friends teased him for the childish antics he displayed inside the club.

The Ford Explorer they drove was in the parking lot with very few other vehicles around considering the late hour. As the men approached the vehicle, Al, who was anointed the designated driver and who was the least intoxicated of the bunch, removed his Glock pistol from his waistband before hopping into the truck. There was a police cruiser travelling south on Côte-Vertu Boulevard with two officers who yielded before continuing on their merry way. The gangbangers paid no attention to the local protectors, considering the opposite directions in which the vehicles were travelling. With their hip-hop music blasting, the gangsters cruised west along Gouin Boulevard en route to lightening the load inside the vehicle around the surrounding West Island territories.

The police cruiser that drove by the thugs earlier reappeared behind the Ford Explorer at Sources Boulevard and Gouin before the sirens directed them to pull to the side of the road. Officers Pierce Sauvé and Dwayne Campbell used their vast knowledge of the city to intercept the suspected criminals, who had by no means associated the cruiser on their bumper with that of the vehicle noticed prior. Al advised his comrades, who'd begun mellowing out from the marijuana joint being passed around, of their immediate dilemma, although both men were too nauseated to give a fuck. In order to defuse the hostilities that would have certainly transpired, Al insisted Trevor assemble all weapons and secure them in the stash compartments.

"Yow, you guys good?" Al demanded before stopping the vehicle.

"Yeah, man. What the fuck these fools want now?" Jacques replied, sprawled out all over the back seat.

Both Metropolitan officers exited their vehicle and approached the Explorer from separate sides. The officers had removed the strap securing their weapons inside their harnesses prior to exiting their vehicle and maintained a hold of their weapons as they approached. Trevor peeked through the passenger-side mirror at the officer making his way toward the truck and developed an uneasy sense from his approach.

"Yow, guys, these guys up to somme!" Trevor exclaimed.

The officer on the driver's side tapped on the tinted glass with his flashlight and demanded the driver lower the window. Trevor's attention, which was momentarily stolen by the tap on the glass, was focused on the officer who came along the passenger-side after the officer shone his light directly in the thug's face. The same officer proceeded to motion Trevor to also lower his window in order to harass the passenger.

"License and registration, please," Officer Campbell demanded of the driver.

"Why you guys pull us over, man?" Al asked while handing the officer his documents.

"Have you boys been drinking tonight, Mr. Miner?" Officer Campbell demanded while looking over the documents.

The officer at the passenger door asked, "How many of you guys are packed in here?"

"Three of us, man!" Trevor exclaimed.

"How about you? You got any identification?" The same officer spun his flashlight at Jacques in the rear seat. The officers, who hadn't noticed any infractions thus far, were elated to see Jacques sprawled out across the rear seat with no seat belt protection.

"Sir, are you aware that not wearing a seat belt is punishable by a fine or jail time?"

"How much alcohol have you consumed tonight, Mr. Miner?" Officer Campbell questioned.

"Probably three or four Heinekens," Al answered.

The officers glanced at each other before demanding the occupants of the vehicle exit their chariot. It was evident by their tone of voice that their already disgusted attitudes had tightened, and they drew their weapons and removed all occupants from the vehicle. The officers had the men laid out in the street with their hands clasped behind their heads as they proceeded to search the vehicle. At first, the officers neglected to mention their beliefs, which alluded to the thought that they believed weapons were hidden inside the truck. Following their unproductive preliminary search, the officers returned to their detainees for further questioning.

"Yow, guy, if you trying to get me for a DUI, where's the fucking breathalyser test?" Al asked as the officers ripped through the Explorer.

"Listen to me carefully now. I know you boys got a weapon hidden somewhere inside that truck. It would save us a lot of time if you just tell me where to find it," said Officer Sauvé.

"What the fuck are you talking about, man? What gun? Ain't nobody got any guns around here, but you boys!" Jacques answered.

Officer Sauvé casually walked up behind Jacques and stepped directly into the man's groin area. "Is this where you got the fucking gun hidden?" His detainee groaned from the painful infliction.

The streets were barren at said hour of the morning with motorists seldom passing by. Without a weapon found to administer a proper charge, all detainees would have to be released with only a mediocre ticket for non-compliance of the seatbelt regulation. The officers were determined to land a case against these three men they felt were guilty even though they had yet to establish physical evidence. Officer Campbell marched over to Al, kneeled down directly in the centre of his back, and jammed his assigned 9 mm pistol in the back of his head.

"Yow, this is police brutality, man. What kind a shit is this?" Trevor yelled after witnessing his friends being roughed up.

"Shut the fuck up before I come over there and give you some of the same! Now, you're going to tell me what you did with that gun I saw you pull from your waist before getting into the truck," threatened Officer Campbell.

"I don't know what you're talking about, man. I took my keys from out of my pocket. That's all!" Al exclaimed.

"You got five seconds to tell me where that gun is, or I'm going blow your head off and then go find it!" Officer Campbell said.

Trevor listened to Officer Campbell count down from five, before cocking the hammer back on his 9 mm at three. By the time the officer uttered the number two, Trevor who believed his friend was about to be murdered, tackled the officer and knocked him to the ground, before proceeding to apply a few punches to the officer's face. Officer Campbell's partner caught sight of the rebellion against higher forces and fired two rounds from his pistol at the mutineer. The conquered officer pranced to his feet and assembled himself, first retrieving his weapon, which had been tossed astray.

Al went berserk after witnessing his friend's murder on his very birthday and attacked the officer who fired both fatal shots. Officer

Campbell had retrieved his weapon by then and blasted brain matter from the attacking man's skull, killing him before he had the chance to harm his partner. The sight of both his friends' corpses brought instant tears to Jacques' eyes, and he remained frozen to the ground so as not to frustrate his antagonists. The lights went out instantly for Jacques as both officers realized the serious implications one high witness could make. Officer Sauvé removed his backup weapon from the holster around his ankle, placed it in Al's palm, and fired two shots at their previous position before radioing in the call to headquarters.

Part 14

MAYORAL CANDIDATE MINISTER Richard Blanc visited the twenty-fifth police precinct the morning following a rallying of minority leaders who called for investigations into the recent killings of alleged criminals. Minister Blanc was at the helm of the French Independent Party, which was a French-legislated electoral party lobbying for the job to become the mayor of the province Quebec. Candidate Blanc was on the verge of touring the province of Quebec while campaigning heavily to sway voters' confidence before the upcoming elections. TheFrench Independent Party had existed and operated for over a half a century, inaugurating two grand representatives to the Mayor's office throughout its tenure.

News of the aspiring mayor's visit brought an array of reporters to the precinct, which had already been placed underneath the microscope from recent events. Chief Arnold Dubois had the briefing room prepared with a podium in order for the minister to deliver his message as well as an open question period for journalists. The unofficial poll regarding candidates' favourability among the voters had Minister Joseph McArthur of the Liberal Party in fourth place with a meagre 6% voters' average. Minister Blanc was in third place with 19.7% behind the reigning elected mayor, Sir Gerald Lavoie of the Party Quebecois, who held a mere two point margin over David McNeil of the People of Quebec National Party.

Minister Richard Blanc entered the conference room to a huge applause from well-wishers and admirers who vowed to support the candidate during the upcoming elections. Chief Arnold Dubois and a number of well-decorated commanders of the police force, who relished the opportunity to display their stripes and medals, escorted the minister to the podium. Freelance photographers and news reporters seized the moment to capture as many photographs as possible for that one definite front-page photo that summed up the minister's entire visit. As the aspiring mayor shook hands and thanked everyone in attendance on his way to the podium, sceptical voters awaited his vision for cleansing the city of the turmoil that lurked within.

The dust soon settled as everyone who cheered for the mayoral candidate took to his or her assigned seat. A pin drop could have echoed throughout the room before Sergeant Elgin began the festivities by first introducing the entire panel on stage. Chief Arnold Dubois soon took to centre stage and immediately proceeded to announce the guest speaker rather than tangle with the blood-seeking reporters who pranced on issues of police brutality throughout the city.

"Ladies and Gentlemen, *Mesdames et Messieurs*, presenting the next mayor of our lovely province, his Honourable Minister Richard Blanc!"

The audience of eighty-nine applauded for another two minutes before finally coming to terms with the fact that the guest speaker needed silence to speak. The honoured guest speaker stepped before a collection of microphones belonging to the different news agencies in attendance. An impatient reporter for the Gazette pounced on the topic regarding recent altercations between police and criminals, where public outcries were against excessive force administered by law officials. Minister Blanc waved off the reporter and her question by simply swiping his hand over the stilled microphones, denouncing her attempts at the question-and-answer period.

"My fellow Quebecois, it's time for a change! When I pick up my newspaper in the morning and it reads man pops off at cops and then I read on to discover that this maniac had an assault weapon, which he used to injure our assigned protectors, I say it's time for a change! We're currently being governed by a mayor who spends more time in the winter skiing, and more time in the summer hiking mountains, than he does representing the people's best interest. I think our mayor's love for mountains should empower him to simply become a hermit. After all, we hardly see him, anyway, so he's practically one already." The supporters and police staff in attendance all broke into laughter as Minister Blanc took his first cheap shot at the absent mayor.

"Instead of standing alongside our officers today with his support and respect for the valiant job these people do to ensure our safety, Mayor Lavoie is having tea with the Guatemalan President. While our streets become infested with the filth that our police force gets scrutinized for battling, your honoured mayor finds time for a vacation. I'm here, ladies and gentlemen, to offer my continued support to our fine law enforcement officers who go out and tangle with these thugs, rapists, and murderers who believe themselves above the law on a daily basis! The city I once knew and proudly grew up in has changed. Our officers had to change with the times in order to combat these criminals. Come Election Day, you have to show the rest of Canada that you also will change, and that begins with a new mayor of the modern day era who knows exactly what Montrealers and Quebecers need!"

The small crowd rose to their feet and applauded the sentiments of the campaigning minister. Minister Blanc addressed the issues with health care around the province, problems and suggestions for strengthening our schools, ideas for securing new jobs for the people of Quebec, and his personal vision for where Quebec should go. Monsieur Blanc harnessed the affluent officers by suggesting they make their methods of crime fighting stricter, and vowed his continued support toward the work they do. Minister Richard Blanc abstained from the persisting argument aboutsegregation, which was a mandate supported by a great number of Quebecois, and chose instead to conclude his speech by vowing to reduce taxes and jobless rates around the province once elected.

"Minister Blanc, sir, how did you manage to acquire the services and support of Joseph McArthur of the Liberals, and when is the grand celebration for the merger scheduled?" Sandy Walters of the CTV News reporters asked.

The minister replied, "What?"

Jim Clarity finally closed his eyes at 1:28 am after a day of hard work. The chief handler for Minister Joseph McArthur lived the life of a bachelor who moonlighted with the classiest of women, while reserving the pillows on his bed for the undercover men in his life. The former University of McGill student graduated with top honours in his class and continued on to an exceptional career in politics. His bachelor's degree and tainted lifestyle brought him to the steps of an overachieving visionary who had become the voice and power behind gay activists across Canada. At 4:36 am, Jim was awoken by two men seated by the foot of his bed that had sneaked in without raising his privacy alarm. The two Caucasian male wore steel-toed boots and blue denim jeans with leather vests adorning their gang insignias over plain white T-shirts.

One of the two humongous males said, "We really aren't here to hurt you, but give us a reason and you'll truly end up sorry!"

"What is it you gentlemen want?" Jim asked.

"We're just here to show you a movie, that's it," said the same individual.

The other male rose from the foot of the bed, shoved his automatic weapon into his waistband, and removed a DVD from his inner vest pocket. The man walked over to the DVD player and placed the disc inside the machine before snatching the remote from atop the dresser on his way back to the bed. Both men behaved as if they were quite at home as they made themselves comfortable alongside the nerve-shot assistant.

The man with the remote joked, "No popcorn?"

The other exclaimed, "Just play the fucking movie, fool!"

The DVD began with a female expressing her sorrow for something she truly did not wish to do, though she had absolutely no choice in the matter. The lady on the disc was a former adultery partner to the man Jim Clarity idolized and praised, while anointing him to the highest pedestal. The female wept as she proceeded to threaten the minister, instructing him of her intent to take their affair public should he continue lobbying for the post of mayor. The female spoke of occasions where she was forced to perform sexual favours despite her constant refusal to participate. There were a number of photos depicting both parties, followed by a live sex session between the minister and his mistress.

The minister's assistant argued, "Where did you get this disc? It's not possible. She's lying! She must be lying!"

The man with the remote declared, "The man's got his dick all the way up her asshole and you're arguing it's not authentic?"

Jim Clarity took a moment to gather himself as the disappointing thoughts surrounding the mortal man he represented soaked in. Both intruders had mellowed into the graphic scenes transmitting through the television, while their host shied away in disgust and chose not to continue watching. Despite the homeowner's objections, the Rough Riders gang members, as was evident by the patches on their vests, chose to watch the DVD in its entirety before finalizing their visit.

"Now, before you start throwing a kiddie's tantrum, listen. You're going to instruct your boss to concede like the lady said, but bring those votes of his over to the French Quebec Party. The good minister has until tomorrow at noon before our lovely Isabella Coy makes that all-important call to the press. Be sure to advise your boss that he'll be more than welcomed in the nest of the new Montreal mayor and as long as his support remains loyal and Miss Coy remains invisible. That's your boss' personal copy of his freak show; I don't need to advise you that copies are easily dispersed. Besides, the liberals alongside the French Quebecers are guaranteed to win. You think about it," suggested the gangster closest to Jim.

Jim Clarity telephoned his boss' security detail and advised them to collect their employer within the hour. The aspiring mayor was awakened by his wife at 4:45 am after only closing his eyes for a meagre three and one-quarter hours. Mr. McArthur's assistant instructed his boss that his chauffeur and security detail were enroute to his home, as they'd entered a crucial phase of their campaign. Jim Clarity promised to debrief his boss in the privacy of their office rather than have the minister endure the embarrassment at home around his wife.

The minister's bodyguard and chauffeur were surprised to arrive and find his client waiting at the front door. Before the chauffeur could exit the car in order to greet and allow his client entry, Mr. McArthur had entered and slammed the door himself. The fury and impatience showed by Joseph McArthur was one never before witnessed by his personal detail, and he had been in the aspiring mayor's employ for more than four years. Monsieur McArthur travelled with the divider closed all the way to the office and refrained from uttering a word during the trip. Once they'd arrived at the Liberals' Headquarters, Joseph stormed from the vehicle without his bodyguard's assistance and flew into the office.

Jim Clarity had everything prepared for his boss, who knew to expect the worst before arriving. The assistant assembled everything inside his boss' office and simply handed the minister the remote before exiting the office. Jim Clarity exited the office to find Matt the bodyguard pouring a cup of coffee before deciding to join the bodyguard during their final moment of peace. The assistant poured himself a cup of coffee, eased Matt's concerns about the minister firing him, and took three sips from the Styrofoam cup before a huge crash sounded inside the minister's office. Matt, as expected, went charging into the office to ensure his client's safety, while Jim continued nonchalantly sipping his cup of coffee. The bodyguard drew his weapon and busted through the door to find that his boss had thrown a metallic ornament from his desk through the television screen after watching an obviously bothersome program. The minister flung the remote across the room, smashing it against the wall, and he swore continuously while ripping pamphlets of himself to shreds and littering the entire office.

"Are you okay, Mr. McArthur?"

"That fucking bitch! God, let that bitch die a horrible death! You fucking bitch! You bitch! You bitch!" The minister screamed as he stumped over to the DVD player, yanked it from the wall, and sent it sailing through a window. Once the minister realized he'd tossed damaging evidence of himself through the window, Joseph marched out in search of the DVD player so as to retrieve the disc. The minister surprisingly returned with a different attitude and the shattered DVD player underneath his arm, while his bodyguard, who never allowed him room to breathe, pursued. Minister McArthur threw the dismantled DVD machine atop his secretary's desk and advised his bodyguard to remove the disc and present it only to him before signalling his assistant to follow him into his office.

"Okay, so which of my cock-sucking nemeses dicks do I have to suck to keep this bitch and this shit quiet?" Joseph demanded.

"It looks like the French Quebecers, sir," replied the assistant.

"Of course. No one else has the power to scare Isabella into stooping to such immoral levels. How long before she goes public? I mean, how much time do I have?" The intellectual minister understood the railroad business side of politics.

"They said tomorrow at noon."

"As expected! Go for the kill when you got the shot."

Montreal's Liberal Party was the chief advocate for gay and lesbian rights across the province. The political party had been at the forefront of environmental issues, prompting major development and changes in a number of manufacturers across the entire country. The group supported marriages between the sexes and were the legislators of the act provided to Congress mandating a law allowing gays to wed. The Honourable Sir Joseph McArthur III had been at the helm of the political party for over eight years, although he failed to be nominated to the Mayor's office three times.

The campaign trail for Chief Minister McArthur had him scheduled to participate in a number of fire drills with the city's twenty-seventh district fire station in the Notre Dame D'Grace area at 7:00 that morning. There were a number of internal primary components who contributed to the development and structure of the Liberal Political Party, who Joseph instructed his assistant to debrief in part before his defection to the Devil's Court. To avoid an unimaginable fiasco that would guarantee his surrender of the mayoral race, his removal from his current position at the helm of the Liberal Party, and possible divorce filings from a wife slated to inherit millions from her ailing father, Minister McArthur took to his only possible solution. The assumption that Minister Blanc plotted such a diverse scheme infringed Joseph who refrained from telephoning his new associates with the minister's decision. The aspiring mayor chose instead to deliver his response during his message to the reporters and supporters gathered to cheer him on during his workoutwith the local firefighters.

An anonymous caller telephoned Montreal's largest news provider, the Gazette, at 6:42 am and leaked information of the minister's intent to join forces with a group which proclaimed themselves the healers of Quebec. Suspense and intrigue brought the entire news kingdom to the twenty-seventh district fire station, where liberal voters had camped out awaiting glorified moments to incite their support for the candidate they envisioned becoming Montreal's mayor.

Minister McArthur arrived at his scheduled appointment to an overwhelming crowd of supporters who acted eager to catch a glimpse of or shake the hand of their commander and general. McArthur refused to comment on allegations being raised by reporters who stormed his transport, demanding his intent to merge with one of his party's three political nemeses. The professional lobbying for mayor shook hands of supporters and neglected those determined to disrupt the cohesive ambiance between voters and their minister.

The training exercises between the brave men who placed their lives on the line daily to rescue victims and property from disaster and the campaigning minister took place at the Fireman's Developmental Facility, located directly behind their twenty-seventh district fire station. Observers on hand believed their minister performed well throughout the event, which saw Joseph compete in fire hose carrying techniques, extinguishing fires, Jaws of Life rescue from a vehicle collision, and proper use of the breathing apparatus. An exuberant Joseph appeared ten years younger throughout the training regiment as he laughed and joked with ordinary firefighters who vowed to support his campaign.

Correspondence between reporters was immediately scaved however, as Minister McArthur paused for questions after his exhibition workout with some of life's true heroes, the politician thought gravely about his family and the seriousness of the situation. The question of the hour was answered by Joseph, who abstained from additional comments related to the issue of his political future. "My childhood dream was to one day become a fireman or the leader of this country. Thanks to wonderful friends like Colonel Dubury here, I've gotten the opportunity to see what it really feels like to be in one of those furnaces rescuing trapped people and sometimes their pets. With the help of wonderful friends, I was able to live out one of my childhood dreams, and I am happy to inform you that come next election, with the assistance of Minister Blanc and the Français Quebecois Party, we will live out my second fantasy as rulers of the province!"

Part 15

THE SOUTHERN TOWNSHIPS of Quebec such as Shawville, Aylmer, and the Gatineau areas across to Papineau, were territories that reported the most volatile acts against humanity during a campaign dubbed by Rough Riders as "the persuasion tour." The diverse scheme intended to capture the voting interest of key activists against the French Independent Party and was handed to the gang leader with a "whatever required" order. Members of the strongest gang across Canada made house calls to neighbourhood leaders, business owners, and clergymen who were believed to carry a trusted voice among the voters of their communities.

In Hull, Quebec, eleven-year-old Adrian Lavoie awoke late for school and headed for his first pit stop of the day. While peeing, the thought of his mother awarding him additional time beneath the covers intrigued Adrian, who had always been taught to be assertive and prompt. The silence around the remainder of the house was unusual for a moderate day, where his parents always rushed him off to school before tending to their own ambitions. Adrian flushed the toilet of the third tier and ignored washing his hands or face before walking down the hall toward his parents' domain. The young lad became frozen with fear as he entered his parents' bedroom to find both parents hacked to death. The dismantled body parts around the room, along with the colour of red blood against the walls, hypnotized the young lad, who remained frozen for a few minutes. Although Adrian had never before witnessed a corpse, the assumption of anyone reviving without an attached head seemed farfetched even to him. With both eyes filled with tears, Adrian slowly walked back to his bedroom, from where he placed the critical phone call to emergency personnel.

At 1:29 that morning, Adriana Lavoie repositioned herself from the arches of her back to a kneeling position while her husband manoeuvred himself to enter from the rear. The lovers' sexual intimacy began with the stimulation efforts of Andrew Lavoie's tongue fluttering across his beautiful wife's body as she sucked and jerked his penis while grinding on his mischievous index finger. A half hour later came the moans and groans attributed to the passions of lovemaking between the pair as Andrew sank his colossal penis into her vagina. Adriana Lavoie repeatedly reminded her egotistical husband to lower his outburst, due to her charismatic flattering overly stimulated him. Perspiration ran from Andrew's body like an open faucet, bringing about a clapping sound with each contact of their bodies. The compassionate husband caressed every tender curve of his wife's body as he reached over and kissed her refined shoulder blades. The sexual escapade between the Lavoies' crept into its second hour, with both performers raging as if backed by Ecstasy or other performance enhancers. Adriana took hold of her husband's right hand and placed it beneath her crotch, instructing him to also caress the clitoris while stroking. Andrew followed instructions and gingerly massaged the tip of Adriana's clitoris, which sent his wife into a cosmic frenzy. Andrew Lavoie found himself caught in the reverse role as he became the sensible lovemaker reminding his partner of proper discretion.

Adriana and Andrew completed their ordeal and fell to the mattress like ducks shot from the sky. Andrew kissed his wife's tender lips as he reached over her for the Du Maurier pack of cigarettes on the night table.

A deep voice from the frame of the door asked, "Want a light?"

"*Ahhh*!" Adriana screamed, who believed her husband to be the only male inside the house.

A strange voice said, "Shut the fuck up, bitch, before I come over there and slap the scream out of you!"

"Who the fuck is that?" Andrew questioned as both he and Adriana grabbed for the comforter that lingered by their feet.

"Don't worry about who we are, Mr. Lavoie. The important thing here is that we know exactly who you are!"

Two husky Caucasian men walked into the gloomy bedroom and stood on either side of the bed. The gentleman with the bass-toned voice instructed their female accomplice who lingered in the dark to remove a chair from the room and station herself before Adrian's door. The instructor spoke with clarity as he instructed the female to shoot and kill the couple's son should any mutiny or disobedience develop. The intruders knew the entire household by name, the layout of the property, and key aspects that allowed them entry despite the security system.

The intruders behaved and reasoned like professionals, although their hosts appeared far less confident that they would remain as such. Andrew held his wife tightly in his arms and felt the shivers and trembling of a naked woman who feared and worried about being raped or molested inside her own home. The King of the Castle knew his wife's personal demons, which included some molestation by an uncle at the tender age of three. With such knowledge, Andrew was compelled to convene the negotiations factor in hopes that their intruders sought a monetary solution for their troubles.

"What is it you gentlemen require? Mind you, anything I have to keep my family safe is yours," negotiated Andrew.

The massive thug standing over Mr. Lavoie began removing a Manila envelope from beneath his jacket as Andrew intensely watched both men's every move. The intruder tore open the envelope and removed an electoral ballot from within before slapping it square across Andrew's chest. The addressed hostage lifted the ballot toward the gloomy nightlight plugged into the electrical outlet so as to properly assess the contents of the document.

"Your support for your brother's political aspirations ends tonight. You're going to call our dear Minister Gerald Lavoie and inform him you'll be supporting General McArthur and friends from now on. You're also going to stir up some political friction between those you've already brought into your brother's fold and the remainder of his constituency. And don't worry—we've already removed his advertising plaques from your front yard. Now here, sign the fucking document," ordered the assigned spokesman.

"Associating myself with my brother's worst enemy would destroy everything we ever had. Nothing could ever heal our relationship after that. He would disown me publicly, and the rest of the family, too, if they ever sided with me. I-I-I-I-I can't sign this, I can't do all that!" Andrew exclaimed as he broke into tears.

"Click! Click!" The bullet selection action of the thug's pistol sounded.

Andrew may have struggled seeing the fine print written on the electoral ballot, yet had absolutely no problem describing the model of the weapon braced against his head. Adriana became frantic, believing the intruder about to murder her husband and yelled out in reproach.

"Didn't the man tell you to remain fucking quiet, bitch?" *Whack!* The slap across Adriana's face silenced her immediately.

"As you can tell, we aren't patient people, so before something bad happens to your entire family that you love so much, sign the fucking document!"

"Please, please, I'm begging you! Consider my position," Andrew reasoned.

The second of the male intruders yelled, "Tracy, shoot the fucking kid!"

"No!" Adriana screamed as she sat up and began moving toward her child.

In the blink of an eye, the intruder who held Mrs. Lavoie suspended twirled around in a circle, withdrew a Kenshin sword from the depths of his trousers, and swiped away his victim's head in one smooth motion. Adriana's decapitated head landed on her husband's stomach, who became so frightened that his eyes widened as he gawlked for oxygen like an asphma patient. . The decapitator proceeded to hack away at his victim's stilled corpse, removing both her 38DD breasts from her chest, her arms, and every visible portion of the female. Andrew's reactions were held in check by the contraption squeezed against his head, though he slowly managed to swivel his head around and watched the decapitator transform into a butcher. Litres of blood squirted at Andrew and throughout the room as the sight of his wife being carved up like Thanksgiving turkey drove Andrew into a deranged, psychotic, trance-like state. Once the sought after screams expunged through Andrew's lungs, the loaded weapon to his scull blew brain matter against the pillow that offered him comfort.

"What the fuck is it with you and these fucking swords? We're here to discuss business first, and then send a message should business fuck up. You just cancel business whenever you get fucking agitated, and we all know that doesn't take fucking much."

The bass-toned intruder removed the electoral document from Andrew's grasp and ignored both victims to his accomplice, leaving the catastrophe Adrian found the following morning.

In Saint Justine, Quebec, local farmer Jose Mercier was in the process of ploughing his cornfield when he noticed an off-trail motorbike coming at him through the grounds he'd already ploughed in the distance. *Who the hell could be so stupid?* Jose thought as he brought his John Deere tractor to a halt. The fifty-three-year-old father of five, who was a devoted Christian and community activist, supported the views and concepts of Minister Gerald Lavoie of the Party Quebecois, who fought for the rights and privileges of farmers. The areas surrounding Saint Justine, such as Saint Zachary, Montmagny off Interstate 132, Baie Johan Beetz, and Lac Frontier, were agricultural areas filled with farmers who all supported the campaign of Minister Lavoie.

Jose Mercier owned and operated the largest dairy, grain, and wheat farm of eastern Quebec. The highly respected farmer had four sons who ranged in age from seventeen to twenty-six, and he had one fourteen-year-old daughter who people believed was conceived for the lone female inside the house. Jose had been a farmer all the days of his life as had his father and grandfather before him. From the cattle of Mercier Farm's pumps came litres of Quebec's most nutritious milk, and the soil produced award-winning produce coveted by all.

The trail bike pulled alongside the tractor while Jose continued bickering over the bike rider's course selection. Had the rider been one of Jose's sons, the angered farmer would've probably implanted his galoshes in the lad's rectum, but the stranger jammed a cork in his reaction.

"Didn't you notice that you've been riding on ploughed soil?"

"Whatever. Get down off the fucking tractor!" The bike riderwhomotioned Jose down with his automatic weapon. The sight of the weapon immediately changed Jose's bitter tune, bringing him quietly back to the earth.

"That's not necessary," declared Jose, pointing at the gun as his galoshes made contact with the dirt.

The bike rider remained atop the trail bike with his gun aimed at Jose's stomach and handed the farmer a Manila envelope. Jose opened the envelope and withdrew an electoral ballot with a curious expression on his face. The scruffy-looking thug atop the trail bike used his free arm to point the farmer in the direction of his house, where four men armed with high-powered automatic weapons had his entire family and staff knelt on the dirt in preparation for an execution. Hysteria overcame Jose as he expelled a humongous sigh before bringing his attention back toward the bike rider.

"You and family are all going to vote for Minister Blanc and company. We know you're a very influential man around these parts, so deterring anyone without a Minister Blanc's election plaque on their front lawn from voting for the opposition is also a job requirement. Sign the documents and place them back inside the envelope and our business is complete. And we know everything that goes on around these parts, so if you take your chances with your family by informing the local cops or not achieving your goals, I guarantee you'll see us again."

Jose was signing the documents before the bike rider gave him the instructions to sign the papers. The picture of everything he loved under duress severed his connections to the Party Quebecois and landed him in the trenches of the devil.

In Salluit in northern Quebec, committee members for David McNeil's campaign orchestrated a strategy assembly where they planned to reformat their slogan to involve native Indians, Eskimos, and immigrants who were qualified to participate in provincial elections. The meeting was scheduled after regular business hours due to the heavy workload each member tackled during the peak hours of the day. The headquarters for The People of Quebec National Party was located in an industrial area of town where huge manufacturers of various products manufactured and exported their goods. Eighteen-wheelers, semi-trailers, production machinery, and hard labourers created a huge racket throughout business hours, leaving the nights more adequate for strategy developments.

The mayoral candidate had a scheduled evening in Montreal, where he'd commence by mingling with important business tycoons and politicians, among others, at a gala held at the Queen Victoria Museum slated to unveil historic artefacts from Canadian history. Minister McNeil and his wife, Francine, had a 7:00 pm dinner engagement at The Delta, which was a rotating restaurant built on top of a five-star hotel. The minister and his wife were also being recognised by the Doctor's Association of Canada for their continued zeal to raise funds in support of women with breast or other cancers. The awards celebration was scheduled for 9:00 pm at the Hilton Ballroom, only seven blocks east of The Delta Hotel.

While the boss plays, the workers work, as was evident by the group of eleven strategists strategising formulas for victory in the upcoming elections. A team of five women and six men had gathered around the huge conference table in the boardroom at McNeil's headquarters to debate graphic ideas. The conference table was littered with Tim Horton's coffee cups, fruit, stationery, and the boxes from devoured pizza while the young geniuses devised solutions. Minister McNeil telephoned his election strategists shortly before 9:00 pm to the response of playful workers shooting crumpled paper at each other around the room. A confident and joyous work force always pleased the boss, who expressed his gratitude before continuing with his evening.

The roars from Harley engines outside the QAW building at such weird hour didn't unnerve the late-hour staff, which had become accustomed to high-octane engines passing on a regular basis. Outside the building, however, seven members of the Rough Riders gang dismounted their hogs, retrieved their semi-automatic weapons from the pouches attached to their bikes, and walked toward the office building. The men all wore German chopper helmets with black-and-white striped bandanas covering the remainder of their faces, black leather vests with patches of rank and gang insignias covering white T-shirts, black jeans, and cowboy-style leather boots.

There were three employees of Molly Maid Services assigned to clean the two-story office building before the start of each new day. The lone male among the three cleaners was mopping the service entrance when a member of the Rough Riders gang tapped the glass door with his automatic weapon, seeking entry. The sight of seven, heavily armed thugs wearing masks scared the man, who believed the four-inch glass separation between them thick enough to withstand bullets. The man dropped the mop and began running for a rear exit before the spraying action of Uzis flung him to the ground. One of the two females assigned to sanitation duties was busy sanitizing the bathrooms on the main floor, and nosily emerged to determine whether the blast was from a weapon or from something else. The female suffered the same fate as her co-worker, whose body was the first sight she came across after exiting the male toilet. The third female assigned to sanitation duties was busy cleansing Minister McNeil's office with her iPod earplugs beating iTunes into her eardrums, and the blast went completely unnoticed by her as she continued on with her assigned duties.

The eruption on the first floor had by then caught the attention of everyone inside the boardroom, and they also began frantically debating on the type of sound they'd heard. The strategists were split on the exact action to take, as some were for alerting the police, while others believed such actions were premature without definite proof. Empty magazines were exchanged by the gangsters, who'd spat detrimental bullets at the civil workers, and the thugs all climbed the stairs leading to the second-story conference room. One of the brave-hearted sceptics inside the boardroom quickly volunteered to settle the fears of doubters and determine exactly what was happening. The strategist opened the huge mahogany door that lead to the hallway and froze in his tracks after facing the death squad sent to annihilate him and his peers. Bullets flung the brave soul halfway across the room as the remainder of his crew began hysterically scattering for shelter underneath the conference table, behind the leather sofa, or wherever possible. A large number of the men inside the conference room screamed as loud, if not louder, than the females who were all screaming at the top of their lungs. One of the male strategists was attempting to open a second-story window in order to leap to safety when plastering bullets hammered him through the thick pane of glass.

The mercenaries stormed into the conference room and immediately changed the décor inside the room. The masked thugs transformed the beige-coloured walls to red in a matter of seconds as bullets ripped through flesh and everything else inside the room. There were lonesome cries that silenced as the battalions exploded, bringing to an end the joyous laughter that once filled the room. Three of the mercenaries took a brisk walk around the room to be sure of their kills by pumping additional bullets into stilled corpses.

The third maid was cleaning Minister McNeil's office next door and narrowly escaped a scatter shot, which bore through the gyprock wall and into the minister's laptop on his desk. The sudden crash that occurred only inches from her around the desk frightened the maid to the ground, where she yanked the earplugs from her ears and gazed around the room. The maid threw her hands over her mouth to prevent herself from screaming as she overheard the devastating screams of people being massacred in the room next door. Once everything silenced, the maid nervously began seeking somewhere to hide, fearing the killers may search around for additional targets. The woman quickly ruled out the minister's personal bathroom and closet before using her gymnastic talents to squeeze herself into a filing cupboard. From inside the cupboard, the woman listened as the death squad went from room to room in search of other victims before total silence was had throughout. The maid, terrified, waited an hour and eight minutes after the killers had gone before sneaking a peek out the cupboard and informing the authorities.

In Poste-de-la-Baleine, Quebec, Pastor Guy-Francis Bouillon, who had been the lifelong minister for Gerald Lavoie, held a memorial session for Andrew and Adriana Lavoie, who were also brought up in Pastor Bouillon's Anglican Church before relocating to Hull, Quebec. There was a stellar audience of family members, family supporters, well-wishers from miles around, voters, and government officials who all turned out to commemorate the lives of two of their own. News reporters swarmed the festivities with press coverage, which generated from an incident that occurred over a hundred miles away. Citizens and friends created a shrine outside the main gate of the Lavoie's family home, where they laid seas of flowers, greeting cards, and teddy bears to convey their heartfelt emotions toward their neighbours. The house of God, built to accommodate three hundred people, was over capacity by nearly two hundred, with patrons choosing to stand and mourn rather than return home.

Pastor Bouillon soothed the hearts of grievers, who were all still shocked by the horrific manner in which the couple had died. Preacher Bouillon uncharacteristically cursed the doers of the act against the Lavoies before rendering forgiveness unto the sinners who terminated the lives of two wonderful human beings. The clergy leader believed it healing for the soul to have personal friends convey their sentiments, and thus opened the floor for grievers to publicly express their thoughts. A line up of well-wishers slowly formed to the left of the altar, with the majority of spokespersons being close relatives of the deceased. Each of the thirteen female speakers who volunteered a kind word broke down mid-speech and had to be aided from the podium except for Adriana's sister, who brought everyone inside the church to tears with a poem inspired by her personal reflections of the deceased.

There was a genuine expression of love, hurt, and regret throughout the ceremony, which lasted well over five hours. Patrons consoled each other as the various speakers shared their personal memories of the murdered couple. Mourners joined in a prayer asking for justice and righteousness for the couple before conveying their respects to the family inside the church. The night ended with Pastor Bouillon reminding his congregation to "Hold firm and trust in God, for only He can truly take a life."

Pastor Guy-Francis Bouillon had always maintained an apolitical stance on the issues of voting, yet encouraged support of the Lavoies' political aspirations through subtle messages during his sermons. The clergy leader loved the Lavoie family for their devotion, which stretched over thirty years and continued on through three generations. Pastor Bouillon acquired flocks of supporters for the Party Quebecois through his continued praise and glory about the magnificent work done by Lavoie family members around the surrounding neighbourhoods.

The pastor personally closed the doors to the church at 11:41 pm before retreating to his domain only feet away from the house of God he governed. Pastor Bouillon partook of a spaghetti meal prepared by Sister Mary, the Sunday school teacher, who ensured the sixty-four-year-old celibate preacher had his daily meals. The pastor ate and washed the utensils he'd dirtied before retiring to his bedroom for the night.

An upset stomach caught Pastor Bouillon seated atop the toilet reading his Bible at 12:43 am, though stomach gripes offered him less time to read than he'd expected. A sharp point to the gut forced the pastor to cringe forward as he muscled and tightened his buttocks in an attempt to expel the cause of his stomach ache.

Two muscular intruders stormed into the bathroom, snatched the aching pastor from his toilet throne, and dragged him directly from the house. The fright shocked the defecation process into immediate termination and frightened the old man, which generated a mild heart attack. The unexpected intrusion rendered Pastor Bouillon unconscious as the two men dragged him along his tiled floors and into the church where he'd soothed the hearts of hundreds only hours before. The two assailants hoisted the unconscious pastor to the primary crucifix of Jesus Christ that hung inside the church before proceeding to douse the entire church with gasoline. Pastor Bouillon regained consciousness by inhaling a huge gasp of oxygen before the pain of his lower extremities being set ablaze forced him back to unconsciousness. The sight of his congregation hall burning, along with the scent of burnt flesh seeping up his nostrils, brought on a second heart attack that immediately killed the Anglican pastor.

Part 16

Nicholas insisted on formally introducing Kadeem to Montreal's reggae dance hall scene, especially after receiving word that his favourite sound system was scheduled to perform that very weekend. Triple B Records Promoters, along with Island Vibes Crew, presented, live in concert from Jamaica West Indies, the Mighty Stone Love, Metro Media, and Matteron Sound at the spacious E&B restaurant. The line-up of selectors was not one to be missed by avid reggae adorers across the island, hence the boss' interest in attending. Nicholas rarely mingled with such a rowdy crowd due to the high chance of someone succeeding at assassinating him, yet he chose to throw caution to the wind and party with the regulars.

With the decision made to attend the soiree came the daunting task of finding the perfect attire elegant enough to express one's exquisite taste. The young gun hands, such as Damian, Tank, and the crew of shooters, all fancied the modern youth hip-hop generation style of jeans, sneakers, and baseball hats, while Nicholas and his red brothers opted for the elegant fashion designs by famous creators such as Kenneth Cole, Armani, and Chanel, just to name a few. Four top designers stacked with runways of creations were brought to Kevin's mansion, which was like an impenetrable fortress, heavily guarded twenty-four hours a day. Designers Ralph Lauren, Kenneth Cole, Armani, and local talent

Carlton Daly spent the majority of the morning of the soiree fashioning their designs for a customer with whom they'd become quite familiar. The location for the showing of the designers' fashions was prepared inside Nicholas' humongous family room before the proprietor decided to house the event on his stylish veranda, which stretched halfway around his mansion.

"Blood-clatt my youth, you do thing with style and elegance! Kenneth Cole, Armani, Mr. Lauren, a chill and beat Heineken, burn weed with the man them like is a family thing, a so man must live nice respect my brethren!" Killa said as they relaxed on lawn chair while enjoying the fashions.

"Life nice all now even though we have a big war a go on right now, but things soon nicer man, as soon as we eliminate da pussy hole yah!" Nicholas commented as he tossed a magazine featuring Martain on the cover at Killa's lap.

Killa stared deeply at the portrait of his friend's enemy, hating and despising the man more with each passing second. The words that highlighted the story said, "The Island's most feared gangster," prompting Killa to race to page thirty-eight for further details on the story. The article spoke of Martain's huge flock of followers, his many women, motorbikes, businesses, and leisure activities.

"So how you no manage to kill him yet?" Killa asked.

"A just time, me boy, just a matter a time. That piece Aspire!" Nicholas said as he pointed at the jacket suit ensemble being modelled.

"This is a nice piece!" Danny declared, who quickly indicated to Esquire his interest in acquiring the garments.

Two of the four designers brought a few outfits for Nicholas' son to try on, which divided the proprietor's time between the adult fabrics and his son's personal fashion show. Junior, Kevin's son, would occasionally appear from the rear wearing designer outfits for his father to choose from among. The young lad modelled the GQ assortment of exquisite linen with confidence and vigour before appearing with tears in his eyes over an army fatigue outfit he despised wearing. Junior walked out on his personal stage degenerate and slouchy, unhooked the buttons to his vest and tossed the vest at his father. "I told them I don't like this suit!" Junior complained as he marched back into the changing room.

Everyone who witnessed the rage of the young lad broke out with laughter over the manner with which the boy handled himself. Nicholas' arrogance was evident in his son, who, like his dad, accepted no form of bullshit or disrespect. With no motherly figure present except for his personal nanny, Miss Emma, who remained devoted to Junior, the boy grew among that ratchet knife-wielding, ice pick-stabbing, gun-shooting maniacs his father embraced as family. Miss Emma was, in fact, responsible for maintaining discipline around the compound, and criminals were terrified of being caught swearing or behaving unmannerly around the seventy-four-year-old woman. Miss Emma, who was a devoted Catholic, tolerated the massive weaponry that was exposed by guards and gun hands around the compound, yet knocked gangsters across the head for swearing or indulging in any form of propaganda while she was present. The maid, who watched over Kevin's only child, had protected and cared for the child since he was the tender age of seven months. Without regard to the Esquada boys and Damian, Miss Emma had been in the trusted employment of Nicholas longer than any other worker on his roster.

"Miss Emma, you know the boy don't like them sort a things. See him a walk right out of them on his way back!" Nicholas joked while chuckling over his son's actions.

"What happen to Junior's mother?" Killa asked.

Nicholas buckled over the first few words to leave his lips. which indicated that the subject was a difficult topic for the single father. It was evident that the topic was one of personal affliction for the boss, who rarely let anything affect his moods. Nicholas was considered cool, calm, and collected by his assistants, and they had never seen him frown or murmur over any incident, regardless the magnitude.

"Martain and his peers—them have a gentlemen's club downtown. When me start, me hunt for the pussy hole, that spot there was the first place me go look for him. He was somewhere else still, but one of the pussy holes who beat me into a coma over turf shit was flossing on his birthday or some shit. From me see the boy that was it, him have to pay back the piper. But before me step to him, the little filly I was rapping to slip her phone number into me pocket and tell me call her. Because me had to cancel the pussy hole who put him hands on me, me didn't want call still, in case she decided to set me up for a little money. Still me give her a link and it so happen that is one a the best move me make in this country, 'cause she no stop give me info on where to find the pussy hole, Martain. Have the boy Martain a run 'round the city with no safe place to lay him head for weeks, every girlfriend, family member, any house him dock into a pure gun shot. Me get message say him a hide out with some blonde chick in South Shore, directly in front them police station. Tall building with about seven or eight floors and she lived on the fifth, so no chance for a drive-by and spray the place. But the buoy, Martain, think him smart and set up an ambush with shooters on the fourth and sixth floor, plus the entire police station as backup. Anyways, me, Danny, and Tank drive go look for the buoy. Once we see the building location, we decide to leave Tank in the vehicle with the engine running by the southern exit, which was furthest exit from the police station. Danny and I walked into the building a few seconds before an old lady stepped off the elevator on her way out. We take the elevator up to the fifth floor and start walking toward apartment 509 before Danny's Indian senses began kicking in. To him, things seemed too easy for a man who no leave him heavy convoy nowhere. Same time Tank while waiting notice three fresh replacements arriving for duty, and couldn't get in touch with me over the phone, so him decided to follow the replacements in case them try get the drop on us. The replacement body guards walked up the stairs to the fourth floor and enter some apartment up there, while Tank wisely decided to lay low and watch what transpired. Knowing I was that close to Martain after everything the pussy put me through clouded my judgment still. Me drop two shells in the dead bolt lock and came in the apartment, spraying everything in sight. Is once me get into the apartment, I realise that Danny was right, it was a little too easy to get to that fucking biker. When me busted in, the blonde chick frightfully jump off the sofa with her TV remote in her hand and frighten me, so I laid her ass out across the fucking coffee table. We spray up every room in search of that biker bitch but couldn't find him. On our way out the front door, a pure gunshot greetings Danny and I receive. We ran up in a roadblock in the hallway, where five heavily armed bikers decided we weren't exiting the apartment. Luckily, those five guys came up from the fourth floor with Tank overshadowing their every move, or they'd have held us there 'til the cops came and got us. Them boys dumped a bucket of bullets on us inside the apartment, but as we start looking for alternative escape route, we overheard shots being fired at the pussy them, from their rear. Tank showed up right in the nick of time and created a window for us to escape, because had he not shown up, the rest of guards from the sixth floor plus them police friends who were storming the building would have definitely cancelled us. Martain revered me so much that he'd only spend time with the young lady when his dick was hard. Apart from that, he made sure the gun hands were around at every waking moment of the day. I believe the first time we actually spoke together was right after that incident. Martain called me crying to inform me that him personally take out a bounty on my head. I told that bitch that, unlike him, I will definitely be the one to send him back to his maker." The boss man expressed a translucent smirk, though memories of the incident were painful, and he paused for a couple of tokes off the marijuana joint.

"After a few months, me little mole in the Rough Riders family got pregnant, and that was when some jealous gossipers found out she was the one feeding me information. Between the strippers them gossiping about the little man's affairs, and the drunken bikers spilling more than them beers, I stayed knowing where to find that pussy hole. Martain took the betrayal by KJ's mother so serious that him called me and threatened me that he was going to kill her entire family, which he did, before he mutilated her. I kept her locked up at home with guards galore whenever she decided to go out and do a little baby shopping. I thought knowing what Martain and friends did to her mother and sister would scare her from wanting to leave the compound, but Stacey swore she was a gangster and refused to be intimidated by anyone. The moment for Junior's birth arrived and we do the hospital thing, but his mom experienced some complications and had to stay over in the hospital for another few days. The doctors didn't like the idea, but I kept round the clock guards interrogating everything the nurses did pertaining to Stacey. Four days later, they evaluated her and decided that she was well enough to come home with Junior. Me sign them out and tell Damian to push the wheelchair with Stacey so me can carry Junior in the little carriage, while Tank and the Rass go carry the vehicle 'round front. Walked through the huge sliding glass door from the lobby to the street, when three apprentices in a Chevy Trailblazer attempted a drive-by through the drop-off zone. Fucking idiots trying to speed through somewhere where vehicles ahead of you are creeping at least five kilometres an hour. All me could do was lay low with Junior, but me could hear Damian squeezing off rounds out the German luger. The pussy dem ran up into the back of a Mazda 6, crashed them vehicle, and then try shoot their way out to safety."

"Don't tell me say them get away?"

"A police cruiser was parked right in the parking lot with two on-duty officers who claimed them brought some unconscious pedestrian to the hospital. Sometimes I question whether or not them two officers were staking out the drive-by to clean up the garbage after them assassins finished their work. Still, them shot the front passenger before him could get out the vehicle and claimed that the driver got pinned by the airbag before a stray bullet lick out the back of his head," added Nicholas.

"What happen to the third shooter?" Killa asked.

"Neither one of the police gave chase, so them claim him escape, though him manage to accomplish his task still, 'cause after me get off the floor, check Junior, who was screaming his head off, me realize that Stacey was slumped over in the wheelchair. Damian roll over off the ground and start scream her name, but the wheelchair prevented her from hitting the ground like everyone else and she pick up two shells in the chest. Junior lucky she was too weak to carry him, or mi would bury mi gal and mi son at the same time. Me stand up over her while the doctors rush in to treat her and is like me couldn't move, all them telling me to step to the side so they can help her. All I'm imagining is Martain telling me by any means necessary a message I've since then called him to relayed and will live to see come through." Nicholas relit him extinguished joint and inhaled a huge cloud of weed toxins into his lungs before slowly exhaling it through his nostrils.

"I know you like that suit, my boy, clean, can't stop grinning from ear to ear. Hah!" Nicholas shouted to his son, who walked out wearing a brown Armani trouser with a golden fabric shirt sporting Asian tigers. "Go tell Miss Emma to put that outfit among you choices!"

"Me sorry to hear say is them sort of fashion you lose your baby mother still, and knowing one a the pussy them who pull the trigger is still alive must grieve you!" Killa sympathized.

"I said the police were under the impression him get away because them didn't pursue, but the Rass and Tank were pulling in the drop-off zone when the buoy them pull off them stunt. Rass Ijah watch the police them move in on the Trailblazer before deciding to pursue the batty boy attempting to escape. Fucking scared pussies got lucky, come to a killing and end up running like bitches. After the beating me receive at the boys them hands, that was the second-worst tragedy to hit me in this country, and all caused by the same motherfucker. Me glad when Ijah check in and tell me him camp outside the pussy them hideout, although me personally had to attend to my son's needs. The boys brought him over right after I put Junior down for a nap that evening, but I was so vexed that I end up beating that boy stink, 'til the baby made a squeak through the monitor in my pocket. And, after all, that I still had to send Damian to attend to the baby, because I was drenched in blood by that time."

"Boss, the Africans them a wait for you inside your office," exclaimed a member of Nicholas' perimeter guards.

"Yeah, tell them say I'll be right there! You boys continue enjoying the festivities. I've got some unexpected business that just turned up. I'll try to be as prompt as possible still," said Nicholas, who left to attend some personal matters.

The boss obliged all his guests by purchasing an array of garments for himself, the Esquada brothers, Junior, and Killa, whose eyes were altered from his typical thuggish look once the creativity by some of La Monde's finest were displayed. Nicholas thanked his guests for their presence and bid them farewell should they depart before he'd concluded his other affairs while instructing Kane to properly compensate his guests.

Nicholas and Danny shunned the festivities and began walking toward the boss' office when KJ crept up in between the two men and held both their hands.

"Uncle Danny, are we still going to camp outside all night?" KJ asked.

"Of course, Junior, and don't forget we got to set up our tents and fire equipment later this afternoon," said Danny.

"Are you coming camping with me and Uncle Danny tonight, Daddy?"

"Sorry, son, but I got a little jam to go to later, but I'm definitely in the next time. All right, bad boy? Now, can you please go harass some of your other uncles? Thank you!" Nicholas answered.

"All right, Dad, I'll let you guys off the hook for now, but don't forget I'm in the shadows like Night Man!" KJ exclaimed as he scurried away.

There were two Nigerian descendants inside his office patiently awaiting Nicholas' presence as he and Danny entered the chamber. Polite greetings of sturdy handshakes were shared among the men who gathered around Nicholas' desk to discuss business. The darker of the two black men placed a Hitachi briefcase atop Nicholas' desk before gradually opening it to reveal the contents.

"The last time I was here, I talked with you about the problem I was having with this Officer Renick and his partner. I can't play soccer or do anything without these cops bothering me every minute of the day. You said fifty thousand to have them taken care of. There is that and enough money for three keys inside the case," exclaimed the apparent head boss.

"No problem, Hakeem! Danny, send for the products for them and tell Marcel them they got a green light," said Nicholas.

Executing Orders

Officer Renick and his partner, Doug Battier, were members of the drug squad unit and the SWAT Division at the Thirty-First Police Precinct in Lachine, Montreal. The dynamic duo of crime busters were a constant thorn in the asses of drug dealers and crime offenders within the perimeter of their patrol. The two officers had never participated in or orchestrated a raid on the public without substantial arrests and seizures, which they dubbed as trophies throughout the local news programs. Their latest procession against crime came only a week prior where they stormed and closed one of Hakeem's prized drug bases in Lachine. The officers raided the high-tech drug base loaded with cameras, sensor equipment, and surveillance by paid neighbours, knowing they wouldn't catch a dealer on the premises, yet wanting to send a message that dealing drugs would not be tolerated around Lachine. Hakeem, however, chose to relocate his affairs from the third to the fifth floor and reopened shop an hour after the drug squad left.

The ongoing feud between Hakeem and members of local law enforcement had brought the Nigerian to his final trump card, after which remained nothing less than surrender. The two officers in question were spotted in the alleyway behind Hakeem's prized drug base, which he refused to close despite opposition from activists and others. Officers Renick and Battier were gathering information on the number of known drug addicts to enter the premises at 11 Sacre Coeur Street, from where Hakeem acquired 65% of his spoils. The unmarked cruiser from which the officers gathered their information was a turquoise Chevy Malibu that had been seen around by offenders avoiding the long arms of the law.

The alleyway ran between rows of buildings inhabited by welfare recipients and lesser fortunate patrons of society. An M&M produce delivery truck sneaked up behind the focused officers before the driver abandoned the vehicle. Two minutes after the man abandoned the truck, a Greyhound tour bus pulled directly in front the officers' Malibu and blocked their vision of the building they were surveying.

"Partner, I'm telling you without a doubt, that's fifteen smokers in as many minutes," declared Officer Battier.

"Look who's running up into the hot spot! If it ain't our old friend, Twizler. We'll definitely get some answers about whatever we need to know now!" Officer Renick said.

"Where did this fucking idiot come from, and why are there no windows in the frames?" Officer Battier said.

The officer's question was answered as eight heavily armed mercenaries popped into the window frames and began plastering the Malibu with bullets. Both officers ducked low from the unseeing eyes of bullets. "We're under attack! We're taking serious fire! Help, help! Oh, my God, I think they just shot my partner!" Officer Battier yelled through his two-way radio.

Two ignited torches sailed through the side windows of the Malibu and quickly lit the vehicle's occupants ablaze. The screams of men enduring torture could be heard for blocks, and the stinging sounds of copper slamming against metal kept them at bay. The entire ordeal, which horrified residents, lasted a mere seven minutes, yet left the entire neighbourhood infested with police combing through the aftermath for clues on who orchestrated such an ambush. Both victims died after receiving burns throughout their entire bodies, properly roasted like Thanksgiving turkeys.

The Party

Nicholas' SUVs sandwiched the Mercedes Benz 600 he was aboard as they came to a halt in front the venue that hosted the dance hall event. There was a rolled red carpet similar to that at the Oscar event, and numerous thugs evacuated their vehicles and immediately surrounded the boss' carriage. Nicholas' entourage treated him like an important dignitary as they quickly scurried him into the building under tight security. Killa was aboard the boss' luxury carriage when the guards practically lifted Nicholas from his seat, yet chose to remain aboard and accompany the drivers on their valet duties. The drivers in the vehicles began circling the block in search of parking before deciding to station the vehicles directly in front a car dealership only a few yards away. As Killa and the remaining three drivers exited the carriages, Killa caught sight of a 323 BMW parked in the alleyway across the street. The black automobile could hardly be seen in the dark alleyway except for the chrome insignia and trimmings. Four men suspiciously exited the vehicle, intensely checking out their surroundings before proceeding to conceal artefacts beneath their clothing.

"Yow, Tank, we a carry them things in wid we?" Killa asked.

"Don't watch no face man security a wi people, we well protected in these places!" Tank answered as he and the remaining drivers commenced grooming themselves before moving toward the dance hall.

Killa removed his Glock 9 mm from the stash pot built into the rear armrest and shoved it into his waistband. The thought of guards with metal detectors and other devices in no way swayed the thug's decision as he charismatically mingled with his associates as if all was well. The movements of the four suspicious men, who Killa positively believed armed themselves for a mission, didn't go unnoticed by the wanted Jamaican, who'd prefer to be caught with a weapon than without one.

"Buoy, a tonight you a go see some big batty and sexy gal, remember mi tell you!" Tank exclaimed as he playfully shoved Killa by the shoulder.

"A them things deah me used to king, nothing but the finest," acknowledged Killa, whose attention momentarily swayed from the alley.

The gangster took a sneak peek over his left shoulder at the alley. Strangely enough, instead of the avid partygoers materializing from the dark alley, the men completely disappeared from radar as the window to the alleyway closed.

Tank and the other two drivers were well greeted by the security personnel, who pointed out that the entrance fees had been taken care of and that their associates awaited their presence at the top of the stairs. Killa slouched behind as the chauffeurs scurried up the stairs to the party zone, and he again attempted to see who the four secretive men were. Without catching a glimpse of the people he sought, Killa decided to join his friends and ran up the stairs. The remainder of troops had cleared security, and they began wondering where he might have run off to before he materialized at the security check. Killa could see Tank pointing at him, indicating he was the final count as he walked toward the security personnel.

"Arms up so I can check you, please," said the security personnel.

"You don't need to check me still, me can tell you straight me have it pan me!" Killa declared without so much as a smirk as he walked up toward the guard.

The man looked puzzled at first as he thought about the consequences of trying to disarm this thug in front of him. The club's rules specifically forbid any form of alcohol, weapons, and illegal substances and mandated they be confiscated before entry. However, the thug to be disarmed looked like an untamed gorilla, and knowing the pack with whom he hunted would discourage the National Guard from intruding. The security guard stepped to the side like Moses parting the Red Sea and allowed the stylish gangster entry without provocation.

Props and acknowledgments came from the DJ on the ones and twos, who spotted Damian and his entourage of thirteen. Nicholas remained constantly surrounded by his personal strike force, who allowed no one within three feet of the boss. The crew of fourteen hustlers took over the far left corner inside the vicinity before a small scouting team went off for refreshments.

Massive amounts of females of all makes and models paraded their attributes as they danced. The music selector had the entire club ablaze, and men were not shying away from the challenges of the females, whom sceptics would say behaved and danced provocatively. There was a smoking ordinance inside the club, which was difficult to believe because of the huge clouds of marijuana smoke floating about the ceiling. Nicholas' scouting team, who went off in search of refreshments, soon returned with bottles of Hennessy, Pepsi, Guinness, Heineken, and a pack of Red Bull energy drinks.

The guards around Nicholas weren't only watching out for their boss' best interest, but they were also managing time for their personal desires. Not one female who passed by the dog pound went by without someone tugging on her arm or using some type of dialect to gain their attention. Ganja baseball bats began blazing all throughout Nicholas' mini camp as the thugs began drinking, partying, and enjoying the festivities. Killa stood by Nicholas' side all night, and the boss attributed his attention to ensuring his friend's enjoyment, as well as the fact that the position offered him a better view of the entrance.

West Indians from the Caribbean are overpowered by the musical creations of their islands, such as Salsa, Meringue, Calypso, Soca, and Reggae, to name a few. Trinidadians, Barbadians, Haitians, Jamaicans, and so on all celebrate their carnivals by declaring national holidays for which their citizens are eligible to party for days on end. The travesties that occur at such festivities are almost immoral, as patrons push the boundaries with sexually explicit behaviour. The party-goers inside the hall were all flamboyantly dressed, with the ladies wearing some of the skimpiest outfits, while the men adorned the latest fashions. The female dancers who sought to exhibit their dancing skills, soon neglected the restrictions protaining to their attires, as they performed dance manouveres which in most cases exposed their privates. There were ladies grinding on their male counterparts, whinning while balanced on the top of their heads and performing sexually enticing features, which caused the men to gather around.

A number of hustlers came over to Nicholas throughout the night to acknowledge the man most respected for his stance against the Rough Riders. Huge quantities of liquor were sent over from the various high rollers inside the party, who all admittedly considered Nicholas "The One."

"Yow me haffi let out some a this liquor from out a mi system!" Nicholas declared as he grabbed Killa around the neck. "Don't think I don't see you a watch that thing in the white all night!"

"You need fi mind you own business!" Killa joked as he began walking alongside Nicholas.

Jasper, Damian, and Rass Ijah all broke ahead of Nicholas and Killa as the remaining thugs held down the fort. Tank soon decided he also needed to empty his bladder and set off behind his peers, who'd gained a few paces on him. Killa and Nicholas continued their laughing ways across the huge dance floor as they made their way to the men's facilities across the hall. There was a wall that hid the facilities which was opened on both sides, offering patrons easy access from both directions. For the first time since entering the hall, Killa caught sight of the four individuals he believed changed their minds about entering the soirée. The woman and three men were located toward the opposite end of the wall Nicholas and company walked around. There was a look of alertness about the four, and they appeared surprised to see Nicholas without many bodyguards. Kadeem was no Bill Gates, yet when it came to proficiency at one's job, he was as masterful at his craft as the Microsoft genius himself.

Kadeem believed something was afoot, and he decided not to enter the facilities should an ambush be the plot. The wanted Jamaican instead hugged the wall and attempted to inconspicuously watch the movements of his suspects, though visibility was indeed poor. An object similar to that of an automatic weapon startled Killa as someone jammed the round mouth iron into his ribs. Killa looked down at the weapon jammed into his ribs before looking down into the face of the five foot four little-man holding the weapon.

"Just relax yourself, breatherin'!" The Haitian man had a huge smirk on his face.

It was evident that his abductor didn't want the sound of gun fire to alert both Nicholas and his peers as the other three assassins moved into position to sniper off anyone exiting the bathroom. Kadeem's eyes grew wider with each tick of the clock, knowing that at any second his friends would exit into a trap. With his eyes fixed on the door, Kadeem felt himself about to pull away from his captor, which would definitely have resulted in a bullet to the ribs, yet he was content to die if it meant saving his friends. Killa looked down at his captor before making his move and realized the man was coughing up blood. Tank was on his way to the facilities and, realizing Killa's dilemma, piercing his twelve-inch blade into the man's abdomen. The Haitian assassin slithered to the ground and fell at the heels of a woman whose attention was fixed on the happenings around her. The woman soon stepped on the deceased assassin before screaming once she realized that he'd been killed.

The claps of gunfire erupted as the scream startled one of the assassins, whose twitchy fingers thumped two shells into the bathroom door. Once the assassin realized he'd possibly foiled the ambush, the man charged into the bathroom with the door quickly closing behind him. Following the initial sounds of the assassin's weapon being discharged, there were two huge blasts like that of a .357 Magnum that flung the assassin back through the door he'd entered. Killa armed himself and used his weapon to blast continuously at the remaining pair. The second bullet to be discharged from his weapon laid out the male assassin across the party floor as ruckus and hysteria ran rampant. The lone female assassin screamed in terror as she blasted bullets at Killa, who was forced to duck behind the wall for protection. Tank removed the deceased assassin's weapon from his grasp as the onslaught by the female assassin kept them at bay. The female began moving toward a rear exit as other members of Nicholas' party ran toward the gun battle. In an attempt to escape, the female assassin found herself erratically shooting at the hostile crowd as her window to accomplish the slaying drastically diminished. The fright of suffering the same fate as her accomplices terrified the assassin, who attempted to clear the path through the exit with gunfire. Her attempt killed a pair of girlfriends fleeing the violence as flares from other weapons around the hall terminated the assassin's hopes.

Part 17

YVES BUCHARD KILLED more of Nicholas' allies and Defenders since the beginning of the war than any other soldier in Martain's arsenal. Since Nicholas murdered his dearest friend, Pierre "The Moose," Yves had waged a personal campaign against all who defied the Rough Riders' laws and vowed their termination. The Defenders gang of thugs had fought for control over the distribution of recreational drugs around their West Island neighbourhoods for years, yet failed to implement a strategy capable of eliminating their competition. Their adversaries, on the other hand, had implemented strategies for the destruction of their enemies, whom they believed prevented economic growth.

"*Oui, monsieur!*" Yves answered as he spoke with someone over his cell phone.

The bikers' enforcer looked across the train coach at the two men he'd been surveying since the train departed the Bonaventure train station in Montreal. The Amtrak passenger train destined for Grand Central Station in New York City had being used by the pair of Columbian runners for years to smuggle large amounts of money into the United States. The two Spanish natives had absolutely no idea they were being followed during their return trip to Miami, Florida via New York after their two-day excursion at Nicholas' mansion. "I will do exactly as you request, sir!" Yves said before the conversation was terminated.

The two Columbians were under the employment of one Ernesto Lopez, who handsomely rewarded both men for collecting his drug payments. The pair made a substantial number of trips during the year, over the course of which they retrieved nearly a hundred million dollars in payment. The money was casually wrapped among clothing inside a huge traveller's pack to avoid detection by the border patrol in search of various contrabands. Without a mandatory searching law of travellers' belongings at the border for railway cargo, intellectual smugglers transferred their black market items without the hassles of being scrutinized.

Yves watched the men place the money sack inside the overhead compartment as casually as if they were taking the garbage to the corner. The men were conservative in their actions despite the fact that they were carrying ten million in cash. For the first hour of the trip, Yves pondered over how he'd separate the sack from its handlers, who stood guard like centurions. Should a situation arise, however, Yves was prepared to dispense a bullet to the head and chest of each individual before vanishing amidst the hysteria. Whatever the result at attempting his goal, the biker assassin knew he'd have to accomplish his mission between the train clearing Immigration and breaking at its first stop following.

One of the smugglers, who had kept his head buried in the day's Gazette thus far, began scanning various faces around the coach and intently stared at Yves for a few seconds. The Columbian native believed the biker to be a prominent businessman due to the tailored business suit, the dark hair with a smooth, shaved face, his posture, his demeanour, and the laptop on the desk tray. Yves played his role to the T, and neither smuggler believed him to be a threat to them.

The smuggler seated toward the aisle soon arose from his seat and walked toward the restaurant and bar area. Yves asked the student traveller seated beside him to watch over his belongings while he visit the onboard facilities. The biker assassin followed the smuggler to the bar, where the Columbian threw back two shots of Tanqueray before purchasing himself a third and a single for his partner. The train attendant was passing out declaration forms for each passenger to fill out to assist with the smooth transition through Customs. Those eating or partaking of the Happy Hour specials were told to complete the INS forms and return to their assigned seats before the train pulled into the Custom's checkpoint.

By the time Yves returned to his seat, the train was in the process of halting to allow the Immigration inspectors time to board. A quick glance at his targets showed both men comfortably seated with empty liquor glasses before them. *Seemed they needed the shots to settle their nerves,* thought Yves as he began preparing his documents for inspection. The Immigration officers who inspected the train were diligent as they proficiently interrogated each passenger while ensuring their travelling documents were in proper order. Two men and a female were removed from the company of those aboard with zero dispute or quarrel about the claims. Following the Immigration officials' detainment, the train remained stationary for another few minutes before the passengers of Amtrak 565 slated for New York City were sent on their merry voyage.

With the only point of concern behind them, the Columbian smugglers believed they were successful and began their premature celebration. The same aisle seat centurion who earlier visited the bar seemed eager to gulp down a few more as he bolted to the bar before regular transactions were announced. Yves followed the man, who had become totally complacent after the first few rounds, although he was unable to get within arm's reach of the smuggler. There was a young couple between Yves and the smuggler, with the female boasting about her young fiancé taking her to Atlantic City to be wedded. The tight corridors along the train offered enough space for two bodies at a time, which made it impossible for the biker to force the smuggler into a detour. Yves had selected his weapon of execution before leaving his seat, which was an eighteen-inch carving knife that he'd used to carve up a lot of his enemies.

The smuggler made it safely to the coach that housed the restaurant and bar, which was two cars behind the coach in which their seats were assigned. The Columbian, who possessed that hazy look of an alcoholic, seemed furious to find he was not the first to arrive at the bar as he jumped on one of the bar stools. A negotiation soon erupted over the purchase of an entire two-litre, 40% alcohol content bottle of Tanqueray, which the vendors weren't at liberty to sell. The celebrating Columbian settled for a tray with a few shots of his favourite liquor as he began his trip back to his centurion duty position. As the joyous smuggler passed the toilet facilities, Yves ambushed him by gagging him and dragging him into a toilet compartment. The blade of his eighteen-inch butcher knife sank deep into the ribcage of the smuggler, who died once the garlic blade pierced his heart.

With his plot in motion, Yves moved to secure the package he'd come for after eliminating half the hostiles. Due to the late hour, the lights about the passenger cars were dimmed to allow fatigued passengers the opportunity to rest. The biker assassin returned to the coach they were assigned and sat directly beside the second smuggler, who had begun dozing off from fatigue.

"What took you so long?" demanded the smuggler in Spanish as he turned to look at the goodies brought to him by his friend.

"*Uhhh!*" The smuggler groaned as Yves pierced a vital organ beneath the man's armpit. The biker assassin summoned the train attendant and demanded a blanket for his friend, whom he claimed fell ill along the journey. Once the attendant returned with the blanket, Yves covered the deceased smuggler, who had blood pouring down his arm, before collecting his prize in preparation to depart the train. There were two bikers waiting for Yves as he exited the train at the first stop in the United States. The chauffeurs allowed one of their top gunners to relax and snooze as they drove him back across the Canadian border following a successful operation.

Damian attended high school at James Lynn High in Montreal, where he encountered a number of his close friends. One such friend was a Caucasian male named James Tea, a French-Canadian boy from Saint-Constant, Quebec. James joined the Canadian Armed Forces during his junior year and never wavered from the discipline acquired therein. Despite his honour and his courage to defend his country, James' upbringing taught him the value of a buck and the hustling skills desired to acquire that buck. Hence, the opportunity with his prior connections was a match made in heaven, as the army's elite maintained an offshore bank account.

Nicholas had placed an order for some rather sophisticated, high-powered weaponry modified to improve the American soldier's way of life. At the time the order was placed, the weapons, which ranged from long-range sniper rifles capable of extinguishing one's target from a mile and a half away to rifles that eliminated their targets around corners and flat-out, kick-ass automatics that forced one's opponent into submission, were only available to the U.S. military. However, five months after the original order was placed, Damian received a confirmation phone call that the order had been filled and was ready for pick-up.

The items ordered by Nicholas came to a grand total of Can$350 000.00, which was handed to Damian to complete the transaction. Nicholas advised Damian to ride with Killa and two others of his choice to the address in Ottawa, Ontario. The hour and a half ride to Ottawa saw the men as never before as they joked around about women, social affairs, and guns. The men joked about memories they possessed where they were forced to either flee or stand and fight during a gun battle. One of the men who hopped into the huge Chevy Suburban truck was mocked for peeing on himself during a shoot-out against Rough Riders representatives a few years prior.

Damian recounted the precise story of why it was that certain individuals never journey away from their nests unless they were detailed to a mission. "King Man, an Italian breatherin' of the family, opened a top-of-the-line clothing store downtown, right in the centre a Rough Rider's city. The man dem decide that nobody naw stop them from going anywhere, 'cause it's like there was a civil war on where one side of the town a fight against the other half, so every man stay strap."

"You mean like now!" Killa said, who hadn't witnessed a day without the brandishing of firearms since he began defending the cause.

The comment brought a mild chuckle from the occupants inside the vehicle, who all knew the statement to be completely true. "Fi real, still them Kloffie yah decided them going shopping with a bunch a chicks. Splurging and shit all over the place! But you see how downtown is, though—big enough to where you can davel a little, but it's only a matter of time before word gets out, and when it does, I swear it's almost like the cops block off road, and you'd better have a few extra clips 'cause that type a show down. This fool's walked out the spot and a biker boy put his big dutty Desert Eagle to his temple and pull the trigger. Them swear say Panta 'dead, cause is like everything freeze, the bags them in him hand drop, him legs get weak and him flatter to the ground, not to mention him bladder release an wet up himself. The biker boy 'til this day in him grave a wonder how the gun stick, 'cause after that a pure gunshot for about half an hour. A channel-surfing cousin a do when him call me and show me the big shoot-out, a happen live on the CFCF news station, that's why him always a watch the news fi see what a go on."

"You really piss yourself, breatherin'?" Killa laughed.

"Man, when I felt that blue steel next to my head, man, everything just went loose, man. I couldn't hold nothing in, man. I had to check my drawers after, man, 'cause I swore I shit myself, man. Man, it was crazy. Laugh all you want, but that was real, man!" Panta confessed, who laughed at himself for his boo-boo, though he jumped on Damian for revealing his most awkward moment.

"Your ass lucky you still alive to talk about it," stated the driver, who cruised along at a soothing 130 MPH.

As the gangsters neared the Castle Man's introduction sign off the 417 Trans-Canada Highway, the distance sign to Ottawa read fifty-eight kilometersto the capital. Damian telephoned his connection to advise him of his current ETA, which was an estimated twenty-five minutes at the speed they were travelling.

Once they arrived in Ottawa, the capital city of Canada, the men exited the 417 Trans-Canada Highway at the first sign, which read Walkley Road, and veered northbound. The location selected was an abandoned warehouse once used by the premier shingle producer in Canada. The men had done prior dealings from this location, which was ideal for the soldiers whose base was only a few miles away.

Sergeant James Tea had always included the same three officers of the Petawawa RCF base in his illegal dealings, though a few higher-ranked officials had to have their pockets greased in order for such high-powered machinery to go unaccounted for. The sergeant's allies were Private Doug Hayes, Private Lucien Harbour, and Gunnery Sergeant Matt Sikes. The higher-ranked officials involved in the scheme were in on the deal since the debut, and their disassociation would be imminent should any accusations or actions be taken against the group. However, the constant flow of money kept the players' interest acute, as everyone perceived the sure payoff.

The army officers arrived before their business counterparts and arranged the viewing of the products they had brought. Within minutes, the buyers for the hardware entered the northeast hangar door and proceeded toward the arms dealers. The ambiance was perfect for the transaction and both parties were eager to attain their portion of the transaction. Damian first hopped from their chariot and greeted their business counterparts before introducing everyone else. Killa emerged from the 4x4, inspecting the surroundings all throughout before joining his friends at the vehicle's bumper. After Killa was introduced to the soldiers, their relaxed nature calmed Killa's nerves, and his entourage began inspecting the weapons, which was the cause for their travels.

"How the fuck come you in the army and you getting fat when all that training is supposed to keep you slim and trim?" Damian asked of Gunnery Sergeant Sikes.

"I can't speak for everybody else, but my training is eating and firing weapons all day and all night," responded the sergeant, who found the comment slightly funny.

"Yeah, that's right, Sarge, we told you that exact same thing," said Private Harbour.

"Woo, me can't wait 'til them pussy in Montreal fuck with us!" Panta hollered as he keenly inspected the M-16 automatic rifle with the 40 mm grenade launcher attached.

"Killa, feel how nice and light this is!" Damian said as he tossed Killa one of the M-203 automatic weapons. Killa nonchalantly looked at the high-powered rifle, as his interest had been stolen by the almighty AS-50 sniper rifle.

The orchestrator of the deal was handed the briefcase containing the full payment. Sergeant James Tea opened the attaché case and began inspecting the deal sealer. From out of the blue, a loud shout came from across the warehouse.

"Nobody move! Hands in the air! Now!" A loud shout came from the southwest section of the warehouse.

Basic soldiers and Military Police began springing up from sewer covers, flying in through windowpanes, and charging in on foot as the participants of the illegal transaction began looking around at each other. Killa removed the safety switch from the weapon tossed to him and began emptying the clip at their antagonists. Young Panta needed no invitation to join the offence as he moved to the front of the pack, believing his weapon sufficient enough to ward off all comers. Their initial outburst caused the invading forces to prematurely scatter as bullets ripped through those who refused to seek shelter. The attacking soldiers returned fire once the opportunity became available, and it became immediately evident who had undergone proper weapons training. Panta's brown eyes widened after his M-16 automatic rifle indicated the bullet chamber had been emptied, though he quickly selected a grenade for launch as back-up. The sharpshooters of the army base tattooed Panta as he released a detrimental grenade that killed an additional five soldiers before he succumbed to his injuries.

Gunnery Sergeant Matt Sikes had, like his assailants, taken a solid vow to not bear arms against his countrymen and allies of war, which was a promise he intended to keep. The eighteen-year veteran of the armed forces threw his hands high in the air and fell to his knees in gesture of a peaceful surrender while bullets sounded all around him. The gunnery sergeant could be seen shedding tears with his eyes tightly closed as the thought of the humiliating procedures to come devastated him. "I didn't mean to! I'm a true soldier, you hear? A true soldier!" Sikes exclaimed.

"Sarge, get your face in the cement before they put you there!" James screamed from among Killa, Damian, and Tank, who were holding fast their position.

Killa caught sight of four army personnel attempting to flank them by circling the warehouse and attacking from the rear. The men broke away from their platoon, which was being overpowered despite their large numbers by six armed and defiant men. The rush to locate protection against the attacking Military Police had brought Damian to overturning the table of weapons, which only hid those seeking a safe spot from the eyes of men, not bullets. Killa dragged the high-powered, fifty-calibre AS-50 into position and illuminated the night scope to gain sight into the dark. Twenty feet away through a soiled pane of glass, Killa was able to catch sight of the men making their way to furthest end of the warehouse. The gangster timed the men along the cement wall and fired once he believed the platoon had reached a zinc-sheeting portion of the wall. The humongous blast tore out a twelve-inch gap from the wall and remarkably blasted two soldiers into Neverland. The two soldiers became confused and decided to abandon the mission, fearing they would not be allowed to reach the specified coordinates.

Private Lucien Harbour and Private Doug Hayes were using the Hummer they rode as protection against the onslaught of bullets being spat at them when a stray bullet struck the gasoline tank and caused the vehicle to explode, killing instantly the evasive soldiers. With their numbers dwindling against a determined force, Killa and the remaining deifiers began moving to the Chevy truck while renderingan audacious amount of cover fire.

Tank was the first into the vehicle, igniting the engine while supporting his friend's escape. Killa was in the act of retrieving a few weapons despite the hostile environment, such as the lightweight M-203 automatic to compliment his AS-50 sniper rifle, when he stumbled across the briefcase containing the payment. While everyone else moved to the escape automobile and administered suppressive fire against the MPs, Killa ensured the trip wasn't a complete waste as he dove into the SUV loaded with artillery and collaterals.

James and Damian, who were the farthest from the SUV, began moving toward the escape automobile, though the MPs seemed determined to block their return. Killa had never before fired a grenade launcher, although the gangster did not need the instruction manual for any weaponry. The ghetto war veteran launched a missile at three MPs who held his friends suppressed from the final tilt to the vehicle. The missile struck the barrier that protected the soldiers, blasting everything sky-high.

The commanding officer for the Military Police grew furious at the notion that his intended targets might escape despite his superior manpower and rank. A few soldiers of his convoy had positioned themselves behind supportive beams, ensuring them the ability to return fire at a bunch of thugs who'd managed to dominate despite their meagre numbers.

"Fuck!" The commander yelled, and he and the three men of his immediate squadron tucked their heads protectively beneath the barrier that supported them as bullets crashed into the objects around them.

One of the MPs posted atop a second-tier walkway opened fire at Damian as he attempted the final tilt at manoeuvring into the SUV. A bullet from the soldier's AK rifle struck Damian in the right shoulder and flung him into a very compromising position. Tank caught sight of Damian going down and emptied the remainder of his automatic rifle's magazine at the soldier who'd wounded his boss' cousin. Tank sought to award his brethren enough time to safely board the SUV, thus while his assault hindered the soldiers from striking at Damian, Tank yelled at his the injured thug 'to get in the truck'!.

Damian struggled to his feet, awkwardly drew his pistol with his left hand, and began staggering to the rear truck door. The commanding officer for the Military Police rose to one knee and managed to align Damian into his firing scope, slightly smirking with the knowledge that he was about to cancel one of the arms buyers. The commander squeezed the trigger and appeared to be watching the bullet as it pierced thin air en route to its intended target. Damian's friend who orchestrated the arms deal, noticed that he way about to get killed by the Military Police, and shoulder tackled him into the SUV.

"Get the fuck out of here!" James yelled as he rinsed bullets through the open door at his estranged family.

"Don't let them get away!" The frustrated commander yelled as the surviving soldiers popped bullets at the escaping SUV.

As the SUV sped through the huge hangar door, the commander in charge began sequestering the communications officer in order to alert all public officials of the fleeing thugs. There were nine MPs unaccounted for before further investigation revealed the communications officer and his equipment had been blown to smithereens alongside fellow soldiers. Said discovery increased the commander's anxiety as he stood over the kneeling gunnery sergeant before putting his boot to the side of Sikes' face. "Someone put this traitor in irons and get him out of my sight. Sergeant Docket, I want you to access the weapons and see to their transfer back to the base. The rest of you soldiers gather the dead and the rest of the equipment. Let's go, gentlemen, today. I don't want to be out in this night dew longer than I have to," ordered the commander.

While the commander prepared the official documentation detailing what transpired for the Review Board, his squadron followed orders and retrieved their government's property scattered throughout. Other officials from various organizations began arriving on the scene, such as the Royal Canadian Mounted Police, high-ranked colonels and generals, along with ambulances and mortuary vehicles. Within three quarters of an hour, an Admiral Tate, who vowed to uncover those behind the arms-dealing scenes, dispatched the vehicle assigned to transfer the stolen weapons back to base. The Ford Econoline 350 truck that was packed with the weapons slated for sale was also used to transport the weapons and personal effects of the soldiers killed in the conflict earlier that night. Two senior privates were assigned the task of returning the truck to the Petawawa Army Base with zero thought of adding additional escorts or detail.

The occupants of the Ford Econoline truck had no idea their skirmish with bad boys had piqued the interests of news reporters who were being held at bay a few paces away by local police officers. As they passed through the police barrier, a swarm of reporters corralled the truck, seeking confirmation of what they had heard transpired. The soldiers, who'd lowered the windows of the Econoline truck for ventilation against the humidity, were forced to seal up the cab to avoid the pressures of those seeking answers. Once the soldiers cleared the reporters' checkpoint, they immediately reopened the windows and selected their favourite dial on the radio as they cruised back to the base. Private Lee Chow brought the Ford Econoline 350 to a halt at the traffic light at Walkley Road and St. Laurent Boulevard, a whole second and a half before a bike rider pulled along the right side of the truck. A white brunette out on an early morning jog caught the attention of the two soldiers, who keenly watched her jog from the right sidewalk all the way across the front of the truck.

The slender, subtle curves of the six feet two inch cantaloupe ass in tights with a twenty-eight cup exercise tank top and her luscious long hair bundled into one jogger captivated the soldiers who drooled over her. As the female jogger passed before Lee Chow's window frame, a weapon sounded and the private's companion fell on his right shoulder. Before completely looking around at his companion, Lee wiped a slab of brain matter from the side of his head before realizing what had become of his friend. The private shrugged the body from his shoulder and immediately threw his hands in the air once he caught sight of the musket aimed at him.

"Out the vehicle, baby!" The soft female's voice sounded as she crept up behind Lee with her pistol to the back of his head.

Part 18

THE GAZETTE REPORTED a story that originated in Montreal, Canada, though the actual events occurred halfway across the world in Shanghai, China. The economic trade arrangment between Canada and China reported the discovery of a corpse, which was found hanging from a meat rack among exported beef on a huge cargo ship slated for China. Inspector No. 374, Lee Han Sung, was checking the refrigerated container's supply when he came across the nude and badly abused corpse of a man strung up with a baseball bat lodged in his rectum. There was dried blood covering the entire body, with huge lacerations into the skin from head to toe. The discovery startled Inspector No. 374, who raced to his superiors and revealed his findings.

Though said discovery frightened Inspector Lee Han Sung, the corpse was not the first of such to be found. In fact, an open investigation was being pursued by a joint team of investigators from both countries lobbying to terminate the human anatomies being sent to the butcher's market. The forensic report indicated the man had been killed and refrigerated in Montreal before being stacked among the frozen cattle voyaging to the mainland China. Photos were taken of the man's face in order to properly identify him, although investigators had to first consult a sketch artist to reconstruct the man's disfigured face. The sketch of the corpse was run through an international database, which provided investigators the true identity of the victim.

The Chinese authorities made evident the fact they had no wrongdoing in the tragic death of the Canadian male so as to avoid any future disruptions between the two countries. The body was flown back to Canada at the country's expense, although Chinese officials saw to it that the corpse was placed on an immediate flight out. An insider at the Chinese international dock, who quickly jumped on an opportunity to pocket a few bucks, leaked word to the press while the Agricultural Department contemplated whether or not to release the story.

The frozen corpse, who was later identified after officials decided to release the story, was the eighth Canadian victim to be found overseas packed into small crates or strung up inside containers. "Unsafe meats or Contaminated foods" was the headline for the story in the local press, which soon sparked an outcry from residents lobbying to terminate free trade arrangment between the two countries. Certain officials of parliament began demanding that the shipment of beef be returned after being exposed to a human corpse that carried possible life-threatening bacteria.

Brogan Alfonso was the man credited for slaying Yves Lafleur, who was the former Rough Riders leader, and he had remained a constant thorn in the bikers' ribs since its conception. Brogan headed the mighty Defenders crew, which competed strongly over territory with the Rough Riders' western division. Since the brutal slaying of one of the Rough Riders' most feared leaders, Brogan had survived nearly a dozen attempts on his life, ranging from sniper shots to bomb explosions. The lives of his family members had also been targeted by biker extremists who believed that if you couldn't catch the prize, you fucked up the runner-up. The latest victim to fall to the Alfonso family curse was Brogan's youngest brother, Brandon, who was just in the wrong place at the wrong time.

Brandon was on his way to spend some time with a female he'd recently met at a party when an altercation between he and some patrol officers turned ugly. The twenty-year-old youngster had used public transportation to voyage from the West Island to the Atwater Metro Station in Little Burgundy. Brandon exited the Metro at Atwater Street and quickly hustled ahead of traffic to cross the road, although the traffic light wasn't on amber. There was a squad patrol parked halfway up the block, and the officers at first appeared uninterested in the jaywalker. Brandon continued his journey to the female's house, but before the young college student, who took no interest in his brother's choice of career, could walk the next block, the patrolling officers were on him.

The officers busted around the corner with their lights flashing as if called to an immediate emergency before driving onto the pedestrian pavement directly in front of Brandon.

"Get up against the car and place your hands on the hood!"

"What the hell did I do?"

"What? You didn't notice the red light when you ran across the road?"

"Sorry, I was in a hurry," exclaimed the lad.

With his hands on the hood of the car, young Brandon twitched at the touch of the searching officer, who asked, after first ensuring there were no weapons available, "Now, you don't have any sharp objects in your pocket that might injure me, do you?"

"Not at all, sir," Brandon responded.

The officer checked Brandon's pockets and found nothing except for a bus pass, a few dollars, a wallet, and keys. The young man had his school identification, which properly identified him among other documents to prove his eligibility to be in the country, yet one photo clip found of he and his elder sibling brought his demise. Once the officers saw the photo clip, their nasty attitudes got nastier and the whole cycle flipped against Brandon.

"So you're a gangster!"

"Come on, man! I'm a student. It says so right there on my ID. You can even call the school if you don't believe me," said Brandon.

"You posing big time with gangsters, you must be a part of the crew," suggested the driver, after sneaking a peek at the documents.

"It's not like that. He's my brother," Brandon answered.

The officer who searched Brandon unexpectedly jammed the butt of his metallic flashlight into the student's lower spine. The young lad's limbs gave way, and he crumbled to the turf like fallen leaves come autumn.

The officer smacked the handcuffs on and said, "You're under arrest for disobeying the traffic signal. You have the right to remain silent, anything you say can be used against you in a court of law. You have the right to an attorney of your choice if you so choose. If you can't afford one, one will be appointed to you by the courts. Do you understand these rights I've explained to you?"

The officers went through the motions of an actual arrest due to the fact that a few bystanders had begun hovering around. Before witnesses could begin speculating, the officers scooped Brandon from off the turf and flung him into the rear of their car. That was the final time anybody saw Brandon alive.

Sofia Alfonso wept every night her youngest son was missing while she mainly prayed for his body to be recovered in order to properly commemorate the young man for his vast achievements. The fifty-seven-year-old widow had grown accustomed to the results of any family member going missing after thus far losing two other members of the family to violence. Brandon was just the latest casualty of a war that had absolutely nothing to do with the future engineer, considering the family sustained the loss of one other brother, a cousin, and an uncle, who, like Brandon, lived a crime-free life. Once Brandon had been missing for the first six hours without a trace, Mrs. Alfonso was convinced that she'd seen the last of her son and went to church to pray.

There were two other members of the Alfonso clan also who met their demise on the battlefield skirmishing against their primary enemy. Brogan's brother, Joey, and cousin, Todd, were killed defending their family away from home, and, as such, RIP West Island Defenders Syndicate was stamped on their memorials as a tribute toward their everlasting memory. Brother Joey, who was the third of five boys, was killed in the largest street shoot-out in the city's history. On one side of the road were Rough Riders extremists, fully armed with automatic weapons, exchanging bullets with Defenders lynch men, who were trapped like fish out of water. Pedestrians fled for their lives in the centre of downtown while these two vigilante movements scattered shots heinously at each other. At the end of said battle, nine gangbangers, five Defenders, and four bikers were brought to the morgue, along with two officers who should have followed the crowd and fled in the opposite direction of the spitting bullets.

Cousin Todd, or "Loco Extreme" as he was referred to by his gangbanging family, spent two weeks in Afghanistan as a Coalition force member. While battling the Taliban Insurgent Forces in the war-torn country, Private Alfonso was shot in the ribs and narrowly escaped death after his convoy was ambushed in a small town outside Kandahar. The private was sent home after the incident and released from the army, and so he returned to Montreal to be among family.

The family motto, which was "Defend to the end your family and blood," plunged Todd into the middle of the war between his family and the Rough Riders after he came to his cousin Mikey's assistance one cold winter evening. A well-planned hit was arranged for Mikey, who had orchestrated the plot that destroyed a storage depot that belonged to the Rough Riders organization. Espionage levels of intelligence were brought to Mikey's attention suggesting that the storage facility was being used to store exquisite antique automobiles. The automobiles had been stolen from their wealthy owners and sold to foreign businessmen, and they sat awaiting export in the storage facility. The stolen car industry made the bikers an annual $500 million, which, like most of their fundraisers, went to "The Society" as payment for their judgment as overseers. The shipment of cars contained twelve rare collectibles that were all stolen from selected owners—eccentric millionaires who simply spent their money buying items the general population couldn't afford. Mikey and a number of his bandit friends broke into the storage facility, stole a 1964 Aston Martin, and set fire to the remaining structure. Non-distribution of the vehicles in turn cost the bikers respectability, money, and public inquiry into the business affairs of the bikers' club.

News reporters flocked to the U-Haul storage and rental facility located close to the pier on Old Notre Dame Street after word leaked out that the unsolved mystery behind the disappearance of countless millionaires' toys had been unravelled and solved, with fingers being pointed at the Rough Riders gang. Investigators concluded after checking the VINs of each vehicle that the vehicles were indeed being sought after, and further investigations were on the way. A few hours after the story broke, the attorney to the Rough Riders organization released a public statement implying that the club had sold the storage/rental facility to an undisclosed client who wished to remain unanimous. Days after the arson ordeal, reports reached the Rough Riders captain that Mikey had been spotted parading the town in the re-stolen '64 Aston

Martin. The order was immediately given to terminate Mikey and everyone who aided in the exposure of a major enterprise.

Cousin Todd received his honourable discharge for bravery from the army and sought to join the police cadets before discovering that the criminal histories of certain individuals in his family prevented those dreams from becoming a reality. The ex-soldier of the 39th Battalion located in Surey, Quebec, believed in hard, honest work and devoted himself to working construction while attending college. Todd was returning home from classes one evening when he stumbled upon three uniformed officers harassing Mikey behind the Lola's confectionary store on Sources Boulevard. The officers lay awaiting Mikey and two of his partners after they'd entered the convenient store to purchase cigarettes and soda. The officers preferred confronting the men in a situation where they had the upper hand, and they waited for all three men to enter the vehicle before swooping down on them.

"The cops!" Ryan yelled, who, along with Johnny, bailed from the front section of his automobile.

The lone rear passenger was caught attempting to flee the vehicle and soon found himself trapped in a lion's den. A search of the detained revealed a Glock 40 shoved into Mikey's waistband, with two extra clips in the adjacent pocket. The uniforms and badges disclosed the men's ambition, but none of the officers aboard cruiser 516 were afraid to exhibit their Rough Riders insignia tattoos. The arresting formalities dispersed the crowd, which was convinced of the young banger's guilt by the fleeing of his friends who also occupied the car.

Matters grew worse for Mikey once he was placed in the rear of the cruiser with both hands tied behind his back. The officer seated in the rear could barely wait for the cruiser to go into motion as he repeatedly rammed his metallic baton/flashlight into Mikey's ribs. The long ride to the Cop Shop Mikey expected was short and decisive as the coppers simply circled the building and parked in the rear.

After cracking a rib or two, the rear officer demanded, "You fuckers like to take things that are not yours? I'm going to ask you one time only—where's the car?"

Mikey could feel a distinctive change in the amounts of oxygen he was allowed to inhale, and he crouched over in an attempt to protect his ribs. The groans he muffled were difficult to transform into words, and every muscle in his body tightened for what might transpire. The officer came down in the centre of his back with a thundering blow, which prompted Mikey to sit upright with pain gushing to the tips of his toes. All at once, the cruiser came to a halt as the punishers' friends decided to join the party.

All Mikey could hear being yelled by one of the front passengers was, "Get his ass out the back of my cruiser before he starts bleeding his shit all over my seats!"

The door opened and a boot to the right arm pitched Mikey directly from the seat out onto the pavement. Todd came by after the officers had had their way with Mikey, who could only manage to crouch in order to protect himself. The student was seeking the shortcut through a hole in the fence behind the confectionary store when he caught a glimpse of the winter jacket the beaten man was wearing. With all three officers putting a clubbing on Mikey, they had no inkling that they were being watched, and Todd began looking around for means to equalize the battlefield.

From the glooms and shadows of the dark came a soda bottle, which opened a huge laceration above the driver's left eye. The officer grabbed for his face as if a flash fire had burned off the skin. Todd used his combat training to manoeuvre himself before hurling his second article at the frightened policemen. By the time the brick collided with the head of the shotgun-riding officer, the decision had already been made to abandon their prey and run. The coppers released a few scattered shots aimed at convincing their antagonists to remain at bay while they hastily made their escape.

After personally witnessing the evil that those who had sworn to defend so mindfully commit, Todd changed his perspective on life and joined the vigilante movement. "Loco Extreme" soon changed the tactical approach to dealing with the enemy as he inaugurated the art of bomb explosions. Within the coming weeks, Todd became one of the most infamous men in the Defenders' history after levelling the Rough Riders' clubhouse with a bomb that drew national attention, prompting government officials to question whether it was related to overseas terrorist activities or if bombs were now a part of the daily lives of Canadians. Todd made his enemies cower, prompting more phone conferences between bikers than ever before registered in their history.

Todd was assassinated, along with a hooker he'd only recently acquired, by an officer of the law who pulled him over, claiming he'd run a red light. The officer collected Todd's driver's license, car registration, and proof of insurance, returned to his cruiser and pretended to be issuing a ticket before returning with his side arm cocked and ready to fire. The officer shot and killed Todd before turning the gun at the lone female, who had her index finger shot clean off after attempting to block the shots fired at her with both of her hands. The officer checked Todd's vital signs to be sure that he'd died and tossed the weapon used to kill both victims onto Todd's lap before returning to his vehicle. The copper cancelled the flashing lights and slowly left the scene, without so much as a call to emergency assistance to report the incident.

Part 19

MISS SAMANTHA TEA made her living by cleaning office buildings after hours for Molly Maid Services. The morning following her son's altercationwith his fellow brothers in arms, Samantha returned home completely unaware of the developments. There was a huge commotion with members from the press, law enforcement personnel, and emergency handlers parading in front of the maid's apartment building. At first glance, the thought of a disaster such as fire striking her building went through her mind, and her health condition prompted her to gasp for additional oxygen. The single mother of three was bombarded with reporters immediately after exiting her co-worker's vehicle a few feet away from the pile of emergency wagons. Neither of the janitorial employees figured the huge crowd they speculated about previously was awaiting one of them, and an array of questions fluttered in from the many reporters scattered across the walkway.

"Are you hiding your son the traitor inside your apartment, Ms. Tea?"

"Can you tell us why are there MPs searching your apartment?"

"Have you been in contact with your son?"

"Do you know where or did you instruct your son to hide from authorities?"

There were also parents of a couple of the young men who'd lost their lives in the shoot-out among the vultures scavenging for something to report. Those grieving parents were sure to voice their anger at a parent who had struggled to provide for her children and had taught them wrong from right since Day One.

An angry father yelled, "What kind of a fucking parent are you? They should try you instead of your butcher son!"

A grieving mother cried, "Your animal murdered my son! I want you to always remember that! Murderer, murderer, murderer!"

Another female shouted, "I pray they find your son and give him the same opportunity he gave my boy!"

Samantha's entire focus was on her youngest son of thirteen years, who was her sole responsibility because he was still a minor. The maid hastened her pace to the front entrance, having to use force to clear a path through the hounding reporters and hecklers. Once inside the building that prohibited loiterers and solicitors from entering, Samantha rode the elevator to her tenth-story apartment, hesitant to find out if her premises were being searched by law officials.

There were law officials from the Canadian Army Military Police, the Ottawa Police Department, Royal Canadian Mounted Police, and gentlemen in suits and other personnel in green uniforms strolling all over her hallway whose job classifications Samantha did not acquire. An officer who was stationed at the end of the hall halted Samantha as she stepped from the elevator. The maid franticly identified herself before she was allowed to proceed onward. The fatigued maid, who'd been toiling since 10:30 the previous evening, hastily found her son, who'd received the fright of his life when the SWAT team barged into his home.

"For God's sake, what the hell is going on around here?" Samantha screamed once she'd gained a hold of her son.

"Mom, they're looking for James! They said he ran off here after some shoot-out last night! Mom, they scared the Jesus out of me and I think they made me pee my bed!"

An officer in a green suit walked over to Samantha and her boy and introduced himself. The officer was placed in charge of apprehending Sergeant James Tea in order for the Awoled soldier to be court-martialled and sentenced.

"Hello, madam. My name is Christophe Lavoie. I'm with the Army

Corrections Division, and I have been placed in charge of capturing your son. I would very much appreciate your cooperation in this matter so we can apprehend James without any further altercations," began the French native officer.

"Did you boys find James anywhere on the premises?" Samantha asked.

"I'm afraid we didn't, madam."

"Okay, then. You and your gun-wielding buddies ran up in here, scared the shit out of boy, nobody removed their shoes and so now my house is filthy, and now you're trying to get me to snitch on one of my other boys? Well, a bunch of know-it-all reporters just tarnished the shit out of me. I came home to relax, take a pee, have a cup of tea, and get some rest, but you and your evidence-collecting friends won't let that happen. Now I want everybody out of my house right now, before I catch a case for fucking up one of you, and I'm definitely serious!" Samantha angrily yelled.

"Here is my card in case you decide to assist us in this matter!" Monsieur Lavoie indicated as he scampered behind his peers.

The officers were in the process of evacuating the premises when Samantha's home phone rang. Speculations of it being the man they sought hindered a few members of the Military Police, who awaited confirmation of who the caller was. Samantha walked over to the phone in the hallway and answered it. The caller was her girlfriend from work who had dropped her off who sought to uplift her co-worker's spirit after receiving the full disclosure of what occurred.

"Lord have mercy! Are you okay, baby? Those vultures wouldn't even allow you to get into your building. You know I had to get home to the baby, or I would have kicked a hole through them reporters for you!" Samantha's co-worker exclaimed.

"Grace, I feel like I'm a criminal in my own home. All sorts of police all over the house, in my panty drawers and Lord knows where else!"

The officers exited Samantha's domain once they became satisfied the caller was not the man they sought. Samantha's friend, Grace, who had been watching the morning's news-cast, suggested she tune in to CBC for further details on the story. The references toward her son immediately overwhelmed Samantha, whose attention was focused on the fact that her high school pupil declared he was leaving for school.

Moments after the clack of the door sounded, Samantha realized her teenaged son had unknowingly departed for the vultures before she could advise him to abstain from school for a few days.

"Oh my God, Gracie! My baby left for school!" Samantha exclaimed as she flung the phone onto the sofa and ran out the front door.

Samantha opened the main entrance to the building and found her son being gang-rushed by the slew of reporters camping out in front her apartment building. The frustrations of the morning brought a vicious mother to the forefront as Samantha began slandering the reporters who had earlier taken advantage of her.

"You parasites stay away from my boy, and if any of you have any problem with any of my children, you bitches know where I live. As a parent, I raised my children knowing right from wrong, and if later in life they decide to mess up, I can't guide them forever. When my boy was throwing his life on the line for this country, he was something to you then. Now a little mishap occurs and he's public enemy number one. Stay away from me and my family and that is all I have to report!"

James Tea sat with a bottle of Canadian Club whiskey while watching the skit of his mother against the media. There were muscled guards racing around him as the voice of a doctor in an adjoining room yelled for additional support. The loud murmurs of Damian could be heard throughout the house as a physician attempted to save his arm, which was almost severed from his body. The physician could be heard barking instructions at the apprentices who aided him due to their inability to stabilize the patient. Damian scratched, punched, and kicked those attempting to subdue him as the wound with the unbearable pain that had rendered him unconscious twice before threatened his existence with the huge amount of blood lost.

James was a twelve-year veteran of the army who knew and understood the penalties and consequences of his actions. James expected to be named the principal conspirator behind the mishap that occurred and would welcome an eternal life sentence behind bars, although he knew the contrary was imminent. There was such a stir inside the guest house/guard quarters attached to Kevin's mansion that morning that it lead to the soldier believing he was still on base with the family he'd gone to war with. A number of well-dressed men came marching down the stairs from the third level as the intoxicated soldier raised his bottle of liquor in appreciation of his mother's valour before reacquiring the taste of the Canadian Club whiskey.

"That's right, Mom. Tell them motherfuckers like it is. Fuck them all, anyways. I don't need them!" James yelled.

The men walked to the main house and entered the premises from the side door that led to the grounds. They met with Kevin and went over a few details regarding their tasks before exiting through the main entrance. The men surrounded and ushered their client into an awaiting SUV before dividing their remaining bodies between the two vehicles. The identical SUVs speed off along the half-mile before reaching the main guard's gate, which was always tightly guarded by a number of well-armed men who also patrolled the terrain surrounding the property. After clearing the main guard's shed, the men had to yield another quarter-mile down the road and wait for the hidden patrol along the border line to remove a chain of metal spikes from across the roadway, which was the first line of defence against intruding vehicles. The SUVs drove another few feet before entering the roadway at Oliver West road that lead to the highway. St. Jean Baptist Fairway was one of the two frequently used routes into Chateauguay, with the next being the Pont Champlain, which was over thirty miles away. There was the Champlain River separating the island of Montreal from its Chateauguay neighbours, with the all-important Mercier Bridge being the sole means of crossing for miles.

Kevin received a phone call from his prized nemesis, Martain Lafleur, who called to offer his condolences on the retirement of his arch rival. Martain had organized a demonstration of force that was practically a page torn from Kevin's war doctrines. The overzealous Frenchman had in his possession the very long-range cannons that Kevin had speculated would terminate the war, with an ingenious plot to gain victory over a foe he'd rendered formidable.

"Genius, genius, genius! I've turned the tables, but I must give you credit on a plot well planned. I've got you now, you son of a bitch. Let's see you get out of this one, you black piece of shit!" Martain who believed Nicholas was aboard his convoy lamented.

Martain had anchored the two stolen AS-50 automatic sniper rifles atop the Mercier Bridge's overhead framework and equipped them with sharpshooters capable of centring a penny from a thousand yards away.

The phone call Martain made was synchronized by the Rough Riders' captain as a mean of inputting his final injection into the thorn that had ached him for far too long. With the termination of his dictation came an onslaught of bullets onto the travelling SUVs from a standpoint ahead which no one inside the SUVs were given time to decipher. The AS-50, fifty-calibre armour-piercing bullets completely severed heads from their shoulders, tore through the windshield, seats, and anatomies like tissue before striking engines and erupting fuselages in explosions. Once it became evident that the vehicles had been completely destroyed, the shooters armed the timer on an explosive device attached to the weapons before attaching themselves to a harness deployed from a hovering helicopter. The weapons used to deliver the tyranny that obstructed thousands of morning commuters were destroyed as the C-4 explosive blasted aspects of the weapons into the Champlain River and onto the roadways below.

Kevin knew his opponent well enough to take him at his very word. Once the threat had been administered, Kevin's fear for his son's safety saw him immediately disconnect the link between Martain and himself in order to alert those in charge of his son at home. The decoy, which was meant to trick onlookers, featured a Rastafarian attired as Kevin, along with his usual two-vehicle entourage. Kevin's reduced security force was equally as deadly as any twelve-men protection force armed to the teeth with guns, bombs, and more guns.

"Killa, link up Crazy Indian and the convoy and tell them to watch out!" Kevin exclaimed as he nervously awaited a response on his home phone line.

The telephone was answered by one of Kevin's Indian maids named Hyacinth, who relieved the gangster's mind with her mild and relaxed tone. The maid calmly followed her employer's orders, which were to notify all security personnel of a possible breach and ensure his son's safety. Kevin had developed a fascination in safety chambers after watching a film where the essential concept saved a family from invaders who'd broken in with evil intentions. The gangster insisted his son be placed inside the chamber with adequate help and support to protect him fully.

"Me can't get no signal from the phone in the van," alerted Killa after attempting the call a few times.

"Boss, I was just talking to Leo, and his cell went dead, too," the chauffeur advised after Killa's revelation.

A silent calm fell over the four occupants inside the dark, limousine-tinted Mercedes 600 Benz after the final judgment on who had been attacked became evident. Kevin withered away into the soft leather contours of his seat as he puffed the fumes of his marijuana joint through the rear sunroof. It wasn't long before a conniving smirk grew on Kevin's face, which was generally the indication of a brainstorm plot by the boss.

Killa whispered to his long-time associate, "Why you pull for a decoy today of all days? Something you never did before?"

"Knowledge come through all source, mi buoy," began Kevin as he inhaled a cloud of toxins into his lungs before slowly blowing it through the open vent. "You see the shipment me send you fellows to pick up? After the altercation between you all and the batty buoy them, someone walked right in and snatch them up the shipment without so much as a bullet being fired. With this important meeting this morning, me had to make sure 'bout some speculations me have. Everything else is just elementary."

The longer ride along Interstate 30 to the Champlain Bridge took an extra hour, yet safely brought Kevin and company into the city. The Honourable Sir Joseph McArthur had personally contacted the only man he believed capable of disrupting the plots of a secret organization intent on dominating once again the ruling and handling of the Quebec government. He invited Kevin to his personal home in order to avoid the prying eyes of the public. Minister McArthur had a fully scheduled day ahead of him, and so he chose the early portion of the morning since it was his only grace period that day.

The AK assault rifle that Apache had lying across his lap was so huge that they wondered if the guards assigned to the counsellor would allow them free entry. The 500 Benz came to a halt at the guard's gate, only for the guard to pinpoint where their host awaited them. As the vehicle pulled up to the main house, the minister's wife walked out to greet her husband's guests. Kevin and his entourage with their big guns and all marched behind the main lady up to their million dollar house. Should this intended meeting be a hoax, Kevin and company, after their morning's loss, were not willing to take any further chances. Proper introductions were made once the French doors were closed behind those involved, and the minister personally invited his honoured guests into his luscious home. Tank chose to remain near the front door in order to maintain a constant visual of the vehicle to make certain that no one tampered with the ride. Killa and Apache joined the minister's wife for a cup of tea inside the day room as she watched her favourite morning program, *The View*.

"Suzy? Tea for everyone, please," the lady of the house said. "So, you gentlemen are thugs from the south side?"

The Honourable Joseph McArthur and his esteemed guest both retreated to his office for the business of the day. The minister went right to the business he'd invited Kevin over for as he began with confidential tales from the past. Kevin refused the beverages and went right to the chairs and conversation, with business always the first selection on his plate.

"This country was founded, and then retained, by a bunch of men who own three-quarters of this city and 60% of this province. These men have placed into one of the highest offices in the land a mayor who has left the office in more disarray after ripping off the economy and small businesses around the province. The laws they've made are purely for their advancements, and now—"

"You've joined their den of lions! Why exactly is that, Minister? Because Richard Blanc is obviously the devil you're addressing," Kevin argued.

It became apparent to the minister that he was consulting with an intellectual of the handlings of government affairs. "My case is difficult in the sense that I have a family, and may I just say that my extra activities after work are not ones I'd want my wife and kids to hear about!"

"So they've got you, but you refuse to go down without a fight?"

"I'm a fighter, which is why I'm a liberal. Those pussies like Lafleur and Trudeau and friends aren't about to win like that. I already told my wife, and our little conversation here has given me the strength I needed to face my public! I may cost my party and followers an election and probably have to resign the post, but I won't give another party my voters like that!"

The name "Lafleur" was the minister's trump card, and he played it like a true politician. With government's backing, the already ruthless gang of thugs known as the Rough Riders would eventually possess God-like capabilities and the means to govern fully.

"Lafleur? You wouldn't be referring to Martain Lafleur's dad, Michel?"

"He's one of the heads of their covenant, as they so like to call their little gang of billionaires. They've bled this province from the bottom up since the beginning of time and are still as thirsty as ever, with their 'rule the underground to the senate' moto. . Michel Lafleur is the only man to find himself being chased by an entire police force doing two hundred and fifty miles per hour on the highway, then was released with an apology after the highway patrol finally pulled him over. . You would expect handcuffs or detention or something, but nah, the officers simply returned his documents and apologized for interfering."

"So what exactly do you need me to do, sir?" Kevin asked.

"That son of a bitch Blanc has been using the Rough Riders' power to influence key voters around the province. I know it for a fact, but I just can't prove any of it. What I'd love for you to do, because it's obvious I found the right man, is to find out whatever you can about these home invasions and shitty tactics they're using so we can shut them down before the final votes are tallied."

"I have been hearing a buzz about something like that. Don't worry, I'll get to the bottom of all this."

Part 20

MARTAIN LAFLEUR SAT back and watched the events which occurred earlier that morning on the newscast courtesy of the special footage he awarded the CTV news station. The entire household surrounded the boss celebrating as the flick played continuously on the huge Panasonic seventy-two-inch LCD flat screen television inside Martain's living room. The video was shot from angles that made it impossible to identify the shooters or the exact hardware used to mash the demolition. Liquor was being consumed in large quantities as the Rough Riders partied early into the morning, way before the sun actually appeared in the skies. The snipers who blasted the SUVs and their contents were being placed on high pedestals, and Martain paid the bounty to the assumed winners of the prize. After paying the snipers, Martain continued partying with his crew, and he vowed a city-wide party for all Rough Riders.

The liquor, the humongous marijuana joints laced with cocaine, the ambiance, the belief that his prized nemesis was to be placed beneath the soil, and a sense of freeness to party with the female after a year of abstinence all combined and influenced Martain to contacting his accountant, Luc Savage. The two had secretly discussed the don's intentions after ridding himself of his primary distraction against his affairs, and Martain felt invigorated enough to invoke his plans.

Luc had his girlfriend in a compromising position with his head planted deep between her legs. You could hear the moans and groans of his girlfriend throughout his apartment as she grabbed the bulk of his hair and tried to pull him up on top of her. All her attempts to remove her lover from the dining table failed, although she craved a thumping instead of the cheese-tasting escapade he had to offer. The personal ringtone Luc assigned to announce Martain's calls brought the accountant from beneath the sheets faster than the speed of light, and the bewildered female stormed off into the bathroom.

"You fucking bitch! You can't even fuck me right! You seem better off fucking Lafleur than me, because your ass is always available every second he calls!" The Female cursed then slammed the bathroom door.

The accountant quickly covered the speaker portion of the phone while praying his gangbanger client, who alone furnished Luc's lavish lifestyle, hadn't heard the disrespectful comment. "Morning, Mr. Lafleur. How are you this fine morning?"

"You mean you haven't seen the news broadcast all morning? Half the city is over here partying. Ass a matter a fact, that's exactly why I called you. Remember that little business we spoke about regarding the celebrations after my guaranteed victory?"

"Are you referring to the centre town affair?"

"Exactly. I want it announced immediately that this weekend we're bringing back the block party in the centre of town. Get the particulars together and come party with me and the boys afterward."

The accountant ensured the call was disconnected before reconvening the developing argument with his girlfriend. After tossing the cellular phone atop his bed, Luc attempted to enlighten his girlfriend on the errors of her actions.

"I'm tired of telling you these people aren't the type of people you fuck around with. I swear I'd throw your ass to the wolves if he ever overheard your comments and sent someone to deal with the disrespect!" Luc threatened.

The beautiful young lady the accountant had in bed came storming from the bathroom, fully dressed and fiery as ever. The female shoved her lover from her path with such brutal force that the accountant tumbled atop the bed as she collected her personal belongings and headed for the exit.

"You don't have to worry about giving me up, because I won't be here for you to give up, you thirty seconds fucking asshole!"

"Come on, baby, you know that's why I have to lick it a little longer. Don't leave, baby. I'll get some pills or something to lengthen the time, baby. I'm an asshole, baby, I know, but please come back!" Luc begged as he stood in the middle of the open doorframe, naked as the day he entered the world.

While members of the Rough Riders gang partied in anticipation of the glorious times to come, Martain found he'd gotten an erection from watching the destruction of his nemesis' SUVs. The Riders' point guard, therefore, remained in front of his massive television with a groupie sucking on his dick while the tilt of the SUVs being shot up played continuously. The original sounds of hogs or Harley Davidson motorbikes, which disappeared with the years of war, blew through the tailpipes of Iron Horses with the sweet sounds of yesteryear. Word had spread that the glory years of the Rough Riders were back following the slaughter of the only man to impede the Rough Riders' sovereign rule over the underground. Generals from across the province and beyond all rode the distance to convey their sentiments to the biker don after years of battling the same foe. Lanes of bikes spread across Martain's lawn, with many more entering the property through the huge, well-guarded metal gates.

"Yow, boss, it's like Christmas all over the city. I saw some of our Aryan and skinhead brothers showing homage by beating a bunch of Haitian small-time hustlers downtown. The word hit the city like mad, and now everyone is trying to show good faith before we begin inflicting our brand of martial law!" Ivan announced as he walked into the day room and gave his man a fist pump. "I see you celebrating in fine style!" Martain's long-time friend and gunner added.

"Only way we do it, bro, after almost a decade fighting that black fuck! Roll me up one of your specialities, because today we party, but tomorrow we remind everybody of the way it was before our sovereign rulership was questioned." Martain slapped the groupie on the right side of her head and signalled her to exit the room. "That was nice, girl. Make sure that I can find you when I'm ready."

"No problem, Mr. Lafleur," the very lovely blonde answered.

"It appears the Feds are going to head the investigation into the stolen military weapons, but there is also supposed to be some special detective for the army who apparently is on some related case. Find out what exactly this detective is searching for; maybe we can help him with it so he doesn't need to unpack his luggage. I'm waiting on Luc to bring my passport stamped and showing I was in the States throughout this entire ordeal, because this is one multiple homicide certain prosecutors would love to hear my name mentioned with."

"So when do we start going after the rest of Nicholas' bunch?"

"Let these so-called investigators do their work and go home satisfied, and then after the election when we're rulers of the entire land, we'll massacre them wherever we catch them. Before all that, I want you to get me a copy of the autopsy report. I must see the fucking name Nicholas Henry on that list. I must get that final assurance. And one more thing: Luc has a big-mouthed bitch he's fucking. I don't want to ever hear that voice again. She knows a little too much!"

"You're still one the most thorough people I know. Even the newscasters reported that Nicholas was among those killed. You got a lifetime to watch this piece continuously, so let's take the full party outside, because you know it's never a real party unless you're present."

Martain hated the idea of being drawn from in front his skit, but he had to admit that it had been ages since he'd been himself. The biker don had remained hidden thus far from the majority of his party crashers, who all attended to celebrate with Martain just as they'd bled and suffered losses with him. However, the don had no inkling that the handful of gangsters he'd celebrated with earlier had grown to such a massive crowd. The sun had made its morning debut in the sky to a crowd of bikers all intent on partying the day away.

The atmosphere at Nicholas' estate was somewhat different following the loss of eight veterans devoted to eliminating the corrupt system of the Rough Riders gang. This was the single deadliest attack against Nicholas' coalition forces, considering never before had they experienced such a high mortality rate. Nicholas returned home to an estate in mourning, with teary-eyed guards grinding their teeth in anticipation of a retaliation attack against their nemesis. Each security guard had bloodshot eyes from a mixture of the Hennessy, heavy tears, and marijuana. The guards at the first checkpoint informed Nicholas that he had a few long-distant guests awaiting him at the mansion.

There was a Lincoln Town car parked along the guests' parking spots that commanded three car slots. Nicholas, despite the horrific events, showed a pleasant gesture for the first time that day as he realized who his guest was by the flare and excellence of his chariot. There were regular sounds of dominos clashing against the tables and dice smashing against the wall while patrons' bids were replaced by the chants of cultural reggae from artists such as Jah Cure, Jah Maison, and Richie Spice, while those in mourning grieved their loss.

Nicholas' demeanour never swayed, whether he was enraged at the world, staring down the barrel of a gun, or having sex with one of his many concubines. In fact, the only person to totally alter his emotions was his son, Junior, who always managed to brighten his father's gloomy days. Before attending to his guests, Nicholas made a pit stop at the guards' house to settle a matter of extreme importance. The boss walked into the unit assigned to his guards and gun hands, went directly up the stairs to the sleeping quarters and dragged a gun hand from the comforts of his bed. The young man was whacked across the head with a police yardstick, which immediately opened up a huge gash across the gun hand's head. The young man was still groggy from being dragged out of bed before becoming discombobulated by the whack across the head.

"What did I do wrong?" The gun hand begged as he staggered to the bedroom door with licks falling like rain.

Killa had chosen to remain on the main floor, not knowing his boss' intent as he marched up the stairs without hesitation. The loud screams from Zebb getting the shit kicked out of him alerted everyone to the situation before the bloodied body of the person whom Nicholas blamed for the ambush came toppling down the stairs. Zebb's body fell head-over-heels down the long staircase and landed lifelessly on the living room floor. Nicholas pursued while instructing people on the main floor to raise Zebb to his feet.

"Please, boss, don't kill me! I didn't have a choice! They were going to—*ahh*!" The gun hand screamed as another guard put his Timberland boot to his ribs.

"You went from doing no wrong to apologizing for the wrong you did!" Nicholas declared as he planted the yardstick into Zebb's ribs. The boss proceeded to credit their loss to the Alliance of the traitor in their midst and the Rough Riders' mercenaries who carried out the hit. Nicholas vowed to avenge the deaths of the men lost before leaving the traitor to his band of misfits.

Nicholas and Killa walked into his entertainment lounge where his guest was being served a glass of Napoleon Brandy on the rocks. The waitress had just handed Nicholas' guest his drink and was about to return to the maids' quarters when she observed her boss and confidante. The waitress turned back to inform the guest that his sandwich would be ready momentarily when she observed the guest removing his pistol from the holster beneath his jacket. The glass of brandy had been released from the guest's grasp, and it smashed against the floor while moist liquid shot from the waitress' vagina. The woman found herself staring down the barrel of the guest's pistol with absolutely no capability of expelling a sound.

The shocking revelation of Nicholas' guest brought the three men to a showdown position, with the waitress in the middle terrified to death. Ernesto Lopez saw a face that had haunted his dreams for a number of years and was a split second from blasting when he saw the fear he'd lived with for years in the eyes of the young Indian, beauty. Killa instantly remembered the man he'd held hostage and robbed, although he believed Nicholas had sold him to the hyenas and thought of cancelling his mentor with his weapon pointed at Nicholas. The notion of Ernesto killing Killa frightened Nicholas, who simply aimed at Ernesto to negotiate his actions.

"E, what are you doing? This is my friend I told you about from Jamaica!" Nicholas yelled.

"I know him, all right!" Ernesto replied.

"Then put the gun down before one of us fires accidentally!" Nicholas said.

"Sir, I know I've wronged you, but give me the chance and I'll make things right some way or the other!" Killa advised.

As the guns slowly descended, the waitress' feeble legs gave way, causing her to tumble to the ground. The three men rushed to the woman as she fell only inches away from the broken liquor glass. The tense situation between the three men was calmed due in part to conscious reasoning, the trust factor, and the capability to move forward despite the curves life throws you. Each man apologized to the other as they attended to the maid, and it became evident to Killa the manner of love and respect Ernesto had for his long-time acquaintance.

The doctor who attended to Damian was lounging out by the pool with a small group of thugs, smoking and carrying on before he was summoned to help with the fainted female. Once the doctor saw Nicholas, he immediately began offering his diagnosis on his young cousin's recovery prognosis, which was quite positive and upbeat. The doctor quickly relieved the minds of the three men who ran to the Indian woman's side after declaring that the maid had simply fainted.

Killa helped the doctor to lift and move the maid to a more comfortable resting area while Nicholas and Ernesto went for a walk. The two ancient friends hugged and complimented each other, Nicholas on the esteemed gut which Ernesto had developed, and Ernesto on the luscious dreads cascading down Nicholas' back. Nicholas owed his long-time mentor, boss, and friend for all he'd been able to attain and accomplish after being forced to flee the United States in order to escape captivity.

"It's really good seeing you, my boy. For years, I've been saying, 'One day, I'm going to visit.' It might be a little late, but I'm here. I brought a surprise for you with me, but I have absolutely no idea where it went."

"Where did all this grey hair come from? I must admit it fits you— gives you that distinguished millionaire look. How you like that new 550 Benz I sent you for your birthday last week?"

"Kevin, I love it, my boy. I don't even allow my chauffeur, Rahoul, to drive it, because that came from you, so I drive it myself!" Ernesto exclaimed as he looked around for the surprise he'd promised Nicholas.

"How is business running?"

"Those federal boys stay knocking at my door! If it wasn't for my legitimate affairs, I would be rotting away in some federal institution somewhere. Remember the detective boy, Carbonelli? With blond hair, tall, with some dark blue eyes, who swore he'd lock us all up?"

"Ehee!"

"That's one white boy who stays determined to find you and lock me away no matter what, according to him. Apart from my problems with the Feds, who are the only disrespectful bastards on the continent, you know respect is due right across the board.. I receive no quarrels and business is always fair. Still enough about me. We can finally discuss permanent solutions to your problems."

"I received some important information this morning that is going to put things into proper prospective real soon. Tell me something: who is the highest-ranked person you know?"

The two men walked like brothers, arms around shoulders, as they travelled throughout sections of the house. Their stroll took them along the maids' corridor on the first floor as they discussed matters of personal security. Kevin's cellular phone kept sounding every few seconds with concerned friends seeking confirmation on the latest rumours. With Nicholas assumed dead, the movement against the Rough Riders would hardly be considered viable by the other key participants involved. Eventually, each drug kingpin from the Africans, Indians, and the Defenders would either have to resign to the consequences or team up with the devil in order to retain that constant dope traffic.

Nicholas had devised a plan he believed adequate to defeat Martain and his band of marauders, although the finer details weren't exactly hammered out. Hence, given the opportunity, Nicholas confided in his mentor, boss, and friend, Ernesto, a veteran of multiple drug cartel wars, who offered suggestions on how to attack a force almost twice the size of Nicholas' outfit. Ernesto, regardless of insurmountable odds, always believed in his once Chief of Business Administrator, especially regarding matters involving firearms. Ernesto promised Nicholas all the men available to travel he could find to assist in the final judgment his long-time understudy so passionately spoke of. In fact, Ernesto was in the midst of donating as many mercenaries as possible to the cause when both men became conscious of a rather strange sound. At first, the faint muffles sounded in the distance, yet gradually augmented the closer both men got to young Junior's nanny's quarters.

Junior's nanny was a seventy-four-year-old widow whose husband drank himself to death at the tender age of thirty-six. The old Catholic nanny had been in Nicholas' employ since Junior was seven months old and had become a staple inside Nicholas' home after vowing never to return to the horrors she endured inside the house she had shared with her husband. Nicholas was sure the woman had taken a life of celibacy and curiously pushed her door ajar to investigate the cause of the mysterious sounds. The door swung open to reveal Nicholas' long-time mate, who'd spent his last eight years in federal prison, the one and only Swarty.

Although at first glance the massive human before Ernesto and Nicholas stood completely naked with his back to the door, the Roman letters strutting across his back pronounced his name loud and clear.

"Swarty!" Nicholas yelled to his friend, who had the grandmother of eight in a rather precarious position. It was evident by the lack of clothing and the manner in which the big man worked his waistline that Swarty was engaging in sex, although his partner could not initially be identified because she simply could not be seen. The sound of his ancient partner's voice startled Swarty, who ejected from his partner and spun around without consideration of the actions he'd been performing.

"Miss Emma!" Nicholas murmured.

"Excuse me, boss, but I send out big boy in five minutes," insisted the nanny as she pulled the straying Swarty back onto her.

Part 21

KANE BECAME A different man after their father passed away. Without Eagle's constant supervision, the young native Indian began trafficking drugs throughout the reservation. Eagle was never against the sort of work Nicholas did for a living, yet he stood fast against the distribution of drugs among his people, who he believed suffered enough turmoil and poverty without the interference of such things.

"The white man brought my people alcohol and all the vile things of this earth to wipe us off God's planet. Look at us today. Nobody wants to do anything but sit around and wash down the poison they brought us. No way. Bring that stuff across the bridge where they can afford the high it brings, but not to my people!" Eagle warned the day the mention of the unconquered market was first brought up. Nicholas had always respected the wishes of Eagle, even after he'd moved on to the spirit world. However, the youth in Kane dispatched all sense of humanity and compassion after seeing his father's mutilated corpse.

Kane had been drinking and smoking heavily while partying the day away with a number of his warriors at the annual neighbourhood multicultural barbeque. The event was sponsored entirely by the Defenders and held in the Pierrefond district of West Island. The party was a yearly event where members of the community, gang members, and specially invited guests gathered to commemorate the multicultural society they'd built. There was a certain young señorita belonging to one of the prominent gangsters in Brogan's army who managed to captivate the intoxicated Indian, who seldom found time for any female not of the Nubian complexion. Kane was enchanted by the female the instant she stepped from her BMW coupe with her expensive Coach handbag, which she tossed over her shoulder to create room for the box of liquor she carried in her arms. The young native Indian sent one of his posse members to assist the female, who politely refused the offer. Kane watched the female intensely as she made her way to the gate of the soiree, where fellow girlfriends surrounded and aided her with the box of liquor.

There was a huge sound system strung up with humongous speaker boxes around the children's and the adults' poolsides, with local DJs playing the latest in hip-hop. Kane entered the pool area to the arousing accolades from fellow thugs who all welcomed both he and his entourage, who were among the honoured guests. The organizers of the event orchestrated matters to cater for the children in a completely separate portion of the pool, giving the adults more freedom to do as they wished. During the greetings process between the Indians and fellow Defenders, Kane sneaked a peek over Chico's shoulder and caught the young damsel sneaking off to play with the children who were all enjoying the pool and various activities.

The peaceful atmosphere was an opportunity to witness a tranquillity never before observed by certain roughneck shooters within Brogan's elite. The thugs laughed and joked among themselves as if they were of the same household since birth. Regardless of the peaceful assembly brought about by the gala, each and every thug stood ready to defend his home turf with his pistol concealed in his waistband and heavier firepower inside their vehicles around the parking area. Despite their era of warfare, it was beautiful to witness men openly enjoyed the company of friends as they played dominos, gambled cards, and celebrated among themselves.

Brogan chose not to attend the festivities following the recent occurrence between his friend Nicholas and the Rough Riders. The Defenders' boss chose safety and remained home under heavy guard, not knowing if similar weapons used to create the tarnish along Interstate 10 were still in the possession of Martain and company. The news inserts on the deadly attack were repeatedly broadcasted, although the reports on those deceased remained unclear. Nicholas himself had decided to go underground and remain dead until his grand resurrection, where he hoped to land his nemesis a crushing blow.

The multicultural festival went on regardless as the theme of "Community First" brought hundreds out to enjoy the festivities. The kids had spent the majority of the day eating various foods and treats while having the time of their lives without their parents. The parents, on the other hand, were all engaged in some illicit or candid affair with farfetched thoughts of their children. The young teenage boys who weren't attempting to score a date with the young señoritas were off either getting high on chemicals of their choice or shooting hoops on the basketball court next to the pool. There were a lot more physical activities occurring in and around the children's pool area, with only a few adults vying for a dip in the warm waters. Most of the men chose to drink, converse among themselves, or play social games while watching the ladies tour about in their sexy swimsuit outfits. The women, on the other hand, did as ladies in packs, which was to gossip about everything from their Gucci bags to who their favourite actor was sleeping with.

Khai, Samuel, Malki, and Kevan from Kane's rebel Indians struck up a challenge against members of the Defenders after Khai submitted that the Defenders had no skill or flair atop a high powered motorcycle. A large number of spectators soon gathered around the parking area to witness bone-chilling antics atop motorcycles as gangsters illustrated their control over their monster bikes.

An ace shooter named Juan Sanchez said, "All right, who's putting up what? I got a hundred here that says Defenders all the way!"

"You boys poor around here or what? I got five bills that says the Indians are taking it all. Now who's got balls to take my money?" Jericho said of the Sioux tribe.

"Easiest money I'll make all week! I got my boys' back Get ready to pay me, Jerry!" Carmichael yelled.

Khai began the stunt show with a rear-wheel wheelie, which he maintained from one end of the parking lot to the other. Such an amazing feat was topped by Eddie, who began with a rear-wheel wheelie before switching to the front wheel for his grand finale. The Hurricane bike Eddie rode held him hunched over the handlebars as he rode the front wheel for almost a hundred yards. The surrounding crowd cheered for Khai's spectacular antics, yet screamed for the grand theatrics Chico performed.

Malki positioned himself over the front fender of his motorbike and took off on that lone wheel down the long parking aisle. Once the ponytail-wearing Indian got to the end of the parking area, he immediately switched atop the bike and, with the same wheel extended high into the air, rode back to the starting point. The crowd may have chosen to render a biased decision against Khai, but they were impressed to the point of shouting at the antics of young Malki atop his Ninja.

Carlos Alvarez, who was the lone child to Felix and Maria Alvarez, went against his parents' wishes by joining the neighbourhood gang of thugs instead of acquiring a trade and working. The twenty year old attempted the same difficult manoeuvre his counterpart had succeeded, and crashed his bike after it tossed him a good twenty yards. Friends of the young daredevil rushed to his side, as he was a bit slow getting to his feet. However, once the wooziness cleared from Carlos' head, he immediately pounced to his feet and indicated he was okay.

Kevan had those in attendance in awe as he handled his Suzuki like a piece of paper by standing basically on the side of the bike and riding with the bike almost touching the ground. He brought it to a standstill before bouncing off either wheel like a bouncing ball, and then flipping the rear of his bike completely around after coming to a pin stop on the front tire. Samuel joined in on the act during Kevan's performance and brought the house down as both men exchanged handlings of their bike in mid-pass. Both men began at separate ends of the parking lot and charged at each other. A third of the way along, both men mounted their bikes and slowed down to make the bike switch. The crowd went ballistic as both men returned to the point where they began before swapping the bikes again with the same amazing tactics.

The competition seemed finalized; however, Young Jit of the Defenders had one manoeuvre he simply had to perform. The youngest of the Defenders' shooters began with an ordinary ride before flipping himself upside down to where he was sitting on his head while riding. While the crowd continued its usual frenzy, Khai came back with his second stunt, which brought the noise decibels to their all-time high.

Khai began by lifting his front tire off the ground before bringing himself to a handstand while operating the motorbike.

"Give it to the Indians! They killed that shit!"

Another spectator added, "Oh, shit! Did you see that? That was tight! Indians! Indians! Indians!"

"Indians! Indians !" Everyone who appreciated the demonstrations shouted.

Two teenage kids from the West Island territories rode their BMX bicycles into the centre of the action and began dazzling everyone with their style and pizzazz. The teens were jumping onto parked cars and flying off articles while always landing safely on two tires. The young men twirled, twisted, and flipped their way into the good graces of the crowd, who were previously completely blown away by the men on the metal horses. The youngsters took over the crowd after a few gimmick tricks and impressed those who chose to remain, while the majority returned to party by the pool area.

While the youth of the future dazzled friends and neighbours, the contestants who participated in the bike skills contest high-fived and congratulated each other as they boasted about their individual accomplishments. Bets were paid by satisfied betters who joked about matters as they walked back toward the pool area. The men who participated in the motorbike contest had friends hold their weapons who returned the goods once the gimmicks were over.

As the gangsters returned to the pool area, an old Hyundai went by on the main road a few yards away with a loud bang caused by the engine backfiring. Some of the brave-hearted thugs reacted as if they were a Canadian platoon in Afghanistan as they all but scattered for safety. Several of the gangsters performed evasive manoeuvres as they withdrew their weapons and sought cover by either running to it or somersaulting at it before checking to verify the cause of the noise. Those who didn't even flinch began teasing the less confident in the group, who they assessed would definitely abandon their comrades should they be given the opportunity to see danger forthcoming.

The entire high-powered bike contest transpired without Kane watching a single bit of how his boys took the bragging-rights trophy. Instead of morally supporting his allies, Kane's intrigue had barely wavered from the enormous beauty he beheld in the park area, and he sought the proper opportunity to insert a phrase. The white Bikini Village swimsuit the señorita wore made it impossible not to stare at a physique undoubtedly carved out by the Almighty Himself. Besides, under his full-frame Armani sunshades, it was impossible to tell at what the Indian was staring.

Kane watched the female as she entertained a bunch of girls between the ages of nine and fifteen. The radiant señorita, who appeared to be in her mid-twenties, genuinely cared about the children enough to where she spent the duration of her time entertaining them. The Indian bad boy leader from Chateauguay was in dire need of information about the woman he'd spent the entire time admiring, yet remained a bit sceptical about whom to interrogate for the information. Once the gentlemen who participated in the bike rally returned from the parking lot, the perfect opportunity presented itself, and Kane motioned Chavo to join him.

As luck would have it, the female was a cousin to Chavo, who volunteered every bit of information possible. Chavo was delighted to hear a man of Kane's stature actually interested in his cousin, Alyiah, especially since he hated her boyfriend, who was a personal bodyguard to Brogan, the crew leader. Kane discovered that her love for the children came long before she became a social worker who worked with displaced and abandoned children. The more Kane learned about the beautiful señorita, Alyiah, the more intrigued he grew, and he removed his American Express card from his wallet and informed Chavo to pass it on directly to his cousin.

Khai and the other victorious stunt men began debriefing Kane on what tricks they performed in order to claim the entire winning pot and trophy. The Indian boss could all but get excited for his victorious riders, whom he knew endured countless scratches, bumps, and broken bones in order to perfect their craft. Kane's associate Jerrico went around with the bottle of Silver Patron they'd been abusing and refreshed every man's plastic cup as the boss toasted and congratulated his troops on a victory well earned. During the congratulation speech, Chavo dragged his cousin Alyiah over to introduce to Kane. Although Chavo was the one dragging his cousin along, Alyiah resembled the enforcer as she squeezed his humongous earlobe, while pretending she had no interest in accompanying him.

A long, black-tinted limousine sandwiched between two General Motors Tahoe SUVs pulled in front of the gate before coming to an abrupt stop. Almost everyone with interest looked to see who the client was aboard the limousine, with the latest rumours circulating that both Nicholas and Brogan were absent because they were both mutilated inside the vehicles on I-10. Brogan had speculatively sent a messenger to declare he would not be in attendance, while the highlighted footage of Nicholas' motorcade being annihilated ignited the curiosity from associates of both men. The men from the rear Tahoe climbed from their vehicle and positioned themselves around the limousine to ensure the client's security. Once the security personnel from the Tahoe were revealed, everyone looked in astonishment because they expected Nicholas to emerge from the limousine.

Killa stood at the door to the limousine and awaited confirmation from his client tapping on the window to suggest he was ready to exit the chariot. James Tea, Ernesto's personal bodyguard, and one of Nicholas' gun hands all stood guard around the vehicle while spectators craned for a look at the occupant. It wasn't long before the crowd returned to whatever activity held their attention after their intrigue subsided with the Columbian who stepped from the limousine. While your basic pedestrians returned to the fiesta, major players throughout the game sought to learn more about this mystery man who commanded the respect and honour of Nicholas' most proficient shooter, Killa.

The limousine and front Tahoe sped off once the occupants who bailed from the vehicles had gotten safely into the pool area. Once inside the actual grounds of the cultural event, Ernesto opted to tread about with less security at hand in order to lessen the stares and discomfort of the local patrons, seeking to casually enjoy himself. Ernesto remarkably chose Killa over his personal bodyguard, who rarely left his boss' side.

"I know you Jamaicans have a pride about you that can never be disputed. I also saw that Kevin trusts and knows you to the point where he is willing to bet his last dollar on you. I want to know if this is the life you saw for yourself, and are you happy about your choice?" Ernesto asked.

"I believe we're all dealt a deck of cards, and it is up to you how you play the game of life, because, like it or not, until God come for Him world we all go dead out like the roses. Cancer, bullet, gunshots—

all amounts to the same thing. As long as you enjoy the ride, don't complain!" Killa answered as they stopped to watch a dance recital by a Latina group.

"I see myself in you more than any other man on this earth. Like you, I come from the ghetto, ambitious and hungry to get make a better life for myself and my younger brothers and sisters. The first time I gripped a pistol was off a dead drug dealer's chest after some padres filled him up with lead and left him to die. I took that pistol and brought my family their first steak meal ever! Never before had my mother eaten a T-bone steak, and I swore to have her eating like that every day. I got caught stealing purses at seventeen and they were going lock me up and teach me a lesson. Luckily for me, the drug cartel wanted to destroy the local police station and sent a hit squad out to cancel the twenty-six officers on the force. I was beaten for nearly an eternity before the eruptions of gunfire sounded in the station. The hit squad went through and killed eighteen officers, including the three who were inches from breaking my arm. Once I got that invite to join these militia drug traffickers, life and everything changed, and the rest, like they say, is history!" Ernesto revealed.

Following the performance, both men walked over to a vendor's stand to purchase beverages and nutrition from a lady of Spanish persuasion. Ernesto had asked Killa, who he referred to by his given name, whether or not he'd ever tried a taco or burrito, to which Killa responded, "Them things there is not on the Jamaican menu!" The big boss chuckled to himself after Killa responded and walked up to place the order before the vendor froze him in mid-order.

"Oh, my God, no! El Chacha, is it really you?" The vendor covered her mouth in amazement.

Brogan was surfing the Internet inside his home office when Nicholas arrived with his rugged entourage. The black-tinted limousine accompanied by the Tahoes entered from the rear to Brogan's mansion in order to remain under the radar. After the morning's debacle where key military personnel of Camp Nicholas were brutally ambushed and killed, nobody expected the man himself to be among the day's commuters. However, Nicholas had important matters to discuss and came in person, which symbolized the integrity of his message.

Tension reigned throughout the city as the rumours of Nicholas' slaying provoked racial clashes, between minorities and Caucasian French Canadians. There were guards in numbers around the property brandishing humongous weapons as if they had been placed on military alert. Once Nicholas' entourage identified themselves at the rear gate, safe passage was given to them to the rear door where they were met by Brogan's girlfriend.

"Hi, Nick. Brogan asked me to escort you to his office," said the half-drunk female wearing a dark, see-through lace robe over her two-piece bikini swimsuit.

The female showed Nicholas' entourage the section provided for gun hands and bodyguards, where a number of men participated in the enchanting boxing challenge provided by Nintendo, courtesy of the Wii console. The two men at the helm were perspiring as if they were actually engaging in a battle of momentous proportions as they slugged each other across a huge, seventy-inch LCD screen mounted on the wall. The three-minute rounds went as typical boxing exhibitions, with both combatants fatigued to the point where they actually sat down between rounds to conserve energy while jawing off at each other about what they were going to do to the other the following round. The excitement had even the corner attendants fanning the flames, and one corner manager was overheard accusing the other of being enraged for not being at the multicultural gala while some amateur grinned on his girlfriend. The other corner responded by insinuating that no man could ever take their claim and it was the other side that needed to worry about their women. *What the hell is going on in there?* Nicholas thought to himself, as he proceeded onto the boss' office.

Brogan's girlfriend quickly calmed the boss' fears as she explained, "That's the troop's favourite pastime event." Nicholas' peeps settled in and engaged in the drinking and social affairs such as dominos while their boss continued on to handle the matters forwhich he'd visited .

Nicholas believed that cockiness on the Rough Riders' side had given way to the opportunity of a lifetime. The bikers' wishful desire for the eradication of their most prominent nemesis had created carelessness with their announcement to reinstate their blockbuster event, which had been cancelled since the beginning of the war. The Rough Riders sought to revive an event of gross proportions by basically shutting off the entire downtown of Montreal from Atwater to St. Denis along the

St. Catherine route. Such an event was first introduced to the city by Martain's late uncle and ex-leader of the Rough Riders, who rocked the entire city with the biggest party downtown Montreal had ever witnessed. From Martain's late uncle's biker party, where countless musicians and art performers showcased their talents along the long stretch of downtown, came the idea to host jazz festivals as an annual event, although Martain intended to engineer a day of bonanzas never before witnessed.

Nicholas envisioned total annihilation of his enemies should his plot be executed as the blueprints indicated. The plot accessed by Nicholas was diverce and complex, where he calculated every aspect of the assault, ranging from their interaction with every security detail, to the featured clash involving their nemesis. The importance of Nicholas' visit was to hammer out strategic manoeuvres before implementing the task with those involved. Through their discussions, the proper manoeuvre was determined on exactly how to engage the hundreds of police officers assigned to protect the public. Further speculations were drawn on what routes to offer to whom, though it was agreed that the absent party would tackle the final and easiest leg of the deal. The two bosses sat and talked for hours, with the sole disturbance being Killa telephoning to assure his boss that they need not return to pick them up from the multicultural affair.

Part 22

THE PARKING ATTENDANT parked the Tahoe and handed Killa a parking tag the moment they pulled in front the fabulous, five-star Queen Elizabeth Hotel on Rene Leveque Boulevard in the centre of downtown. The concierge opened the rear doors for the passengers seated in the rear, and Killa quickly ushered his four passengers inside the hotel. The choice of hotel spoke resoundingly for the men who made the choice, as merely entering such lavish facilities moistened the crotches of their female companions. The financially endowed guests walked to the reservation counter and requested two separate penthouse suites with adequate amenities to suit both men.

Ernesto Lopez had the honour of reuniting with one of the only women he ever truly loved, although they'd been separated for nearly sixtyyears. As a young ambitious thug growing up in Columbia, Ernesto was ruthless after poverty showed him little in the means of survival. Carmen came with the best of times during the early days of a child's innocence, when a young boy ran the school playgrounds careless and free before the proper distinction of having nothing sunk in—an era where young Ernesto learned that, unlike him, a great multitude of children brought money for lunch. Back in those harsh, early years, his mother sent him to school with empty pockets, and the government assistance programs were what allowed him the opportunity to fill his stomach. Carmen was the light toward which Ernesto strived, though she, too, came from a poor and broken home. They shared a youthful love for the short period when Ernesto attended La Matador Junior High school before dropping out to support the family. It wasn't long after Ernesto's departure before Carmen was sent to reside in Canada with close family members. Circumstances prevented the two from continuing any formal means of communicating, as even a mere phone call was somewhat of a delicacy to Ernesto.

Ernesto rented a double-room suite on the penthouse floor for three nights at a rate of twenty-two hundred dollars a night, and he insisted the receptionist keep his credit information handy, as he might be telephoning to lengthen his stay. The big boss then motioned Killa over and sneaked five one hundred dollar bills into the palm of his hand and insisted that he find a partner to serve as his honoured guest during his stay at the hotel. Killa immediately withdrew his cellular phone and telephoned his long-time girlfriend, whom he rarely saw on account of his lengthy hours at Nicholas' estate.

After the receptionist finished registering Mr. Lopez, the lovely French accent graciously welcomed their guest and his lady friend to the majestic Queen Elizabeth Hotel. Kane Esquada tossed his Platinum Visa card atop the counter, along with his driver's license, as the female proceeded to register both Kane and his companion. While registering Kane's entourage, who also opted for the same duration of time at the hotel, the receptionist handed out brochures that highlighted different amenities provided by the hotel for their honoured guests. The pamphlet highlighted their massage therapy session, the health and fitness gym, pool facilities, sauna, deluxe bar, and a five-star kitchen which were all hospitably offered to guests at the hotel. The receptionist also proceeded to inform the bunch that each room came with a hospitality kit featuring a hot bar, free robes, and comfort slippers, along with several other offers they'd find appealing.

Kane was another man all together, and his interest barely shifted from the magnificent creature he captured from the multicultural gala in the West Islands. The thought that the female belonged to another man who frankly wasn't aware of the new developments didn't matter to the Indian warrior in the slightest as he drooled over her every action. There was an unhappy glare in the beautiful señorita's eyes that Kane intended to transform, and very little else mattered from that point on. The Indian warrior had successfully swept the beautiful señorita off her feet the moment she returned his credit card and her cynical cousin held in restraint. The female later revealed that she had taken notice of Kane, but it was not until he begged her to marry him, which was the first statement he made to her, that she felt the genuine sincerity of his actions. Kane's finesse stunned the gorgeous señorita, who was silently searching for an escape from the nightmare of a relationship she was in.

Oh, my fucking God! Is he for real? I got a handsome, genuine man standing in front of me who is capable of protecting me both physically and financially. I really don't want to lose something special. Ah, fuck Eddie. Those were the exact sentiments to flit through the señorita's thoughts as Kane proceeded to strengthen his argument by tossing his motorbike keys at one of his troops and insisting she become his chauffeur.

The Queen Elizabeth Hotel was second to none throughout the province of Quebec, with its eighteenth century English decor throughout the hallways, chambers, and suites, exquisite service, and knowledgeable staff, topped by first-class cuisine that had intrigued and fascinated visitors for centuries. The hotel was a favourite to a number of National Hockey League teams, whose members highlighted their games in Montreal every year, as they must attend games on their season schedule. While Kane submitted his information to the receptionist, Ernesto continued waving his magic wand by summoning the concierge and bribing the man by squeezing three one hundred dollar bills into the palm of his hand. The proud Quebecois, who appeared as mighty as the hotel he supervised, quickly transformed into a sheep, as the persuasive money in his palm brought all his responses from there on to an approving nod. Ernesto ordered three bottles of the hotel's finest champagne for his chambers and a complimentary bottle for Kane and his lady friend, along with some other items.

The double-room suite that Ernesto rented was "divine," according to Carmen as she entered the suite. Poverty throughout his early years had fuelled Ernesto's thirst to experience personally the magnificence and splendour produced by each country from continents around the globe as he travelled to places he only dreamed of as a child. The hotel suite was similar to most regular apartments around the globe, with a living room, full kitchen, and two bedrooms with individual bathrooms. The concierge was at the front door with the items Ernesto requested before anyone could remove their shoes from their feet or survey in its entirety the luxurious suite.

Killa's date had not yet arrived, but that did not hinder the party spirit of everyone else involved as Ernesto immediately popped a cork of one of the three bottles of Dom Perignon delivered to him. The concierge had a maître d' assemble the cutlery and essentials prior to the arrival of the feast that Ernesto pre-ordered from the lobby. Carmen was still in awe as she walked around the apartment and admired the exquisite, handcrafted furniture that was all imported from England. A sense of royalty surrounded Carmen as she admired the magnificent penthouse view overlooking the beautiful city of Montreal.

Ernesto asked everyone to raise their glasses as he proposed a toast. The elderly yet jubilant Ernesto threw his arm around Carmen's shoulder and looked out into the night sky at the outstretched streetlights across the city. "To friends of old who are reunited with the joys of the present, I salute you and feel blessed being in your presence this wonderful evening!"

"Salute!" Killa confirmed, while Carmen laid her head on the shoulder of the man on whom she'd had her first crush.

The alerting rings of the telephone couldn't disturb the seventy-seven-year-old Ernesto and his seventy-five-years-young female companion as they wandered off to admire the enchanting city view. Kane who could barely wait to seduce the beautiful senorita he envisioned spending his life with, bidded everyone a good evening following the drink, and trotted off to their personal suite. Killa raced to the telephone in anticipation of it being the receptionist calling to announce that his date had arrived. Once it became clear that the call was indeed to announce the female's arrival, Killa waited intensely by the door for his date to exit the elevator.

Mocha had completed her studies at Concord University and was looking forward to returning home to Brazil to begin her illustrious career as a doctor. Killa had attempted to change her mind from returning home by offering to finance her own personal private clinic, which she graciously refused. The reasons for Killa's objection to Mocha's lifelong dream soon stepped foot from the elevator wearing a pair of Gucci jeans, a fitted T-shirt, leather boots, her Gucci purse hanging off the shoulder, and an evening sweater tossed over the left arm. The five feet seven inch, one hundred and twenty pound delight may have been adorned in moderate attire, but her sensational curves and eternal beauty made it impossible not to stare at the South American bombshell.

"Kadeem!" Mocha exclaimed as she ran toward her boyfriend, whom she hadn't seen for almost two weeks.

"Shhh!" Killa remarked as he placed his finger over his lips to motion his request.

The two embraced and French-kissed in the doorway before joining their host in the lavish apartment. Killa had grown accustomed to, although he had long outgrown, the hails of people referring to him by his actual name. For that one evening, Kadeem Kite was a mere mortal, without the qualities that terrified people in some instances. Mocha was very well received by Carmen and Ernesto, who both indulged in a conversation in Spanish with the young graduate. Killa properly involved Mocha into the bonding aspects, by fetching her a glass of the bubbly and anointing her with a toast to congratulate her on successfully completing her studies.

Both Carmen and Ernesto were utterly impressed by Mocha's decision to put the needs of her people first before all else and return with the knowledge and capability to help the poor and needy sufferers of the slums. Ernesto insisted on footing the bill for the facilities from where she would offer assistance to the lesser fortunate people of whom she so passionately spoke. "Any cause that is aimed at bettering the lives of the less fortunate is a cause I'll happily support all the days of my life!" Ernesto promised, who was always a man of his word. The feast that Ernesto requested soon arrived, and all four acquaintances sat down and dined like long-lost friends and lovers.

Without the unscrupulous eyes of the public, Kane was engulfed in vagina the second the door closed behind them, as he fell to his knees and immediately began dining. The Indian warrior had his proposed fiancée draped against the door as he licked every inch of her pelvic area. Alyiah ripped the hair band from Kane's long hair and twirled her fingers around in his hair as she cringed under the erotic tingles flowing through her body. There were immense groans and murmurs by Alyiah, who made no attempt to deviate from the pleasures she felt.

The extravagant exhibition of pleasure portrayed by Alyiah froze the concierge who was about to knock and announce the complimentary bottle of Dom Perignon sent over by Ernesto.

The interruption by the concierge offered key insight about the woman Kane had all but decided to marry. As the raptor sounded at the door, Alyiah had Kane attend to the matter as she scampered off to "freshen up for her future husband," according to her. The sound of the champagne delivery tickled Alyiah's ears, and she promised Kane an alter-ego performance once intoxicated. Without further emphasis, Kane answered and collected the bottle from the concierge and quickly filled two glasses to the brim, almost causing himself to trip and spill the alcohol in a hasty attempt to experience the transformation foretold to him.

Halfway through the bottle, Alyiah who rarely drank didn't wish to appear cynical or impulsive, hence she admitted her shortcomings to Kane. . With her intoxication, however, came a totally different woman from the more conservative version of herself. Alyiah was like a sex-crazed maniac as she attacked Kane and ripped every piece of clothing from his body. Kane, in response, quite frankly surrendered and offered himself as a sacrifice as Alyiah made him an offering which only magnified her stance as the future Mrs. Kane Esquada.

Immediately after sex, Kane who later declare that he'd been dumbstruck by love and knew he had to put that ring on her finger," had the hotel's receptionist locate a priest who would perform their wedding ceremony. The Indian warrior solicited a priest from the Anglican church two blocks away to tie the knot between Alyiah and himself.The priest agreed to perform the ceremony, though he first had to advise the couple that their marriage wasn't conclusive until the legal documents were filed.

Kane believed the odds weren't in his favour as he tapped on the door to the suite Ernesto rented in an attempt to conjure up a best man for his wedding. Ernesto and Carmen had partaken of supper with their honoured guests, who were busy banging the headboard through the wall inside their bedroom suite. The romantic attraction between the two elderly lovers was more symbolic of the times missed as they emotionally compensated each other for those missed moments. Ernesto answered the door after ensuring the visitor, and he became elated at the honour of standing for a man on his most important day.

Pastor Larry Forbes was happily compensated for even considering the ceremony at the unprecedented hour of 2:40 am, while his church received a healthy donation. Alyiah accepted Carmen's offer to stand by her side only after her biological sister remorsefully declined due to the fact she had no one to babysit her three siblings. Therefore, dressed in formal attire produced by the Gentlemen and Ladies Apparels Department inside theQueen Elizabeth Hotel, the Esquada wedding party stood before Pastor Forbes in holy matrimony.

Pastor Forbes performed the ceremony, although the wedded couple would have to return to sign the documents. Mr. and Mrs. Esquada were treated to the grandest of gifts, as the Queen Elizabeth Hotel opened their grand ballroom and popped a romantic CD into the disc player for the wedded couple to dance the night away. Both Carman and Ernesto joined the newlyweds on the dance floor and continued their affair before returning to the privacy of their suite.

Eddie got word that his girlfriend Alyiah left the multicultural festival with Kane and went ballistic at the news. Once the news was received, Eddie left Brogan's estate with two of his closest friends and went in search of his so-called property. Eddie was a prominent soldier for the Defenders, who hustled throughout their territory as a delivery boy for the products they sold. As they cruised around the city, reluctant to cross the Pont Mercier Bridge and continue their search on Indian soil, Eddie received a phone call from an informant who disclosed the church where Alyiah was to marry.

Eddie was late disrupting the wedding proceedings, as he arrived after the wedding party had returned to the hotel. Pastor Forbes rarely found himself awoken at those hours and decided to prepare a few items for early morning mass before returning to the comforts of his bed. Eddie and his cheerleading squad broke into the Anglican church and attacked the pastor, who was assessing the amount of choir magazines across each aisle. The disappointment of not catching his supposed girlfriend, who had neglected mentioning her intentions to part ways and move on, infuriated Eddie, who simply began pistol-whipping the pastor just for being involved in the proceedings.

"Where did the couple you married tonight go?" Eddie asked, before the clergy member slipped into a state of unconsciousness.

The pastor was beaten for almost three minutes before he got an inclination of what the intruders wanted. The bloodied clergyman, despite his antagonist's hideous actions, blessed and forgave Eddie as he lost consciousness. Eddie's accomplices weren't as comfortable pounding on a priest as they would have been a Rough Riders member, and they bolted for the exit before Eddie got through with his interrogation. The two Defenders members who accompanied Eddie looked puzzlingly at each other as a single shot sounded back inside the church.

An irate Eddie telephoned the informant who disclosed Alyiah's supposed location the first time and insisted the person find her present coordinates. The informant advised Eddie that he'd get back to him as soon as some information became available, and he began waving around his magical telephone wand. Within minutes, the informant responded with the correct information, although the actual suite number was not a definite.

The busboy who worked the graveyard shift at the Queen Elizabeth Hotel was toking on a marijuana joint behind the hotel when Eddie and his two misfits crept up on him. Eddie behaved like some rich aristocrat as he began threatening to have the busboy fired or arrested and charged for possession should he not respond to a few questions. The busboy confirmed that a couple from the hotel had indeed gotten married and were loaned the ballroom where they were currently partying the night away. Eddie noticed the slightly ajar service door and motioned his companions to subdue the young busboy. The young hotel employee believed they were making progress, and he hoped to hinder the person he perceived important from informing his supervisor. The only thing the busboy received was a knife to the abdomen, which paralyzed him immediately and sent him crashing to the floor.

Eddie and his accomplices covered their faces with ski masks and barged into the hotel in search of Alyiah and her new husband, Kane. The Defenders interrogators forgot to request the clear route to the ballroom during their question-and-response session with the injured busboy. The service entrance led to the employees' lounge across from the kitchen and managerial services, with the ballroom located to the very end of that corridor. As Eddie arrived near the managerial services chambers, a female employee stepped from the bathroom next door and surprised all three men, before one of the intruders frantically blasted the woman right back into the bathroom.

The initial gunshot echoed through the empty hallways and alerted everyone within the vicinity. Kane had heard enough gunshots through his lifetime to unquestioningly identify the sounds he heard, and he was confident certain criminals were about. The Indian warrior had begun moving his wife toward the alternative entrance when the three masked marauders busted into the ballroom. Protecting his wife was his priority, and Kane raised his pistol and fired two shots at the intruders, who all dove and hit the turf before themselves returning fire.

The masked intruders intended to cause their targets obvious bodily harm as they blasted holes into the beautiful architecture, aiming to create lifeless corpses. Kane noticed the ski masks covering the faces of his attackers, and he ordered Alyiah to run for her life. At the debut of the shooting, one of the masked marauders was shot in the gut, while attempting to evade bullets by diving to the ground. The Defender who got shot began hollering and screaming for his friends not to let him die, although Eddie impulsively wanted to pursue his targets.

The masked intruders could not afford to leave their ally to die inside the hotel, nor could they leave him to the authorities for fear of him being identified and triggering a full-scale war. Therefore, the two other Defenders aided their friend to his feet and escaped through the nearest exit door. As for Kane and his bride, the Indian warrior immediately chartered a local taxi to carry them to familiar grounds at his home across the bridge in Chateauguay.

Part 23

THE SHOCK OF being shot at had Alyiah's entire body shivering as if she was suffering from pneumonia. The thought that she could have been wiped clear off the face of the earth terrified her, and she clung tightly to her new husband's arm. Kane gripped his new bride tight as he threw both hands around her and apologised continuously for exposing her to the graphic reality of his life. The warrior Indian hopped into the first taxi he saw after the incident and headed directly to the sanctity of Chateauguay.

Once over the Pont Mercier Bridge, Kane instructed the taxi driver to find the closest Tim Horton's because he sought to soothe his wife's tense nerves with a cup of hot chocolate. As they travelled along Saint Jean de Baptist Boulevard, the driver observed that Alyiah appeared a bit ill and offered humour as a remedy. The driver insinuated that the vast number of cigarette and cigar huts significantly outnumbered Tim Horton's fast food restaurants and delis around the entire Indian reservation. There was a vast difference in the quality of tobacco produced by the government of Canada and that of the Indians! Hence, a grave number of cigarette-puffing Quebec taxpayers were inclined to make the short journey in order to purchase the cheaper generic brand produced by the Indians. As such, there was an array of cigar and cigarette shacks along the main roads around the reservation. The couple in the rear of his taxi chuckled over the statement, although it was evident that the female was still quite shaken from her ordeal.

Despite his recent brush with death, Kane appeared unflappable as he ran into the Tim Horton's restaurant to fetch the items he deemed vital to strengthening his wife. As soon as Kane exited the taxi, Alyiah began confessing to the driver as if he were her priest from church. The frightened young señorita told the driver she had just recently tied the knot, but questioned whether she'd made the right decision. The female neglected to mention the incident that brought her to her dilemma, although her gibberish at times made her sound at bit nostalgic. During her flapping-at-the-mouth session, Alyiah suddenly thought of a piece of evidence vital to solving the masked intruders' identities, and she went racing from the taxi into the restaurant.

Kane collected the beverages, a few doughnuts, and his change from the servicer and was about to exit the restaurant when Alyiah rushed him as if she'd discovered the cure to mortality. The Indian warrior's new wife disclosed her belief about whom she perceived to be the attackers who attempted to snuff out their life forces on this their most memorable day. Alyiah had caught a glimpse of their attackers as Kane fought to preserve their lives, but the ruckus confused her thoughts to where she could hardly make sense of what actually happened. Given the time and ability to reflect, Alyiah analyzed the entire evening as she recalled it before determining and rendering her final judgment on who exactly attacked them.

"Honey, I know exactly who tried to kill us tonight!" Alyiah began, before collapsing in Kane's arms at the thought of the implication she was about to disclose.

Kane guided his wife out the restaurant before she caught the attention of those eavesdroppers seeking a wisp of gossip. The pair of Esquadas stood in front the restaurant, where Kane made sure his wife wasn't delusional before curiously deciphering her information.

"Baby, I know the bullets and stuff startled me to where I screamed in fear of losing my life, but before I turned to run, I saw something familiar that identifies the shooters!" Alyiah commented.

"How can you be so sure about who it was?" Kane asked.

"Because I personally bought one of the shooters the Triple B T-shirt he had on," chuckled Alyiah over her words.

"You're fucking kidding me! You mean that was your ex?" Kane demanded.

"Yes, and I guess the other two were his little stoolies," Alyiah said insightfully.

"It's all right, baby. The Champlain River is not one that many people cross over into Chateauguay, and I guarantee they won't get that chance again! I promise!" Kane soothingly declared.

The Indian warrior was about to re-enter the taxi when four Kawasaki motorbikes roared into the parking lot and drove toward the yellow cab. Almost instantaneously, Kane began walking toward the men, who were all fully decked out in cyclist gear, as if he knew exactly who they were. The Indian warrior was a few paces ahead of the four riders when he suddenly dipped, made a one hundred and eighty degree turn, and began bolting toward the awaiting taxi. Two teenage high school seniors had just walked from inside the Tim Horton's and were heading to their vehicle in the parking lot when Kane scurried by the inattentive lads. Before the actual eruption of bullets was heard, Kane was positive he'd been struck, and he lay directly in the path of the oncoming riders. The two senior students went flying as if they'd gone skydiving from twenty thousand feet in the air. Once Kane made it into the taxi, he knew the youngsters he'd run past saved his life, although they paid the ultimate price.

With his patented 9 mm barking cover fire at his antagonists, Kane crashed on the rear seat and immediately yelled to the taxi driver, "Hit the gas!" As fast as Kane ordered the driver to flee the scene, he was back dousing his attackers with lead as he opened the rear window and snuck his hand through, while discharging his weapon. Kane managed to separate one of his attackers from his iron horse as the taxi went screeching out onto the main roadway. The heavy firepower from his antagonists, who were armed with Uzis, forced Kane to protect himself and his wife by shielding them in the rear seat as bullets shattered glasses and ripped into metal.

"Are you fucking crazy? You could have been killed! Why would you possibly walk toward people who are trying to kill you?" Alyiah angrily demanded.

"Two of those guys are wearing my warrior riding apparel. I thought I knew them!" Kane answered.

Reports of the incident were made to the different agencies of law, which scrambled police and emergency technicians to the scene. There was an Indian police officer parked three miles from the incident with his radar speed analyzer surveying the traffic, although his interest was being captured by his female partner on his cell-phone. The taxi and pursuing motorbikes sped by the monitoring cop at speeds exceeding one hundred and fifty miles per hour, with a significant amount of ammunition being dumped on the taxi. Officer Yukon Geronimo ended his phone sex chat and threw on his sirens as he engaged the disruptive vehicles wreaking havoc along the roadways. The repeated announcement informing all emergency personnel about the murders at the Tim Horton's blasted over the air waves the moment Officer Geronimo turned up the volume on his transistor radio. The officer listened to the report and the description of the assailants before informing the dispatcher that he was, in fact, giving chase to the shooters. As the convoy of victims, mercenaries, and police sped by Anjou Boulevard, a provincial police officer joined the chase alongside Officer Geronimo, who was also being doused with bullets from the bike riders.

The provincial cruiser, unlike the reservation patrols, was equipped with two officers to combat the tough situations on the reservation. The provincial officers joined the chase and immediately turned the tables as the bikers had bullet-spitting trailers interfering in their affairs. The barrage of bullets fired at the riders soon decreased their numbers as another of the mercenaries went crashing along the roadside. Kane squeezed his pistol trigger until the hammer cocked back, which signified he had run out of bullets. The Indian warrior held his newlywed tightly as they crouched on the back seat of the taxi, hoping the police would rid them of their antagonists. A detrimental bullet from one of the bikers shattered the taxi driver's skull against the dashboard, as the speeding taxi bumped up off the sidewalk and went spiralling in midair, before crashing against a huge pine tree. The bikers who devoted themselves to eliminating the Warrior's leader had to flee the scene as more police cruisers began emerging from all coordinates.

There was utter chaos aboard the vehicle that transported Eddie Cortez and his crew of mercenaries. The shooter, who was shot in the stomach, was twenty-year-old Miguel Torres, a high school dropout who lived for the thrill and excitement brought about through hustling. The driver, Marquez Dominguez, like his counterparts, was grass-rooted in the west end and rarely visited the centre of town. Hence, the directions to the closest or any hospital was to them like finding the nearest police station. The Toyota Camry they utilized drove about the centre town region as they searched for signs or indications of a hospital. With bloodstains throughout the car and on the clothing of everyone, Eddie thought it best they refrain from asking for directions to a hospital and complete the search themselves.

Miguel exclaimed, "Come on, Eddie! Fuck! Just pull over and ask someone for the fucking hospital! I'm bleeding to death here, can't you see?"

"He don't look too good, Eddie. I think we should pull over and get some directions!" Marquez added.

"Are you both stupid? Don't you think they got the entire downtown searching for us right now? If it wasn't for your ass, we would be on that highway back to the West Island right now! Instead, we gotta be riding around this stinking town searching for a hospital!" Eddie declared.

"Don't let me die, Eddie. I don't want die! Please don't let me die! Drop me off by an ambulance or something, but don't let me die, please!"

"Just hold on, M-Ten. We gonna find a hospital real soon," Eddie advised.

The driver looked back through the rear mirror at his allies and shook his head as Eddie ripped open Miguel's shirt, exposing his horrific wound. The bullet struck at the very base of the chest and slightly above the navel, which caused the victim severe pain as blood gushed from the wound. Marquez knew that without immediate attention his friend would certainly succumb to his wounds anddie, yet there still remained no sign of a hospital. As the driver returned his focus to the roadway, a blue, square sign with a giant "H" indicating the route to a hospital flashed by attached to a light post.

The driver said, "I just saw a hospital sign. We'll be there in a few minutes, M-Ten!"

"Hold on, my boy, you can't die yet. Nobody else I know rolls an L like you!" Eddie confessed. "You remember the time we met those sisters? The old and young one from Lavalwho we sent to Columbia for business? Remember what happened the first night we took them back to their house? You rolled a couple Ls and got them fucked up out their minds before they started sucking our dicks and shit! Yow, I took the bigger sister up stairs, left M-Ten this fool fucking this chick in the living room up the ass and her father comes home! The man walks in and sees this fool piping this chick, walks over, and taps him on the shoulder! You know what this fool says to this chick's father, who was probably having a heart attack? 'This ass too sweet! If you want to switch, you have to give me a few minutes to finish busting up this ass.'"

Everyone inside the vehicle laughed at the amusement, before Eddie continued his story. "M-Ten , the man couldn't handle it. He raced up stairs for his revolver and would have blasted this fool, who until now didn't even turn around to make sure I wasn't tapping him on the shoulder. Luckily for him, the father walked in on me and his older daughter on the parents' bed. That chick would have given me the world and I chose this bitch over her. Before I got down to tearing that ass up, though, that chick gave me her daddy's gun, a box of bullets, and all the cash out the safe. I had to push that man's own revolver down his throat in order for us to get up out there that day. You have never seen a father before who sits back and allows his daughters to pack their shit and leave with no arguments!"

"Hospital two blocks ahead. How we gonna do this, Pump E? We might as well drop him off at the emergency entrance. Someone is guaranteed to wheel him inside once they find him in the state he's is!" Marquez suggested.

Miguel began convulsing and grabbed on tightly to Eddie's hand as if grasping for added strength to help combat the pain. The wounded gangster's eyes expanded as if they were about to pop out of the sockets as Miguel attempted to communicate with his peers. Instead of words, a river of blood spewed from the injured thug's mouth, and his body began trembling before the life force exited his body.

"M-Ten! M-Ten, wake the fuck up!" Eddie yelled as the final breath exited the Young Gangster's body. Eddie pounded the young gangster's chest in order to jumpstart his heart, yet all his efforts went in vain, and Miguel's blank stare professed to what he'd succumbed.

Marquez pulled to the curb and stopped the vehicle two street blocks away from Montreal General Hospital. The lifeless corpse of his ally was slumped across Eddie's legs, and Eddie began vowing to avenge his death. The survivors aboard the Toyota Camry immediately headed for the safety of the west, and along the way, they drove to a familiar dumpsite to destroy the evidence. There was an old chop shop on the border of Lachine and Pierrefond across from the Old Garmin Steel Factory where the Defenders typically dumped vehicles they wished to hide from law enforcements. The old Frenchman who controlled the Slater's Junk Yard and Chop Shop had done a lot of business with the mischievous bunch who supplied 85% of the stolen vehicles dismantled inside the shop. Hence, for a meagre fee, extra services such as total annihilation of property by explosions, chemicals, or fire could easily be arranged. The proprietor at the junk yard charged the vigilantes one hundred dollars before providing the essentials such as gasoline and a ride home after the ordeal. The bloodied and enraged gangsters drove the Camry to the furthest region of the yard, doused it thoroughly with the fuel, and set it ablaze with the corpse of their fallen comrade inside.

The Press Conference

The media coverage of the Rough Riders' free event celebration for the public was ridiculous. Numerous news agencies from around the world flocked to the conference room at the Bell Centre, home of the Montreal Canadiens. The promotional event was opened purely to media in order for the celebrities and important officials to respond to questions regarding the event. There were thousands of fans around the Bell Centre awaiting a slight glimpse of their favourite artists, who all arrived in flare and style. The strictly Canadian performances event had humongous stars performing in the same show for the public in the centre of town. At the announcement of the scheduled performances, sceptics declared that such a line-up would be impossible to achieve with such little advanced notice. Therefore, as superstars such Celine Dion, Nickelback, and Wolf Parade stepped from their limousines to enter the media affair, it was no surprise to witness those same sceptics snapping photos.

The ambiance was somewhat inappropriate for someone seeking the top position in Quebec politics, yet Councilman McArthur sought every means necessary to gain a leg up on his opponents. Mr. McArthur excused his presence by suggesting that his thirteen- and fifteen-year-old children requested to join the festivities in order for them to get the opportunity to experience their favourite performers live. Thus, the councilmember was centre stage, praising the secret contributors to his campaign while magnifying his personal status in the polls, especially among the younger voters.

"Good day to everyone present! I'm here to help kick off this spectacle of magnificent music for the citizens of Montreal, Quebec, Canada!" The councilmember paused for the huge cheers and applause from around the room. "Before we proceed with the questions, I'm told that each performer will be available for questions, so please be patient; you will be able to get your questions in. This event was once an annual affair that was started by a late high school friend of mine, Mr. Yves Lafleur, who passed away a few years ago. Today, I'm here with my children, whom I've been telling about this show since they were babies. I've told them about the glamour and finesse of times past, where people couldn't wait 'til the next year to experience this spectacle again. I pray this festive engagement returns to its annual form, because I'm looking forward to standing right here next year as your host and your premier of this province! Long live Quebec and its sovereign father, Canada!" Councilman McArthur proclaimed.

The cameras belonging to the paparazzi and freelance photographers snapped furiously as reporters dove into questions pertaining to the rumours surrounding the campaign trail. Councilman McArthur shunned all references to politics as he insisted the event remained paramount for discussion. Mr. McArthur was sure to advise the public that a security team would be in place at the venue for precautionary measures only as they expected very limited incidents of violence. When asked whether or not he believed an attack inevitable, Councilman McArthur responded, "I'll certainly be there with my kids!"

Minister Richard Blanc's wife, Francine Belle Blanc, was devastated to find out her husband had a secret mistress who he confessed to fondling more times than he'd sexually appeased her in almost three years. The political celebrity, whose grace and mannerism had always disdained her husband's foes, decided, like most supportive wives, to remain encouraging and vigilant by her man's side. The Blancs discussed the effects and turmoil of Richard's decision, which was to confirm the slutty gossip in the tabloids instead of subletting their party's priorities for power-seekers. Following their decision on how to proceed, the minister informed his personal liaison of his decision to remain an independent political party.

Minister Blanc was not booted from his family home for his promiscuous affair because Francine chose to save face instead of awarding the media more ammunition for their newspapers. The minister, however, was tossed his pillow and a comforter and sent to the guest chambers until further notice. At 11:47 that evening, while Richard watched the day's news, Francine walked into the room with her eyes filled with tears and handed him the telephone.

The minister, who appeared to be dozing off to sleep, asked, "Who is it?"

Francine remained quiet as the tears ran down her face. The minister had been with his wife long enough to know her boiling point, which was quite evident by her breathing like a fatigued horse.

"Hello, Minister Blanc, how can I help you?" The minister asked in French, the language of his forefathers.

"Daddy! Daddy, I'm sorry!" The voice over the phone broke down crying.

"Guinevere? What's wrong, honey?" Richard demanded of his twenty-two-year-old daughter, who was away attending University in Vancouver, British Columbia.

"*Daddy!*" The female was obviously under duress.

The phone was snatched from the female, who sounded like her mouth was being muzzled close by. Mrs. Blanc covered her mouth in order to avoid from screaming as she fell to her knees beside the bed. The voice of a French-accented male came over the phone as the minister sat up in curiosity and concern of his daughter.

"Good evening, Minister. I'm not going to beat around the bush. It has recently come to my attention that you've changed your mind regarding the offer made to you! I personally believe young Guinevere here is a beautiful young woman. I'd like to get to know her under different circumstances, but for now that's all up to you!"

"What is it you want? Please don't hurt her!"

"Like I said, that's all up to you and how well you take directions!"

"Whatever you want, he'll do it!" Mrs. Blanc shouted in the background.

"Nice! Just what I want to hear. Now, if you and your wife ever want to see this girl again, I want you to …" The caller threatened.

Part 24

MARTAIN HAD A viable concern after the autopsy technicians reported "Inconclusive evidence to positively identify the deceased." The biker boss' corporate analyst advised him that politics played a role in the proper disclosure being released and, as such, a concrete summary of the findings would not be possible. The analysis proceeded to argue that, because they were so close to Election Day, every party leader would rather bury a topic such as Nicholas Henry than lose grounds in the election polls. The explosion of both vehicles disfigured the anatomies of all eight men, leaving only those with Canadian dental or medical history with the possibility for identification. Martain sought the advice of his closest analyst before wholeheartedly agreeing to proceed with the momentous event.

Police officers from the downtown precinct began sealing off adjacent roads to St. Catherine Street at 10:00 on the morning of the Rough Riders' grand celebration. Roadblocks prevented motorists from occupying the busy commercial and tourist portions of town, which are the districts that operate twenty-four hours a day, seven days a week. A number of semi-tractor trailers with volunteers began dropping off and installing musical equipment along the highlighted route directly after the officers secured and safeguarded the venue. There were huge sound systems set up every four blocks, with one main stage set up inside the industrial park across from La Baie shopping centre. While various infamous DJs excited the crowds throughout the highlighted route, the main stage would showcase some of Canada's most famous superstars, such as Nickelback, Arcade Fire, Wolf Parade and others.

There were a few events scheduled by the organizers that catered mainly for the children and their biker peers. Ronald McDonald would be at and around the McDonald's at the corner of McGill Boulevard and St. Catherine Street from 11:30 am until 6:00 pm, taking pictures with kids while collecting and lobbying for donations to help the sick children of the Ronald McDonald House. There were artists along the highlighted route who would paint patterns on the children's faces for free, as well as magicians who thrill the crowds with glorious magic beginning at 11:00 am. Hamburgers and hot dogs were offered to the children under the age of thirteen at more than twenty food stands along the route. Free beer was only offered to members with the patch or insignia of the Rough Riders on their jackets, as it was their day to feast, celebrate, and enjoy fully the atmosphere.

Nicholas' ambush went into action the moment the word was given to commence the spectacle. A number of the police officers who aided in the road blockage were actual members of the Defenders posse and Nicholas' mob. While a crew of police officers swept the area, which was a customary security measure before important delegates or persons of stature visited an area, twenty-four mercenaries outfitted like officers branched off into higher level buildings and businesses along the route. The glory was for no single man included in the ambush, and thus every crewmember involved was given equal share of the duties. While some of the mercenaries who outfitted like constables of the greater metropolitan city of Montreal sought higher grounds, a large number still mingled in the crowd, serving as decoys for the event slated to transpire.

Kane and twenty of his Indian Warriors were outfitted like the Rough Riders' merciless misfits. The Indian Warriors astoundingly resembled their biker nemeses with their patented leather jackets decorated with patches of various valours, plain denim jeans, leather cowboy boots, and the hog of the road, a Harley Davidson motor cruiser. Apart from their vehicles and attire, some of the Indians also wore fake beards, tatoos and mustaches, which undoubtedly molded the bikers' characteristics. The Warriors awaited their cue to join the battle, which was to come during the grand introduction of the host and all his merry men. Nicholas planned to have his imposter bike riders integrate with the last leg of Rough Riders to enter the festive area and flank his enemy like great war generals through history.

Scores of people from all walks of nations poured off each Metro station from Atwater to St. Laurent in anticipation of seeing their favourite rock bands for free. Bus loads of out-of-town visitors and local transit takers also ascended into the centre of town, while vehicle owners were forced to find parking miles from the spectacle. The streets, which were semi-tranquil during the early morning, were remarkably transformed to the vibrant atmosphere to which downtown is accustomed by 10:40 am. The trans-continental highway, I-20, had been backed up with traffic since 9:00 that morning with impatient motorists attempting to enter the downtown area. The pedestrian ambushers drawn up in Nicholas' plan took basic transportation like the metro and city buses to the gala. Theirs was a mixture of men and women involved in Nicholas' plot, as the Alliance forces came out in full to annihilate their prized enemy.

Nicholas had met with both generals from his Alliance force only once to discuss the plan, which would have been practically foolproof had not their opponent been Martain Lafleur. The biker leader expected an attack from the remaining rebel forces, who he believed must make use of their one and final opportunity to strike a blow. Moreover, Martain expected the political party they endorsed to jog away with the election and hereby hand over a "do as you wish" license to help his rebel movement in defeating the Alliance insurgents. Martain had implanted a number of insurance policies inside the crowd to mainly serve as backups should his combatants be unable to weather the storm.

Five minutes into the spectacle, the Rough Riders' event was already being heralded as the greatest event in Montreal's history. For a single day, the poor and less fortunate felt as important as the financially secure, and they partied side by side with everyone. Nicholas sat inside the Starbucks on the corner of St. Catherine and Atwater Boulevard, indulging in a cup of mint tea with Killa as the roaring engines of Harley Davidsons sounded in the distance. Both men, like many others of the ambushers' group, had to disguise themselves in order to not give themselves away to their opponents, who knew them quite well.

"What's this rumour me a hear 'bout Kane get shot after two time the other night?" Nicholas asked as he sipped a bit of hot tea from his cup.

"We so busy with Boss E. leaving and thing that mi forget totally to mention it! You want see is like di man come check we for a witness in his marriage!" Killa commented.

"Marriage? Kane married somebody?" Nicholas asked.

"Yah, man! Some shorty from the West Island who him thief from one a them Defenders boys. I gotta give it to him still, cause the gal pretty and sexy like money!"!" Killa implied.

"Yeah, mi get a text from him wha night, I guess that's his urgent message. Mi have to talk to him 'bout that still, 'cause at a time like this, them things there can divide we, when we need the unity!" Nicholas conveyed. "I wonder which man gal him took away?"

"When Kane called we and mention that we need to leave the hotel, him did say the man them who rush him a wear ski masks, to hide them identity," Killa announced.

"Hold on, hold on, tell the gal behind the counter fi turn up the TV?" Nicholas said after glimpsing news footage of the Honourable Minister Richard Blanc, who was holding a press conference to disclose his and his political party's future intents.

"We've embarked on a historic journey which will without a doubt empower us to make those changes we've always preached about. As was rumoured, my electoral party has joined forces with Minister McArthur and the Liberal Party!" The minister paused in mid-speech to accommodate the cheers and applause generated by loyal supporters of the party, who were willing to follow their leader to the ends of the earth.

"Once a politician, always a politician!" Nicholas said, who wasn't surprised to witness the minister rescinding his pledge.

"Same so mi tell yu, you can't trust them politicians for nothing! From mi live a Jamaica mi no fuck with them, cause come election time is the only time them know ghetto youths. Is them bring the most big guns inna di ghetto, then turn 'round and send soldiers fi go kill off the same youths them what them did give the guns them to. That's way from me make a money to buy my things, mi just buy mine 'cause me able fi a buoy come talk 'bout, carry back him things, you crazy!" Killa said.

The roars of what sounded like a million Harleys began showboating in front the restaurant. The two men, or cross dressers for the day due to the fact they were dressed in women's apparel, such as tank tops featuring fake breasts, women's sneakers, make-up, and long brunette weaves that pranced off each man's shoulders. Both men arose from their table and grabbed their full-sized Louis Vuitton purses from off the floor as they went out to view the bikers' spectacle. The gangsters in drag, depending on who you ask, made awful-looking women, although a number of men either tooted their horns or asked for the contact digits. As Killa and Nicholas stood in front the coffee house watching the display of Rough Riders parading down the centre of downtown, a few riders offered to take the ladies for a bike tour, although they were all declined.

Nicholas received a report on his two-way radio regarding the number of transports and bikes cruising along in the parade from one of the analysts he had in place at all of the surrounding entry points to downtown. The caller was unable to produce a definite number of riders, but she did manage to report that the Harleys in the parade were astoundingly scattered along a perimeter of six city blocks, an entire army by any standard. The female watchdog also reported that the senior advisors were scattered between the fourth and fifth blocks, with their Commander-in-Chief well protected among members of the fourth block. Nicholas desired such prudent information for the finalization of his tactical strategy as he sought to invoke his toughest firepower especially on those key areas.

Nicholas contacted Brogan, who was relaxing in the serenity of a luxury suite at The Embassy Suites hotel, located at 2866 St. Catherine Street West. Brogan was camped out as a sniper at a vantage point from where he expected to massacre as many Rough Riders members as possible. The chief for the Defenders misfits had just finished his oversight on the positioning of his troops who were scattered from edifices to the streets all along the highlighted route.

"Yow, Brogan, come in!" Nicholas requested over the radio as he adjusted the volume so his conversation couldn't be overheard.

"Go ahead, partner, I'm right here!" Brogan answered.

"The fishes, them entering the pond as we speak! Mi just receive the clarification that the head groupie them a swim around the fourth and fifth pond, but overall them stretch out over six ponds' length. Inform the fisherman dem, no fishing 'til the captain give the go-ahead, 'cause we definitely a catch some big fish today!" Nicholas instructed as he spoke in their assigned code talk.

A male pedestrian was walking by the gangsters dressed in drag and caught the final sentiments on Nicholas' tactical update. The white male had set out, like everyone else, to listen to the delectable lyrics of their favourite rock bands. The thirty-five-year-old bachelor could not ignore what sounded to him like the desperate plea of an attractive filly that he perceived was somewhat sex-starved. The indulgent heterosexual male diverted from his path along the St. Catherine Street sidewalks and rudely took Nicholas' left hand into his palms. "Let me spend the—" began the intolerable male before Nicholas formed a fist with his phone in his right hand and clobbered the man, knocking him out cold as he fell on the seat of his pants.

"Copy that, General!" Brogan responded as static filled the airwaves over the phone, which came about by Nicholas' TKO.

Almost everyone who witnessed the TKO of the woman-heckler, particularly the females travelling along, cheered and applauded the valiant effort of the assumed female gender. The thought of breaking his radio disturbed Nicholas, who desperately needed his radio to dispatch the troops. As Nicholas pondered over solutions to reacquiring certain numbers that weren't embedded into his memory but simply stored on his SIM card, a little girl who was skipping along the sidewalk in front of her parents stopped and bent to her knees in order to retrieve the many broken sections of his phone. As Nicholas stared at the little eight-year-old girl, he began envisioning his son, whom he hoped would grow up to become a productive member of society. The thought of innocent children being wounded bothered Nicholas, who had devoted his life to the extinction of the greater evil. The generosity of a child brought the little princess to returning Nicholas' broken phone. For her troubles, the mastermind behind what was secretly dubbed 'The Extinction Project' gave her ten dollars for her pocket.

"Thank you, miss! That was a hell of a right hand!" The young girl stated, then went right back to skipping down the sidewalk.

"Pass me yu cellie?" Nicholas asked of Killa, who was sizing up the competition.

"Hold this!" Killa responded as he immediately passed over his phone.

Nicholas telephoned Danny Esquada, whose number he'd dialled more often than anyone else's inside the country that it was imprinted into his memory. The phone numbers belonging to Kane and Brogan were given to Nicholas by his personal advisor, who was in charge of dispatching their personal troops at the safest and at the most volatile areas. Killa tapped Nicholas on the shoulder and pointed to the convoy surrounding Martain, which consisted of twelve riders wearing tailored Icon Leather suits specially designed to harbour heavy weaponry and to protect the wearer with its bullet-proofing capabilities. The personal security surrounding Martain was expected by Nicholas and his constituents, but there were six uniformed police officers assigned to the detail who weren't foreseen in the planning. Martain appeared cocky and dismissive as he briskly sat up in the saddle of his Harley as onlookers fought to capture a photo of one of Canada's most notorious mobsters.

"Let's walk!" Nicholas directed, and they began strolling through the huge crowds gathered along both walkways within the entertainment zone. Nicholas then telephoned Kane and his band of pretenders, who were mainly supposed to flank the enemy before engaging the battle and giving chase to the fleeing cowards.

"Yow, Kane, congratulations, mi buoy! Later we buss some juice, but right now, creep and come in, 'cause everything set!" Nicholas exclaimed.

"This the day we waiting for a long time! Say no more, Chief, we en route!" Kane answered.

Kane and his band of Warriors looked similar to Rough Riders with their multiple tattoos, fake beards, and wigs gushing through the air as they cruised along Atwater Boulevard. The graciousness of the biker gang crowned them royalty for the day, and patrons heading to the soiree cheered Kane and his portrayers as they rode by. The Warriors rode up the hill and turned left two lights before St. Catherine

Street before proceeding three blocks west and then north back to St. Catherine. The actual bikers were two blocks ahead of Kane and his Warriors, who didn't want to interact with their nemesis before they'd gotten within inches of the event.

The royally majestic treatment being showered at members of the infamous gang lessened their fears that any attacker would proceed with his intents after witnessing the godly love being flung at them. Therefore, the centurions who toiled at the rear of the convoy of bikes found more interest in gawking at beautiful women than ensuring their rear was actually clear. Kane and his Warriors sneaked ever closer as the train of Harley Davidsons entered the highlighted route, which was obvious by a huge banner hanging across the road that advertised the event, along with ear-blasting hip-hop echoing through huge speakers of the first sound system along the route. DJ Mes, a well-known personality within the city, rocked a crowd of young hip-hop generation students who'd gathered around the trailer that was provided to each DJ.

A single shot erupted at a distance, although it sounded to observers as if it originated from the northwest rather than along the trail. Those who actually heard the shot paused and waited to see the reactions of others before deciding how to respond to the disturbing sound. The spectators in the crowd grew somewhat nervous out of fear of retaliation against their hosts by members of Nicholas' cabinet, who were believed to have lost their general. There were thousands of sceptics who loyally supported their favourite rock stars, although they believed the event to be the perfect setting for a mass slaying.

The horrific screams from females were almost as loud as what sounded like a cannon, which blasted the biker at the helm of the parade completely off his Harley Davidson chopper. The bikers drew their arms and immediately looked to the buildings as incidents began transcending among patrons in the crowd. All at once, windowpanes along several edifices from Atwater Boulevard to Guy Street began breaking as the ambushing forces rained down showers of bullets. A few bikers attempted to utilize the banks of the sidewalks as cover before discovering first-hand that some of their so-called police security were actually enemies in disguise.

Pure chaos erupted with what seemed like police killing police, civilians killing bikers, and bikers killing randomly, while the innocent became causalities of war as they attempted to flee the battleground area. Civilians began breaking through windows in order to escape the bullets at their backs, as they broke into businesses either closed or open. Inconsiderate escapees were seen pushing aside children, elderly folks, physically impaired, the handicapped in wheelchairs, and even trampling over patrons who fell while attempting to flee the massacre. Ronald McDonald was greeting people along the route before being forced to kick off those humongous clown boots in order to run for his life once the fighting began. There were the tragic sights of a few parents' corpses protectively cradling their infants as their children either suffered the same fate or cried uncontrollably.

Rough Riders were falling like ducks of a hunt as bullets sought them from high and low. Kane and his Rough Riders-mimicking bunch began opening fire at the riders in front of them, who were fast realizing the severity of what they'd gotten into. The surrounding buildings echoed the sounds of gunshots and magnified the decibels, which sounded similar to humongous cannons being blasted from the decks of war ships. Those who were fortunate enough to escape during the initial surge kept their backs to the bullets and, in most cases, ran directly to the serenity of their homes.

The leading pack of bikers never made it to the event centre as bodies littered the downtown streets from McGill Boulevard back to Atwater. There was an exchange of gunfire along every street block for seven blocks as chaos and anarchy bewildered officers, who became as ignorant as the public they were scheduled to protect. Police officers soon became uncertain withwhom to battle, as the alliance vigilanties who pretended to be cops, began targeting corrupt officers as well as bikers. The first infringement against Montreal's protective forces occurred at Metcalfe and St. Catherine, where two Jamaicans disguised as police officers bushwhacked a group of four officers and killed them all. The disguised Jamaicans pretended that they were assisting a young lady, waited until their believed targets had walked by, then shot them dead from close range by scattering their intestinesacross the sidewalk. The report of police killing police changed the prime directive, as the real Defenders of Montreal became confused about who their actual predators were. Along another street block, two sexy-ass females attired in skimpy outfits opened fire at another bunch of officers, slaying every one of them instantly.

Reports of disrespect against Montreal police officers were being transmitted across the band waves at an unrelenting volume. Where it wasn't reported that officers were killing officers, it was said that civilians were partaking in the deed of eliminating the security obstacles. Hence, the protection that should have been awarded the host of the event found that they needed protection from the entire city, which had obviously gone mental. Nicholas' plot on how to puppeteer the officers at the event worked brilliantly, as soon similar altercations provoked officers into killing biker members who were merely trying to protect themselves from the assassins decimating their population. Remarkable amateur video footage made by a number of fleeing civilians captured actual police officers, who normally run toward disaster, racing the pack and out in the lead as they fled for their lives.

The street block between Côte-des-Neiges Boulevard and Guy Avenue was one of the two blocks entrusted into the defence contract of the Defenders. Eddie Cortez chose the best vantage point along that route, which was inside the tallest edifice on that block—the fifteen-story welfare building. The overall strategy devised by Nicholas was relatively simple: to eliminate all foes in your vicinity, especially the chief commanders over various sectors throughout Montreal. Should the ambush strategy pay gross dividends, those who survived would be much easier handled and the eradication mission would persist until the last Rough Rider was killed.

Nicholas and Danny Esquada were flowing through the crowds along the right side of St. Catherine Street like hot metal through butter, and they slew every enemy counterpart they encountered. The two men killed swiftly in poetic harmony as if they'd perfected their art of Indian Warrior silent assassination. The automatic weapons that rained bullets from above aided drastically the Warriors' advance as they inched ever closer to Martain's motorcade, which firmly held off all mediocre attacks. Killa, on the other hand, found it tougher to manoeuvre through the crowds along the left side of the road as his convoy that consisted of four of Nicholas' loyalists trailed their boss who was on the opposite side of the road by a few feet.

There were portions along the trail where huge bullet exchanges rumbled on continuously for nearly an hour. The Barrett automatic weapons stolen from the military held all attackers at bay with their capability of piercing cement walls and various sheets of metal. However, the limited amount acquired by the bikers encouraged their ambushers to continue the assault.

Martain's entourage was forced to dismount their Harleys, while members of the opposing forces found it difficult to overpower them, with their seemingly more powerful high teck weapons. . The Rough Riders' head honcho was tossed from his Harley Davidson, yet instead of immediately acquiring shelter, Martain, along with his security force, coupled up in the middle of the street and began pouring bullets at every police officer, Defender, member of Nicholas' personal strike force, as well as pedestrians. The full body armour cycling suits they wore were fitted with matching bulletproof boots and helmets; hence, while bullets practically bounced off of them, they shook the very core of their attackers.

Eddie Cortez had an alternative plan that purely called for the demise of his newest nemesis, Kane. The vengeful Defender assured Brogan and others he was prepared before the battle began, yet chose to stand and watch his comrades get slaughtered instead of ensuring them the advantage. As the battle raged on between Martain's defensive forces and their ambushers, Eddie glanced out the window at the fearless biker boss as he yelled furiously and dared his attackers to kill him.

Martain angrily shouted as his attackers' bullet response dwindled, "You fuckers dare to ruin my shit? I'll kill all of you bitches! Come on, come on!" The AS fifty-calibre, high-powered rifle braced against Eddie's shoulder could have ended it all for Martain with one shot, yet, instead of accomplishing the primary objective, Eddie chose to settle his personal grudge. The largest slaughter of activists against Martain's Rough Riders occurred beneath Eddie's watchful eyes as he conspired and waited patiently for a glimpse of one specific target.

Without sticking your head through the office windows, there was no means of viewing more than ten feet in either direction. As such, it was impossible for Eddie to calculate the exact moment Kane would be passing in order to acquire the single shot he'd waited for. Eddie placed his lookout, Marquez, outside the building along the northern section behind the huge garbage containers filled with rubbish. Marquez was supposed to inform Eddie the moment he saw Kane and his band of pretenders instead of actually reporting the discovery in person. As the startling eruption sounded at the door, Eddie grumbled as he walked over to unlock the barrier.

"I told your dumb ass to call me the moment you see those red-skin freaks! Don't tell me you lost your dam cell phone again?" Eddie argued as he opened the door.

The indignant sniper's hands fell lifelessly to his side as a chrome .357 Magnum was thrust directly against his head. "I—I—I!" Eddie mumbled before *boom!* The pistol exploded, lifting Eddie from his Timberland boots and flinging him halfway across the room.

Kane tossed Marquez, whom he'd held securely in a choke hold, into the office where the Defenders' sniper had set up operations. Marquez, who was a bit woozy from a blow to the head, had a massive amount of blood gushing from the wound as he went tumbling over chairs prearranged for customers. "Keep an eye on our little friend," Kane instructed his companion, Big Bear, who was a massive six feet eight inch, four hundred and thirty-two pound beast.

The sounds of emergency sirens could be heard forming a perimeter around the entire area. The Montreal police were delicate in their handling of the situation after confirming reports that members of their family turned their weapons against their very own. Barricades were set up to prevent anyone dumb enough to enter the war zone from actually attempting the suicide. News reporters from every media possible waited by the safety barriers installed by police for word on when it was safe to proceed onto St. Catherine Street.

The collision between Martain and Nicholas had finally transpired, and neither gangster sought to retreat. Martain had full confidence in the protection of his armour as well as his superior firepower, and he aimed to finally rid himself of the one itch he could never scratch. The two crime bosses trash-talked for a few ticks, which led many to believe they were fueling each other's rave, when in fact they were actually calming each other's nerves. There was a moment's calm along said stretch of St. Catherine Street, and Killa, who advanced along the opposite side of the road, realized his personal associates had all been terminated. Despite the calm within Nicholas' entourage, gunshots rang out in abundance along other city blocks as the gangsters reloaded and prepared for their showdown.

"You ready to die, you black piece of shit?" Martain yelled.

"I'm not here to talk and make friends, bitch!" Nicholas answered.

The middle of St. Catherine Street, of all places, became like *Tombstone* with Wyatt Earp and his brothers blasting against the Clancy pose. Before a single shot could be squeezed off by either team, Danny fired an arrow directly into the throat of one of Martain's centurions. The frightened guard dropped his weapon and grabbed for his throat as he began gasping and sucking for oxygen. Martain and company responded by awarding Nicholas' entourage with pure lead, which saw them scattering for protection, knowing the damage capability of the Riders' armament. Kane did the job awarded to Eddie as he centre-scoped one of the Riders assaulting his friends and squeezed the trigger. The fifty-calibre bullet that struck one of Martain's guards plastered the man against the Roots store wall, and that was all the demonstration his peers needed before grabbing their boss and forcing him to retreat.

Part 25

THE WEALTHY BILLIONAIRES of the secret society called an emergency meeting to discuss the atrocious events that occurred during the Rough Riders' day of celebration. Each member of the covenant received his summons through an ancient method, which was simply a note tied to the foot of a pigeon. The members would all read the note before properly burning the evidence in order to prevent the material from being acquired by infiltrators. Whenever there were matters of importance to be discussed, each man would be awakened between 4:15 am and 4:20 am by a phone call which indicated they had mail. The society member would then proceed to their bedroom window, where they were certain to find a pigeon with a summons attached to it's leg.

The location of the chambers of the covenant was known only to the members who'd been attending secret assemblies since their induction into the secret committee. Each member had his personal entrance from the limited number of secret accesses built around the city. There was a short distance to travel between the entrances and the assembly hall considering you had the knowledge of where to find an entrance and how to open it. A typical voyage to the covenant was like sifting through a maze where the different corridors and open spaces were enough to discourage any explorer. The quarters of the assembly hall were built beneath the city by French King Louis X1V , who sought an escape route should any attacks occur. The secret chambers were not merely lavished quarters, but were instead a mixture of grace and horror, considering the dungeons and jails integrated into the architecture.

There were jail cells and a dungeon that provided evidence of the horrors that transpired in the years past. Inside the cells were heavy chains and shackles hanging from the ceilings with the skeletons of the humans who suffered the ordeals still in their graves. There were whips and multiple weapons of torture inside one chamber that was obviously an interrogation room. Here, deep beneath the Metro and the underground pipes was where the rulers of all evils and kindness throughout Quebec convened their assemblies.

Michel Lafleur would visit his barber on assembly days for a trim and receive his two hundred dollar pampering before disappearing, thereafter entering the bathroom. There was a secret entrance to the domains of the covenant inside Lloyd's Barbershop at 6450 Sherbrooke Street West that was known only to Michel Lafleur and three other men. Michel would enter the bathroom facilities after his pampering and ensure there was no one else inside the washroom before pushing in three specific bricks among the many used to build the wall which would open the door that granted access to the assembly hall..

On the day of the assembly, Michel arrived at his barber for his 6:00 pm appointment. There was a man awaiting his haircut from the barber who complimented Lloyd while the barber first attended to his son. . Lloyd Bathurst had been a barber for forty years, and he personally trimmed Michel's golden locks for thirty-seven of those years. Michel had never once been asked to wait for his haircut, and Lloyd's barber chair was always cleaned and awaiting the owner's most valued customer. As Michel entered and went directly for his barber's chair, the kid getting his haircut shouted to his father as if some humongous hockey star walked into the shop, "Look, Dad! It's Mr. Michel Lafleur!"

The little boy frantically persisted to gab about "the most magnificent car race" he had ever seen, which was actually an SAAQ highway patrol chase between the boys in blue and Michel. Apparently, for his fortieth birthday, Michel received a Lamborghini Diablo as a present from his brother, Yves Lafleur. On the night of his birthday gala, Michel was caught by his ex-wife, Theresa, having sex with a female from the guest list. Theresa, despite the festive affair, vulgarly assaulted her husband for the disrespect before jumping in her Porche Carrera and exiting.

Michel wasn't fazed by his wife's reaction to his demeaning stunt. In fact, he and his new-found beauty jumped into his most expensive present that year and abandoned his guests to continue their private celebration. For five days, Michel and his sex partner toured the sections of the northeast where French-speakersdominated the countryside. The pair awoke the first morning in Quebec City and found a separate town to awake in every morning after.

On their journey home, Michel decided to exercise his newest toy and set a new record for the fastest time to Montreal from the provincial border near the Laurentians. The Lamborghini sports car roared as it massacred Interstate 30 at speeds described by the Highway Commission as "dangerous" and "suicidal." Michel's lady friend readjusted her seat and reclined to a more comfortable position. As she put it, "You gotta allow boys to be boys!" Pedal was far from metal, yet Michel's Diablo was screeching by commuters as if they were crawling along like ants. The music system inside the well-tuned machine sounded with absolute clarity, and the Solo 11 laser detector Yves had installed beeped every so often to indicate it had obstructed the speed assessing of another highway trooper.

There was a police helicopter on its way into the mountains to search for illegally grown marijuana, which is a yearly battle fought by the Royal Canadian Mounted Police and outlaw producers throughout Canada. The Lamborghini was spotted by the pilot of the helicopter, who alerted his astonished crew aboard and began recording the event before radioing his allies on the ground. The pilot gave the vehicle's description and requested troopers from as far away as fifty miles ahead, as it would be impossible for any trailing vehicle to catch up to the raging Lamborghini.

Michel raced along Interstate 30 at speeds in excess of two hundred kilometres per hour. There was an unmarked police cruiser travelling along discreetly behind an armoured Brinks Security truck destined for Montreal, and Michel sped by the two vehicles as if they were motionless statues. The undercover officer immediately engaged in the chase, but, not wanting to embarrass himself, chose not to activate his siren and speakers. Michel noticed the increased speed of the brown

Chevrolet Impala, yet paid it no attention as it quickly became a dot in the mirror.

The billionaire was flying by exits so quickly that they simply began identifying each off-ramp by the most recognizable numbers. As they approached Exit 238 south of Quebec City, Michel noticed four cruisers preparing to enter the Interstate. The Lamborghini Diablo flew by the police cruisers that were aligned behind a tractor-trailer that was slowly entering the highway from the onramp. By the time the cruisers got onto the highway, the Lamborghini was nowhere in sight, and the officers activated their lights and sirens before attempting to catch the fox. The undercover officer who had secretly engaged in the chase joined the flock of predators intent on catching and prosecuting to the fullest the reckless driver and passenger.

Commandant Danzel was seated behind his desk at the Surette Quebec Headquarters when a roadblock demand came in to the dispatcher. A ranking official's authorization was needed in order to coordinate an event of such major significance. The dispatcher was somewhat amused that the officers seeking the roadblock were reportedly chasing a ghost they believed was still mutilating the highway! The officer making the request sold his position to the commandant by implying the Lamborghini was travelling erratically on the highway and bursting at speeds of up to two hundred and fifty kilometres per hour! Directly after receiving such a report from the field officer, Commandant Danzel ordered a blockage of Interstate 30 between Exits 221 and 220.

The Royal Canadian Mounted Police who answered the direct order to place a barricade across the extremely busy Interstate 30 responded as professionals who had been properly trained, considering they'd simulated the incident during training. Four police cruisers stretched across the width of highway while allowing a meagre pathway for basic traffic to slide through. The officers were given information about the situation, including the possible make of the speeding vehicle and its colour, without an actual number to distinguish a license plate.

Michel could see in a distance the flashing lights of sirens attached to the roofs of three police cruisers that were as tiny as little flies flickering around in the dark. Without alerting his guest, Michel smirked to himself as he reached for a cigarette in the glove compartment of his vehicle. The thrill of the lightning speed of the Lamborghini, along with the fingernail pinch of cocaine sniffed by the female, empowered her to express her rejuvenation, and she unbuckled Michel's trousers and began administering fellatio. Michel rambunctiously muzzled his head across the seat's headrest as the stimulating sensations of her tongue electrified his senses. The billionaire moaned and closed his eyes with pleasure before opening his eyes to a pending disaster.

There were six vehicles attempting to arrange themselves in order to pass through the police barricade as Michel came blasting around the corner. With his limbs showing signs of paralysis from the shock treatment being awarded to his genitals, Michel rammed the brakes and gripped the steering wheel tightly as the road beast came screeching to a halt inches from the Ford F-150 truck ahead.

RCMP officers surrounded the Lamborghini Diablo faster than Usain Bolt winning the one hundred metres sprint. There were weapons drawn and pointed at the driver while officers uttered threats and instructions before the fellatio-performing passenger came up for air and frightened the law enforcement professionals who believed the driver was the lone occupant.

"Oops!" The female exclaimedbefore throwing her hands in the air to comply with the orders being dictated to her.

Despite the weary officers threatening to shoot and maim the driver, Michel picked up his cardholder from the armrest console and slightly lowered his window before handing a Mountie his license, registration, and proof of insurance. By then, the trailing group of RCMP officers had joined the traffic stop and began assisting by offering protective cover for their allies. Motorists became concerned after the traffic was altered and by what seemed like a police station of officers engaging two motorists. People were seen attempting to capture the event on their cell phones, while others settled for still portraits with their cameras. It did not, however, take long for officers to resume the flow of traffic, and the entire incident went down as if it were planned.

The officer who collected Michel's driver's license was not at all amused by the billionaire's cockiness, and insisted the driver open the door and step out of the car. Michel, under the pressures of blue steel packed with lead casings, refused to obey the orders despite the officer's threat to blow his head off. Once the officers realized that Michel was not about to corporate, they went after his passenger in order to terrify the woman into allowing them entry.

"Lady, open the door and I promise you won't go to jail with this guy, because he is going to jail, and we are going to impound the car!"

The speeds at which Michel was travelling were punishable with jail time, immediate seizure of one's vehicle, and a first offense suspension of driver's privileges for three months. While his officers attempt to negotiate with Michel, whom they preceived was on his way to the pound one way or the other, the officer who'd collected the driver's license returned to his cruiser to update the terminal on the ground situation. The officer entered Michel's information into the cruiser's computer system and was about to unleash a series of fines when Commandant Danzel radioed in with executive orders that ran counter to what the Mounties were trying to accomplish.

Commandant Danzel said, "Listen to me carefully, Mounties. The man you gentlemen are trying to detain cannot under any circumstances be arrested. You gentlemen are to release Monsieur Lafleur immediately, and I suggest if any of you have offended him in any way, shape, or form, be sure to apologise or find another occupation! That's an order! Am I clear?"

"But sir, the regulations specify that we sieze Mr. Lafleur's vehicle and his license,for his antics".

"Did I ask you about the man's antics? I said return his documents and send him on his way immediately".

"Understood, sir," exclaimed the Mountie, who immediately went to inform his allies.

The RCMP battle drones who were inches away from requesting the Jaws of Life in order to pry the door open changed their tune, and they began sounding like long lost friends reunited after decades apart. The Mountie, after correcting his allies' speech, walked over to the Lamborghini and offered his apologies before returning the billionaire's license. The recorded version of the entire incident was uploaded to Youtube by Frank Riley, and it caught nearly ten million hits after the first day. Audiences around the world could not believe that someone who defied more than two dozen officers scattered among eleven vehicles and a helicopter would just simply speed away after speeding at more than one hundred and fifty miles over the legal speed limit.

The young lad brought a smile to the mogul's face as he went on to partake of the gathering held by his brethren. There was no assembly of the brotherhood prior to the covenant being called to order as members would typically arrive inside their quadrants, don the sacred black robe, be seated in their assembly glory, and await their time to be hailed, which brought the Chair into the Hall of Conference. Each member was brought into the Hall of Conference in sequence as the chairs would mechanically manoeuvre into the dim slots designated for each member. The gloomy lighting, dark quarters, and mysterious outfits made it impossible to see the members across the aisle, and walls shielded those both to the left and to the right of members. Each member was given the opportunity to vote on matters, and votes were made with one of two chips—one for and one against. There was a mediator whose voice was always heard on topics, although he was never visible. Members were allowed to argue once awarded the floor by the mediator, but proper etiquette and respect for peers were laws never to be violated by members of the covenant.

The Meeting

"Gentlemen, our beloved city has been attacked, our way of life challenged, and our very existence questioned. Our very rulership over this province has been mocked and degraded by a foe which we've for far too long allowed to thrive. These vagabonds who've killed innocent women and children along with our selected police officials must be dealt with accordingly. Our continued partnership with the various syndicates who govern this country depends upon our ridding this province of these lowlifes. As members of the sacred covenant and the core of this nation, you've all basked in the glories and accolades awarded this cabinet. Today, we've entered a new age and a new era where our might and vigilance will once more shine the beacon for all Quebecers and Canadians. As is evident by the numbers in the political polls, this nation cries for leadership that only comes from true leaders, and we will give it to them! Here today, we've installed a graphic image transcender that will offer everyone a clear and precise picture of this Nicholas Henry," said the mediator.

There was an octagonal platform placed in the centre of the floor with three humongous cables attached to a computer monitor in a separate room. A perfect image of Nicholas was transmitted to the platform where everyone could visibly see the outlaw standing with both hands by his side as the imagery rotated above the platform. The cabinet members around the chamber, who were all seated inside their cubicles, saw first-hand the vigilante blamed for the massacre that transpired in the centre of town.

"Make sure you all take a good look, because as it's a new day with new times, I throw the first hundred thousand in the pot for whomever brings the head of that man on a platter!"

"Blood-clatt! Make me get in on some of that action.Let me check my figures, there is eighteen of you in here at a hundred thousand a piece, that 1.8 million just for my head Don't be alarmed; you boys looking at the real thing now, not some imagery, so make sure you take a good fucking look!" Nicholas mocked as he walked into the centre of the chamber with two 9 mm pistols at hand.

The mediator, after leaping to his feet in order to highlight his protest, insisted, "Sir, I don't believe you were ever awarded the floor!"

Nicholas found the outburst offensive and grew ferociously annoyed, as he raised his left hand and hammered two rounds into the man's chest. The loud blast from the weapon indicated to everyone the severity of the moment.

"Have you any idea who we are?" Michel Lafleur demanded.

"Actually, if I don't everyone else inside here, I'm positive about who you are, Michel Lafleur!" Nicholas retorted, and he turned his weapons at Martain's father and awarded him a permanent sleep. The same weapon that terminated the mediator, blasted three shells into the old man's chest through the pane of glass.

The sounds from the explosions agitated members of the secret cult, who all began voicing their complaints despite having an enraged murderer in their midst. Nicholas walked over to Michel and stared at the French mogul for a few seconds before hammering two more shells into his corpse.

"See, I believe it is unpatriotic for any country, province, or what have you to have an undermining government while the heads of state, who were voted in by the people, forcibly have to submit to some high-powered, greedy force who will go to any means to achieve whatever they want. The rest of the country may be duped by the suave means through which you gentleman do business, like kill all who oppose and buy out whoever can be bought, as long as the end result provides whatever you seek. You men don't give a fuck! You all have a hand in almost every money, equipment, legal, and illegal transaction that happens in this city. But all that isn't enough, is it? Now you want to take it one step further again by stealing the city mayor's job."

One of the members demanded, "What exactly do you want? A seat on this counsel?"

Another member in his native tongue interjected, "Holster your tongue, Monsieur Raymond. We are the leaders of this great nation, not some fraternity you became a part of in school! We are lords whose veins pump pure French blood. White is the colour of our skin, and we will never integrate anyone of lesser stature!"

"I wouldn't sit with you pathetic invalids to save my life! See, understand this—it is a new era, like the little man said, but this is one era you gentlemen won't get the opportunity to experience!" Nicholas said, and he exited the chamber's centre and had six shooters run in to clean up the mess.

A senior counsellor argued, "We are the advisers to the government of this nation. There will be anarchy throughout this country without our oversight! You can't treat us like second-class citizens! I'm talking to you, boy! Don't walk away when I'm—!"

The explosive sounds of high-powered automatic rifles sounded throughout the chamber as the shooters went around and killed everyone inside the room. Nicholas thereafter entered Monsieur Lafleur's compartment from the rear entrance with a razor-sharp machete at hand. The corpse of his enemy's father was slumped across the table inside the compartment, and Nicholas positioned himself before beheading Michel with one clean swipe.

Part 26

THE CITY HELD an elaborate ceremony for its civil servants killed in what was described in the Gazette as, "The day Montrealers mourn." The prime minister of Canada attended the ceremony, where he laid a wreath at the foot of the altar before addressing the large crowd of mourners. Various dignitaries, preachers, widowers, and friends poured out their emotional grievances while those in attendance and millions around the country mourned along with them. The event aired on local and international news stations, which also highlighted footage from the talks between the prime minister and law enforcement superiors for the province of Quebec. Prime Minister Daniel Couture was adamant in mentioning drastic changes in leadership should those responsible for the debacle not be brought to justice. The number of law officials killed, according to the prime minister, was unacceptable, as was the number of civilians who lost their lives that tragic afternoon.

After the gun smoke cleared the air, 1,524 bodies laid about the downtown streets. The majority of those killed were innocent bystandards, who only sought the experience of witnessing their favourite artists perform.

"I can't believe this is downtown Montreal. I swear it's more like a battleground after a clash," remarked one reporter after personally seeing the carnage. There were more than five hundred Rough Riders, more than three hundred Metropolitan police, and more than six hundred innocent victims, plus seventy-six coalition members from Nicholas' entourage killed in the encounter. The entire city was left incensed by the vile and wicked actions of hateful men insistent on settling their differences wherever they encountered each other. The news agencies that featured the story were all puzzled as to the motive behind the numerous officers killed, although the slayings eventually brought merit to a news report filed by the W Five News program some two and a half years prior. In the report, the accusations of civil police accepting bribes, performing assassinations for the mob, and transporting illegal articles were simply the tip of the iceberg. The implications, although proven accurate by investigators, were expelled as being inconclusive due to the sources from which the accusations originated. When questioned about his officers' conduct, the ex-captain of the police force refrained from directly answering the question and instead chose to demerit the drug addicts and criminals who allegedly testified against his law enforcers.

A number of Nicholas' coalition troops sought the parade event to settle past grievances they'd endured on certain police officers' behalf. There were officers more hated than the true foes of the coalition, and thus they were placed on the extermination list and marked for death. There were, on a number of occasions during the attack, circumstances where Nicholas' coalition members broke off their engagements with Rough Riders in order to settle personal conflicts with police. The stigma that grieved the law officials was exactly how precise and keen the attackers were in their endeavours to massacre all friends, acquaintances, business associates, and members of the infamous gang. After tallying up their initial body count, government officials later found that nine of the uniformed deceased officers were actually coalition members attired as police.

A massive length of Police line do not cross yellow tape stretched out across an amazing perimeter of seven street blocks. Forensic investigators blocked off a significant percentage of downtown for sixty hours before any agencies or businesses were allowed to reopen for business. Investigators combed every section of the crime scene collecting items from spent shells to bloodied knives, as they retrieved precious evidence for use during prosecution. The determinations of who fired what weapons were made, along with the information desired to seal perspective convictions.

The guarantee made be Minister McArthur was scrutinized by one local reporter who was among the few allowed to film the disaster area. The reporter suggested that the minister, who stated that he'd be jamming with his fellow Montrealers, undergo a lie detector test, as he believed McArthur had first-hand information about the ambush, which was the reason for his absence. The minister refused to comment on the allegations that his spokesperson decried as, "ridiculous andreprehensible." Minister McArthur chose instead to stand alongside the top brass behind the municipal police of Quebec, business owners, and neighbourhood activists who held a news conference to stipulate what injunctions would be imposed against the organizers. Law officials also scrolled through hours of video footage from an array of cameras throughout the downtown areas in order to positively identify shooters they believed must be brought to justice.

The days following the horrid incident saw police change their tactics and increase their resolve at bringing that closure that thousands so drastically desired. Officers combed and searched the streets for all the patriotic gangsters caught on tape exercising their rights to bear arms and busted them as they pleased. For the first time in their existence, police officers raided several institutions belonging to the Rough Riders club, where they seized drugs, weapons, and ammunition while taking into custody bikers wanted for multiple crimes ranging from drug trafficking to bench warrants. Royal Canadian Mounties went to Martain Lafleur's establishment in order to bring the gangster into custody for weapons violations after his arrogant proclamations in the centre of town. The Mounties, after sounding the buzzer for a few minutes, forced themselves in to find the mansion had been vacated only minutes before as was evidenced by the cigarette butts burning in the ashtray.

Ten minutes before the Mounties arrived to incarcerate Mr. Martain Lafleur, a Fed-Ex deliveryman was announced at the front gate with a package labelled "DAD." Martain had his guards bring the deliveryman, along with the package, up to the main house, which was like an armed fortress with over fifty heavily armed bikers. His late misfortunes had the biker boss short-tempered, and he sat around a plate of pure-cut cocaine that he'd been snorting in excess. The Fed-Ex deliveryman walked into a den of lions where even the lionesses appeared thirsty for a kill.

"What the fuck do you have that is so fucking important you have to disturb me?" Martain questioned.

"Bring that shit over to him," instructed a guard, who shoved the man in Martain's direction.

"I-I-I-I got a package for you," declared the delivery man.

"Who the fuck is it from?" Martain asked.

"There—there is no sender's name, sir."

"Then you open the shit, and you'd better hope it's not a bomb," joked Martain, whose head bobbled around his shoulder as if he was suffering from fatigue and a lack of sleep.

The deliveryman reached into his pocket and withdrew a small pocket knife which was barely capable of cutting a tiny hair. The man opened the knife and was about to open the box when all around the room guns started clacking as the holders pulled back their weapons' hammers in anticipation of firing. The deliveryman was so terrified he actually messed up his pants as his bowels gave way and released. Disgraced and ashamed, the deliveryman lowered his head as he cut the masking tape from around the box. Even though the deliveryman slowly opened the package, the sight of what was inside the box frightened him enough to where he dropped the box atop the centre-table and simply dashed out of the room with his hands squeezed tightly over his mouth.

Curiosity brought Martian to his feet, and he peeked over inside the box that rested at the other end of the table. At the sight of his father's head inside the box, Martain's mouth fell wide open, and he fell back onto the chair behind him. The biker boss threw his right hand over his face to cover his eyes as he began weeping over the loss of his dad. Inquisitive bikers around the room gathered to observe what frustrated their leader, who had his face covered and the handle of his pistol tightly gripped. The telephone atop Martain's desk began ringing, and after he removed his hand from his face to answer the call, everyone else realized that he had been crying.

"I know you dream about killing me as much as I dream about

burying you, blood-clatt! In case you haven't been counting, you are the only one still breathing from our introduction that cold day in the tailor's shop. You make me even have to bring your father in our private affairs!" Nicholas calmly debated.

"You're dead! You hear me? This world isn't big enough for you to hide! You think you and a couple of punks can cripple an entity like the Rough Riders? You think you got clout because you bumped off a few of my riders and killed my father? I got almost a million warriors at my disposal. You want to fuck with us, all right! All right!" Martain definitively threatened.

"Calm down, because I want you to understand that there is a shift in power taking place here. Ain't going to be no more laws from your old regime. We're going to regulate this business properly," Nicholas assured.

"Ha ha ha ha!" Martain laughed. "You aren't the first to challenge the only imperial entity in Canada, and you won't be the last. This is French-Canadian territory, and the French-Canadians will forever rule it, regardless of what you think. Frankly, you're right; all I dream about is killing you, and the time has definitely come!"

"Is that a challenge? 'Cause we can meet anywhere and settle our private differences quick!" Nicholas asked.

"It's time for the better man to run this shit once again!" Martain remarked.

"You have ten minutes before some Mounties arrive with a warrant for your arrest. Them about to lock you up, you blood-clatt, for that joker stunt you pulled downtown. Next time, wear a disguise, you dumb fuck! Personally, I believe locking you up is a slap on the wrist, 'cause where I'm going to send you is no fucking bed of roses. Meet me on Saint Helen Island at eight o'clock tomorrow morning!" Nicholas instructed.

"I'll be there. Bet your life on it. I'll be there, you fucking coward!" Martain agreed.

The metropolitan police of Montreal received a tip indicating the stench of dead bodies emanating from deep inside the sewer system. Investigators followed maintenance engineers deep into the sewers from which the reports were heralded in order to dismiss the claims and reassure public confidence. City officials had been drenched with reports of missing individuals, especially since the bikers' parade, where many families and friends were forced to scatter in order to avoid being slain. There were individuals reported missing who were either found in hospitals or were wandering the streets confused. That was the case with four witnesses who either had someone's brain mattersplattered over their faces or the memory of a loved one's facial expressions after they'd been brutally dismantled. Retrieving individuals reported missing practically became a matter of national security following the reports filed by sixteen wives of the members of the secret society who'd exhausted all means of finding their husbands before alerting police officials.

Investigators were sceptical that ridiculously wealthy men such as those being reported missing would have vanished off the face of the earth without at least one bodyguard squeezing off a few rounds. With all their scepticism about where they believed the husbands had run off to, investigators were compelled to begin an investigation after the men had indeed failed to respond to their various communications devices and had exceeded the maximum time allowed for any human to disappear without justification.

The sewer technicians believed they were experts in deciphering the maze of tunnels beneath the city that were built centuries prior, but they were surprised to come across a secret entrance hidden since the creation of Quebec's greatest city. Neither of the technicians had ever before seen hidden passages around the tunnels they'd maintained for decades. There was no disputing the source of the odour the engineers had reported as the scent of rotting decay grew ever stronger. The entry led directly to a secret passage, which eventually came to a dead end where the bodies of the missing billionaires were found.

The exclusive list of men found inside the sewers included owners, presidents, and CEOs of a number of key enterprises relevant to the daily operations of the entire province. Found dead were Sir Marcus Herrera, retired president of the Water and Sewage Department, General Donald Drummonds, former chief of the Canadian National Security, Sir Ronald Bell, ex-head of the Canadian Espionage Division, Sir Joseph Artours, the first president of the Tobacco and Alcohol Federation of Canada, business tycoons. Michel Lafleur of Lafleur Enterprises, Steve Harding of the National Banking Association, Leonard Miller of the Miller products of beers, Stewart Bagels, retired Director of the Hydro

Quebec, Gerald Severe, former president of Boeing Air Dynamics, oil tycoon Lloyd Roberts, voted the richest man in Canada, plus other former members of the government and businessmen.

Director Paul Carbonelli, who had justifiably achieved awards of splendour for his years of dedication and service to his country, was watching CNN news footage describing the second national funeral event to be held in Montreal, Canada in less than a week. Many departments within the Canadian government were affected, which created a trickle-down effect that wavered down to the U.S. FBI Director's "Code Yellow" threat alert status. The slaying of such high-profile businessmen, especially Sir Gerald Severe, who was paid handsomely by the United States for the valuable information he'd provided, warranted an investigation according to the U.S. Secretary of State. Executive orders were handed down to the FBI director to form a strike force team in order to assist the Canadian Mounties who were being overwhelmed by two entities constantly bucking horns.

The extravagant funeral events in Montreal overshadowed other major developments of importance, such as the victor of the mayoral contest. The front pages of every mainstream newspaper featured some grieving, emotional individual who had been deeply saddened by the death of one of so many icons. The news of the combination duo winning the coveted job of mayor wasn't even printed on the front page of certain local newspapers since the historic drama which shook the city maintained precedence. The newly appointed co-mayor, Minister Richard Blanc, secretively arranged for the integration of FBI special forces agents whom he expected to be progressive against the different divisions of gangsters without the political interference of the secret chamber. Minister Blanc had a few dark secrets he'd rather never resurfaced since they'd destroy him publicly, even to the extent of a prison sentence.

An undercover RCMP agent was sent from Quebec City to Miami, Florida, to brief U.S. agents on the turmoil between Nicholas Henry and Martain Lafleur. The RCMP agent brought mug shots of both Nicholas Henry, which stemmed from the incident at Carlton's tailor shop, and Martain Lafleur, who was arraigned after an ex-girlfriend reported to police that he'd sexually molested her with his Smith and Weston pistol Canadian officials were able to acquire the identity of key players in the war between the Alliance and the Rough Riders, through the different surveillance cameras around centre town. There were distinctive video footages of Martain, Brogan and several influencive gun hands, blasting their weapons and killing indeviduals, The importance in integrating the Americans was because they had the technology to compare and distinctively match the disguised photos of Nicholas and others, with those on file. Canadian government officials also knew that certain law representitives would seriously abstain from arresting members of the biker club, in fear of the reprisal from such dangerous men. Everything and everyone related to those who offended such killers were fair game, and for officers with families, the price to pay was far too great. . While the Americans could easily flee to the bosom of their borders, every Canadian official knew directly the qualifications of the mobsters involved, as well as the exclusive posse of men who followed these killers.

An example of the level of intimidation came after police investigators reviewed taped footage that caught Martain in the act of murdering a few hysterical youngsters who were merely attempting to flee the violence. Martain was clearly seen, regardless of the fact that he was covered with bullet-resistant armour, incapacitating both ambushers and fleeing spectators trying to get out of harm's way. Regardless of the airtight case, lawyers inside the prosecution office shied away from the glories of imprisoning one of Canada's most infamous gangsters because they knew, should they be fortunate enough to survive the trial, death would be imminent. The case was eventually snagged by a rookie named Sarah Finch. Sarah craved the opportunity to display her talents while polishing her resume and impressing the superiors.

The RCMP agent stood before the six men assigned to the detail, along with Director Carbonelli who joined in simply to show his moral support. The Canadian agent was using the CNN network as a means of illustrating the activities presently inside Canada, where the actions of one of the men spoken about caused the city to close down in order to commit some well-known figure to the grave. The agent soon dimmed the lights and began showing still shots of the two gangsters on a projector machine.

Once Nicholas Henry's face popped up on the screen, Director Carbonelli briskly walked from the briefing room. The director of the

Miami division of the FBI walked directly to his office and instructed his secretary to follow suit. Once inside his office, Director Carbonelli began instructing his secretary on a number of matters as he planned on being away from the office for a few days.

"Mary, I want you to cancel those six U.S. Airways tickets to Montreal and call Jim over at the Air Force base and tell him to fire up the private jet! I'll personally be going back into the field, which means I'm joining this little escapade. I'm leaving Colonel Brittle in charge, but you already know how to handle that issue. Call me if anything arises, bring those treasury forms in here for me to sign, and get the Secretary of Defence for me on the phone!" Carbonelli instructed.

"Right away, boss!"

Part 27

THERE WAS A gathering held at Nicholas' estate to commemorate the soldiers who had fallen in battle, as well as those who were about to sacrifice their lives. Nicholas had made arrangements for young Junior to be sent to the only person he truly trusted, which was Ernesto Lopez, in case the unforeseen should occur. Prior to such lifestyle changes, Junior was transported to Killa's girlfriend, whose three months pregnant stomach was just beginning to form an arch under her clothes. Killa had convinced Nicholas that, should anything unfortunate happen to them both, the desire for him to secure his loved ones was as grave for him as it was for his boss. Hence, Junior was brought to lay low with Mocha while the heavy female hitters in the crew protected them.

Killa connected Junior's Nintendo Wii video game to Mocha's living room television in order for the young lad to enjoy himself while he awaited his father's return. Junior's nanny, who also made the trip, sat and challenged the young gamer to a boxing match, which seemed for the moment to settle the nervous youngster's anxiety. Junior was terrified he would never again have the chance to hug his father, who he knew was going off to war as soldiers have done since the beginning of time. Nicholas may had involved his young son in matters well beyond his years, but as a patriot and a realist, the gangster lived by a strict code of conduct, which was to "put God the Almighty first, respect and love your fellow man, don't disrespect no woman, and never leave home without your gun!"

Mocha was so nervous that her bowels would not allow her to leave the toilet. The expectant mother summoned Killa into the bathroom, where she poured out her heart in an attempt to alter his plans. As a first-time mother, Mocha expected her child's father to play a commanding role in the child's life, yet there he sat, weakened by the fact he may never hold his own child. Killa empathically sat on the ledge of the bathtub and listened to Mocha's outcry, although he'd rather walk through Hell's lava pits than miss a gun battle of such magnitude. Mocha went from reasoning with him to exploiting her love for her boyfriend as she furiously tried to channel her needs into him. Tears poured from Mocha's eyes as she cleansed herself and crawled on feet and arms over to her baby's father. The expectant mother, after realizing the determination in Killa's eyes, grabbed onto her boyfriend and began instructing him to return home to his family.

Killa passionately kissed the lips of the only female he'd laid with on Canadian soil. The gangster lovingly rubbed the tummy bearing his unborn child before slowly reaching down and kissing Mocha's navel. Killa paused by the stomach and whispered, "Daddy will always love you," before continuing to kiss upwards until he landed a breast in his mouth. Mocha's body temperature rose as she grabbed for Killa's crotch and began unbuckling his pants. As passion grew, Mocha yanked Killa on top of herself and guided his penis into her vagina after sliding her panties to the side. There was absolutely no lack of passion between the expectant parents, who growled and grabbed for each other as if they were wild wolves mating. Two hours later, after the entire St. Patrick's field orchestra, the international circus and all its clowns and animals, Formula One racing teams, and all their sponsors passed through, the lovebirds finally decide to rest and come up for oxygen. As Killa exited the premises, the ladies providing security ganged up on him and pinned him to a corner.

"You a listen me, rude buoy. You have a decent young lady who love you very much. Make sure you come back to her. I'm sorry—I mean *them*!" Gwen exclaimed.

"It a go be a boy, eh. I just know!" Joan commented before being rudely interrupted by Eva.

"Shut you pussy 'bout you know. You don't shit you obea working bitch!"

"Don't hate, bitch, you know me have the gift!" Joan argued.

"Must the man thieving gift you a talk 'bout!" Gwen commented.

Killa sneaked out the back door the moment the ladies spurned up one of their legendary arguments that were always a compound of foul dialect aimed at topping each other's insults. As Killa raced down the stairs toward the awaiting SUV, Eva called to him and stopped him in his tracks.

"I love you. Y'all my family, so make sure y'all come back home safe," encouraged Eva.

"Yah, man, not even a scratch!" Killa boasted before hopping into the vehicle.

Nicholas' estate was like a pool party at the Playboy Mansion, with countless females partying about the grounds wearing the skimpiest of bikinis. The table, which was generally stacked with the complimentary marijuana and alcohol for invited guests, had an array of very potent drugs such as cocaine and Ecstasy for the special visitors on said celebrative affair. The main mansion was always off limits to basic visitors, and Nicholas had always been careful as to whom he allowed within such close proximity of his son. The gathering was a means for the troops who had orchestrated a brilliant ambush attack against the Rough Riders to regroup, collect their thoughts, party a little, and prepare for the upcoming battle that would determine whether the regime of sanctions or one of free enterprise would thrive. Nicholas had never been one to leave matters to chance, and such was his motivation in creating an attack formation guaranteed to bring forth victory.

The complete alliance of Defenders, Indian Warriors, and Nicholas' Rude Buoys all prematurely celebrated a sure victory that seemed much easier with the killings of several high profile bikers. After witnessing the death of the final bodyguard who combined with his mates to serve him his worst ass-whoop since birth, Nicholas wasn't content until he'd completly dismantled the biker gang. There was one final piece to the entire puzzle that Nicholas was intent on configuring as his life's masterpiece the moment Martain Lafleur ceased breathing. While everyone enjoyed the festivities around him, Nicholas sat watching the news as he oiled his pistols and reminisced about how close he came to either killing Martain or being killed by the biker boss.

The jubilant screams of ladies being pestered by drunk, disorderly, and horny men were heard throughout the party grounds, as patrons danced around the pool while others simply sat with their feet dipped in the water. A Defender gangbanger who'd gotten drunk off Petron Tequila and high off Ecstasy was told by a peer to "find a bathroom or something," after the man was interrupted attempting to engage in sexual affairs with a female on a lawn chair. There were a few thugs inside the pool who weren't about to reassess their achieved advances any other place after softening up their victims enough for nature to take its course. Those who had sweethearts or faithful relationships were either seen yapping away on their phones with their loved ones or gambling a game of poker.

Three helicopters materialized from over the horizon and suddenly began raining fifty-calibre bullets and laser-guided rockets at Nicholas' estate. One helicopter approached from the west and came up behind the mansion while the others came up from the east, spitting bullets at everything that moved. The timing of the attack by the helicopters couldn't have been more perfect considering that the outpost guards capable of eliminating such threats were all relieved of duty in order to attend the function. A few armed centurions returned fire at the non-relinquishing hovercrafts that maintained their altitude and distance while annihilating everything within their paths. The fugitive James Tea put his military training to good use as he sheltered himself and the female he was with by hiding behind one of a few support columns built to hold and stabilize the huge building structure.

The screams of ladies and frightened gangsters sounded about the grounds as people attempting to outrun bullets found out quickly the task was easier thought of than accomplished. People attempting to leap from the pool met similar fates as those standing forthright against such a spectacle, believing the automatic rifles they had at hand were capable of destroying these hovering, ammunition-spitting beasts. The entire pool and its surrounding areas was painted red with the blood of Alliance members and a vast number of their honoured guests.

Nicholas was pinned behind one of the huge columns as bullets skipped overhead and into the cement column that shielded him and all around his extremities. Thoughts of there being a traitor in their midst grieved the Jamaican rude buoy who sought to bring the fire-breathing dragons crashing to the ground. There was a bazooka rocket launcher inside the weapons depot that was approximately twenty feet across the room. The attack formation of the helicopters told Nicholas that the informant must still be among them, as such a strategy seemed impossible. A huge explosion erupted at the mansion after Nicholas' gas tank was struck by rockets meant to level the luscious home.

Killa saw the huge fireball shoot into the air as he turned off the main road onto the private driveway which led to Nicholas' estate. The Jamaican Bad Man immediately turned off his CD player that pounded some Carribean dancehall tunes in order to listen to the destruction that was taking place. Killa stopped the SUV at the guard's station and ran into the checkpoint as if the cure to his problems lay inside there. The rude buoy affiliate soon exited with a ground-to-air rocket launcher, puffing as if he was experiencing a heart attack while moving to a vantage point to release his brand of destruction.

The two hovering hueys that attacked from the east had laid waste to the majority of party hicks, and the single chopper stabilized some eight feet off the ground for the six bikers aboard to evacuate. The objective of the bikers who exited the chopper was to seek out, find, and assassinate any survivors found without interference from intruding local police. Killa threw his personal Barrett automatic rifle over his shoulder, positioned himself, adjusted, aimed the bazooka at one of the two eastern hueys, and blew the helicopter right out of the sky. The pilot who flew alongside the annihilated aircraft panicedand took off before Killa could reload his weapon and score one hundred on his exam.

Experience taught the veteran pilot to elude the situation, regain the vantage point, and reengage the enemy after you've secured the above. Killa, however, began moving to another sniper's kill point immediately after dousing his first helicopter, as the art of war had taught him that camouflage and confusion protects soldiers. By the time the huey got through its manoeuvres, Killa had vanished from sight, which left the existing pilots nervous, not knowing from where exactly the threat emanated. The pilot, who was forced to change his positioning, began randomly firing rockets at areas he believed possible for the sniper to hide. A second rocket was fired from the guards' housing unit, which struck the paranoid pilot's helicopter the moment it skimmed above the six advancing bikers' heads. Nicholas, who was given the time to collect the bazooka, had timed perfectly his direct hit, which destroyed the chopper and killed three bikers. The bikers were forced to scatter in order to avoid the crashing helicopter, which unfortunately dismantled in a manner which inflicted catastrophic wounds to three of six.

The latest revelation frightened the third pilot, who immediately reported the situation back to base. Before the pilot could finish his report, the surviving three bikers who were flung to the ground were being attacked and beaten by the very survivors they were sent to kill. The survivors were bashing in the skulls of the bikers with baseball bats, rifle handles, lead pipes, and any other destructive material they could possibly get their hands on as huge flames lit up the evening skies. The pilot moved to intercept the angry mob, but then noticed what felt like acid burning his shoulder as rifle shots began piercing the skin of the helicopter. Beneath the pilot and his Systems Failure alert flashing across his monitor inside the aircraft were Bad Buoys Damian, Tank, Brogan, and Kane emptying magazines of bullets into the skin of the helicopter. The systems alert warning forced the pilot to veer off to the south and attempt an escape, which seemed less likely with each passing second. The helicopter began smoking as the pilot, who'd been shot in the right shoulder, muscled the failing aircraft in an attempt to return to base. Everyone who survived the ordeal gathered on the lawn and watched as the helicopter swayed and dipped until it went down and crashed in some thick brush some two miles away.

There were no words to describe the sorrow Nicholas felt as he looked over the field of bodies scattered across his football field-sized lawn. Other survivors began moving to help their injured allies, which, in most cases, was an unfortunate waste of time. Those who yelled for help all clung to life by a mere thread, as their bodily injuries were so severe that a priest may have been a better choice than to call 911. Killa stood frozen at the sight of the massacre as men he'd had the privilege of knowing and battling alongside laid lifeless across the lawn. Bodies were dismantled and chopped up as if someone had taken a dull and rusty machete and butchered them like ground beef.

"*No!*" Kane screamed as he checked around for his brother, only to find Danny had suffered the same fate as many of their allies.

287

Nicholas ran to his friend's side, regardless of the fact he had to step on corpses and body parts in order to get to him. Danny was one of those unfortunate victims who managed to stubbornly still be breathing despite the fact he'd been completely chopped in half by a fifty-calibre shell. Nicholas' eyes immediately filled with tears at the sight of his friend with his internal organs lying callously on the grass. Both men bumped foreheads together and held each other behind the back of the head as they said goodbyes secretly to each other in an appreciative manner. Nicholas held his friend until the final breath exited his body, at which time he rose to his feet, looked around at the survivors, and pulled his cell phone from his pocket.

"I'm sure you can appreciate me returning the favour, though I didn't expect you to still be alive," Martain boasted.

"Would that be with this hit on me, or the countless failures in the past?" Nicholas cynically answered.

"I don't want you dead yet. That's my job, and tomorrow I'm going to make sure I finish the job properly!" Martain threatened.

"You couldn't kill me if I lay down helplessly across a train track. Your informants finally ran out, just like your coward-ass followers. They didn't do a blood-clatt thing. Tomorrow you a go still haffi answer to my nine!" Nicholas warned.

"Oh well, that little nigger, Nigel, already out served his purpose, anyways. Everything else is only technicality," Martain assured.

Nicholas looked over at the Defenders' gun hand to whom Martain referred as the young lad stood nervously over some of his deceased allies while sucking the air out of a cigarette. If body language foretold guilt, then young Nigel was definitely guilty of a thousand sins as he fidgeted about the grounds.

"Oh, and one more thing: I don't think you're going to want to stick around there until the U.S. Marshalls arrive. Shit could get sticky!" Martain warned.

The Alliance Army of one hundred and eighty-seven Defenders, fifty-nine Indian Warriors from Chateauguay, and thirty-one Rude Buoys were reduced to thirteen, like Jesus and his twelve disciples. Nicholas instructed his survivors to gather the necessary items as he gathered with his chief personnel to discuss their strategy. Brogan had lost a great deal and saw no reason to "commit suicide," as he perceived an attack against the Rough Riders to be suicide. Nicholas understood his general's concerns, and thus he began telling a story about the type of city he originally believed Montreal to be, and the type of city it had become, which was a far cry from the communist laws of the Rough Riders. Nicholas reassured his troops that they would be victorious despite the peril they faced as he set out on a mission of immense importance.

It was 12:00 on the morning of the battle at an old warehouse in Ville St. Pierre, Montreal.

Nicholas used his influence to orchestrate a general meeting with all minority ethnic group leaders who'd suffered under the tyranny of the Rough Riders, yet tasted success through the defiance of the Alliance. The secret meeting was called so abruptly that no entity had the services available to infiltrate it; Kevin invited everyone exactly an hour before the event, gave them the area in which the meeting was to be held, and then texted the exact address an half hour prior. The meeting was an all-star event where the bosses chauffeured themselves and drove into the warehouse, parked, and listened to the speaker before exiting at the termination of the speech. Nicholas centred the many vehicles that belonged to prominent businessmen of the city who were all faced with the same dilemma he battled against.

"Ladies and gentlemen, I want to thank you all for coming tonight, because here tonight is our final opportunity to rid ourselves of this band of misfits we've been forced to honour and strengthen with our dollars. Tomorrow, a handful of warriors and I are going up against this immovable force that believes it can never be altered or destroyed. Until the final breath is blown from my body, I refuse to believe that. I had an army well prepared to kill every one of those sons of bitches before they struck us a few hours ago and killed off most of my brave fighters. In a few hours we can change this whole island, or we can just go back to the way things were and accept it the way it is!" Nicholas exclaimed, before stepping into his vehicle and departing the scene while everyone else followed suit.

Ile Ste. Helene, as the French refer to the island, is easily accessible by the Metro, which had a special route dug underneath the Champlain River to reach it. The special Metro had two stops before turning back around and returning to the primary boarding, which is Berri-UQAM

Metro Station. There wasn't anything significant about the island, such as population, because nobody lived on the rock. However, there was historic significance and major reasons visitors flocked to the island. The amusement park, La Ronde, was filled with roller coaster rides and excitement in the summer and ice skating and tobogganing-type sports for the winter.

Nicholas' scouts reported that Martain had confidently boarded the single train he requested for the transportation of his troops onto the island at 7:00 am. Nicholas requested two trains to transport his troops, which Martain believed was a mental tactic, especially after receiving the body count from the huey attack from one of the forensic investigators on the scene. The report given to Nicholas stated that Martain had up to two hundred troops, which was a staggering number considering the number of bikers killed during their parade.

Nicholas arrived at Berri UqamMetro Station at 7:08 am with his army of twelve fighters prepared to tackle their primary nemesis for the final confrontation. The Metro trains to the Island of St. Helene were all deemed inoperative by the transit worker on duty, who was forced to comply with orders or suffer being torched by a flammable contraption installed inside her work booth. Nicholas waited for a surprise he promised his troops until 7:47 am. When it appeared that the surprise he promised would not arrive, it prompted his fighters to wonder if their leader was stalling because he was afraid. In time, Nicholas accepted his fate and boarded the Metro with his allies, who believed in the cause for which they fought and would gladly give their lives for it.

The confrontation between two Canadian gangs went as followed: both armies would line up across from each other like armies of ancient times and exchange whatever miseries they so desired until the charge was sounded, at which time, both armies would attack each other or shoot each other to death. A clash between two Canadian gangs hadn't occurred since the 1800s, where British Columbia orchestrated the barbaric event. The battle would last until the last man or team was left standing, at which time said entity would be crowned "Montreal's Underground Rulers."

Nicholas and company exited the St. Helene Metro Station and walked toward the wall of bikers some fifty yards away. As they exited the station, the Alliance members began removing their individual weapons from bags and elsewhere as they loaded and prepared them for battle. The line of thirteen allies resembled a stone being dropped into a pail of water as they advanced fearlessly up to their enemies. Nicholas, along with his troops, walked up to the massive bully and stopped some twenty yards shy of their combatants, while both sides began sizing up one another. The grin on Martain's face was the first noticeable factor among his army men as Nicholas approached while surveying the multitude. The grin only managed to widen the closer Nicholas came as Martain's whole attitude spelt victory.

"I'm glad to see you came and brought all my enemies to their funerals, because you're all going to die here today!" Martain insinuated with a huge smile on his face.

"You fucking coward, you send some helicopters to do your dirty work!" Brogan shouted.

"Of course, it worked, didn't it? Ask Nicholas here, or should I say *Kevin*, if he wouldn't have done the exact same thing!" Martain boasted.

"You know I would, but we past that now. It's time for us to settle this issue once and for all!" Nicholas said.

"Everyone is always in such a rush. Why you boys in such a rush to die? Take a minute and savour that last breath of fresh air, and you all might as well tell me what you want me to tell your girlfriends and families, because I'm going to visit them all real soon. Pop a couple caps in those snotty-nosed rug rats of yours, some dick in those bitches of yours, and those old folks, y'all get the idea! Must admit I never thought it would be this easy to kill the Dream Team, but here y'all are about to quit breathing for the rest of your lives."

Martain walked around behind the protective shield of his bikers while speaking, being cautious to the Indian Warriors' ability to strike with pinpoint accuracy, knowing that he alone was his nemesis' primary target. As he spoke, a Metro arrived in the docks, where 240 African, Chinese, Indian, Lebanese, South American, and many other nations of people descended from the underground train. "Such stupid bravery, and all easily avoided had you fools just simply paid homage to rulers of this fucking game in this city! Now look at the pathetic crumbs I've reduced you to! No man is above my law. You've all witnessed that before, and you're all going to witness that permanently!"

"Shut the fuck up! Like I promised you, breatherin', you a dead motherfucker!" Nicholas insisted.

"Who the fuc—?" Martain couldn't believe the audacity of someone he held in his grasp.

Martain peeped over the six foot, giant shoulders surrounding him at a very difficult task, as the original thirteen dramatically increased to hundreds. Members of the Rough Riders army, who merely attended the show of force as intimidators, began reversing to the rear of pack as the opposite army trumped the intimidation factor.

The format of the battle had changed to where individuals sought to exchange blows in physical combat rather than simply massacring each other in a horrific gun shoot-out. Nicholas had spent the greater part of the evening visiting tribal leaders of every nation throughout Montreal in an attempt to convince them about the importance of supporting his cause against the Rough Riders. The revolution was one that addressed every nation, as the Rough Riders had their laws implemented throughout the land.

"That over there is you talking, as usual. This over here is the communities of Montreal all standing up to tell you to go fuck yourself! Enough of the Rough Riders' laws. From now on, it's all about free trade. Whoever want to sell whatever them want, go right ahead. We also replaced the retired secret covenant, 'cause real gangsters need to handle real gangsters' shit. You feel me, now a war mi come, so let's war, pussy! Attack!" Nicholas yelled with a resounding charge that invigorated his followers.

With that, Nicholas sounded the charge of battle which released the fury that was brought on by the newly formed Alliance. The loud roars of the attacking Alliance forces appeared to frighten some members of the bikers, who weren't sure if they should attack or turn and run. Martain raised the Mini-14 automatic weapon he'd paraded around with and sprayed a number of bullets directly at Nicholas. The scattered bullets bore a hole through Nicholas' right shoulder and shredded the front of his Versace shirt, exposing the bulletproof vest which protected his chest. The single giant among the Alliance forces, who was a six foot six inch Nigerian, toppled onto his face as a single stray bullet struck him in the head.

"Kevlar, motherfucker! It won't be that easy this time!" Nicholas warned, despite the fact that not everyone came similarly equipped.

A few fighters from both ends went down instantly from gunshot wounds, and within the squint of an eye, both sides were within arms' reach of each other. Thugs wielded axes, machetes, knives, baseball bats, swords, pipe irons, chain saws, guns, scissors, shanks, self-altered weapons, fists, and feet at each other as they fought like barbarians scrapping for wealth. Men were soon covered in their own blood, the blood of some friend, or an antagonist they'd mauled to death with either their bare hands or a foreign object.

Killa had a machete for close confrontation that he swung like a farmer reaping sugar cane. The Jamaican Rude Buoy had five Glock 9 mm pistols shoved all throughout his waistline, which he sparingly used to ward off threats he believed significant enough to damaging the blueprint. The battlefield was nothing pretty, nor were the men engaging in war as both sides carved, decimated, and disfigured each other in an excruciating manner which left most of those deceased adequate only for closed casket funerals. The screams of men being brutally murdered sounded across the board as combatants fought for their very existence.

Nicholas, Kane, and five Warriors fought as men with proper training, and they made the art of killing look simple. Kane had his tribunal dagger, which he creatively manoeuvred like an extension of his arm. The rigorous training by Eagle, who had prepared his pupils for this grand battle, had motivated them enough to the point that failure wasn't option. Nicholas had a dagger he'd bought on a fishing expedition to the Sioux Land, along with a Manchurian Axe that was made in Alberta by the Navajo Indians. The pioneer against the Rough Riders had trained extensively at the advice of Eagle, who believed a man should be capable of protecting himself against his enemies. Eagle taught Nicholas how to feel his way around a battlefield, which was a trait that, if properly manoeuvred, became somewhat of a sixth sense. At one point during the battle, Nicholas felt the spiritual force of his deceased friend, Danny, and Danny's father, Eagle, as he avoided or altered offensive strikes while connecting with his defensive counters.

Martain had enrolled in self-protection courses since he was old enough to kick a soccer ball. The biker boss had studied various disciplines of martial arts, such as Karate and Tae Kwan Do, and he was quite capable of protecting himself. Those who fought alongside the Rough Riders' boss were always cognisant of his well-being since he meant a great deal to the continued existence of the club. A representative from almost every culture that formed the Alliance group attempted to kill or injure the longest-reigning ruler of the biker club. Martain Lafleur was legendary throughout the underground; hence, whoever was credited with killing him knew his name would be guaranteed to be written in the history books. For such an honour, many men threw away their lives recklessly, and they shunned their responsibilities to strike a blow at Martain.

The battle raged on for nearly two hours, and it wasn't until the hour and thirty-ninth minute before the sound of an intruding helicopter was heard in the skies. The RDS Broadcasting Station received information of a brutal battle and sent their traffic update helicopter to investigate the claims. The footage captured by the helicopter, which wasn't allowed to hover over the fight zone due to gangsters blasting away at the hull, was disturbing to viewers who thought they were watching a taping of an overseas event. There were bodies scattered across the plains with few anatomies left intact as the majority suffered cut off hands, legs, feet, and body parts which shouldn't be exposed, causing the vultures to gather around for the feast.

Martain glared over at Nicholas as the field of over four hundred shrunk to twenty plus men. The two warring groups had surrendered a great deal of their soldiers to the cause, with the Alliance mob still maintaining a slight edge in numbers. The helicopter distraction gave both parties the opportunity to re-evaluate their stance as they retreated to their individual quadrants in preparation for the final conflict. The eighteen remaining bikers, along with the twenty-three Alliance members, were all tired beyond comprehension, and yet their genuine hatred for each other fuelled their fighting spirits. Martain and Killa were the only combatants who, although covered with blood, weren't actually injured or wounded. Kane, Tank, and Brogan, among others, slumped forward or fell to one knee as they grabbed or attended to their wounds. Nicholas, despite the bullet that went directly through his shoulder, appeared physically stealthy, although his breathing demonstrated his fatigue. The Alliance forerunner stood tall in front his troops as those who redirected the helicopter dropped the weapons they used to do the job. Martain also stood vast before his troops as the two leaders stared each other down like raging bulls priming to attack.

The unspoken fury that transcended from both men soon brought their remaining faculties to their sides as both gangs stood fifteen feet apart, soliciting the other to attack. Suddenly, without any warning, both groups collided with each other in what only could be described as an artistic masterpiece. Killa found himself submerged in a battle against an opponent who actually had a Chinese sword that he'd used to carve his way through the first round of the battle. For the first few ticks, Killa was forced into a defensive posture as the Asian wielding the sword poised to decapitate him. The Asian had Killa in reverse mode as he bobbed and weaved his body in order to avoid the chops being swung at him. While backing up, Killa tripped over the corpse of a slain Nigerian and fell flat on his ass. The trip caused Killa to lose his machete, which went flying as he collided with the ground, and his opponent moved in for the kill. The reluctant Jamaican's eyes opened wide as he anticipated the blade piercing his skin, and he grabbed for the first object within arm's reach. The Asian biker was poised to run his sword through Killa when the Rude Buoy came up with the deceased African's spear and jammed it into the Asian biker's belly. The man froze his actions, and he grunted like a bear before expelling his final breath. Killa tossed the biker to the side, collected his machete, and charged into the raging battle.

There were bikers intent on slaying the leader of the opposition as was evident by the two separate stab wounds which Brogan received from cowardly opponents who attacked him from behind. The Defender boss was engaged with the Rough Riders' west division captain when a biker private who shed his opponent began moving in from behind to jam his fifteen-inch blade into Brogan's back. The attacking biker was inches from killing the Defenders' leader when Killa chopped off his arm from an angle, which tossed the arm and the knife it held into the air before they landed a few feet away. The surprised biker's mouth fell wide open as he watched in slow motion his arm leave the base from which it was attached before flying away like a bird. Before the biker's arm holding the knife could hit the ground, Killa had swung his judgment stick again, removing from his shoulders his opponent's entire head, which fell with the same astonished expression. The Rude Buoy proceeded to help Brogan, who wasn't one hundred percent, as they disfigured the Rough Riders' west division captain.

Nicholas and Martain engaged in a classical battle the moment they clashed into each other as they vowed to physically rip each other's head off. The two men were drastically improved in skill from their original encounter, which was actually a show of power by the Rough Riders. The memory of everything Martain and his goons did to him replayed continuously in Nicholas' head as he sought to slice and dice the biker boss. Martain had armed himself with a dagger and a meat hacker to complement the dagger and axe of his opponent. The *ching-ching* of metal colliding echoed for nearly five minutes as both leaders went back and forth at each other. The battlefield had decisively been conquered by the Alliance, and those who'd been victorious in their struggles began assisting their mates who were less sturdy in their conflicts.

The six surviving Alliance members gathered to watch the battle between Nicholas and Martain that had been raging on for thirteen agonizing minutes in a seesaw affair. Killa thought back to his days on the playground in Jamaica where his battles against future friends and foes occurred. The Jamaican Rude Buoy thought of a manoeuvre that was done to him by Stamma, which, had the altercation not been interrupted, may had won him the match.

"Remember the slide-and-pop move what Stamma lick mi wid? Put it pan the buoy!" Killa instructed after observing the proper opening for the technique.

Martain had Nicholas in a chokehold while attempting to plunge his dagger into his throat. Nicholas had been disarmed of both his axe and his dagger after the biker boss smacked him with a three-punch combination directly after catching him with a stunning kick to the side of the head. Martain faked as if he was leading with his blade before bringing that colossal kick to the side of Nicholas' temple. The combination of blows staggered Nicholas, who only managed to remain conscious through the cheers and encouragements of his friends. Martain fought valiantly as he attempted to end the battle by piercing his blade into Nicholas, who was on the verge of being killed by the man he hated the most.

Nicholas, from the standing position, folded his legs like a Muslim crouching to pray, which released him from Martain's secured grip. As he fell to the ground, Nicholas grabbed the blade from Martain's grip with his countered weight against Martain's one-handed grip. The manoeuvre by Nicholas was so smooth that it caught Martain complete by surprise, and he looked down at what was a sure kill. Nicholas knew that Martain wore a vest beneath his clothing that might interfere with him puncturing one of his main arteries. The Rude Buoy leader therefore rammed the blade directly up the crotch of his revered enemy and left it stuck directly between his testicles and buttocks. The jolt of electricity that shocked up Martain's intestines froze the biker boss in his position, and he fell to his knees and grabbed the blade's handle, unsure of what removing it might do. Nicholas arose to his feet while gripping the closest pistol in his vicinity.

Three Black Hawks and a military helicopter approached from all four directions as Nicholas held his weapon aimed at Martain's head. Chief Carbonelli of the Federal Bureau of Investigation grabbed the loud speaker aboard his chopper and announced his company.

"This is Agent Carbonelli of the Federal Bureau of Investigation. I need to see everybody's hands in the air! I have an Immigration Deportation Order and a Federal Warrant for the arrest of Kevin Walsh—" barked Agent Carbonelli over the loud speaker.

"Shoot him! Shoot him and shut the fuck up! For Christ sakes, he's got a gun pointed at my head! Somebody shoot his ass! I need help! Shut the fuck up and shoot him!" Martain begged as the loud sounds of the helicopters muffled his voice.

"Good-bye, Martain!" Nicholas said.

Boom! Boom! Boom! The weapon fired in Nicholas' grasp.

Part 28

NICHOLAS AND HIS surviving cast were all taken to the RDP Central Jail for processing prior to their early morning rendezvous with the presiding judge. The Alliance members were transferred to the central holding facility by the biggest prisoner convoy ever formulated, and law officials took all precautions with their high-profile prisoners. The Patine Central Jail was a twenty-story edifice that mainly held prisoners going through transfers or court-appointed individuals. There were different levels for various stages of criminals, and the most violent offenders were held on the top two floors. With the arrival of each member of Nicholas' coalition to his range came humongous cheers and applause, and rumours already circulated about their triumph.

Patine Central Jail didn't offer the housing amenities of permanent holding institutions such as Bordeaux, where inmates were allowed to walk from one activity to another. The transition jail held its visitors captive for twenty-four hours a day, with an hour of exercise only offered to those who visited for more than three days. The cells held two men reasonably comfortably, three meals were provided each day, and showers were given on Thursdays. Nicholas and company were not, however, treated to the fine hospitalities of the jail, as they were summoned and transferred to the court for early arraignment.

The elaborate motorcade that transferred Nicholas and company to

Montreal's Palais De Justice courthouse, resembled that of the United States president, with it's vast amount of police detail and armoured vehicles. The posse that defeated the great Rough Riders crew was reunited in the Bull Pen, which was located in the basement of the Palais De Justice building, where they high-fived, fist-pumped, and hugged each other in appreciation. There Nicholas addressed his peers, and he assured them that none of them would spend a moment incarcerated, as he'd always been the type of person to cover all angles.

"Where is James?" Tank asked, who noticed that the soldier was gone.

"His army buddies most likely came and picked him up. Remember, he ain't a regular civilian like us," Kane answered.

The on duty sergeant soon walked over with a list of names of Nicholas and his Alliance team who were scheduled for a private hearing before the Honourable Antoine Bryere. There is a nervous tension that develops inside every man who is slated to pass before a judge who bears the power to reprimand that person or grant them their freedom. Such emotions weren't apparent by the confidence emanated by the Alliance members, and they gave fellow inmates the strength to withstand their impending process. The men rode the prisoners' access elevator up to the third floor, where, instead of a repeated process as was in the basement, they were rushed directly into the Judge Bryere's courtroom.

The courtroom was nearly barren, with only Judge Bryere, the prosecuting attorney, Agent Carbonelli, and Nicholas' high-priced attorney present. The guards who led the accused into the courtroom remained for a moment before the judge instructed them to vacate his chambers, as the matter was one of extreme confidentiality. News media personnel packed the hallway outside Court Room #305, desperate to capture the photos of men who'd become infamous. Discovery disclosures were often sent to media relations in high-profile cases such as The Canadian Government vs. The Alliance. However, Judge Bryere issued a gag order which prevented any leaks of information pertaining to the case. Entry to the courtroom was prevented by two correctional officers who allowed no one within ten feet of the entrance.

Inside the courtroom, Judge Bryere politely asked the gangsters before him to take a seat as he read over a letter that was handed to him moments before they entered. The judge also held a cellular phone to his ear, which was unusual for a presiding judge while seated on his bench. Nicholas' lawyer signalled his clients that everything was proceeding accordingly as he confidently sat behind the defence table. Judge Bryere terminated his phone conversation, and then summoned both legal counsels to approach his bench. The judge was insenced as he grimaced at the members of the Alliance who sat serenely awaiting his decision.

"Chief Prosecutor Ramous, I trust you've spoken with your superiors and understand the critical junction we've come to in this case," demanded the judge.

The prosecutor exclaimed, "Yes, sir, I most certainly understand!"

"Okay. Mr. Paventrum, I guess your clients are free to go pending proper documentation," ruled Judge Bryere. "You gentlemen have been struck with the hand of the Almighty, because I don't believe any trial would be necessary to convict you men of all these charges, especially premeditated murders. I guarantee, should I ever catch one of you back in my courtroom, it will be the last time you freely see the light of day! You gentlemen are all free to go."

"Wait a minute, Your Honour. I'm Agent Carbonelli of the Federal Bureau of Investigation, and I have here a warrant and a deportation order for Mr. Kevin Walsh, aka Nicholas Henry, in connection to the deaths of U.S. Marshalls on American soil. Mr. Walsh's extradition has been signed and approved by the Attorney General of the United States, and I have every intention of honouring this warrant," Agent Carbonelli argued.

Judge Bryere took the documents from Carbonelli, who maintained a vacant stare at Nicholas as if he was attempting to intimidate the Rude Buoy. Nicholas smiled at Carbonelli before raising his handcuffed hands and applauding the agent for his years of dedication. Carbonelli was content with seeing Nicholas confined, and he envisioned removing from the infamous FBI's Most Wanted list the third most sought after fugitive.

"These documents appear to be in order. He's all yours, Agent Carbonelli!" Judge Bryere disclosed.

"What the fuck? What kind of shit is all this, Judge?" Damian yelled, who leaped to his feet the moment the judge gave his ruling.

"Your Honour, I don't believe you have the power to sign an

extradition order for Mr. Henry. Furthermore, this is all new to Mr. Henry's defence team, and thus we request the necessary time to file an injunction in this case!" Nicholas' attorney protested.

"Are you attempting to lecture me on the requirements of my job, Mr. Paventrum?" Judge Bryere asked.

"No, sir. I'm simply unaware of these charges against my client and need time to formulate a defence," Mr. Paventrum explained.

"This case has not provided your typical pre-trial hearing. I personally believe our taxpayers deserve more accountability from their government, but then again, in the long run, what difference am I making? You may state your grievance with the committee, but I'm releasing Mr. Henry into the custody of the U.S. Marshalls. Thank you, and have a nice day!" Judge Bryere said, and then he stormed from the bench for his personal chamber.

The corrections officers who led the men into the courtroom returned to bring the men back to the holding facilities pending their release documents by the Bureau of Corrections. Nicholas was in Killa's ear the moment the judge rendered his final verdict regarding his future, and the outlaw issued his desires and wishes pertaining to his son. Killa vowed to protect and raise young Junior according to his friend's wishes while continuing the growth of Nicholas' empire during his absence.

The prime minister of Canada hung up the phone with Judge Bryere after instructing him on how to proceed against the surviving Alliance members. The prime minister was at home where he'd summoned his entire cabinet for a viewing of a private DVD he'd received via a Fed-Ex courier. The DVD disclosed years of political manipulations by the secret covenant, assassinations orchestrated and performed, business affiliations where political figures accepted bribes and payoffs, personal favours involving building contracts, real estate developmental contracts from the days of our founding fathers, and the most compelling disclosure of all, which disclosed all former appointees to political offices through the vigilance and roughhouse tactics of the secret covenant. There was incriminating evidence, documented and filed, which proved the Rough Riders were the puppets at the end of the string who were controlled and manipulated by a bunch of old geezers. There was a single detrimental aspect that would have shaken Canada's very core, which implemented Sir Robert Borden, whose picture graces the Canadian hundred dollar bill, implementing him as a member of the secret fraternity. The entire DVD, which would have been a political nightmare for any regime had it been publicised, came with specific instructions that stated, "DVDs will be sent to all news media should the Alliance survivors not be released!" The embarrassment that loomed, especially after the recent slayings downtown Montreal, was believed to be too stressful for Canadians by a prime minister who sought immediate closure to the whole ordeal.

The governing cabinet weighed its options and decided to release without restrictions the accused gang members who were caught with their hands inside another woman's panties, guilty as hell and proud to admit it. The floods of the heavens would have poured had the prime minister not accepted the deal after watching the powerful bargaining chip held by mysterious foreigners. The prime minister was cognisant of the reprisals against the newest appointed officials in Quebec, who were mentioned on the DVD among those illegally appointed into office since the beginning of Canadian democracy.

The prime minister telephoned Mayor Richard Blanc, whom he believed might be the sole voice of reason to which French Quebecers were willing to listen. The Canadian prime minister withheld mention of the scandalous DVD as he encouraged half of the first joint mayor to take the lead on the arising issue. When asked by Mayor Blanc, "Why are video-recorded killers being set free?" The prime minister soberly explained, "Our hands are tied behind our backs, Richard. God dammed in-house affairs!" The mayor refrained from any further enquiry as he intellectually deciphered that Pandora's box had been opened, which, if exposed, brought the possibility of impeachment charges. With that, Mayor Blanc issued a press conference where he, along with Police Chief Arnold Dubois and RCMP Commander Lucien Lapierre, answered tough questions from the media regarding the decision to release the Alliance members without restrictions or impending incarceration.

Police intervention was necessary for Brogan and his liberated friends, who exited the courthouse to a huge mixed crowd of protestors and admirers who anointed them or believed they should be locked away with the grimiest of criminals. The police officers had to form a pathway from the front entrance of the Palais De Justice Building down the long steps along St. Antoine Boulevard to four Chevy Suburbans being driven by the ragamuffin ladies of the Alliance. The loud roars of a thundering Porche Phantom came to a screeching halt in front the awaiting SUVs before the luscious, long-legged Alyiah pranced from the conductor door. Kane smiled at his wife before fist-pumping his mates and assuring them that he'd be in touch, and he hobbled down to his awaiting chariot. Killa, Damian, Tank, and the rest of the crew all hopped aboard the identical SUVs, while completely ignoring the crowd and media personnel asking questions. The vehicles all sped off down St. Antoine Boulevard before veering west on the Ville Marie Express Way.

The moment Killa hopped into the SUV, he began checking for young Junior, but believed the female left him secure due to the hectic pressures they'd face. It wasn't until the SUVs were speeding along Interstate 20 that Killa asked about the young lad of whom he had been placed in charge. The female driver apologised for the news she was about to deliver before recounting an incident that had occurred only moments before where they were ambushed and hijacked by a bunch of females who took young Junior hostage.

Commander Carbonelli and his strike force drove into Hangar #11, where their private plane awaited them at Dorval International Airport. The commander was jubilant after apprehending a suspect he'd chased for more than a decade, and he advised his central command that they were "returning with the package." The commander came off the phone and looked back at Nicholas, who appeared tranquil for someone about to get buried.

"I'm going to ensure they put you in a hole so far underground that if you ever come up for light you're either dead or getting transferred to an even deeper hole! I told you I was going to get you, didn't I?" Carbonelli bragged.

Nicholas remained quiet and smirked at Carbonelli as if he still had an ace card up his sleeve. Once they entered the hangar, Carbonelli's men took up positions around the area, which was standard procedure to ensure the area was secure. Carbonelli waited for the area secured report before attempting to transfer Nicholas from the car to the plane. The Jamaican Rude Buoy was shackled at the ankles with handcuffs which were attached to a chain around his waist.

While Nicholas shuffled along across the hangar floor, with his feet shackled and hands handcuffed, two black Hummers pulled in front the huge doors with a series of armed, uniformed men dismounting. Carbonelli's special forces agents surrounded their prisoner and removed every safety clip from their automatic weapons as they prepared for an intense gun battle. The armed men who dismounted from the Hummers all wore dark, lime green uniforms, which was the colour of the Canadian special forces uniform.

The Americans were under strict, "react only when attacked" orders which prevented them from just opening fire at the approaching figures, regardless of the huge weapons they carried. The armed Canadians walked directly up to Commander Carbonelli and handed him a note. Carbonelli read the note and said, "No fucking way,"as he withdrew his side pistol and jammed it directly against the head of the Canadian who handed him the note. The sounds of hammers being cocked echoed inside the hangar as both sides prepared for the altercation.

"Sir, may I remind you that you're still on Canadian soil, and I doubt you guys have enough ammunition to hold off my boys and whatever reinforcements respond to our SOS?"

Commander Carbonelli was furious that he was about to lose the man he'd lost, found, and then lost again, but he agreed to the terms. A confrontation with their next-door neighbours and allies would not be in the best interest for their public relations, and so Carbonelli tossed the restraint keys of Nicholas' confines at the intruders and boarded the plane with his peers. The Canadian special forces soldiers who negotiated Nicholas from the Americans removed the thug's bondages before ushering him into the dignitary cabinet of the vehicle. The Hummers sped off with Nicholas comfortably relaxing as he smiled a gracious smile to himself before sparking up a huge cigar handed him by the negotiator.,

"Excuse me, Mr. Henry, but the prime minister would like to have a word with you over the phone," said the shotgun rider.

The End

Jamaican Slang Dictionary

These are Patquois words that I've used throughout the novel

Dat = That
Dem = Them
Dutty = Dirty
Gwan = Happening
Inna = In the
Kloffie = Idiot
Mi = Me
Onnou = You guys
Outta = Out of
Pan = On
Sai = Say
Shotta = Shooter
Somme = Something
Wi = We
Wha = What

CPSIA information can be obtained at www.ICGtesting.com
Printed in the USA
LVOW132139070613

337567LV00001B/36/P

9 781449 041687